A Howl on the Wind

Book III
of
The Milhavior Chronicles

by
Jonathan M. Rudder

Athor Productions
PO Box 652
Granite City, IL 62040
www.athorproductions.com
info@athorproductions.com

Published by:

Athor Productions
PO Box 652
Granite City, IL 62040
USA

First Softcover Printing, September 2005, Athor
Productions (ISBN 1-932060-05-7)

Printed in the United States of America

ISBN 1-932060-05-7

For Reyna,
May the Light of the Dawn
shine ever upon your path.

Milhavior – West Lands

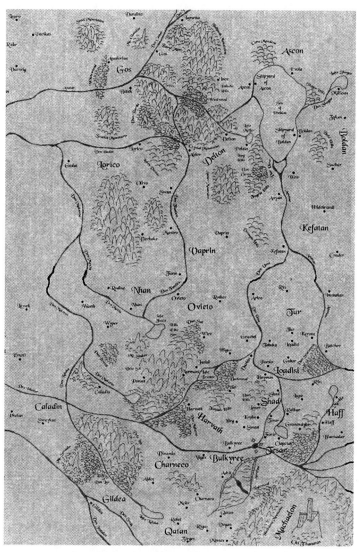

Milhavior – East Lands

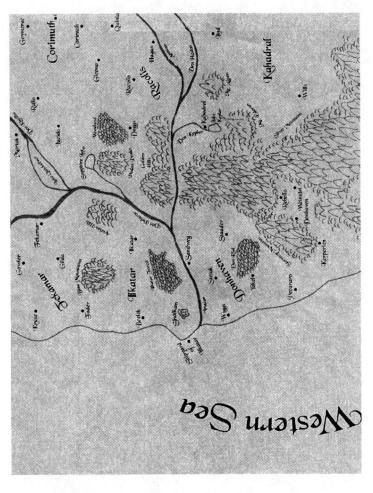

Milhavior – Northwest Quarter

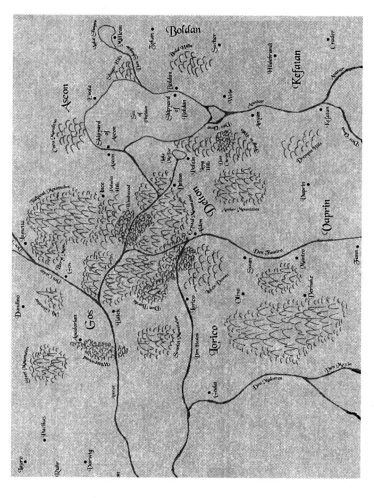

Milhavior – Northeast Quarter

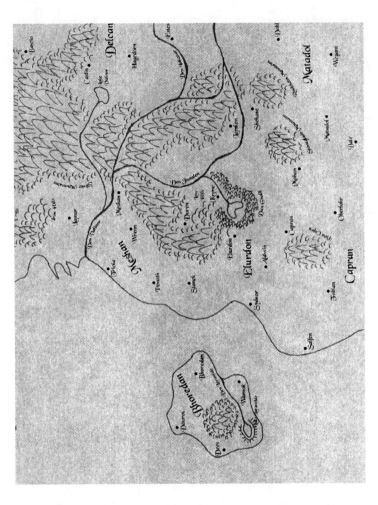

Milhavior – Southwest Quarter

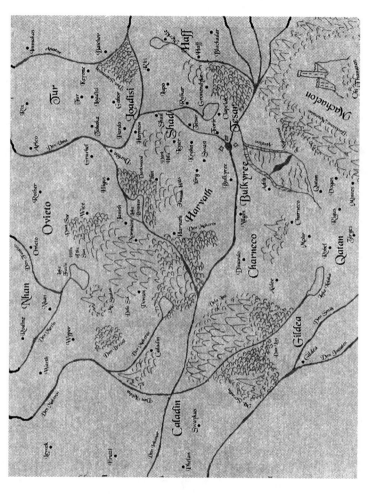

Milhavior – Southeast Quarter

Chapter 1

He had walked the paths of En Orilal, the Mortal Realm, for more than seventeen hundred years, from the gleaming, marble-paved streets of Athor—his true home, the Holy Isle—to the cobblestone roadways of the grandest cities in Milhavior to the mud and waste-mired paths of poor, rural villages and hamlets. Across the trackless wilderness, he had passed into the frozen Far North and into the Shadowed barrens of Machaelon in the south, though never beyond to Mingenland of old, the land of his forebears. He was old, very old, and at the moment he felt every year weighing heavily upon his frail shoulders. Weariness and concern was marked in every line and wrinkle on his aged face, and his lids half-hooded his grey eyes. It was taking every ounce of his strength to purge the disease from his patient . . . a very long and slow process.

Odyniec sat beside the woman's sickbed, holding her hand, looking down at her deceptively young face. Despite her struggle with the Plague, induced by the Sorcerer Brugnara, she retained the appearance of a girl no more than sixteen or seventeen years of age and the Elvin beauty inherent to her Trostain lineage. However, she was still fevered and by no means out of danger. The Wizard tugged on his long, white beard, which flowed over his chest and spilled onto his lap. If he had been delayed but a day more, he would not have been able to save Mattina at all.

A knock at the door of his small chamber rattled him from his thoughts. He cast an annoyed glance at the door, perturbed at the untimely interruption. He glowered in silence for a brief moment before snapping, "What is it?"

The door squeaked open, and a young, brown-haired page poked his head in, gawking at the Wizard in awe. The supernatural was nothing new to the people of Lener Keep. Like everyone else in the nation of Shad—or Lener, as it had been dubbed after the overthrow of the Great Father, Brugnara—they had lived unceasingly beneath the ever-looming shadow of the sorcery and dark magics of the Deathlord's minions, but the Wizard and his Dawn King were something new and, in a way, frightening to them. Instead of darkness and shadow, instead of the pain and stench of death, they brought a glorious light and a renewal of life such that they had never experienced before.

Odyniec could not blame the page for staring, but his concentration had been broken, which had put him into an unpleasant disposition. Nevertheless, he forced a little of the sharpness out of his voice. "Well? Speak up, boy."

"P-Prince Brendys requests your presence, sir," the page stammered in reply, his young voice squeaking in fear.

Odyniec sighed, casting his weary gaze back down at his patient. Only two days had passed since Brugnara's defeat, and still Brendys would not allow himself to rest, to recover from the injuries inflicted on him by the Great Father's minions. But he understood. Brendys worried about his wife and child. Yet Brendyn would certainly live, though he would likely bear his terrible scars for the rest of his life, and Mattina would very likely survive as well, as long as she remained under the Wizard's care.

Odyniec lifted his gaze to the page and replied a little more gently, "All right, boy. You may go."

As the boy disappeared from view, the Wizard grasped his rune-marked staff and rose to his feet, moaning as he stood. "I am getting too old."

After giving Mattina one last quick examination, Odyniec left the room and headed down the corridor towards the Keep infirmary, where Brendys and his son were being cared for. He had intentionally requested chambers near the infirmary so that he could treat the wounds of the Bearer of the Flame and his offspring, not trusting to the ministrations and strange medicines of the Leneri physicians. *Little more than heathen shamans*, he mentally noted with disgust.

As he entered the chambers of healing, he found Brendys leaning against the sill of the room's open window.

Brendys turned at the Wizard's approach, his shoulder-length, black hair lightly blown by a warm draft. His closely-trimmed beard framed a bruised and scarred face, but he seemed more at peace than he had the day before. Nevertheless, there was a slightly haunted light behind his deep-blue eyes.

The Horsemaster spoke quietly, for his young son was asleep in the bed to his right. "Master Odyniec, thank you for coming. I have been hearing some troubling things."

"I can only imagine," the Wizard replied. He himself had heard many of the rumors which were beginning to make their way throughout the city. Many were outrageous. Others ... others were *unhealthy*. "Speak your mind."

Brendys hesitated uncertainly for a moment before replying. "The Leneri have begun to spread rumors that *I* am the Heir of Ascon. I remember stories my father told

3

me as a child . . . the *Annals* refer to Ascon's Heir as the Hawk of Justice."

The Horsemaster's gaze focused on the Wizard with an intensity he had never felt from the man before. "You have often spoken in riddles and vague allusions, Master Odyniec. This once, I ask you to speak plainly . . . *am* I the Heir of Ascon?"

Odyniec knew at once of what he spoke: when Brendys had used Denasdervien, the Living Flame, to slay Brugnara, the Dawn King had manifested himself to the people of Lener Keep as a great hawk of gold, which descended upon the Black Altar upon which young Brendyn was bound and where Brendys stood, Elvinsword in hand. The messenger had declared the coming of the Hawk of Justice.

Truly, the message had been misinterpreted by the Leneri. The Wizard smiled reassuringly. "For once, you have asked a question to which I *can* answer plainly. Nay, you are *not* the appointed Heir of Ascon. You are precisely what you were told years ago: the Bearer of the Flame who will light the way for the Heir's return."

Brendys wrinkled his brow in confusion and turned back to the window. "But the hawk which descended upon the altar . . . the voice said. . . ."

The Horsemaster's words were cut off by a startled gasp. Brendys glanced down at his sleeping son, then turned back towards the Wizard. His eyes were wide in fear and wonder, and his face had paled. His words came slowly. "The hawk . . . it wasn't for me, was it? Answer plainly!"

Odyniec's smile faded, his grey eyes boring into the Horsemaster's, but he did not reply. He had not thought Brendys wise enough to understand, but clearly he had underestimated the Horsemaster. Until now, only four individuals had known the truth: himself, his former master, King Quellin of Gildea—Brendys's brother-by-

4

marriage—and the Elvinlord Guthwine. It was knowledge that in the wrong hands could be disastrous.

Brendys became faint and grasped the window sill to steady himself. Head bowed, he carefully lowered himself to his own bed, gaping in disbelief, his eyes staring at nothing. Odyniec could only imagine the thoughts running through the mind of the Bearer.

"I must counsel you to keep your knowledge to yourself, Brendys," Odyniec said quietly. "Your own destiny as the Bearer of the Flame already puts you and all around you at risk of your lives. Your understanding, if brought to light too soon, could bring the full brunt of Machaelon's strength against you.

"Do not concern yourself with rumors and wild gossip. You may find them more of a shield than a vulnerability. Thanatos knows you are not the Heir of Ascon, and his minions may be more likely to dismiss rumors, even when the heart of truth is in them."

Without looking up, Brendys nodded.

The weariness that had fallen upon the man was so evident that Odyniec felt a renewed sense of vigor in his own limbs. "Rest now, Brendys. The days that follow will not be easy, and you will need your strength."

As will I, the Wizard reminded himself.

Chapter 2

Less than a week after the Day of Shadows—that Zotist holy day upon which Brendys and his son had been intended to die—and the Great Father's fall, Captain Folkor, King Mathai, and the remainder of the High Steward's warriors returned to Harvath Keep, and from there, they set sail back to Ascon. The High Elves that had accompanied the Men of Ascon and a portion of the Harvathine army remained behind to aid Englar, now King of Lener, in the transition of government. With the Zotists removed from power and the influence of Machaelon all but ended in that land, the remaining Lords readily swore fealty to King Englar, accepting Lener-Shad as the new ruling House.

As days turned to weeks, the wounds Brendys and his son had sustained at the hands of Brugnara and his jailors had healed well, though both of their bodies remained terribly scarred, but those marks could be hidden. And but for a scar that crossed at an angle across his lips and another that split his right eyebrow, young Brendyn only sustained a few barely-noticeable marks on his face, but Brendys knew that even the worst of those would probably fade as the child grew—unlike the old, ugly gash along his own temple . . . a constant reminder of a foolish youth bound by hatred to a life of denial. Now he had a few more to add to that.

He knew he should be thankful that his family had survived this latest ordeal, but he found it difficult while sitting at Mattina's bedside, holding her hand. She had not reawakened since the Day of Shadows, though Odyniec had assured him that she *was* recovering. He heard movement in the doorway and looked up.

His brother-by-marriage walked into the room and sat down on the edge of Mattina's bed. Despite his forty years, Quellin—like his younger sister—appeared no more than a youth of seventeen summers or so, Elvishly handsome. Indeed, he could have been Mattina's twin. His emerald eyes were fixed in concern upon his sister's face. "Still nothing?"

Brendys silently shook his head.

Quellin sighed and turned his gaze on the Horsemaster. "I have been away from Gildea Keep far too long already, but I had Kovar send Amrein with a message to Arella, telling her that I will be accompanying you to Shalkan before returning home."

"Shalkan?" Brendys echoed dully, staring blankly at the Gildean King. His gaze returned to his wife. "Then you will have a long wait. I cannot leave Mattina . . . not again."

"You *must*, Brendys," Quellin replied firmly, though not without sympathy. "Odyniec tells me she must remain here until she is well enough to travel. He will take care of her. But *you* have obligations. Think of Willerth and Kanstanon, trying to manage that farm by themselves. By this time, they probably think you are dead.

"And think of Brendyn . . . *especially* Brendyn. The memories here are too powerful for him. He has become terrified of this place, Brendys. He jumps at every sound and shadow. He needs to go *home*."

7

Squeezing his eyes shut, Brendys pulled Mattina's hand to his lips and kissed it. He knew in his heart that Quellin was right, as usual. Odyniec had told him much the same a few days earlier. The Wizard had also promised him that it would not be long before Mattina rejoined him. Would the mouthpiece of the Dawn King lie to him?

Reluctantly, he nodded his agreement. "Very well. I will go."

Quellin gave a relieved sigh and a sheepish grin. "I was hoping you would change your mind. With both Kovar and I here, Shannon and Sîan are the only ones who can understand Amrein. I am sure they will strong-arm Arella into meeting us in Shalkan."

Brendys's frown deepened, recalling the last time Shannon had seen him. Brendys had assaulted Quellin in blind rage—blaming his brother-by-marriage for Mattina's apparent death—in front of his nephew, who was but a lad of five summers at the time. "Are you sure of that? Shannon must be terrified of me."

Quellin's grin melted away into a solemn frown and his voice quieted even more. "He is. For six years, he has feared you. That is why I *do* hope they come. You have changed, Brendys . . . Shannon needs to see that. In all seriousness, Brendys, it *is* for the best."

Brendys felt a strange mixture of emotions welling up inside of him. He felt grief at the thought of leaving Mattina behind once again and fear of a potential confrontation with a nephew he had not seen in six years. Yet underlying it all, he felt a strange sense of relief at the thought of returning home, a peace which slowly thrust back the flood of terror battering at his heart. Slowly and reluctantly, he nodded, knowing that he could not remain at Lener Keep, no matter what his heart told him. He had a duty to his son which called him home.

"We should leave with Earon and his army in the morning," Quellin said, rising from the bed. "It would be safest to travel under their protection, until we have put sufficient distance between ourselves and the Dark Lands. By now, word of the Bearer of the Flame has surely begun to spread, and the enemy *will* seek you out."

"Brendyn and I will be ready," Brendys replied dully.

Quellin patted his brother-by-marriage on the shoulder, then slipped past him to stand at Mattina's head. He bent over and kissed his sister. He whispered something in old Gildean, which Brendys did not understand, then left the room.

Brendys remained in Mattina's chamber through the night, unwilling to leave her side, fearing all the while that it might be his last moment with her, despite the assurances of Quellin and Odyniec.

*   *   *   *

Though Brendys found parting with his wife a heart-wrenching trial, he honored his promise. In the morning, he and Brendyn, riding Fracas, his grey stallion, joined the Harvathine army as they marched forth from Lener Keep. From a distance, the column, resplendent in multi-colored livery and bright mail emerged from Lener Keep, winding its way south and west to their homeland.

As they rode out from the city gates, young Brendyn turned his liquid, blue eyes up to his father. "Isn't Mama coming with us?"

Brendys felt a stab of sorrow, but quickly put it aside. Right then, he had to think first of Brendyn, and Brendyn needed to be as far from Lener Keep as was possible. The child was tormented nightly by fearful dreams, and his fear did not abate with the coming of the dawn. Brendyn remained almost constantly at his father's side, afraid of the smallest shadow.

9

No matter his feelings in regard to Mattina, this was for the best. There was nothing he could do for her . . . she was in the Dawn King's hands now. He would have to trust Odyniec. Looking down into his son's expectant gaze, he shook his head. "Nay, Brendyn. She is still very ill and must stay here with Master Odyniec for a while longer."

The boy's lip began to quiver, and Brendys hurried to comfort him. Hugging his son with one arm and kissing his forehead, he said with a gentle smile, "It's all right, my son. She will join us soon . . . Master Odyniec promised me. You trust him don't you?"

Brendyn frowned uncertainly for a moment, then nodded in reply.

Brendys gave his son another smile, then cast a worried glance back towards Lener Keep. It was easy to speak of trust, but much more difficult to actually practice it. Some part of him still cried out that he should remain there, and he could not silence it.

"You did not abandon her, you know."

Startled by the voice, Brendys turned his gaze towards Prince Earon who had fallen back to ride beside him. The Crown Prince of Harvath was not looking at him, but rode with his head bowed, his grey eyes staring somberly at his horse's mane.

"You do not leave Mattina out of fear or stubborn pride," Earon continued, his voice low and solemn. "And any fool could see that you would rather stay than be separated from her again. You leave because you must."

Brendys was puzzled at the Harvathine Prince. A melancholy mood had inexplicably fallen on Earon since he had first arrived at Lener Keep. His strange behavior had been punctuated by his persistent avoidance of Brendyn. "Earon, is there something wrong?"

Earon looked at Brendyn, a deep sorrow entering his gaze. Brendys recalled the same expression on the

Harvathine's face when he had first laid eyes upon the boy as he lay in his father's arms upon the edge of the Black Altar.

A red flush rose to Earon's cheeks, and he lowered his eyes again. There was a long moment of silence, and Brendys was sure that the Harvathine Prince had decided not to reply. However, Earon at last broke the silence, his voice ragged with emotion. "When I turned seventeen, my father sent me to Corimuth to study with the Oranite scribes at Corimuth Keep. The local temple there was small, but they were renowned for their wealth of lore. My priorities, however, did not include the pursuit of wisdom and spiritual knowledge with old eunuchs.

"I met a common girl during the Morning Prayers." Earon paused, raising his head, his gaze becoming distant. "Semina was beautiful . . . so beautiful. Her skin was like burnished copper, her hair as black silk, her eyes like onyx. Even her Coriman speech I found beautiful and exotic. I was smitten instantly. From that day on, I spent more time sneaking out of the temple to be with her than I did studying."

Earon closed his eyes, a tear escaping from each eye. "Then she told me she was with child . . . *mine*. I swore her to silence. I could not allow word to spread that *I*, the Crown Prince of Harvath, had fathered a bastard, much less of a common girl. She bore me a son, but I refused to have anything to do with him. I left Corimuth Keep upon his first birthday, four years ago, and have not seen them since."

A disgusted grimace crossed the Harvathine's face. "It is not meet that a Prince should behave thus, so I put them out of my mind, pretending Semina never existed . . . that is, until I saw Brendyn lying battered and bleeding in your arms, and you pronounced him your son. Then—I know not why—my thoughts went immediately to Semina and her child, and I wondered what kind of life they were leading, or whether the boy had even survived beyond infancy."

Earon drew in a ragged breath and turned his grey eyes once more upon Brendys. "I brag about my battles won, but because of my pride, I lost the most important of them all. So you see, Brendys, I am well familiar with abandonment. You have no cause for guilt or grief, for you know you are only briefly parted from Mattina."

Brendys had no response, stricken speechless by the Harvathine's willing revelation.

*   *   *   *

The remainder of the week-long journey to Harvath Keep proceeded uneventfully, though Earon's mood had begun to lighten after his confession, the burden of the past years gradually lifting from his heart. He no longer avoided Brendyn and even ventured to speak to him on occasion, though he was clearly never fully comfortable with the child.

From Harvath Keep, Brendys, Quellin, and Brendyn began their long journey to Shalkan. The Elvinlord Guthwine of Greyleaf Forest and the Dwarf Asghar of the Crystal Mountains in the north—Brendys's friends and companions, both during the Siege of Gildea and this most recent struggle against Brugnara—as well as the two companies of Elves sent by Rasheth Joahin, accompanied them as far as the Elvin kingdom beneath the eaves of Dun Sol, the Forest of the Sun, at the Harvath-Ovieto border. There, they prepared to part company, each for their own homelands.

As Brendys and his companions dismounted and gathered beyond the eaves of Dun Sol, the Caletri who had journeyed with them proceeded into the forest, melting into the wood as though they had never existed, with nary the stirring of a leaf. Brendys knew the strange cloth of their garments and cloaks made it possible for them to blend completely into any natural surrounding, but to see nearly two hundred Elves vanish without a trace was still disconcerting. The tight grip Brendyn's small hands had taken on his arm told him that his son had also found the departure of the Elves more than a little out of the ordinary. Brendys smiled down at his son and rubbed a comforting hand through the boy's shaggy mane, eliciting a nervous smile in return.

To his right, Brendys saw Quellin bow to Guthwine and Asghar.

"When I asked you both to accompany Brendys on his journey to Shad, I did not anticipate that you would be required to help overthrow the government of that same nation," the Gildean King said to them, his youthful face grave. "You went beyond any call of duty and proved yourselves once more loyal companions and friends. For that, I thank you."

Captain Asghar bowed his thick body at the waist, his bald, pink pate gleaming in the sunlight, his long, red beard burning like copper. "'Tis nothing, Your Majesty. The Elf and I are ever at your beck, I am sure."

"Speak not so boldly for others, Dwarf," Guthwine said with a frown. His musical voice had a stern ring to it which caught everyone's attention. The Elf allowed a brief moment of unsettled silence before breaking into a smile, his sky-blue gaze drifting to rest upon Brendyn. "I do not regret my decision to come, however, for had I not, I would not have been afforded the opportunity to pay homage to the little Prince."

Brendyn blinked at the Elvinlord in confusion, then his mouth slowly dropped open in wonder as understanding finally dawned on him. He turned his astonished face up towards his father. "Is Lord Guthwine telling the truth, Papa? Am I really a Prince?"

Brendys smiled down at his son, but before he could answer him, Asghar blurted out, "Why of course, lad. Your mother is King Quellin's sister, making her a Princess, which in turn makes you a Prince."

Brendys stifled a laugh, his cheeks burning with the effort, greatly amused by the situation. He was fairly certain that the Dwarf was the only one of the adults present who did not at least suspect the truth. In fact, thinking back to the moment when his companions had arrived at Lener Keep and found him holding Brendyn, he recalled how Guthwine had knelt before them in a display of fealty to the proclaimed Hawk of Justice, whom Brendys knew to be his son. Even Quellin, King of Gildea, had called the boy his *Lord*.

For Brendys, the moment suddenly lost its humor as he recalled the dark look that fell upon the face of the High Steward, Mathai of Ascon, when Guthwine had knelt before Brendyn, fulfilling an ancient prophecy. *All Kindreds would kneel before the Hawk.* That was what Guthwine had said, and it had not settled well with King Mathai.

Brendys recalled as well Mathai's almost violent reaction when his father, Brendyk, many years before had worn the family crest when Brendys and Mattina were wed at Gildea Keep . . . a crest that Brendys now knew was descended from the arms of the House of Ascon. If Mathai truly understood the implications or not mattered little. It was clear that he at least suspected and did not approve. If that were so, the High Steward could be nearly as dangerous an enemy as any of the Deathlord's minions.

"Papa, I thought you were just making fun when you said you thought I could be a King!"

Looking down into his son's vibrant, blue eyes and seeing the glow of wonder upon his young face made it hard for Brendys not to smile, even through the pall of

14

gloom his thoughts had cast upon his heart. With his thick, tousled hair and dust-smudged cheeks, the child looked more a common waif than a Prince. Brendys found himself at a loss for words, for he was uncertain how to respond to his son.

Asghar, however, was ready with an answer. The Dwarf guffawed loudly and said, "'Tis not likely, lad!"

Brendyn looked at him with a puzzled frown. "Why?"

Asghar gathered his composure and placed a meaty hand on the boy's head, ruffling his hair. Brendyn flinched, but did not retreat from the Dwarf. "Ah, lad, your uncle is King of Gildea. For you to be King, he would first have to die, as would your cousin Shannon, for he is the heir to the throne. And after Shannon, your father would have to perish, for the crown would fall to him next. Thankfully, I do not think we will see such days come to pass in your lifetime."

The Dwarf's words struck Brendys like a hammer. A chill gripped his heart and his mind reeled. It had never occurred to him what price he might have to pay to bring the Heir of Ascon to the High Throne and fulfill his destiny. Now that price had become painfully clear. Brendyn could not ascend to the throne unless *he* died.

Numbly, Brendys raised his face towards the sunlit sky, a flurry of conflicting emotions warring within him, though none could manifest themselves. He felt suddenly empty, drained of life and strength. He felt betrayed, forsaken, yet an odd sense of peace countered his anger and pain, a resigned acceptance of his destiny. Indeed, had he not himself offered the Dawn King his life in exchange for that of his son?

Lowering his gaze, he noticed that everyone was staring at him. Quellin looked worried, and Brendys was sure that he had also drawn the same conclusion. Lord Guthwine's expression was almost as tranquil and unreadable as ever, but Brendys thought he detected a slight hint of amusement behind that placid mask. Asghar looked from one to the next in complete bewilderment, certain that he had missed something.

Brendyn grasped his father's hand, looking up in fear, tears welling up in his young eyes. "Papa . . . I don't want to be a King."

Brendys smiled sadly at the little boy, understanding at last his duty as the Bearer of the Flame, the destiny he had so long refused. *My son, there is no other way.* To Brendyn, he said, gently squeezing the child's hand, "Don't be afraid. All will be well."

Asghar cleared his throat in a not-so-veiled attempt to draw attention, then muttered, "Brendys, is there something you should be telling me? I seem to be making an ass of myself, without knowing why. . . ."

"Need you ask, Dwarf?" Guthwine replied with a smirk. "You dash the child's dreams by telling him dreadful stories of how everyone around him must die for him to become King, and you think your companions should be pleased?"

Asghar's face reddened as he barked back, "We Kjerek are a practical people, Elf. We do not believe in promoting false hopes within our offspring."

"Do you not?" Guthwine returned, his amusement growing. "Do you not still tell your children tales of days a-past of the glory of the Silver Mountains and repeatedly declare your intent to claim your realm of old?"

Asghar's scowl deepened as he glared at the Elvinlord. His voice rumbled dangerously as he replied, "Do not mock me, Elf. Such is not a *false hope*. Be it in my day or be it the honor of my descendants, the Throne of the Silver Mountains shall be reclaimed, and my line shall once again make the Delvelord's Threshold its home. The stench of the Kubruki shall not taint its halls forever."

16

Brendys had been grateful for Guthwine's interruption—it had drawn the Dwarf's attention from his original question—but now the subsequent debate was growing dangerous; however, the Elvinlord put his fears to rest. His expression turning serious, Guthwine looked squarely into Asghar's face. "I must beg your pardon, Dwarf. 'Twas but an ill-timed jest on my part. I must confess that there are none who dwell as distantly in the past as my own people. Indeed, as times grow darker, many Caletri retreat further into the once-was, shutting out what will be.

"The days of the Elves are ending and the days of Man beginning. My people face terrible choices: to hide within our borders until the Shadow of Thanatos consumes all that is, to walk the Road to Elekar and abandon this world, or to help bring order to this world so that Men may inherit a legacy of peace ere our days have ended."

Guthwine turned his sky-blue eyes upon Brendys, a half-smile curling his lips. "I made my choice when first I met you, Brendys of Shalkan. For better or worse, I have bound my fate to that of the Bearer of the Flame."

The Elvinlord turned and swung up onto his horse's back. He looked once more at his companions and raised his hand in farewell. "Fare you well upon your journeys, my friends. May the Light of the Dawn shine ever upon your paths."

Guthwine turned his mount's head towards Dun Sol and spurred him forward. The stallion sprang forward, quickly crossing the short distance to the wood, Elf and horse vanishing beneath the eaves of the forest.

Brendys sighed, then turned back to his remaining companions. "And thus is our company parted once again."

"Ah, but such is the way of it, Brother," Asghar replied, his muscular shoulders wilting in sorrow. He tossed his hood over his head, but not before Brendys saw tears beginning to well in the Dwarf's dark eyes. Brendys was surprised how quickly and freely the gruff warrior could shed tears. Asghar clasped Brendys's forearm with a strong hand. "Alas, I, too, must go my own way. The Crystal Mountains beckon me home, and I must heed their call."

Brendys smiled fondly at the Dwarf. "I think I begin to understand a little what it is to be . . . how is it you say it? *Kjerkena?* Farewell, Brother . . . Elekar willing, we will meet again before long."

Asghar clapped Brendys roughly on the arm, then looked down at Brendyn and ruffled the boy's hair again. "Aye. Be well, Brothers. May Kolis Bazân grant you strength in your journey."

The Dwarf bowed to his Kjerken and again to Quellin, then mounted his pony and rode away northward.

Brendys, Quellin, and Brendyn rested briefly there at the eaves of Dun Sol and took a meal before continuing their own journey north and east.

*   *   *   *

The journey across the Free Lands was peaceful, for the strength of Thanatos had been weakened once more with the death of his High Priest. The weeks saw them pass from Harvath into Folkor's home country of Ovieto, then through Nhan and Kahadral. A month after leaving Harvath Keep, they arrived at Hagan Keep in Racolis. Lord Dell greeted them with more joy than Brendys had seen from the man since the death of his son, Kradon, twelve years earlier. Word had first come that Brendys had been lost in Shad, the victim of Shadine treachery, but soon after, news that the Bearer of the Flame had been revealed reached Dell's ears, and he knew that Brendys lived.

After a brief rest at Hagan Keep, Brendys and his companions resumed their journey to Shalkan. The chill of autumn had fallen on the land. Thankfully, Dell had provided the travelers with clothing appropriate for the weather, making the remainder of the journey that much easier for them.

The nearer they came to Shalkan, the lighter Brendys's heart became. He told Brendyn about his home, about old Gwydnan—the former kitchenhand from the Shipyard of Ilkatar—and Kanstanon, his ward, now grown to manhood and at work in Brendys's stables. But most of all, Brendys spoke of Willerth, his devoted servant, and he spared his young son no detail, for he knew Brendyn, more than anyone, would understand Willerth's deepest pain—and Brendys knew that such empathy would be needed, for there was one last trial that had to be faced before they could finally take rest.

At last, they entered the confines of Barrier Mountain.

A nearly-forgotten sense of peace and security fell over Brendys as they crossed through the Eastern Pass into the sheltering embrace of his beloved Shalkan. They traveled through the day, reaching Ahz-Kham late in the afternoon. As they passed through the town, they were greeted by surprised shouts from the citizens, for they, too, had believed Brendys dead.

The sun was beginning to descend below the western ridge of Barrier Mountain, casting a great shadow across Shalkan, when they came within view of Brendys's farmstead. The Horsemaster reined Fracas to a halt and stared at the large spread of land, at the house where he was born and raised, excitement mixed with a small amount of trepidation filtering into his veins.

Home. But *was* it anymore? His parents and their old house servant, Farida—the people who had raised him— were gone. Was there anything left for him there?

"Papa?" he heard Brendyn say. "Is that home?"

In the distance, Brendys could see the silhouette of a man walking to the house from the stable—Kanstanon returning after finishing his day's work in the stable, he was sure. The pleasant glow of lamps lit the windows of the house, inviting him with its warmth. As the front door opened to allow the stablehand inside, Brendys thought he could faintly hear the sound of children's laughter drift out of the house, breaking the still of the evening.

"Aye, Brendyn," Brendys answered his son, the traces of a smile testing the corners of his lips. "That is home."

He turned his gaze towards Quellin. "Unless another has taken my land in my absence, it sounds as though your assumptions were right. Arella and the children did indeed come."

"Aye," Quellin replied with a nod. He cast a nervous look at his brother-by-marriage. "I should tell you that in the excitement of the moment, I *may* have left a detail or two out of the message I sent them."

Brendys raised a brow. "Such as?"

Quellin gave him a lop-sided smile. "I may have forgotten to mention Mattina and Brendyn."

Brendys nodded in reply, an impish grin crossing his bearded features.

They continued to the farmstead without further ado, riding in silence. By the time they reached the house, the sun had dipped below the peak of Barrier Mountain, bringing night to the farmstead. They tethered the horses to a hitching post outside the house.

Quellin dismounted first and hurried up the porch steps, eager to see his own wife and children. Brendys climbed off Fracas, tethered the horse, then helped his son down. He glanced up as Quellin entered the house. The sounds of surprised voices burst out through the open door.

Before Brendys could move towards the porch, Brendyn grabbed his hand. The boy wore a frightened expression, and his small voice trembled. "Papa . . . I'm scared!"

The Horsemaster knelt before his son and smiled. "Why ever for? This is your home, Brendyn . . . you have no need to be frightened here."

"But . . . but maybe they won't like me. . . ."

Brendys laid a comforting hand on his son's small shoulder. "Of course they will, Brendyn. You just remember what I told you and everything will be all right."

The boy responded with a silent, uncertain nod.

Brendys kissed him on the cheek, then stood up and walked to the house, Brendyn following slowly and timidly behind him. As Brendys walked up the porch steps, he could hear the excitement of Quellin's reunion with his family, but when he stepped into the doorway, the room went abruptly silent. He glanced around the room, taking in a sight long-missed, a hollow feeling growing in the pit of his stomach. Nothing had changed in the months he had been gone. The furniture, Mattina's portrait, the old clock . . . everything was the same.

No, not the same. The shadow of Brugnara's sorcery had been lifted, the pall of grief dissolved. This was the way his home was meant to be.

Quellin held his daughter in one arm, with his other draped over his son's shoulders. Arella stood beside them with her arm around her husband's waist. Her long, golden hair and brown eyes gleamed in the light of the hearth. Only in her mid-thirties, she was beautiful to behold.

Her daughter, a few months younger than Brendyn, had inherited her hair and eyes. Shannon, now eleven summers, had the chestnut hair and emerald eyes of his father and aunt and showed every sign of inheriting his father's slight build. His silver crown, ever-present, sat upon his brow, tilted at an angle. The children were unmistakably Quellin's, for they exhibited the Elvin beauty of their Trostain lineage.

In the front room, behind the Royal Family of Gildea, stood Kanstanon and Gwydnan. Willerth was not present. Everyone but Quellin and Gwydnan wore expressions of surprise and wonder. They had known from Quellin's message that Brendys was alive, but he had changed so much in appearance, with his closely-trimmed beard and shoulder-length hair and the new scars which adorned his face, that no one recognized him immediately.

Arella finally stepped forward to embrace her brother-by-marriage. When she pulled away, she looked him in the face, examining the new scars. "Brendys! Thank Elekar . . . we had thought the worst when Quellin told us you had fallen into the grasp of a Sorcerer."

"I have scars in both body and spirit that will never fade," Brendys replied solemnly, squarely meeting her gaze. "But I will live."

Arella's concern deepened. "Brendys, why didn't you come to us when we first thought Mattina died? We would have been there for you."

Brendys glanced at Quellin, grim memories rising up within his mind. "I *did* come, Arella, if you recall . . . and I regret that I did. I owe you and your family a long overdue apology."

"Nay, Brendys, you do not," Arella replied. "You were not yourself . . . I understood that from the beginning."

Brendys nodded slowly. "Indeed. And that is why I could not stay, why I could not heal . . . I had to find myself first."

She gave him a curious look. "And did you?"

"Aye," Brendys replied, straining to keep a grin from his lips. "And even more than I imagined possible."

Before Arella could respond, Brendys turned his attention to her children. He gave Quellin a nervous glance, at which the Gildean King set his daughter on the floor. Quellin nudged his children forward with his hands and a stern nod. The pair stopped at arm's length from their uncle, afraid to go nearer.

Brendys reached a hand out and gave his nephew's shoulder a gentle squeeze. "I want you to know, Shannon, how sorry I am that you have only seen me in grief and anger. I should like the opportunity to prove that I am not a monster."

The fear did not entirely leave Shannon's gaze, but he did give his uncle a silent nod of acceptance.

Brendys then looked down at his niece. "You must be Sîan."

The little girl nodded, no less wary of her uncle than was her older brother.

"I had no doubt," Brendys said, taking her hand in his, finally allowing a gentle smile to stretch across his face. "You are every bit as beautiful as your mother."

He bent over and kissed her hand, eliciting a blushing smile from the little girl's lips.

A quiet, hesitant voice drew the Horsemaster's attention to the stairway on his left. "Master Brendys. . . ?"

Brendys looked up to his left. Willerth was standing halfway down the staircase, firmly supporting himself on the handrail with one hand, while his other clutched the Elvinsilver pendant at his breast, a stunned look on his face. He was a little thinner than Brendys remembered, and his eyes were dark and sunken from a lack of food and sleep. The light of the lamps caused the tears welling in his eyes to glisten.

Brendys's own eyes misted. His servant had not looked so haggard since he had first come to Shalkan . . . not even during those bitter years when Brendys thought Mattina dead. The Horsemaster nodded slowly in response to the young man's question. "Aye, Willerth . . . I'm home."

Arella drew her children back as Willerth nearly fell down the remainder of the stairs, rushing to reach his master. He threw his arms around Brendys's neck, weeping. "I'm sorry, Master Brendys . . . I'm so sorry!"

Brendys drew the slight, young man away. "Sorry for what, Willerth?"

His servant bowed his head, avoiding the Horsemaster's gaze. "If I had known I was sending you into my father's clutches, I would never have convinced you to go with King Quellin. Never. . . ."

Brendys took the young man by the shoulders, fixing his gaze on his servant. "Willerth, it would not have changed anything. I *had* to go, and regardless of what I went through, I do *not* regret the decision for a moment."

Willerth looked up at his master in confusion. "How did you escape him?"

"I didn't," Brendys replied. His gaze turned grim. "Your father is dead, Willerth . . . truly dead. He will never again trouble the Mortal Realm."

His servant's grey eyes grew wider. "But . . . Master Gwydnan said. . . ."

"That only the Bearer of the Flame could destroy Brugnara," Brendys finished for him. He reached beneath his cloak and drew forth Denasdervien, cradling the weapon in both hands before his servant's bewildered gaze. The Horsemaster's eyes flicked towards Gwydnan. "The Hawk of Justice has been revealed."

His last statement had the effect he had hoped for. For a moment, however brief, the old man looked genuinely surprised by the revelation. Then his features became unreadable once more. Brendys had always felt there had been more to the old man than what he had been allowed to see. Now, he was certain.

"Master Brendys!" Willerth gasped, gawking at the mirrored surface of Denasdervien's Silver-gold blade. "I *hid* the sword . . . how did you. . . ?"

Brendys returned the weapon to its sheath. His steady gaze held his servant's. "I walked the Road to Elekar, Willerth, and found him waiting for me. I could no longer deny that which was set before me. I received Denasdervien from the hand of the Dawn King himself. I *am* the Bearer of the Flame."

Stunned silence once more blanketed the room. Even Quellin was startled by his revelation. Brendys had spoken of his experience in the dungeons of Lener Keep to no one, not even Odyniec. The only witness, Montine, the young Temple Servant who had betrayed Brugnara to aid Brendys, lay beneath a grave at Lener Keep, having given his life to save the Bearer of the Flame.

Brendys felt a slight tug at the back of his cloak and his smile was renewed. He placed a hand on his servant's shoulder. "Willerth, there is someone I would very much like you to meet."

Removing his hand from the young man's shoulder, he reached behind himself and drew Brendyn into the house, then closed the front door. He rested both of his hands on his son's small shoulders, prominently displaying Mattina's ring—the ring Willerth, himself, had given her—before everyone present. "This is Brendyn . . . my son."

If the silence had been complete after his previous revelation, it was deafening now. Arella and her children turned to look in amazement at Quellin, who grinned and nodded once in reply to their unspoken questions.

Willerth stared in equal astonishment at his master's child.

Brendyn looked up at his father. "He doesn't look like a little boy to me."

Brendys shook his head, his gaze steady upon Willerth. "That is only how I remembered him, Brendyn. Nay, he is a child no longer."

The boy shifted his curious gaze to Willerth. "Was the Great Father really your papa?"

Willerth glanced anxiously at his master, then returned his gaze to the boy. Swallowing back painful memories, he nodded silently in reply.

Brendyn frowned deeply, a tinge of sympathy entering his young voice. "Papa said the Great Father hurt you. . . ."

The boy lowered his head and his voice. "He hurt me, too."

Brendys watched as his servant slowly dropped to his knees before the boy. Staring in horror, Willerth reached out a hand and lifted the boy's chin. His eyes followed a ragged scar running up the child's neck from beneath his collar. He traced the mark with one finger, then pulled Brendyn's collar back far enough to reveal a portion of the boy's shoulder and chest and the map of deep and ugly scars drawn there by the Great Father's scourge.

With a strangled cry of grief, Willerth nearly collapsed in anguish and shame. He covered his face with both hands as he wept, his shoulders jerking violently with every choking sob.

Arella and Kanstanon both started towards the young man to comfort him, but Brendys waved them back. He looked down at his son, who was staring back at him with a sad frown. Brendys gave the boy an acknowledging nod.

Brendyn stepped towards Willerth, slipping his arms around the young man's neck. "It's all right . . . they don't hurt anymore."

Willerth wrapped his arms around the boy, hugging him close, but crying harder.

Brendys knelt beside his son and his servant, placing a hand on each of them. He lowered his voice to a whisper that only they could hear. "Willerth, six years ago you told me you were afraid. You asked me what you would do when the child came. He is here . . . have you found your answer?"

Willerth looked up at his master with a tear-stained face, struggling to regain his composure. He swallowed, then replied in a hoarse voice, "You were right, Master Brendys . . . I am *nothing* like my father."

Brendys smiled and nodded, rubbing his servant's shoulder.

"What about Mattina?" Arella said, glancing past the Horsemaster as though expecting her husband's sister to also appear. "Where is she? What happened?"

"She is still at Lener Keep with Odyniec," Brendys replied, the shadow of fear and longing again falling upon his heart. He rose to his feet, turning his gaze to the rest of his dumbfounded guests. "I suppose I owe you all a better explanation."

He headed for his favorite chair in the front room. "It is a long story. . . ."

Chapter 3

Brendys sat at his desk in the library, pouring over a letter of invitation from Kosarek, King of Racolis. The Throne of Racolis wished Brendys and his son to come to Racolis Keep to celebrate Brendyn's seventh birthday. It was the fifth such invitation the Horsemaster had received in the last two months from various Kings and Lords, and he was certain it would not be the last. Brendys's name had spread like a wildfire across Milhavior when he had been revealed to be the prophesied Bearer of the Flame, harbinger of the Heir of Ascon, and everyone wanted him to grace their halls with his presence for one reason or another. He did note that there was no such invitation from King Mathai, but that did not surprise him . . . the High Steward seemed to have taken a strange disliking to Brendys and his son.

Nay, there is nothing strange about it, Brendys thought bitterly. Whether because Mathai suspected the truth about Brendyn or simply viewed Brendys and what he represented as the Bearer of the Flame—the return of the rightful Heir of Ascon to the Thrones of Ascon and Milhavior—as a threat to his power, the reigning King of Ascon clearly did not receive him with the excitement and joy that the rest of the Free Lands exhibited.

He wearily rubbed the ragged scar on his right temple as he read the newest communication. His inclination was to refuse Kosarek's offer. He had hardly had a moment to rest after returning from his ordeal in Shad—*Lener*, he reminded himself. It was the custom of Milhavior for every nation to take the name of the current ruling House . . . except for Ascon. When Ascon was lost, the Dawn King had decreed that Evola, Ascon's brother, could never lay claim to the crown, though his descendants had, over the centuries, evidently abandoned hope that Ascon's Heir would return and reclaim the High Throne.

The very thought of leaving Shalkan again so soon after returning sapped his strength. There was still so much work to be done. Kanstanon, his stablehand, was a marvel with the horses, but he did not have a head for business, nor did Willerth, and though old Gwydnan might have supervised the docks at the Shipyard of Ilkatar, he was not a well man and could not manage the horsefarm alone. When Brendys had returned, he had discovered that the Magistrate of Ahz-Kham was beginning proceedings to annex his land because of debts unpaid and reports of his demise. Fortunately, the excitement of Brendys's return from supposed death had delayed the proceedings long enough for him to make good on his debts . . . with help from Quellin.

The workload also kept him from spending as much time with Brendyn as he would have liked. While he never missed an opportunity to express his love for his son, he knew it was not enough. Brendyn was, more or less, being reared by his servants, and Brendys felt that he was somehow failing in his own responsibilities.

Brendys put down King Kosarek's letter and ran a hand through his black hair, sighing. Truthfully, he could not blame all of his negligence on the farm. There were other matters he had felt the need to pursue, as well. He had delved into the *Annals of the Ancients*, seeking out the prophecies of the Bearer of the Flame and the Heir of Ascon. He still had questions that wanted answering, for he had learned very little of what his destiny truly entailed.

The only benefit of his current situation that he could think of was that it kept him from dwelling on his forced separation from Mattina. In the months after he returned to Shalkan, Brendys had only received one communication from Odyniec, telling him that Mattina had awakened from her long sleep, but that she was still not out of danger. He had received no word at all from his wife. It troubled him greatly, but he did not allow himself to fall into the trap of gloom that he only just escaped from. He had to believe that there was a good reason for the long silence.

He shoved his chair back and stood up, walking to the pedestal holding his father's copy of the *Annals of the Ancients*, a prize Brendyk had received as a gift from the Elvinlord Faroan of Dun Rial in gratitude for breeding services rendered. The great tome was lying open at the last passage Brendys had read. So far everything he had found repeated what he already knew . . . but he could not help but feel something was missing.

The passage Brendys was currently reading disturbed him, for it mirrored the era in which he lived. There was a foreshadowing of evil times in those lines:

> . . . *Gods will rise and fall and rise again, frail shadows cast by the greater Shadow, mere illusions of power to ensnare those who lust for it. Kingdoms shall reel beneath the weight of heedless superstition and foolish unbelief, alliances shall be forged and forgotten, and the cold fingers of Death shall clutch the hearts of the unwary. Still, within the Light of the Bearer's*

Flame, the Hawk of Justice shall arise, a Light from Darkness, Strength from Weakness, Life from Death. . . .

Brendys carefully turned the next yellowing page and stared down in bewilderment. A page had been torn from the book and replaced with a folded sheet of paper. Slowly, he lifted away the sheet and opened it. Hastily scrawled on the paper was a shield bearing the arms of the House of Hagan, the arms borne by Lord Dell. His brow wrinkled in confused frustration as he stared at the page.

"Father," he muttered quietly. "What were you hiding?"

Brendys had little doubt his father had left it there as a sign that the missing page would be found in Dell's possession. He felt a slight pang of sorrow at distant memories drawn into the light of the present. Brendyk, his father, had fallen into a fey mood in the days leading up to Brendys's wedding. He had seemed a man expecting to die.

Perhaps, he thought. *Father had already done what I am doing now and had learned his own fate and mine . . . and Brendyn's. Perhaps he had even seen his own death in these pages.*

Brendys shook off the thought. While he was almost certain he could have found another copy of the *Annals* in the libraries of one the nearby Ilkatari cities or even Dun Rial, his father had clearly intended for him to seek out Dell. His gaze strayed to King Kosarek's invitation lying on the desk. Returning to his chair, he took a blank parchment from the desk, then inked his quill and began to write a reply.

Greetings to Your Majesties, Kosarek and Rosa of Racolis.

31

I and my son graciously accept your invitation to celebrate my Brendyn's birthday in your fair city. The Kingdom of Racolis has always held the respect of my family from the days of Evinrad, my grandfather. Though I am sure you already intend to make this an event of significance throughout the Free Lands, I have taken the liberty of sending special invitations to the following persons, my companions through many trials and hardships:

Quellin, son of Quiron, King of Gildea, and his household

Dell, son of Hestin, Lord of the House of Hagan, Regent of Racolis

Asghar, son of Asghol, Delvecaptain of the Crystal Mountains, Heir to the Throne of the Silver Mountains

*Folkor, Captain of the **Sea-Dog**, of Wice Keep in Ovieto*

Guthwine, Elvinlord of the Caletri of Greyleaf Forest, and his household

Englar, Lord of the House of Lener-Shad, King of Lener

Earon, son of Welmon, Lord of the House of Harvath, Crown Prince of Harvath

Your servant, Brendys, son of Brendyk, of Shalkan, Prince and Regent of Gildea, Lord of the House of Trost, Kjerken of Asghar of the Crystal Mountains, Bearer of the Flame of Elekar.

Despite Brendys's own dislike of formality, he used every title he had ever been given, though he was certain the order was not correct. Kosarek was true royalty. Title and status meant everything. He read through the letter, glowering at his own lack of knowledge of diplomatic protocol, then rolled his blotter across the page.

When he was sure the ink was dry enough, he rolled the parchment, then sealed it with hot wax, imprinting his family crest into the seal with his signet ring. He stared for a moment at the crest: a hawk bearing a heart in one talon and a flaming sword in the other upon the blazon of a sun. He closed his eyes, remembering his miraculous ordination at Lener Keep.

After Brendys had saved his son from death at the hands of Willerth's father—Brugnara, the Great Father, Sorcerer in the service of Thanatos—the Dawn King had sent a messenger in the form of a hawk of gold. The shining spirit had alighted upon the altar, proclaiming the Hawk of Justice, the Light of Elekar's Flame. *The Hawk of Justice.*

Brendys had at first believed the messenger to be proclaiming *him* as the Bearer of the Flame, but the Hawk of Justice was a name given to the Heir of Ascon, and Odyniec had promised him that *he* was not the appointed Heir, only his harbinger. It struck Brendys then that the spirit had descended upon the altar where his son lay. At that very moment, he had known that his beloved and only child was Ascon's Heir, destined to take the High Throne of Milhavior.

Odyniec warned him to keep his knowledge hidden to protect Brendyn, but Brendys did not need the advice. Brendyn's life was already at risk as the son of the Bearer of the Flame. If even rumor spread that the boy was actually the Heir of Ascon, there would be no end of mercenaries and hunters in the employ of Machaelon invading Shalkan.

Brendys withdrew more paper from his desk and began the chore of writing invitations to those he had listed in his reply to Kosarek. He also composed letters of polite refusal to those Kings and Lords that had previously entreated him for similar honors.

Before he was finished, he looked again at the sealed invitation to Earon, an intriguing and somewhat mischievous plan forming in his mind. While the Crown Prince of Harvath had in the end proven a loyal friend and ally, Brendys had been forced to endure his pride and arrogance for many days before Asghar had taken a proverbial hammer to Earon's ego. Perhaps it was time to return the favor. . . .

A devilish grin crossed Brendys's lips as he withdrew another sheet of paper from his desk.

When he was finished, Brendys bundled the sealed letters together, then arose and stepped around his desk. He walked from the room and down the stairs to the ground floor, making his way to the washroom at the back of the kitchen. As he opened the washroom door, he heard a loud splash and surprised yelp.

Willerth sat on the floor beside the washtub, soapy water dripping from his hair and nose, a dismayed grimace on his face. Brendyn sat in the tub, soap suds in his hair, laughing at the drenched house servant.

Willerth looked up with a rueful frown as his master entered the room. "I don't know how much more I can take of this, Master Brendys. Sometimes, I think it would be simpler to tie him in a bundle and dunk him a few times, then hang him out with the laundry to dry."

Looking insulted, Brendyn slapped both arms and legs in the tub, sending a fresh spout of water splashing over Willerth's head. The six-year-old giggled in delight at his victim.

Willerth turned red in the face and crossed his arms, looking stubborn. "That is the end! No more. From now on, Gwydnan and Kanstanon can put in their fair share of bathing the little beast!"

Brendyn blanched suddenly at the suggestion. His brow furrowed and lip quivered as he said, "I'm sorry, Willerth. I'll behave."

Brendys knew his son's apology was genuine. The threat of being bathed by the ever-grumpy Gwydnan was itself enough to bring civility to the most precocious child . . . but for Brendyn, it was worse. The boy's body was riddled with ugly, ragged scars, inflicted by Brugnara's scourge at Lener Keep in *preparation* for his sacrifice—a horrible reminder that he would bear for the rest of his life. Brendyn was very self-conscious about his scarred body and would allow no one but his father and Willerth to see it.

The anger quickly drained from Willerth's face, replaced by a slightly guilty frown, as he looked at the boy. "It's all right, Master Brendyn . . . you know I wouldn't do that to you. But you *could* make it a little easier for me."

The youngster nodded quickly in earnest assurance. "I will . . . I promise!"

Brendys smiled fondly at the pair. Despite his grumbling, Willerth spoiled Brendyn more than anyone else at the farmstead. The servant's loyalty to the child was only slightly less than his loyalty to Brendys. The Horsemaster knew they shared a common bond: Brendyn's physical scars closely reflected the emotional and spiritual scars Brugnara had inflicted on Willerth as a child.

Willerth picked up his washrag, then glanced towards his master. "I'm sorry, Master Brendys . . . was there something you needed?"

Brendys nodded and raised the bundled letters. "When you are done here, I want you to take these to the Postmaster. I will leave it on the kitchen table."

"Certainly, Master Brendys," the young man replied.

As Brendys turned to leave the washroom, he heard Willerth tell Brendyn, "If you are good, I may let you go with me. And if you are *really* good, we *may* stop by the confectionery. . . ."

Shaking his head, Brendys closed the door and tossed the bundle on the kitchen table.

*   *   *   *

He had intended it as a bluff to keep his young charge's jubilant bath-time hijinks to a minimum, and it had been successful. When it came time for Willerth to take his master's letters to the Postmaster, he could not refuse the look of innocent anticipation with which Brendyn assailed him while he saddled his bay gelding, Hashan. At last, he yielded to the boy's silent pleas, and saddled Sprite, Brendyn's chestnut pony. Admittedly, Brendyn had been on his best behavior for the entire ride to the outskirts of Ahz-Kham, though the eager anticipation of his sweet reward showed brightly on his round face.

Willerth opened the door to the Postmaster's outpost and ushered Brendyn inside. As he followed his ward into the building, he closed the door behind him. The postal system had been established by the High Steward a few months earlier as a means for the common people to communicate between towns and cities. Every city was required to maintain an outpost and riders to collect and deliver letters. However, the costs involved were still such that only the wealthy could afford the tariffs for delivery.

Doubling as a general store for the mail-riders, the interior of the outpost was crowded with racks, cabinets, and shelves stocked with rations and travel necessities. As Willerth and Brendyn approached the counter, the young, black-haired Postmaster looked up and smiled. "Willerth, Brendyn, what can I do for you today?"

"Master Brendys would like these sent out as soon as possible, Aden," Willerth replied, handing the bundle of letters to the Postmaster.

"Let me guess . . . Lener Keep, Gildea Keep, or Hagan Keep?" Aden asked.

Willerth grinned. "All and more. King Kosarek has decided to make Brendyn's seventh birthday into a national celebration—Lord Dell's doing, no doubt. I don't think that old crow Kosarek knows the meaning of kindness or cheer."

"No doubt you are right." Aden removed the string from the bundle and slid the rolled parchments into a series of slots on the practically empty rack behind him. "I'm expecting riders this afternoon. I'll make sure these go out."

"Thank you, Aden," Willerth replied. He looked down at his young charge. "Well, I guess I promised you something from the confectionery. Shall we?"

Brendyn nodded in return, beaming in anticipation, hardly able to conceal his excitement any longer.

As they exited the outpost, Willerth said, "I think we will walk, Master Brendyn."

Brendyn curled his lip sourly at the suggestion, but did not argue.

Together, they led their mounts down the main street of Ahz-Kham. As they neared *The Green Meadow Inn*, Willerth cast an apprehensive eye at the two-story building. Even after fourteen years, it was hard for him to forget what he had gone through there. Images of his father's weaselly, unshaven face sprang up before his mind's eye, but he shunted them away almost as quickly. His scars ran deep; however, he had learned to live with them.

When they were almost even with the inn, Willerth noticed two men standing outside it, arguing. Their voices were low, but the tone was clearly heated. One of them, the young man knew. It was his master's old—and very much *former*—friend Languedoc. The lanky man was a year or two older than Brendys, but had the same black hair, blue eyes, and tanned complexion common to most Shalkanes.

The other man Willerth had never seen before. He was nearly as big and muscular as Folkor, captain of the *Sea-Dog*. His steel-grey beard was thick, though not very long, and his eyes had a strange amber hue. Even more unusual was his manner of dress. He wore a sleeveless jerkin and trousers made of wolf hide and heavy boots trimmed with fur. Upon his head and shoulders sat a cowl made of wolf heads—one head topping his own and one resting upon each knotted shoulder.

Languedoc cast a spiteful glance in the direction of Willerth and Brendyn, then directed the wild-man's attention to them with a jerk of his head. After a few more angry words, Languedoc held out his hand and the wild-man casually passed him a small coin pouch, immediately losing all interest in the argument.

An unsettling sensation fell upon Willerth. With his right hand, he gently prodded Brendyn to hurry. "Let's go, Master Brendyn"

They had walked on no more than a few feet when they were brought to a halt by a low, gruff voice. "Ho there, boy! I would have a word with you."

Willerth paused, then turned to face the speaker. Rankling, he drew himself up to his full five feet, three inches and glared up at the stranger. "I may be short, sir, but I am not a *boy* and have not been labeled such by any for many years."

The wild man hesitated a step, taken aback by the slight, young man's response. "I was given to believe that you are the servant of the local Horsemaster, Brendys. Is this not true?"

Willerth gave a curt nod in return. "I am."

"Then you are a boy," the man replied in a reasonable tone, bordering on patronizing. "In my land, *men* may not be bought or sold. Therefore, you must be a boy."

Willerth stared at the man in disbelief. "I am a willing servant of Master Brendys, sir. I was not *bought*. Slavery is illegal in the Free Lands. Now, if you would excuse us, we have things to do."

"Of course," the man replied with a grin which reminded Willerth of the wolf heads he wore. His gaze drifted for the first time down to young Brendyn. "You must be the son of the great Bearer of the Flame. I have business to conduct with your father. Perhaps we shall meet again."

Brendyn did not reply, but only stared fearfully at the wild man. When the man turned and walked back to the inn, he looked up at Willerth. "Who was that man?"

Willerth shook his head, watching the man's back, the chill of apprehension running through his veins. "I don't know, Master Brendyn, but I don't like the look of him. I think we should finish quickly here and head home."

Brendyn nodded solemnly in response, a sweet treat no longer at the forefront of his own priorities.

They continued on to the confectionery, but spent little time there before hurrying back to the farmstead. When they arrived at home, they found Brendys and Gwydnan waiting in the front room.

Gwydnan was nearly red in the face as he argued with the Horsemaster. "I tell you, they could be in trouble. You should ride out after them."

"*Why?*" Brendys replied in exasperation. "I don't expect them home for another half an hour at least. Would you rather I succumb to fear and anxiety and imprison my son in the cellar?"

The old kitchenhand opened his mouth to respond, but stopped when he noticed Willerth and Brendyn at the door.

As they approached, a look of relief crossed the man's aged features, and he leaned heavily upon his cane.

Brendys looked at them, then turned back to Gwydnan. "I told you they would be fine. You worry too much, you old goat."

The old man gave him a sharp glance, then shifted his gaze to Willerth. "Did you see aught of anyone else on the road?"

"Do you mean the wolf-man?" Brendyn piped, while chewing a bite of sweet taffy.

Gwydnan's gaze hardened suddenly, but he said nothing.

Brendys gave his servant a puzzled look. "What is he talking about, Willerth?"

"Did he not come here?" Willerth responded, himself confused. "He said he had business with you."

Brendys shook his head. "No one has been here today. Who was this *wolf-man?*"

Willerth shrugged. "I don't know, Master Brendys. He didn't name himself. He was certainly a strange one though, dressed all in wolf skins. He and Master Languedoc had a row out in front of *The Green Meadow*, then he gave Master Languedoc a small purse and approached us. A very odd experience from beginning to end."

"I didn't like him," Brendyn added with a serious expression. "He looked scary."

Brendys shook his head again. "He doesn't sound familiar. What say you, Gwydnan?"

There was no reply from the old man, for he had left the room while master and servant were talking. Brendys sighed and turned back to Willerth. "I don't think it is anything to worry about. To be on the safe side, perhaps you shouldn't take Brendyn to town with you for awhile, unless I am with you."

Willerth nodded in agreement.

Brendyn stuck his lip out in a pout, but did not fuss.

As Willerth and Brendyn continued upstairs, Brendys sat down in his favorite chair and leaned forward, propping his chin up with one hand, a worried look on his face. *It is beginning already. Elekar, what am I supposed to do?*

Chapter 4

It was night, a night made darker by the all-encompassing shadows cast by the looming walls of Barrier Mountain, but it made little difference to him. He saw as well at night as he did during the day . . . better, in his opinion. He reveled in the macabre sense of power the ruddy light of his beast-form's sight granted him. He thirsted for blood, and tonight he would savor the richest blood to be found in Milhavior. *The second richest*, he reminded himself. The Heir of Ascon would be the ultimate prize, but until he could ferret out the Heir, he would settle with the blood of the Bearer of the Flame.

As he stalked into the farmstead's darkened stableyard, each of his three lupine heads scanning the grounds for any sign of life, he felt a sudden weight upon him, a wall of resistance through which he could not pass. All three of his heads turned their attention towards the house. At the foot of the porch steps stood an old man, leaning heavily upon a cane. It was hard to look directly upon the man, for the Fire of the Dawn burned within him, and in beast-form, the hunter's eyes could not abide it. A low growl rumbled from three throats, but he did not shrink from his foe.

The old man straightened to his full height, appraising the hunter with a critical eye. "Ach, Kerebros of Haff, I guessed it would be you. Least finger on the crippled Hand of Thanatos. Your Lord must be desperate indeed if he seeks to pit *you* against the Bearer of the Flame. But then, Michuda, Iysh Mawvath, and the Great Father have all perished, so that leaves little to choose from . . . a formless spirit or a shapeshifting Man. Turn aside now, Wolf, you cannot enter here."

Kerebros snarled again, frustrated and disgusted. The old man spoke true. He had not garnered enough power to counter the Fire set against him here . . . not yet. But there was time. The old man was weakening. Eventually, he would be able to pierce the veil of protection set upon the home of Brendys of Shalkan. He could wait patiently for the proper time.

Still, the old man's words rankled him. Did he truly believe the Black Hand had been *crippled?* A few minor set-backs; however, the Hand had not lost as many fingers as he evidently believed . . . and there was more power in the *least* of them than he could comprehend.

"You underestimate my master, Gwydnan," Kerebros growled through his beast-form's central head. "Even now, a Storm is rising which you cannot hold back. In the Far North, Krifka has awakened a power which will not rest until it has consumed Mankind, and in Chi Thanatos, preparations are being made for the master's return, yet you have the gall to flaunt your dying Fire? How sad."

Kerebros felt a surge of self-satisfaction at the hint of fear which flickered across the old man's face. It lasted but a fleeting moment, but it was enough to appease the Sorcerer. Three wolf heads leered at the old man. "I shall return, Gwydnan of Athor, and shall taste of the Bearer's blood."

Kerebros did not hear Gwydnan's reply, for even as he finished speaking he was enveloped in the blood-red light of his own power and transported from the stableyard. He would bide his time.

*   *   *   *

Gwydnan stared into the night, wondering that the Sorcerer had found the courage to approach the stead alone. Kerebros was becoming reckless in his old age. He did not share even a minute portion of the power wielded by the other Sorcerers of Thanatos. Had he really believed that he could defeat the Bearer of the Flame in his own home, alone and unaided?

It was a disturbing thought. Perhaps Kerebros had grown stronger in the last couple of decades. He had always relied on brute strength, focusing his magic into creating the hideous beast-form which he favored, but strength alone could not bring him victory against the wielder of the Living Flame. The power which burned within Denasdervien, the living power of the Dawn King himself, could not be defeated by strength of arms. What did the Wolf have planned?

"Master Gwydnan?" he heard Kanstanon's worried voice say from the doorway behind him. "It is late . . . is everything well?"

The old man turned towards the open door. Kanstanon was silhouetted in the entryway, holding a candlestick. Gwydnan felt a tremor of emotion as he looked at the young man, recalling the boy he had raised. The duty of protecting Brendys and his family would soon fall upon the stablehand's shoulders.

Gwydnan had tried to prepare his ward the best he could. He had even taught Kanstanon some things that were forbidden to him, things that should perhaps have been left unlearned. He was not sure yet whether Kanstanon was ready for the responsibility or not, but there would be little choice when the time came.

"We have had a visitor, Kanstanon," Gwydnan answered gruffly. "Do not sleep tonight."

*　*　*　*

The days went by, and at last the seasons passed from spring into summer. No sign had been seen of the strange wolf-man since Willerth and Brendyn had first encountered him, and would have been all but forgotten had Gwydnan not persistently hinted that he might be more than he first seemed. Brendys was beginning to tire of riddles and vague allusions, but neither was he apt to discount the old man's grumbling, for he had long felt there was more to Gwydnan than he had admitted to.

Nevertheless, whatever dangers might lay ahead, he could not simply hide in a corner, trembling in fear. He was the Bearer of the Flame . . . he would have to learn to face whatever challenges were set before him. With the changing of the seasons, Brendys and his son prepared to begin their fortnight journey to Racolis Keep, accompanied by Willerth.

As dawn broke, Kanstanon had Brendys's grey stallion, Fracas, Brendyn's pony, Sprite, and Hashan, Willerth's mount saddled and waiting in the stableyard when the Horsemaster and his son came out of the house. Willerth finished loading provisions onto their pack horse, then joined the rest of the farmstead's occupants at the foot of the porch steps.

"Brendys," Gwydnan said, glowering at the Horsemaster. "I wish you had requested an escort. It troubles me that you journey unprotected."

"We are hardly unprotected," Brendys replied, patting Denasdervien's battered, black hilt.

Gwydnan gave him a sour look. "You hardly be a swordsman, Brendys. I would feel even a little better were

45

Kanstanon and I accompanying you. There be safety in numbers."

Brendyn looked up at the old man. "Aren't you coming with us?"

Gwydnan allowed a rare smile to crack his aged countenance. "Nay, lad. I must stay and help Kanstanon care for the farmstead."

Brendys grimaced. He knew Gwydnan's increasingly poor health was the only reason he did not accompany them, but a sharp glance from the old kitchenhand belayed any comment from the Horsemaster.

"But it's going to be my birthday," Brendyn replied with a sad frown.

Kanstanon gently rubbed the boy's shaggy hair. "We will celebrate again when you return."

"You promise?" Brendyn asked solemnly, looking from Gwydnan to Kanstanon.

Gwydnan nodded in return. "Of course, lad."

Brendys placed a hand on his son's back and guided him in the direction of his pony. "The day's a-wasting. It's time to go."

Gwydnan grasped the Horsemaster by the shoulder, his grip amazingly strong for a man of his extreme age and poor health. His voice was low and ominous. "There are many dangers in the wilderness, Brendys. Beware of *wolves*."

Brendys half-turned towards the old man, focusing his azure gaze on Gwydnan's grim face. He understood the kitchenhand's veiled warning. He had heard similar more times than he cared to remember over the last few months. Nevertheless, a twinge of uncertainty tugged at him for a moment.

He placed a hand on Denasdervien's Crorkin pommel, its Elvin warmth driving away his doubts. With a quick, steady nod, Brendys turned away from Gwydnan and took

Fracas's reins from Kanstanon, easily mounting the grey stallion. He urged Fracas to the eastward road, Brendyn beside him on Sprite, Willerth trailing behind, leading the sumpter horse.

By midday, they had ridden out of Shalkan through the Eastern Pass and into the open lands of Ilkatar. From the Eastern Pass, they headed almost due east towards the Great River, Anatar. They camped in the grasslands of Ilkatar that day and reached the river at the end of the next.

As night fell on the second night, they set camp on the banks of Anatar. After a quick meal, Brendyn fell fast asleep, weary from that day's long journey. Willerth spread his bedroll out on the opposite side of the fire and lay down. After Brendys unrolled his own blanket next to his son's, he reached down to unbuckle his swordbelt. His hand brushed Denasdervien's Crorkin hilt, and the black Elvinmetal sent a jolt of power through his arm. He jerked his hand back in surprise, then gripped the wire-wrapped hilt, feeling its power throb beneath his touch.

Evil was near, though distant enough not to pose an immediate threat. Brendys stared northward. Though cloaked by night shadows, he knew that Ilkatar Forest lay only a few hours from their campsite. He had always felt uneasy about that wood, as though something dark dwelt there . . . Denasdervien seemed to agree.

"Master Brendys, what is wrong?"

The Horsemaster glanced at his servant. Willerth was sitting up, staring worriedly at him.

"Nothing," Brendys replied with as much confidence as he could muster.

Willerth gave him a disbelieving frown.

Brendys sighed. It was no use trying to hide the truth from his servant. Willerth knew him too well. "Denasdervien senses something, but it is not too near."

Willerth stared at him a moment longer, then gave a quick nod and laid back down.

Slowly, Brendys loosened his swordbelt and lay down, but kept his hand upon the throbbing grip of the Sword of the Dawn. In the distance, the howling of wolves pierced the silence of the night. Brendys sat up at the noise and scooted closer to his son, staring warily into the darkness.

Willerth also darted upright, glancing in the direction of Ilkatar Forest. He turned his gaze back to his master. "Don't tell me that was my imagination, Master Brendys."

"It wasn't," Brendys replied, grimly cursing to himself. Though not unknown, wolves were scarce in that region. He had the feeling these wolves had more than a little to do with Willerth's *wild-man*. "You sleep . . . I will take watch tonight."

Willerth stood up and dragged his blanket around the fire and spread it out on Brendyn's other side. He drew a long-knife from his pack and lay down next to his master's son.

Brendys said nothing.

* * * *

For the next couple of days, the travelers followed Anatar along its course, until they reached the point where Den Pelacor branched northeasterly from the Great River. They followed Den Pelacor for three days until it curved almost due north. A smaller river continued northeast, emptying into Sapphire Lake north of the Podan Peaks. At this fork, they forded Den Pelacor and made for the Podan Dwarvinholt, where Delvecaptain Rodi—Asghar's cousin one-hundred times removed—dwelt.

During the entire journey, Brendys kept his left hand on Denasdervien's pommel. The throbbing power did not lessen, nor did it grow through the days, and every night the ghostly howls of wolves broke the silence. The pursuing Evil convinced Brendys to seek refuge at the Podan Peaks, though a similar pursuit seven years earlier had ended with an attack by the Great Father in his Drolar form, resulting in the slaughter of the Dwarvin gatewarders and Willerth's brush with death within the Dwarvinholt itself.

The travelers dismounted and led their steeds up the road leading to the Dwarvinholt's southern gate. As they approached the gateway, lit by red flames billowing from the open jaws of the stone dragons carved into either side of the arched entry, Brendys recalled the trepidation he had felt on his first visit seven years earlier. The great dragon lamps were almost lifelike in appearance, and the red fire cast an eerie glow across the threshold. He looked down at Brendyn and smiled. The boy was pale with fright, staring wide-eyed at the fire-belching dragon lamps.

"It's all right, Brendyn," Brendys said, placing a reassuring hand on his son's shoulder. "They aren't real. They are just stone lamps."

Before they had gone much farther, a deep voice boomed out from the unseen guardpost. "Halt, *Jontn!* State your names and purpose."

Brendys still jumped at the voice, though he had been expecting it.

"Brendys and Brendyn of Shalkan," the Horsemaster called back. "And Willerth, our servant. We seek refuge for the night."

Muted by the thick stone walls, Brendys could hear the gatewarder call for the gates to be opened. The huge, stone portals swung inwards, opening into a large, lamplit entrance hall. Standing just inside the gateway was a yellow-haired Dwarf. The Dwarf stood only a few inches taller than Brendyn, but his shoulder-width was half again that of Willerth's, thickly muscled beneath his chain shirt.

The gatewarder bowed to the Horsemaster and his son, his braided beard almost brushing the ground. "Welcome back to the Podans, Brother. Our gates are ever open to you. Delvecaptain Rodi was summoned deepholt by King Bjerkaas, but I will show you to the guest chambers."

As the Men led their mounts through the gateway, the Dwarf said, eyeing the horses nervously. "You may leave your beasts here. They shall be cared for."

"Perhaps you should lead us to your stables first," Brendys replied. "Fracas will not allow any stranger to handle him."

The Dwarf nodded with some relief. "Very well. It is not far."

Their escort took them to the gate garrison's stable, where Brendys and Willerth saw to their mount's needs, though the stalls were clearly meant for ponies, not horses. Afterwards, the gatewarder led them through the maze of passages to the corridor where the guest chambers were located. As they approached the room, Brendys noted that a stone door had replaced the former wooden one.

The Dwarf, noticing his expression, said, "Our Gatemasters put the door in shortly after your last visit. It can be bolted from the inside. We also leave the lamps lit and guards posted in the corridor when we have visitors. We do not wish a repetition of our last experience."

"Aye, it would be well to keep your guard up tonight," Brendys replied. He placed his hand on the hilt of the short sword at his side, but felt nothing but the usual warmth of the Elvinmetal. "Denasdervien spoke of Evil hounding us all the way from Ilkatar Forest, though it does not seem to sense anything now. I would be particularly wary of wolves."

The Dwarf stared for a moment in reverent awe at the hilt of the Living Flame, then scribed a symbol in the air before him and muttered something in Kjerekil. He raised his dark eyes to meet Brendys's gaze. "No creature, living or Deathless, will enter here this night, else my life be forfeit."

He bowed to Brendys, then said, "May your night be peaceful, Your Highness."

Brendys returned the parting and followed his son and servant into the guest chamber, shutting and bolting the door behind them. He motioned Brendyn towards the bed at the back of the small chamber. Willerth quickly claimed the bed nearest the door—the same bed he had occupied on that fateful journey seven years before, determined to protect his master.

Brendys glanced around the room, memories of those dark days reaching chilling fingers into his mind. His eyes lowered to the floor between the beds where Willerth had lain, chest torn open where he had fallen upon Brendys's crown during the struggle with Brugnara. He closed his eyes. *Scars. So many scars.*

Brendys shivered, but not from the chill of his memories. Hidden forever from the sun, the room was cool as an autumn morning, despite the summer warmth outside the Dwarvinholt. His gaze fell upon his son's peaceful face. Brendyn, his clothes scattered haphazardly on the floor, was already curled snugly beneath the heavy, woolen covers, fast asleep.

The Horsemaster's last journey to Racolis Keep had culminated in a message from Gildea that his wife and unborn child had perished at Brugnara's hand, sending him on a six-year trek through the shadows of Hál. His nightmare ended when he gave himself to his destiny as the Bearer of the Flame of Elekar and put an end to Brugnara's Deathless life. At Lener Keep, he also found that Mattina and Brendyn had survived through Brugnara's machinations and had dwelt there for those six years under the protection of Englar, Lord of Lener.

With a sigh, Brendys undressed, blew out the single lamp, and climbed into bed, gently moving his son closer to the wall. Sleep was long in coming, the fearful memories of this chamber gnawing at his mind, but it did come at last.

The night passed without incident, and in the morning, Brendys and his companions continued their journey, turning eastward to Daggs Keep and beyond, to Racolis Keep. By the end of that day, they reached the southern eaves of Woodland. Denasdervien no longer warned of evil, nor did the howl of wolves pursue them. Brendys was certain that their stalker had turned aside for fear of the forest's inhabitants. Woodland was home to a faction of the Saraletri—the rustic Wood Elves—and Evil would not come near except in force, prepared for war.

Five days after leaving the Podan Peaks, they arrived at Racolis Keep. Night had fallen, allowing them passage through the city unnoticed by its inhabitants. After announcing themselves, they were permitted access to the Keep itself, where they were met by King Kosarek's chamberlain. The King and Queen had already retired for the evening, so the chamberlain escorted Brendys and his companions to their own chambers.

The chamberlain offered to have the kitchen prepare a meal for them, but so weary were they from their journey that Brendys declined, opting instead to go directly to bed. The chamberlain left, but before Brendys and his son could cross the antechamber to the bedroom, there came a knock at the outer door.

Brendys turned his head to look over his shoulder, a slightly annoyed expression on his face. "Enter."

The door opened, and two children darted into the room with excited greetings, followed with a little more dignity by their parents. Brendys caught up his young, golden-haired niece in a bear-hug, then sat her back on her feet and clapped his nephew on the shoulder. Both children possessed the uncanny, nearly Elvin beauty common to the House of Trost.

Indeed, Shannon was already beginning to show his father's blood, for though he was twelve summers, he looked no more than a slender ten-year-old. His taste in attire also followed his father's, tending towards bright, often gaudy colors. His silver crown, ever-present, sat at a cocky angle upon his brow . . . he was a handsome youth and knew it.

Sîan wore a delicate, pale-green gown and slippers. She was a few months younger than Brendyn and had not yet begun to show the extraordinary, prolonged youth of her forefathers that her brother was only beginning to show himself, but Brendys was sure it would not be long.

Arella stepped forward to embrace the Horsemaster and kiss him on the cheek. Like her daughter, she was dressed in a light gown, though hers was a pale brown, with green trim. Her long, golden hair was braided down her back.

Grinning broadly, Quellin greeted his brother-by-marriage with an embrace, then stepped back, looking up at the tall Shalkane. Brendys stared back, shaking his head in wonder. Every time he saw Quellin, the Gildean King looked practically unchanged. Time crept slowly upon him, for though he was nearly forty-one, Quellin still looked no older than seventeen or eighteen summers.

"I am glad you could come," Brendys told Quellin and Arella. His gaze shifted to his son, who had put away all thoughts of sleep and was already chattering gaily with his cousins. "It means much to Brendyn."

"Did you doubt we would come?" the King of Gildea responded with a grin.

"Nay, of course not!" Brendys replied quickly. He glanced down at his son again, his smile fading into a troubled frown as he recalled his true purpose for coming to Racolis Keep.

Arella noted the Horsemaster's expression and placed a hand on her husband's arm. "Quellin, perhaps we should have waited until tomorrow. Surely, Brendys and Brendyn are weary from their journey."

Quellin regarded her briefly, then turned his piercing green gaze back to the Horsemaster. "Brendys?"

Brendys started from his thoughts. "Eh? Oh! Nay, not at all! I just remembered that I have matters I need to take up with Dell."

"Business on an occasion such as this?" Lord Dell's voice answered from the doorway.

Everyone turned their eyes to the man standing in the room's entrance. The Lord of Hagan stood about a hand shorter than Brendys and was of average build. His once golden hair was now almost entirely grey, and his face was lined from nearly fourteen years of grief. He had taken the death of his only son, Kradon, the last of his immediate family, very hard . . . almost unreasonably so. But Brendys understood. He himself had fallen into a dangerous depression when he had believed Mattina dead, though he learned that his darkened spirit had also been influenced by Brugnara's powers.

Dell's greying features split in an unaccustomed, but genuine smile. "Ah, I was not certain you would come so soon after your ordeal."

"I almost didn't," Brendys replied. "But it has been worth it just to see you smile. I don't think I have seen a true smile cross your lips since Kradon died."

The Hagane's smile faltered at the mention of his son's name, but did not vanish entirely. "Kradon set my feet upon a path that I never dreamed I would follow when he revealed to me the betrayal of the Oranites. I saw then how empty and evil the gods were. Then, when you appeared at my court last autumn with your *son*, confirming the rumors that had but barely reached our ears—that the Bearer of the Flame had been ordained by the Dawn King himself at Lener Keep—I could no longer deny the truth.

"Since then, I have studied much and learned much and know that in service to the Dawn King, I shall be reunited with Kradon when the way is opened to the High Realm. So why then should I continue to grieve when Death is not always eternal?"

Dell sighed deeply. "By the gods, I miss Kradon . . . but you were right when you told me that I must live my life, not his death."

He raised his brown eyes to Brendys again. "So, you would speak with me before retiring? What business is so urgent that it cannot wait until morning?"

The Horsemaster glanced at the children, then Arella, before returning his gaze to the Hagane Lord. "Perhaps we should speak of this privately. Quellin, would you join us?"

Quellin gave his brother-by-marriage a puzzled look, but shrugged and nodded. "Of course . . . Arella can watch the children."

His wife wryly curled her lip. "I should have guessed as much. Naught changes in this world. Commoner or Queen, is it ever to be the woman's lot to *watch the children?* What about Willerth?"

The startled expressions evoked on the men's faces by her outburst drew merry laughter from her lips.

"Go on," she said, amidst her laughter. "I have no desire to hear ill tidings or dark matters on a joyous occasion."

But though her voice rang in laughter, there was a spectre of anxiety in her eye. Quellin kissed her on the cheek before joining Brendys and Dell in the wide corridor outside the guest chambers.

When the door was shut, Dell glanced around to verify that no one, including the Keep Guard, was within earshot. When he was satisfied that they were alone, he turned his brown eyes to Brendys. "What is it, Brendys, that is so dire that you did not wish to speak of it in front of the others?"

Brendys kept his voice low. "Not so much dire as secret, Dell. Before he died, my father gave you something . . . I need to see it."

Dell's features suddenly became taut, and he avoided Brendys's gaze. "I do not know of what you speak."

Brendys sighed, then reached into the pocket on the inside of his cloak and withdrew a folded page. "I was studying the prophecies of the Bearer of the Flame, hoping to learn somewhat of what I am supposed to be doing. There was a page missing from Father's copy of the *Annals* . . . I found *this* in its place."

The Horsemaster proffered the parchment to Dell, who took it and opened it slowly to find *his* coat-of-arms hastily sketched upon it.

"I believe Father left it there for me to find," Brendys continued. "To guide me to you. He knew I would never open the *Annals* unless I had sworn my allegiance to the Dawn King."

Dell hesitated, as if to speak, but said naught.

"Dell, I *must* know," Brendys pleaded. "Do you have the page?"

The Hagane Lord's lips parted slightly before he spoke. "It was not for *you* to find, Brendys. I do not think your father held much hope that you would follow your destiny. Brendyk made me swear not to let you see it, Brendys. He told me it was not for you, but that it was your legacy."

Brendys grasped the older man's arm. "Dell, *please!* Do you have the page here?"

Dell hesitated again, then sighed with a nod. "Aye. Part of me was inclined to give the page into Brendyn's own hand on the morrow. You would see it then for a certainty . . . I suppose there is no harm in showing it to you now. Come with me."

In silence, Brendys and Quellin followed the Hagane Lord to his own chambers. Once there, Dell instructed his guardsmen not to allow any to pass unannounced, then bid his companions enter. He came last, closing the door behind him, and disappeared into the bedroom at the far side of the antechamber, only to return a moment later, bearing a folded parchment.

It only took Brendys a cursory glance to know it was the missing page. The decorative, but precise writing covering the outside of the parchment unmistakably marked it as a leaf from his father's copy of the *Annals of the Ancients*. The wax seal locking away the contents of the inside surface had not been tampered with.

The Horsemaster held out his hand to receive the document.

Lord Dell looked down at the page for a moment, then slowly handed it over to the Shalkane. A look of guilt crossed the Hagane's rugged features, expressing a sense of betrayal as he broke his vow to Brendyk of Shalkan.

Brendys took the page from Dell, his eyes gliding over the text on the outside . . . the text he had been searching for. He knit his brow in confusion as he read, for the meaning of many of the words eluded him; nevertheless, the words he did understand spoke all too clearly to him.

> . . . *in those days, great tribulation shall fall upon Milhavior. Darkness shall cover the world, and Death's Legion shall issue forth from the Gates of Hál to ravage the lands. Though its number shall be greater than all the Hosts of the Free Kindreds, the way shall be clear to the Heart of the Shadow, and a Light shall drive back the Darkness, for the Living Flame cannot be overcome by Darkness.*

> *Yet, too, there shall come a time when the Flame is quenched and the Bearer is consumed by the Shadow. The Flame shall pass from Man to Child*

and Child to Son. As one, the Free Kindreds shall pierce the Shadow, but victory shall be fleeting. Upon the darkest hour shall the Deathlord come unto En Orilal, and such is the hour of Ascon's return.

Release not the Fire till Death is nigh, else Darkness shall reign for eternity.

Brendys briefly closed his eyes, then with trembling hands, he slowly broke the seal and opened the parchment. His eyes fell upon the coat-of-arms of the House of Ascon: golden hawk perched upon a naked sword, a golden crown above its head and a golden star below it. The inscription at the bottom of the page describing the charges was all too familiar:

The hawk signifies the House of Ascon. The star is the Glory of the Rising Dawn, the Lightlord Elekar, whom we serve. The crown stands for the responsibility with which we are burdened, and the sword is the High Law by which we rule.

Ascon and his escort had been driven into the old fortress of Zhayil-Kan by the Dark Elf Sorcerer Michuda and his Kubruk legion, there to be trapped for two hundred years. Two hundred years was not a terribly long time in the course of history. How could the Asconi have forgotten their own heritage in so short a time? Neither had a single document survived from that day to point to the ancestry of the people of Shalkan . . . it was almost as though they had intentionally blotted their lives from the annals of history.

It did not matter now. If Brendys had sheltered any doubts as to his lineage, they no longer troubled him. He was beyond a doubt descended father-to-father from Ascon himself . . . a fact he could not reveal to the world around him.

Slowly, he handed the page to Quellin, who gave it a cursory glance as though he already knew what it contained. The Gildean King looked from Brendys to Dell and back again. Brendys nodded, and Quellin returned the page to the Lord of Hagan.

Dell looked at the arms drawn upon the page in bewilderment for only a brief moment before understanding dawned upon him. His eyes widened as he looked up at Brendys. "*You* are the Heir of Ascon? King Mathai has made it well-known by his manner that he bears some enmity towards you . . . now it is clear why. This must be made known, Brendys. The High Throne is yours by right."

Brendys shook his head. "Nay, Dell, it is not. I am not Ascon's Heir. After seeing this, I do not understand how any of us could have been so blind to the truth from the beginning. Repeatedly, we have been taught that the Heir of Ascon would return through the Bearer of the Flame. Now it seems all too obvious what was meant. Brendyn, my son, is the Heir appointed."

Brendys paused, staring at the floor for a moment before returning his gaze to his old friend. "Keep the page safe, Dell. It must indeed be delivered into Brendyn's hand, but not now . . . not yet. I am confident the Dawn King will reveal the proper time to you . . . wait for that day and do not speak of this to *anyone*."

There was a long moment of silence before Dell finally responded. "Very well. Though I do not feel right about this, I shall keep it close to my heart, and none shall hear of it from my lips."

"That is all I ask, old friend," Brendys replied, satisfied with the Hagane Lord's word. He sighed. "My heart is relieved a little at least. I am weary now. I should return to my quarters."

Quellin nodded in agreement. "Indeed. You had a long journey, and it is getting late. We should all adjourn . . . dawn shall come all too soon."

Dell bade his friends a good night, and Brendys and Quellin returned to the Horsemaster's rooms. When they arrived, they found Arella seated alone in the antechamber with her two children. Shannon and Sîan were asleep on the couch.

Arella looked up as they entered. "Willerth has already put Brendyn to bed."

"We should be going, as well," Quellin said, carefully lifting his daughter from the couch.

Arella gently shook Shannon, who awakened, blinking sleepily. "We are going back to our rooms."

Shannon nodded, yawning, and climbed to his feet.

As the Royal Family of Gildea moved towards the door, Quellin turned to look at Brendys. "We shall see you at breakfast?"

Brendys inclined his head. "In the morning."

"Good night, then."

"Good night."

Chapter 5

*B*rendys stood just beyond the blaze of a campfire, where two men and two women were gathered. Just behind them were two large, covered wagons, built like prison wains. By their build, he knew they had to be slavers' wagons. The two men were undoubtedly the slavers.

One of them was a brawny man with the dark, nearly black skin of a Bulkyree. The other was an older, pale man with a thin face and meager build. They both stood behind an old woman who was kneeling before a girl who looked no older than fifteen or sixteen years of age, but who was heavy with child.

The girl, fevered, perspiration soaking her hair and running down her face, cried out in the throes of childbirth. The ordeal went on for what seemed an eternity, until her efforts were rewarded. The old woman held up a newborn infant, a boy.

She started to hand the screaming child to the girl, but instead turned and handed him to the older man. She bent down before the girl again, and a short while later, came up with a second boy. This one lay still and silent in her arms. The old woman looked at the slavers and sadly shook her head.

The older man handed the child he was holding into the girl's arms, then took the second boy from the midwife and walked away.

The girl's fevered gaze followed the older slaver. Clutching her firstborn to her breast, she moaned, "My baby . . . oh, my baby. . . ."

As the dream faded into darkness, Brendys heard a familiar voice, deep as thunder, yet soft and gentle as a cool breeze on a summer day. "Heed the cries of the Silent, for they are the cries of the Kingdom lost."

Brendys bolted upright in bed, his bearded face a mask of confusion. The morning light was beginning to show through the shutters of his room's windows, casting striped shadows across the bed. Brendys did not understand the words of Elekar, for they seemed to have nothing to do with the dream. But the dream itself, he understood all too well. The girl of his dream was his own wife.

A year before, Mattina, under the influence of a Plague-induced fever, had wept in bitter anguish over the loss of her child. Brendys had at first thought she had simply been dreaming, but now he knew better. Now he knew her grief.

He leaned forward against his drawn-up knees and wept bitterly.

"Papa?"

Raising his head, Brendys turned his gaze to the bedroom door. Through his tear-blurred eyes, he could see his son standing within the doorway, Willerth standing behind him with his hands on the young child's shoulders. Brendys held a hand out towards his son, and Brendyn ran to the bedside, clambering up into his father's waiting arms.

Brendys held his son in a tight embrace, the cold pain in his heart eased by the presence of the small, warm body in his arms.

"Master Brendys?" came Willerth's concerned voice. "Are you all right?"

Brendys nodded silently.

Brendyn raised his eyes towards his father. "Why are you crying, Papa?"

Brendys kissed his son on the forehead, then allowed a smile to crack his lips. "A bad dream . . . that is all."

Brendyn smiled back, his blue eyes brightening. Suddenly, he broke from his father's embrace and leapt to the floor. Grasping his father's wrist in both hands, he began tugging insistently. "Then come on! It's my birthday, and I want to go to the fair!"

Brendys smiled at his son's innocence. The boy in no way understood that the fair was itself in honor of his birthday. "All right, all right . . . I'm coming! But first, we get some breakfast."

Brendyn crossed his arms and thrust his lower lip out in a resigned pout. "Oh, all right."

Willerth shooed Brendyn from the room. "First, you get dressed. Do you want the blue tunic and green hose, or the green tunic and blue hose?"

"Blue and green again?" Brendyn complained as they walked out. "I'm tired of blue and green."

"Those are the colors of the House of Trost," Willerth's voice drifted back to Brendys. "And as a Prince of that House, you will be expected to wear them. You might as well get accustomed to it."

He should be wearing white and gold, Brendys thought. He climbed out of bed and donned his own clothes. He neither felt a Prince, nor Bearer of the Flame of Elekar, but they were titles he could no longer deny. Despite the fact that his great destiny seemed to be nothing more than the parenting of a child, he knew there must be something else. There had to be. The Dawn King spoke to him personally through dreams . . . something few others, save the Wizards, could claim.

He was sure he would have to wield Denasdervien more than once before it would finally pass to its rightful owner. The agents of the Deathlord were still active . . . the presence that followed them to Racolis Keep was enough to convince him of that. But apparently even the Sorcerers of Thanatos were unaware that Brendyn was himself the Heir of Ascon, for Brendys still seemed to be the focus of their attention.

Brendys shook the thoughts from his mind. This was his son's birthday . . . a time for celebration, not for dark wanderings. Nevertheless, a melancholy fell upon him, for he knew now that he should be celebrating two birthdays, not one.

With his son and servant, he made his way to the Great Hall of Racolis. Brendys could feel Willerth's concerned gaze upon him all the way to the Great Hall, but Brendyn was too caught up in the bustle of the castle folk and the sounds of the fair drifting in through the windows and arrow-slits of the Keep to notice his father's sullen mood. Brendys let go his sorrow as they entered the Great Hall. As he and his son were announced, he noticed many faces among those gathered at breakfast that he knew well and had longed to see again.

Quellin and his family were there, of course, and among his entourage were Lieutenant Gowan and Kovar, the Royal Falconer, Brendys's comrades-in-arms during the Battle of Gildea Keep. Lord Dell was there, as well, with his chief scout, Novosad, and the twins, Copanas and Lehan. Prince Earon of Harvath had come, as Brendys had hoped, and so had Asghar and Folkor, but he did not see Lord Guthwine or his family among the guests. Brendys was sure the Elves were already out and about, requiring no sleep as mortals knew it and little sustenance.

Brendys could feel his son's growing excitement, for he shared it. He would have liked nothing better than to greet his long-missed friends, but protocol demanded otherwise. Gently pressing his young son forward, Brendys crossed the immense length of the Great Hall to stand before the head table, where sat King Kosarek. The old King was clearly at the end of his life. His already wizened and hawkish features now looked frail beyond account. The wisps of grey hair adorning his head and chin did nothing to help his ailing appearance.

At his left hand sat Queen Rosa. She was an older woman, but was many years younger than her husband and had many good years left in her. Brendys had met her once before and knew she had a gentle temperament . . . quite the opposite of her husband. She seemed to be an anchor for his temper. At her left were two empty chairs.

To Kosarek's right hand, in the great chair at the center of the table where Kosarek himself usually was seated, was Mathai, King of Ascon and High Steward of Milhavior. Mathai wore a beige robe, beaded with silver in an attempt to mimic the strange silver-gold hue of the Elvinmetal Gloriod. Though the King of Ascon was only a few years older than Brendys, the golden circlet upon his brow signifying his rank as High Steward must have weighed heavily upon him over the past year, for his black beard and hair were now showing faint streaks of grey. Brendys was sure he saw a brief frown cross the High Steward's tanned face as he approached.

Brendys and Willerth knelt to one knee before the High Steward and the rulers of Racolis. Brendys gently pulled his son down, as well. "Your Majesties."

"Arise, Prince Brendys," King Mathai's rich voice returned. "It is not fitting that the great Hawk of Justice should kneel to any."

Brendys easily detected the thinly veiled sarcasm in the High Steward's voice. Nevertheless, he rose to his feet, with his son and servant. "I am but a servant, Your Majesty . . . not a King."

He could hear a sharp inhale of breath from a nearby table and was sure it was either Quellin or, more likely, Dell.

Mathai inclined his head with a vague smile. "Indeed."

Queen Rosa, though apparently oblivious to the couched argument between Brendys and Mathai, broke through the tension with a delighted exclamation. "Prince Brendys, you have not introduced the rest of your party!"

"My apologies, Your Majesty," the Horsemaster replied. "May I present to you my son, Brendyn, and our servant, Willerth, whom you and King Kosarek have met before."

Brendys knew he need not have presented Willerth, for the royalty and nobility would ignore the young man's presence as readily as they might fail to notice a beetle scurrying through the cracks in the flagstones of the Great Hall, but he wanted to make it clear that he considered Willerth every bit as important as the mighty Lords and Ladies of Racolis, regardless of whom he might offend.

Rosa clapped her hands together, then motioned Brendys and his son to the chairs beside her. "Wonderful! Now please join us, Your Highness. Prince Brendyn may sit beside me."

"Our thanks, Your Majesty," Brendys politely replied. He noticed, of course, the complete lack of acknowledgment given to Willerth, but that was to be expected. Besides, he knew it would matter little to Willerth, for the young man would not abide any castle servants attending his master while he was there to do so himself.

Throughout the morning meal, Brendys ate in silence, disturbed by an odd sense of tension and foreboding, though only he seemed aware of it. Brendyn and Queen Rosa chatted gaily beside him, Mathai and old Kosarek discussed politics, and the other guests seemed to be enjoying their moment of fellowship, but still something nagged at Brendys. As he finished his breakfast, he dropped his hand to Denasdervien's hilt and felt the ever-present warmth of its power, but he felt something else, as well . . . a vague, nearly undetectable tremor beneath his touch, speaking of a distant or hidden danger.

At last, he was startled from his thoughts by the cheery voice of Queen Rosa. "Your son is simply delightful, Prince Brendys! It has been long since the sounds of children's voices have been heard in this hall, and it is refreshing. Kosarek and I never had any children . . . my husband is not terribly fond of them."

"Then I imagine this great house must sometimes seem a terribly lonely place," Brendys replied softly, hoping King Kosarek did not hear him.

Rosa smiled wistfully. "Indeed, at times, it does."

"Papa," Brendyn broke in. "Can we go to the fair now?"

Queen Rosa chimed in before Brendys could answer. "Of course, dear boy . . . it *is* in your honor, after all."

Brendyn gave her a puzzled look. "It *is?*"

"Of course," Rosa replied. "All of these people are here to celebrate your birthday."

Brendyn's confusion gave way to wide-eyed wonder. "They *are?*"

The Racoline Queen nodded. "Indeed, they are. You are a very special little boy."

Brendys felt a brief chill come over him. Rosa would probably never live to know exactly how special his son was.

"Indeed, I think we should go down now," King Mathai agreed. With a quick glance at the King of Racolis, he added, "If it is not too early for you, Kosarek."

"Of course not, Sire," the aged King replied with as much fervor as he could muster.

"Good. It is just that those of us who are to participate in the tournament should prepare ourselves," Mathai said with a half-apologetic smile, less sincere than diplomatic. His blue eyes turned to Brendys, and the Horsemaster steeled himself for what he knew was coming. "I assume you will be participating, Prince Brendys?"

Brendys glanced around at the faces of the guests. Many had heard the High Steward's words and had turned their attention to the High Table. The Horsemaster drew in a deep breath, knowing his response would discredit him among many of the nobles. "I am not a warrior, Your Majesty. I will not fight."

The remnants of Mathai's smile vanished. "You will not allow us to test our arms against the mighty Bearer of the Flame? Many of us, including myself, have looked forward to the chance to prove ourselves against he who wields the Sword of the Dawn."

Brendys was quickly growing more uncomfortable by the minute, but he would not relent. "Say rather that Denasdervien wields me, Your Majesty. With the Flame in my hand, I doubt any here could hope to stand against me, for all weapons which cross it surely perish. But without it, I could not hope for victory over any of the honored warriors gathered here, for there is no skill in my arm.

"I have wielded a sword in battle but once, as a youth, and then it was hopelessness and rage, not skill, which drove me on. And when I first drew Denasdervien in the courtyard of Lener Keep and slew the Great Father, it was Elekar himself who guided my hand. I beg your pardon, Your Majesty, but I must decline."

The High Steward's dark glare hovered for a moment, then melted away into a conciliatory smile. "Of course.

We understand, Prince Brendys."

He rose from his chair and made his way down from the table, followed by Kosarek and Rosa.

Brendys released a sigh and motioned over his shoulder. Willerth responded instantly to his master's summons. Brendys glanced back at his servant and said in a low voice. "I will at least have to attend the tournament . . . I would rather Brendyn did not."

Willerth gave his master a nod. "I am sure there are other attractions more suited to children, Master Brendys."

"That is a certainty," Brendys replied.

The Horsemaster looked down to find Quellin and his family and escorts waiting for them.

"Shannon and Sîan will accompany you," the Gildean King added. "I am sure they will find Brendyn's company more satisfying than ours."

Shannon looked more than a little crestfallen at having to miss the tournament, but he covered his feelings quickly with a smile and beckoned to his younger cousin. "Come on, Brendyn, there is a fair awaiting!"

Heedless of the milling crowd of nobles, the children dashed off for the entrance of the Great Hall. Willerth hurried around the great table after them. "Slow down there! Wait for me!"

Quellin nodded to one of his escorts, a red-headed young man. "Go with them, Kovar."

The young falconer clapped his fist to his chest in salute, then followed Willerth and his young charges from the Great Hall.

Quellin turned back to Brendys as the Horsemaster joined them. "It is hard to even pretend that I did not notice Mathai's belligerence towards you. I am afraid he knows, or at least suspects. . . ."

"And does not like the thought," Brendys finished for his brother-by-marriage.

"Knows what?" Arella asked her husband.

Quellin glanced at Brendys, but remained silent.

Arella fixed an incredulous stare on him. "For goodness' sake, Quellin, I am your *wife!*"

Brendys laid a hand on her arm. "Arella, he is silent at my behest."

His gaze turned grave, moving briefly to Quellin, then back to Arella. "It is best that you do not know of what we speak . . . indeed, it will be safest for all if this is never brought up again by any of us."

"Agreed," Quellin replied with a solemn nod.

Arella gave an exasperated sigh, then threw up her hands. "Do not feed the fires of curiosity if only to stamp them out again. Oh, very well . . . I will put this conversation out of mind, if you think it best."

Brendys nodded. "I do. Thank you, Arella."

* * * *

With numerous polite excuses for rudely shoving through the throng of nobles and knights exiting the Great Hall, Willerth finally stepped out into the chambers beyond . . . just in time to see his young wards vanish around a corner. He hurried to catch up with them, but drew up short as he rounded the corner, nearly bowling into a young woman.

There was no doubt she was an Elf, for the ethereal light which shone within her could plainly be seen even in the daylight streaming through the windows. Her hair gleamed like strands of pure gold and her eyes were the color of a cloudless noontide sky. She wore a silvery-grey tunic and white hosen, with light slippers the same color as her tunic, and her golden hair was swept back into a braid. Though of a fine cut, her clothing was decidedly masculine, but her own slender figure was nothing less than feminine in nature. She stood eye-to-eye with Willerth, her head cocked in curiosity, but there was no sign that she had been disturbed by his sudden appearance before her, nor by the proximity of his face to hers . . . a few inches at best.

Willerth abruptly took a step back and bowed his head. "Your pardon, My Lady. I should have been more attentive."

The Elvinsilver birch-leaf pendant he wore constantly at his heart slipped from beneath his tunic. The Elfess gently caught the swinging charm, which briefly gleamed at her touch. After a quick examination, she let it go and lifted the young man's chin with her soft fingers. Willerth trembled at the touch, remembering the last time an Elf-lass had laid a hand upon him.

The Elfess wore a gentle smile. "You have changed, but though a man, I still sense somewhat the fear of a boy."

Her light voice was as sweet to Willerth's ears as the song of the nightingale and clear as a silver bell, but her words confused him. He raised his eyes to meet hers and dared to stare into the depths of those shining eyes. Understanding came to him after only a moment, and he gasped out her name. "Aliana. . . !"

"Indeed," the Elvinlady replied, still smiling. "I cannot blame you for not recognizing me, for I have grown, too."

Willerth continued to stare at her as if in a dream. "Aye, you *have* grown . . . if a star could shine more brightly, it might perhaps compare, though I think it unlikely."

A faint tinge of a blush rose to Aliana's cheeks, a sight which made Willerth wonder. The Elves he had met were ever impervious to flattery. But then, no other Elf had pledged to be his wife . . . a pledge the heart of a mortal boy could not return.

With a gentle smile, Aliana took his hand. "Come. Walk with me in the garden."

As she started to turn, his feet followed but for a moment before duty called to him, startling him from his waking dream. "The children. . . !"

Aliana laughed. "King Quellin's falconer followed them. Fear not for their safety, or your duty. I have sensed but the smallest shadow of a darkened heart . . . the children will be safe in the hands of the warrior. I shall vouch for you before your master and the King if need demands. Come."

Willerth stared briefly in the direction the children had gone, torn between duty and the desire to walk with this light who was ever in his thoughts. But the struggle was brief. For the first time in his life of service to Brendys of Shalkan, he abandoned duty for the selfishness of his heart. He allowed himself to be led into the summer gardens of Racolis Keep by the hand of the star that had guided him for ten long years.

They walked in silence for awhile, content to merely stroll though the flowering trees and plants of the garden, hand-in-hand, mortal and immortal. Soon, they came to a balcony which overlooked the southern portion of the city and the festival it held. Willerth felt Aliana's gaze upon him, and he turned his face to her.

"I was certain that time and the forgetfulness of mortality would have driven me from your mind," the Elfess said at last. "And that my gift to you would lie hidden amidst the possessions of a mortal boy until it was discarded or lost."

Willerth marveled at the boldness of his own heart, recalling that ten years past he could barely stand in the presence of this Elf maiden. "How could I forget you when part of you remains ever with me."

He held up the Elvinsilver pendant, the polished metal reflecting the rays of the sun. "This and the memory of your face and your heart have carried me through grief when I did not think comfort was possible . . . gave me hope where I could find none. It is I, instead, who should wonder that you have not put a childish young mortal from *your* mind."

Aliana raised a soft hand to his cheek. "Forgetfulness did not entirely withhold its touch from you, for you do not seem to recall that I, too, bear a part of you."

Suppressing a shudder, Willerth lowered his head in bitter shame. "It is the worst part, I fear . . . the darkness of a past best left forgotten."

"But which will, however, endure, be it only as a fleeting shadow," Aliana finished for him, smiling sadly. "The worst part, you say? Aye, I have seen terrible darkness and pain, but I have also seen love and devotion and a gentle heart. These things I loved in you from the first, and they are foremost in my mind. Strangely, I fear to ask this . . . but do you not bear some love for me, as well?"

Willerth raised his grey eyes to meet hers. He trembled a little, a vague shadow of his childhood fears playing at his mind, but he could not deny what his heart cried out. "I do . . . more perhaps than even an Elf could imagine."

Aliana unashamedly drew closer to Willerth, until their bodies were nearly touching. "That is a high claim."

"But ever true," Willerth replied in a soft voice.

Aliana stared unblinking into his eyes as if trying to read his innermost thoughts . . . whether true or not, Willerth felt that in some way she *could*. Finally, she spoke again. "*Anî âbahnir nâshiymër?*"

Willerth's breath caught in his throat. That was a phrase she had spoken to him when he was but a lad of thirteen summers, and he knew what it meant . . . but this time, she presented it as a question, rather than the declaration she had made of it before. She was asking if she would be his wife. His heart screamed to answer her *yes*, but he could not compel even that one simple word from his lips. Doubt

73

and fear clutched at him. He wanted nothing more than to give himself to this wondrous being, but duty and debt would not allow it. He could not forsake his master for any love.

Aliana saw the struggle in his face and lowered her gaze. "You are not ready . . . I fear you may never be. Perhaps, my own love has blinded me to think that a mortal boy could share such a love."

The look of utter desolation in the Elf-maiden's face tore at Willerth's heart. He raised her chin with one hand, forcing her gaze back to him. "I *do* love you . . . more than life itself! But I . . . I. . . ."

Words failed him and he struggled to find the means to explain himself to the Elfess. "Perhaps, I'm not ready— perhaps you are right, maybe I never will be—but I *do* love you!"

Without thinking, he boldly followed his heart and drew her lips to his. Aliana did not resist, but returned his embrace with passion, a fire kept burning despite distance and mortal years. But after only a moment, Willerth felt a sudden chill, like the vague sense of a nearby threat.

Aliana broke away with an abrupt cry and collapsed against the rail of the balcony, gasping, her face pallid in fear.

Willerth took a step towards her, his concern rapidly growing. "Aliana, what is it?"

The Elfess turned her sky-blue eyes to the young man, but her gaze did not seem focused. "A Shadow . . . a terrible Shadow! There is a great Evil here, an Evil such as I have not felt since . . . since your father!"

Willerth stared at her in shock, then turned his grey eyes towards the fairgrounds. His heart thudded in sudden panic. "*The children!*"

With the adrenaline of terror rushing through him, he dashed back through the garden, seeking a way out of the Keep.

Aliana launched herself after him, quickly passing him by.

* * * *

Brendys sat at King Kosarek's right hand in the stands along the tournament lists, waiting for Kosarek to declare the beginning of the tournament, desperately wishing he were elsewhere. Quellin and Arella sat beside Brendys, looking every bit as disinterested. If it were not for propriety and the participation of Prince Earon and Lord Dell in the tournament, none of them would likely have been present.

Waiting in growing boredom, only vaguely listening to the dry conversation of Kosarek and his nobles, Brendys fell deeper into his own thoughts. He was still having difficulty wrapping his mind around his recent discoveries and the events of the past few years. He placed his left hand on Denasdervien's pommel, feeling the warmth of its power. There was still a slight pulse, speaking of a distant or vague evil, but nothing to fear.

Here he was, the Bearer of the Flame, harbinger of the Heir of Ascon, and his task seemed to be as simple as raising a child. A slight grin played across his lips. *Simple? Hah! I can think of no task more daunting!*

His smile faded. No, there was certainly more to his destiny. The minions of Thanatos would not rest until he and his son were dead. The evil that hounded them all the way from Shalkan was a solid testament to that fact.

The touch of a hand on his shoulder startled Brendys from his reverie. He turned to look back over his shoulder and found a fair face, at once youthful and ancient, staring back at him, framed with golden hair. Brendys's lips parted in a smile. "Lord Guthwine! I was certain you would come."

"But of course," the Elvinlord replied, smiling casually in return. "My family and I would not fail when called to honor the Hawk of Justice."

Brendys's smile faltered a little, and he heard Quellin stir beside him, but Guthwine did not seem to notice.

"Truth be told, I would not be present at this particular event if it were not for your own presence here," Guthwine continued. "I find the joust less than graceful at best. I would prefer to join my wife at the archery contest, for indeed she will have no competition."

That caught King Kosarek's attention. The old monarch turned to the Elvinlord, a look of shock on his hawkish features. "Archery? That is a sport for women and common folk. The joust is the true measure of a man!"

Guthwine cocked his head curiously, his piercing blue gaze fixed on The Racoline King. "Do you then consider me common?"

Brendys took guilty pleasure in watching as Kosarek spluttered in embarrassment. "Of course not! But neither are you a Man."

Guthwine laughed in return. "Nor would I have it said of me . . . no offense intended, my mortal friends."

Kosarek's herald approached the grandstand and bowed. "The challengers are ready, Your Majesty."

Relieved for the interruption, the Racoline King clapped his hands together. "Then let the tournament begin!"

As the first challengers were being summoned, Brendys turned again to Lord Guthwine. "Have you seen Asghar?"

The Elvinlord nodded, still smiling. "Indeed. He, too, dislikes the joust. He finds no pleasure in watching two lunatic Men with flimsy sticks charging each other upon

76

the backs of great lumbering beasts. He is instead participating in the melee, where he can display true Dwarvin barbarism in all its primitive glory."

Brendys grinned and shook his head. "And Folkor?"

"He is watching the melee from the stands," Guthwine replied. "With a roast turkey to keep him company on one side and a pint of ale on the other."

Kosarek's herald again interrupted the conversation to announce the first challengers. "Your Majesties, Lords, and Ladies, I present Prince Earon of the House of Harvath, and Lord Jholer of the House of Daggs."

Brendys turned to watch the mounted knights parade past the stands. Jholer's shield and surcoat were sky-blue, blazoned with a fess alternating red and black, a red dagger, point down, in the base, and a border also alternating red and black. Earon's coat-of-arms was a simpler paly of eighteen—eighteen vertical stripes— violet, gold, and grey.

The knights halted before King Kosarek and bowed their heads to him. The old King gave them his blessing and exhorted them to valor, then they turned their horses to take their places in the list. Earon flashed Brendys and Quellin a cocky grin, then slapped down his helm's visor and rode to his end of the list, taking a lance from his squire.

Brendys leaned towards Quellin. "He is going to be laid flat on his back, isn't he?"

Quellin made an acknowledging sound.

Silence fell on the crowd as the herald raised his baton. Only the sounds of the fair beyond the tournament fields could be heard.

Brendys jerked his hand away from Denasdervien's hilt as the power within the Elvinsword suddenly intensified. He heard a sharp gasp behind him and turned to find that Guthwine's features had gone ashen.

"There is a great Evil near," the Elvinlord rasped out.

"Brendyn!" Brendys leapt to his feet in a panic as Kosarek's herald dropped his arm, signaling the challengers to charge, and pressed through the onlookers, eliciting a number of annoyed outbursts from King Kosarek and other nobles.

Warning his wife to remain, Quellin arose and followed Brendys, accompanied by Lord Guthwine. None of them noticed as Earon, distracted by his friends' abrupt departure, was thrown from his saddle by the shattering force of Lord Jholer's lance against his shield.

When Guthwine and Quellin caught up with Brendys, the Elf grabbed the Horsemaster's arm and turned him towards the merchant's bazaar. "This way!"

*   *   *   *

Kerebros wandered among the myriad booths of the merchants bazaar, his wolf-hide garments drawing more than a little attention, but he did not pay any heed. He was on the hunt, the blood of his quarry was near . . . he could smell it. His amber gaze swept over the crowds of peasant-folk and men-at-arms, seeking out his prey.

He halted briefly beneath the shelter of an abandoned booth, resting in the cool shadows. In his natural form, he may not have been prey to the Curse of Darkness, but he still hated the sun. He hated the warmth and the burning light. When he had completed his task, he would never again have to fear the sun. The world would be plunged into Darkness, and he would be able to wear the form he favored above all others forevermore, feasting upon the flesh of the weak.

"Be not overly eager, Kerebros," a fair, masculine voice said from the deeper confines of the booth.

Kerebros turned to face the speaker, a black-robed figure whose hooded features were completely hidden from view. The Sorcerer scowled. "You take a great risk showing yourself here, demon, while the sun rides high. This is my hour. Go back to the Far North . . . I am sure Black Cragg will give you a much warmer welcome."

"Do not be a fool, if you can avoid it, Wolf," the cloaked figure replied, a hint of amusement in its voice. "Your hunger for the flesh of your own kind will be your undoing. You cannot hope to defeat the Bearer of the Flame through brute strength . . . you must be cunning as the wolf you pretend to be. Prey upon the Bearer's weaknesses until he at last fails."

A grin stretched across Kerebros's lips. "The boy . . . the boy will be his downfall."

"It will not be easy. . . ."

"Oh, but it will," Kerebros replied with confidence. "I will see to it personally."

"We shall see, Wolf," the cloaked figure responded. It raised a gauntleted hand, motioning beyond Kerebros. "There is your quarry . . . let us see how easy it shall be."

Kerebros turned around to find the son of the Bearer standing among a group of others not fifty feet from where he stood. He broke into a grin. "Not yet, demon. Not here. You will see just how cunning this wolf can be."

* * * *

Brendyn and his cousins dashed from one booth to another, sampling various foodstuffs, examining artisans' wares, and participating in children's games and contests. They came at last to a booth containing the wares of a Bard, with musical instruments dangling from the walls and piles of scrolls adorning a single rack. The booth was attended by an older gentleman in the bright attire of a minstrel and a lank, brown-haired youth dressed much the same.

The old man immediately stood to his feet and bowed as the children approached. Despite his age, his voice was still clear. "Prince Shannon, Princess Sîan, welcome to my humble booth!"

Shannon graciously inclined his head to the old Bard. "Thank you, Master Fennis."

The young man beside Fennis placed a hand on the Bard's arm while motioning towards Brendyn with the other. "Master Fennis, I do believe this is Prince Brendyn."

"Is it indeed? Welcome, welcome, young Prince!" Fennis looked thoughtful. "I haven't much to offer as a gift on this your birthday, except perhaps. . . ."

The old man turned and took something down from the wall of the booth. When he faced the children again, he held a small instrument comprised of five wooden pipes bound with twine. "This flute was given me by my master when I was a child learning the Bardic arts. Berephon made his own long ago, so it serves me no purpose but as a keepsake. I would be honored if you would accept it as my gift to you, Your Highness."

Brendyn took the instrument, turning it over in his hands, a puzzled frown playing at his lips. "But I don't know how to play it."

The Bard's apprentice smiled. "Then that shall be *my* gift to you. Tomorrow evening, if your father allows—as I have no doubt he will—I will teach you how to play a song. In fact, I know just the song to teach you."

Brendyn brightened. "Would you?"

"Absolutely. . . ." Berephon did not finish, distracted by a nearby scuffle among some children.

Brendyn turned, following the young man's gaze. About thirty yards away a group of common children led by an older lad he recognized as a castle servant circling another child with clearly hostile intent. It was not clear whether the lone child was a boy or girl because of the heavy winter cloak, muffler, and gloves which hid the child's features.

The older boy, a large lad of about fourteen summers, advanced on his intended victim. "Well, looky 'ere, lads, it's the castle demon! But what's it be doin' wanderin' 'bout in the daylight, that's what I wonder."

"I thoughts demons cou'n't walk 'bout in the sun," one of the other boys called to his leader.

"I says we finds out!" With that the older boy shot his hands out and ripped the cloak and muffler from around the lone child's shoulders. The girl, as Brendyn could now see it was, collapsed with a piercing shriek of agony. For a brief moment, Brendyn got a glimpse of chalk-white skin beneath a sweat-soaked mop of red hair before she curled into a ball, covering her head with her arms. The older boy jumped atop the girl, pinning her arms away from her face. The girl screamed in pain, until her voice hoarsened.

"Unhand her, churl!" Brendyn watched as Shannon advanced on the group of boys, ignoring the protests of Fennis and Berephon. His older cousin's face was red with anger, his fists clenched tight. "Unhand her before I have the guards on you!"

The gang of boys looked in the young Prince's direction, at first mockingly, until their slow minds absorbed his rich manner of dress and the silver crown resting cocked upon his head and realized Shannon had the power to carry out his threat. The whole mob at once turned tail and ran from the scene, leaving the girl writhing on the ground.

Shannon dashed forward, grabbing the girl's heavy cloak and tossing it over her exposed face. Brendyn, Sîan, and the two Bards quickly joined the Crown Prince of Gildea. As Brendyn neared, he could see that the girl was trembling violently beneath the cloak draped over her. At last, with Shannon's help, she came to her knees, her cloak draped around her shoulders with the hood drawn so that it shaded her face completely from the sun.

"Are you all right now, Karel?" Shannon asked, wearing an expression of deep concern. Karel, the much-debated step-daughter of Dell's chief scout Novosad, was the daughter of Titha, a Gildean woman of distant relation to Quellin, and Lord Chol, the Dark Elf who had misused her and was slain by Novosad's companion, Lehan, during the Siege of Gildea.

The girl turned her shaded face towards him, tears of pain streaking her white cheeks grey. She had clearly inherited her mother's red hair and the white flesh, cold black eyes, and Elvin fairness of her father. Her Elvin heritage was further evidenced by the fact that while she was two years older than Shannon, she looked no older than he. Some part of her father's blood was clearly inherited as well in that the light of the sun caused her great agony, though that part of her mother's lineage protected her from the curse of death laid upon all Creatures of Darkness by the Dawn King.

Karel's eyes narrowed and she rasped out in a cold voice, "I did not ask for your help, boy."

She began to cough, the effort to speak too much after her ordeal.

Shannon released her and crossed his arms, pursing his lips. "I know . . . but you did not seem able to do much else for yourself but scream."

As she gained control of her cough, Karel rose unsteadily to her feet, keeping her icy gaze upon Shannon. Her expression softened only slightly. "If you are looking for gratitude, I suppose it *is* in order. You have it then."

Taking up her muffler, she turned and staggered off towards the Keep without another word.

Shannon stared after her, his gaze turning wistful. Brendyn and Sîan exchanged disgusted looks, then turned their attention back to Shannon.

"I just want to know one thing," Brendyn said to his older cousin. "What's a churl? It doesn't sound very nice."

Fennis and Berephon at once broke into laughter, joined quickly by Shannon, while Brendyn and Sîan looked on in confusion.

Brendyn was soon distracted by the sudden chill of a fearsome presence. It was clear to him by the sudden reactions of his cousins and the Gildean Bards that he was not the only one to sense the presence. His wide eyes were drawn to two men conversing in the deep shadows of a booth not far from where the small group now stood. One was wrapped in a black hood and cloak, no part of his flesh visible in the darkness of the shadows, but the other was all too familiar to him: a big man dressed in wolf-skins.

The wolf-man's gaze was directed to Brendyn by the shadowy form in the back of the booth. As he turned his strange amber eyes on the boy, his lips peeled back in a grin.

Brendyn took a frightened step back, bumping into Berephon, as the wolf-man advanced. The Bard's apprentice pulled him protectively closer.

The wolf-man's progress was halted by a young warrior in the blue and green livery of the House of Trost. The warrior's curly, red hair burned in the sunlight, accentuating the grim look on his face. He held his left hand palm out towards the wolf-man, his right hand resting on the pommel of his sword. "Halt and state your business."

Staring down into Kovar's face, the wolf-man's grin faded only briefly before returning. He answered in a gruff voice, strangely accented. "What is anyone's business

83

here this day? I am here for the son of the Bearer of the Flame . . . to *honor* him."

"You can honor him where you stand," the young falconer replied stiffly. "None approach Their Highnesses without the consent of King Quellin or Prince Brendys."

The wolf-man's smile vanished abruptly and completely, replaced with undisguised contempt, and Kovar slid his sword partway from its scabbard. Before the man could speak again, a worried call drew all attention away from him.

"Master Brendyn!"

As Willerth and Aliana arrived, Brendyn broke away from Berephon and ran to his father's servant. The boy clung tightly to Willerth. "He's here, Willerth, he's here!"

Willerth wrapped his arms around the child, his grey eyes glancing around the nearly deserted corner of the bazaar. "Who, Master Brendyn?"

"The wolf-man!"

"Skud!" Kovar bit out.

Willerth looked at Kovar, who was scowling angrily. "Kovar? What is it?"

"He is gone," the falconer snapped back. Kovar sighed and rubbed his forehead. "I'm sorry, Willerth. I let the stranger slip away. I take it you have encountered the man before?"

"Aye," Willerth answered with a worried frown. "You might say that. We need to find Master Brendys."

"You haven't far to search then," Brendys's voice replied from behind him.

Willerth turned just as his master, Quellin, Guthwine, and Lady Reatha, Guthwine's wife, converged on the spot.

"Willerth, what happened?" Brendys asked, gasping for breath.

The young man shook his head. "I am not sure, Master Brendys. Master Brendyn says that wild-man was here."

"Brendyn *says?*" the Horsemaster asked in confusion. "Did you not see him yourself?"

A guilty look passed over Willerth's features. "Nay, Master Brendys. I only arrived myself a moment ago."

Brendys's began to redden in anger.

Kovar spoke quickly in Willerth's defense. "Your Majesty, Your Highness, I am equally to blame. I found the children but a minute before Willerth arrived, and I was not that far behind him when we left the Keep. Fortunately, I did arrive in time to hinder the stranger."

"And I, too, must share in the blame," Aliana added solemnly. "For it was I who convinced Willerth to leave the children to the warrior's care."

"Daughter, it was not your place to interfere," Lady Reatha chided, her tone severe.

Aliana bowed her head in shame. "I know, Mother, but I could not resist the opportunity to speak privately with Willerth."

"Lady Aliana!" Brendys said, startled by the changes in her appearance since the last time he had seen her, despite the gravity of the situation. He sighed, letting go the remaining shreds of his anger. "I cannot then blame Willerth, for it would be a sore trial for any mortal to resist such beauty."

Willerth blushed, fondling the Elvinsilver pendant at his breast.

Quellin turned to his falconer. "You say you hindered this stranger . . . did he try to harm the children?"

Kovar shook his head. "Nay, Your Majesty, if it weren't for Prince Brendyn's fear of him, I would not have thought him hostile."

"Where did he go?" Brendys asked.

Kovar s spread his hands as a gesture of uncertainty. "I know not, Your Highness. When I heard Willerth's voice, I turned away, and when I turned back, the man was gone."

Quellin placed a hand on Kovar's shoulder. "Very well. Send Amrein to search the city. It should not be difficult for her to find this man."

"I must beg your pardon, Your Majesty," Kovar replied. "But King Kosarek's men will not allow Amrein to fly free in the city, else I would have found the children sooner."

Quellin grimaced. "Of course. Did *anyone* see where he went?"

The Bard and his apprentice shook their heads, as did the children.

"Then we have no way of tracking him," Quellin said with a frustrated sigh.

"Maybe the other man could tell you," Brendyn suggested.

All attention focused on the boy. Brendys squatted in front of his son. "What other man?"

"The wolf-man was talking to someone over there before he came this way," Brendyn replied, pointing to the shadowed booth.

"That's right, I saw him, too," Shannon chimed in.

"What did this other man look like, Shannon," his father asked him.

The young Prince frowned and shook his head. "I could not tell, Father. He stood deep in the shadows and was dressed all in black, hooded and cloaked."

At that, Guthwine and his wife jogged over to the booth, followed by the rest of the group. They scanned the ground in and around the booth for a moment, and by the concerned looks on their fair faces, it was clear they had found more than footprints.

Lord Guthwine turned his gaze to Prince Shannon. "There is one set of footprints just beneath the awning, but none within. Were both men inside the booth while they spoke?"

Shannon again shook his head. "Nay. The man in the wolf skins was just where you said, just beneath the awning."

Guthwine's expression turned grim. "Then I can say with certainty that this wolf-man is mortal. The other, however. . . ."

The Elvinlord fell silent.

Lady Reatha looked at her husband with some discomfiture. "Dark Alar?"

"That is my belief," Guthwine replied in a low voice. "It has been many mortal years since I felt such a presence."

"Dark Alar?" Brendys echoed in fearful disbelief. "Do you mean to say a demon stood here in the bright of day, unharmed? Is the Curse of Darkness broken then?"

"Nay, Brendys," Guthwine replied. "If the Dark Alar was shrouded as Prince Shannon describes, it could easily avoid the rays of the sun in here. Still, it is a strangely bold move for a Creature of Darkness. It would still be weakened and vulnerable."

Brendys turned to his servant. "Willerth, take Brendyn back to the Keep. Do not let him out of your sight for a moment."

"Aye, Master Brendys," Willerth replied, taking his young charge's hand in his.

"But, Papa, it's my birthday!" Brendyn protested.

Brendys looked away. It pained him to cloister his son, but he did not know what else to do.

As if in response to his thoughts, Guthwine placed a hand on his shoulder. "Brendys, the Dark Alar is gone, and even if it were to return, it could not harm the children as long as they remain in the light. I doubt as well that the mortal stranger would dare to harm the children in such an open place."

The Elvinlord paused, then continued. "Protect your son, by all means . . . but if you lock him away, he will never gain the knowledge and strength of spirit that he will need when he is older."

Brendys rested his hand on Denasdervien's hilt. It was true enough. He could feel nothing but the normal warmth of the Living Flame. What Evil the Elvinsword still spoke of was distant at best.

Finally, he turned back to his son. "Very well, you may stay . . . but you remain with Willerth and obey him."

Brendyn brightened. "Aye, Papa!"

Brendys was amazed at how quickly the child was able to put his fright behind him. Part of him wished he could be that innocent of the knowledge of evil again.

"And that goes doubly for you two," Quellin told his children in a stern tone. "If I hear that you have run off again, it will be the last freedom you will see for many a day. Willerth's word is law for you. Do you understand?"

Shannon became indignant at the thought of having to take instruction from a servant, but before he could protest, Quellin cut him short with a sharp motion. The Crown Prince of Gildea and his sister both hung their heads. "Aye, Father."

Quellin then turned to Kovar. "You go with them, as well . . . do not let them out of your sight for even a moment."

The young warrior stood at attention and struck his fist to his heart. "As Your Majesty wills it."

Brendys looked at Fennis and his apprentice. "I suppose I should thank you as well for watching over my son."

"If there had been any genuine trouble, I fear we would not have been of much help, Your Highness," the old Bard replied.

"May I present Fennis, Master Bard of Gildea," Quellin said to Brendys. "And you already know his ward . . . Bipin."

The young man moaned in dismay. "*Berephon*, please, Your Majesty. Bipin is a child's pet name."

Brendys grinned. "Call him what you will, Quellin, but he shall be Bipin to me to the end of my days."

Berephon rolled his eyes and grimaced, eliciting a laugh from Brendys. The Horsemaster clasped the young man's shoulder. "It is good to see you again, my friend. Will you be entertaining us in the Great Hall tonight?"

"If that is an invitation, Your Highness, we shall be honored to oblige," Fennis answered for his apprentice.

Brendys looked at them both and inclined his head. "Then we shall see you tonight."

Quellin touched the Horsemaster's arm. "We should be getting back to the joust, though I doubt we are missed. In the meantime, I will have Gowan and some of his men scour the city, just to be certain that our unwanted guest has abandoned the area."

"Reatha, Aliana, and I shall join the search," Guthwine added. "Though I strongly doubt we shall find anything."

Brendys nodded wearily, his left hand still fixed firmly upon the pommel of his sword.

Berephon watched as Brendys walked back towards the tournament fields. "Master Fennis, there goes a man worthy of song."

The old Bard patted his apprentice's shoulder. "Then that shall be your final challenge: to write the ballad of the Bearer of the Flame. When you have sung that ballad before an audience, your training with me shall be ended."

Berephon shot an astonished look at his master, then turned his eyes again to Brendys's receding back. "Then you shall be saddled with me for a long while yet, Master, for I ween the Bearer's story is far from over."

* * * *

Rather than return directly to the grandstand, Brendys and Quellin stopped first at the challengers' pavilions. They found Earon and Dell outside the Harvathine Prince's tent. Earon had doffed his mail and was sitting on a stool, leaning forward with his elbows resting on his knees, while his squire massaged a stinging ointment into his back and shoulders.

"Earon," Brendys said as they approached. "I am sorry, but I had to leave before your run . . . how did you fare?"

Earon's steel-grey eyes glared up at the Horsemaster. "Lord Jholer unseated me at *my* end of the lists, thanks to you."

"Thanks to *me?*" Brendys returned.

"Aye, thanks to *you*," Earon shot back. "What was that commotion about anyway?"

Dell quickly agreed. "Aye, Brendys. We all saw you leave. You have always been impulsive, but when King Quellin and Lord Guthwine followed, it was clear something was amiss."

Brendys's shoulders slumped. He could not lie to these his sworn friends and allies. He took a breath, then related to them all that had transpired, beginning with Brendyn and Willerth's first encounter with the wild-man in Shalkan.

"I will make certain the guard is doubled at the Keep tonight," Dell said when Brendys had finished his tale. "Kosarek needs not be informed."

The Horsemaster shook his head grimly. "It is a sore enough trial to live day-to-day looking over my own shoulder, wondering when Machaelon's next assault on me will be, but that my family and friends are caught in the middle of it all is almost too much to bear."

Dell regarded Brendys with a stern eye. "If your family and friends were not willing to share the risks with you, I would not think much of them. We will not abandon you."

"Well spoken, Dell," Earon agreed with a sudden fervor. He thrust his hand towards Holnar, his Gloriod javelin, which was leaning against the pavilion. His squire retrieved the weapon and presented it to his Prince. Taking the short spear from his squire, Earon said, "I have abandoned too much in my lifetime already."

The Crown Prince of Harvath dropped to one knee and offered Holnar up to Brendys as though it were a sword. "If ever you are in need, Brendys of Shalkan, the Throne of Harvath is ever at your beck and call."

Brendys was taken completely by surprise. He had counted the younger man a true friend since their trials together in Shad the year before, but this gesture was most unexpected . . . and it touched him, for such a humble show of loyalty—no, *fealty*—had to be difficult for the haughty Prince of Harvath. He took the javelin from Earon, then returned it, shaft-first. "Rise, my friend. It is not right that you should kneel to me. I am not even your equal."

Earon arose, returning his weapon into his squire's keeping. He fixed Brendys with a steady gaze. "Nay . . . you are my *better*."

Brendys cast a suspicious glance at both Dell and Quellin, wondering if they had revealed to Earon what they knew of him. In response to the look, they both shook their heads. Brendys returned his gaze to his Harvathine friend, a half-smile cracking his lips. "Before this week is past, you may not think so highly of me."

Earon wrinkled his brow in confusion at the Horsemaster's words.

Brendys did not respond to the look as a wave of dizziness came over him. "I think I will take my leave . . .

I feel the need to rest. Quellin, please convey my apologies to King Kosarek. I will speak with you all tonight."

With that, he turned and wandered back towards the Keep, rubbing his scarred temple.

Chapter 6

When night fell upon Racolis Keep, the city's festivities lessened until all the people had either returned to their homes or fallen asleep in a drunken stupor where they sat. The Keep guests retired to the Great Hall for their own little celebration—a small feast in Brendyn's honor. Though not graciously, King Kosarek had granted Brendys the use of the Great Hall to share the evening with his friends, noble and common alike. The nobility of Racolis and their visitors would have a week to acquaint themselves with the great Bearer of the Flame. Brendys did not see the need to invite any of the pompous louts to his family's gathering.

Brendys did extend invitations to King Kosarek and Queen Rosa, as their hosts, and to King Mathai, out of protocol, but they had all declined. The Racoline rulers had long since retired for the evening and the High Steward clearly had no desire to mingle with the likes of Brendys and his companions. Brendys and his companions could not have been more pleased.

While the meal itself was plentiful, it was not overly garish as might have been ordered by the King of Racolis, but it was good enough to satisfy the guests present. Off and on throughout the meal, Fennis and Berephon played and sang for the guests, and Brendys realized how much the boy he knew as Bipin had grown. Berephon had developed a wonderful tenor singing voice and displayed an amazing knowledge of folk songs and lore.

After awhile, the guests began to eat less and mingle more. Brendys moved among the tables, greeting the guests and reminiscing over times gone past. Asghar demanded to be brought up to date on his Kjerken's life, though there was little Brendys could tell him, for little had happened since their parting in Shad . . . at least, that he felt free to speak of. The Dwarf began to relate all of the gossip of his myriad relations to Brendys, but was interrupted, much to the Horsemaster's pleasure by Captain Folkor, who promptly began a friendly war of words with Asghar after first insulting the Dwarf's landlocked heritage. Guthwine, intrigued, joined the spirited conversation.

As Brendys moved through the relatively small group, he took note of the long-missed faces. Rister, his father's old horse-trader friend, had come all the way from Meyler Roam, just outside of Shalkan. Kovar, Quellin's young falconer and a very old and dear friend to Brendys, was of course in attendance, his great white hawk, Amrein, perched on his shoulder. The great bird was permitted into the Great Hall at the behest of Lord Dell, both as a friend and a guardian, for being descended from the white hawks of Mingenland, she could see both the physical and the spirit world at once. There would be no unknown and unwanted visitors that night, for which Brendys was thankful.

Accompanying Dell were his chief scouts, Novosad, Copanas, and Lehan, brave warriors who had helped free Gildea from the clutches of Iysh Mawwath. Novosad's wife, Titha, and his step-daughter, Karel, were also with them. Karel was a curiosity to Brendys, for as the daughter of Titha and the Dark Elf Lord Chol, she shared traits both

94

mortal and immortal. Many believed she was the inheritor of her father's evil and that she should have been slain at birth, but Novosad could not murder her to quell the superstitions of others. He loved her as his own and would not accept that she was evil. Brendys prayed he was right. Denasdervien still spoke of a distant or vague evil . . . it could very well have been Karel it sensed.

Lieutenant Gowan, another dear friend gained during the Siege of Gildea, was present as commander of Quellin and Arella's escort. He was seated with Quellin's family, as was Lord Guthwine's wife Reatha. The Elvinlady had formed a bond of sorts with Arella over the years since their first meeting at Brendys's grim wedding.

Brendys noticed his nephew sneaking frequent glances at Karel, and it struck him suddenly: Shannon was smitten with the girl. Karel did not, however, seem to return the feelings, for her glances displayed nothing but sheer contempt. Brendys was not sure whether to feel sorry for Shannon or relieved.

The Horsemaster sat down at a table nearer to the Great Hall's entrance, a little away from the others. A few tables to his right, in the shadows, sat Willerth and Aliana, but it was not dark where they sat, for the Elfess's inner light was reflected in Willerth's gaze. Their hands were locked across the table, and they leaned towards each other. They said little, but Brendys expected there was little they needed to say.

Brendys had known from the day Willerth had first set eyes on Aliana as a youth that he had fallen in love with her, and he had known that he had never forgotten her as the years passed. He had seen Willerth often holding the pendant she had given him at their last parting, staring off into nothing . . . that his servant's thoughts dwelt often upon Aliana was clear to him.

A knot formed in the Horsemaster's throat. He almost hoped that Willerth would choose *not* to return to Shalkan. After all the pain Willerth had suffered in his life, he deserved to know the love Aliana had to share. The thought brought him both joy and sorrow.

There were others present as well, some of them escorts for the nobles among them, other comrades-in-arms and friends from the past, but there were many more missing from this gathering. His thoughts went first to his beloved Mattina. He so desperately wanted her back at his side. He trusted that the Wizard, Odyniec, would bring her back to him, but the wait was terrible. If even word had been sent to let him know she was healing, that she was out of danger, that the Plague was in fact destroyed . . . but there had not even been a message of birthday wishes to their son.

Their son. Brendys swallowed back his grief. This feast should have been in the honor of two little boys, not one. Why had Mattina not told him of Brendyn's twin brother? Why did he have to learn of him through the tragic vision the Dawn King had given him?

His parents. Brendys hoped in his heart that Brendyk and Danel could see their grandson from the High Realm and could be proud of their son. He grieved still that he had failed his father in the mortal life.

Farida. The old woman who had raised him and his father before him . . . another beloved soul taken from his life before her time. Brugnara had paid for her murder and Brendyk's, but it did not ease Brendys's heart.

Kradon. Lord Dell's son had been the closest thing to a brother Brendys had ever known, but he too had been slain by the minions of Thanatos at the Siege of Gildea.

Young Brumagin. A boy Brendys saved from death at the hands of Iysh Mawvath when the Warlord of Thanatos brutally murdered Bru's mother and sister, only to watch him sacrifice himself in grief and despair when Gildea Keep was finally freed.

There were too many, both living and dead, who should be here, but were not. Brendys missed them all, but the sorrow did not consume him as it once did. He had learned the hard way that grief could be turned to evil when allowed to take control.

Brendys at once snapped out of his thoughts as Prince Earon sat down on the edge of the table.

"You look like you could use a drink," the black-haired Prince said as he poured wine for Brendys and himself. Brendys was sure Earon himself had already had a little too much wine. "Do not worry yourself about this afternoon's events. We have been through Hâl together and lived. We shall survive *this* as well."

The Harvathine Prince raised his mazer. "To friendship?"

Brendys allowed a slight smile to cross his lips. "To family."

Earon gave him a confused look, but drank the toast anyway.

As they placed their mazers on the table, one of the Great Hall's massive portals cracked open and Kosarek's chamberlain shuffled in, hobbling straight to Brendys, a mixed look of urgency and disgust on his elderly face. "Your Highness, there are two . . . *people* . . . in the corridor. I believe your message said that you wished for them to be brought here at once."

Brendys gaped at the old man. He had not expected them to have been found so soon, much less brought to Kosarek's court this quickly. He turned to straddle the bench and beckoned to the chamberlain. "Aye, of course! Show them in immediately!"

97

The chamberlain looked severely uncomfortable and uncertain. "But, Your Highness, are you sure? I mean, they are . . . are . . . *common!*"

Brendys leaned towards the old man with a cold grin. "*So am I!* Show . . . them . . . *in!*"

"Oh dear!" the chamberlain exclaimed, shuffling back towards the door. "Oh my! Of course, at once, Your Highness!"

Earon burst out in half-drunken laughter. "The old codger should know better than to question a Prince . . . albeit a *common* one."

Brendys's grin vanished, replaced by a gentle and tired smile. "I told you this morning that you might not think so well of me before the week's end . . . I hadn't expected it to be this very night."

Earon's brow once more beetled in confusion. "What *are* you talking about, Brendys? Are you drunk?"

Brendys looked towards the door, drawing the Prince's gaze with his.

At once, shock registered on Earon's face, and he stood to his feet. His mazer slipped from his grasp as he rose, clattering loudly on the flagstones, it's contents splashing out upon the floor, bringing silence to the room. Standing in the doorway was a young woman. Her garments were worn and tattered, her long black hair tangled, her coppery skin smudged with the dust and dirt of an urban peasant's life and a long journey. Her dark eyes, like Earon's, were wide in amazement and fear.

Brendys turned back to Earon and watched as his friend slowly lost all composure. The man began tremble from head to toe, his grey eyes finally misting over. His mouth worked silently for a moment before he was able to gasp out a single word.

"Semina!" Earon lurched towards the woman and threw his arms around her, burying his face in the filthy garment covering her shoulder, weeping openly. "Forgive me! Forgive me. . . !"

Brendys's own eyes began to water as the peasant woman returned the Prince's embrace, whispering tearful words of forgiveness in his ear, gently stroking his thick black mane. He was glad . . . he had taken a risk with a proud man and had been rewarded. He had *not* lost a friend that day.

At last, Earon gathered his composure—or as much of it as possible—and pulled away from Semina. He stroked her cheek with one hand as he stared into the face he had fallen in love with as a reckless youth.

Brendys glanced at the poor, confounded chamberlain and nodded. In response, the old man ushered in the second *guest*. The little boy, perhaps five or six years of age, scurried at once to his mother's side, tightly grasping her skirt in fear. The boy's skin had the same coppery tone as his mother's, his long, unkempt hair was black, his wide eyes steel-grey.

Earon's eyes widened further. Slowly, he lowered himself to his knees. With a trembling hand, he reached out to touch the boy's face, but the child shrank back in fear.

The Harvathine Prince did not lower his hand, but neither did he press forward. His lips trembled with emotion as he rasped out the child's name. "Earek? M-my son . . . *my* . . . son. . . !"

The boy looked up at his mother, wonder and fear in his eyes. Semina nodded and smiled through her tears. Her oddly-accented voice was husky with emotion. "Aye, Earek . . . this be your father."

The boy turned his round eyes back to Earon. Still grasping his mother's dress in uncertainty, he slowly took a step towards the Prince. Semina pried the child's hand loose and gently encouraged him forward. The boy glanced furtively in her direction but continued on until he fell into Earon's arms.

Earon closed his arms about the boy, hugging him fiercely and kissing him on the head as he whispered, "I am so sorry, my son . . . I am so sorry."

Brendys looked up as Dell came to stand beside him. The Hagane Lord looked as befuddled as Kosarek's chamberlain. "By Oran's shining star . . . *how* did you manage *this?*"

Brendys wiped his eyes and grinned. "I'm impulsive, you know."

He glanced at Earon's back and raised his voice. "Dell, do you recall Earon saying something about having abandoned too much in his lifetime already?"

Earon's shoulders stiffened at Brendys's words, but he said nothing in response. After a brief pause, he released his little boy. Slowly, he rose to his feet and looked Semina in the eye, his ragged voice belying the same fervor with which he had pledged his loyalty to Brendys earlier that morning. "I *will* right the wrong I have done to you, I promise you . . . if you will have me."

Startled speechless, the woman gave him but the slightest nod.

The Harvathine Prince turned to face the small gathering. Brendys saw fear in his eyes and knew this was his final test, his last chance to let go of the remaining shreds of his arrogant pride. For a moment, Brendys thought he might fail, but at last, swallowing hard, Earon spoke, forcing strength into voice. "This . . . this is Semina of Corimuth, whom I knew and who bore . . . bore me a child . . . and who will be my *wife*."

He rested his free hand on the boy's head. "This is Earek . . . he is *my* son and *my* heir. . . ."

His final words came with an almost animal ferocity, and he spun to face the chamberlain as he spoke them. "And *cursed* be *anyone* who scorns their right to share my legacy!"

"Oh dear!" the chamberlain squeaked, his eyes wide in fright. He turned and hurried from the Great Hall as fast as his elderly legs could carry him.

As Earon faced his wife-to-be once more, Brendys saw pride return to his tear-stained face . . . but arrogance was lost to love. From the corner of his eye, Brendys noticed Aliana say something to Willerth, then they both rose to their feet. Willerth made his way to the serving tables, while the Elfess approached Semina and her son.

Semina's gaze finally focused on Aliana as the Elfess approached. The young woman's dark eyes widened in fear and wonder. She had never seen any Elf, much less a High Elf, and the sight of this one was almost too much for her after the emotional shock she had just endured. Aliana's immortal glory shone brightly in the dim firelight of the hall, causing her spotless garments and golden hair to gleam in the shadows. Her sky-blue eyes reflected the warmth of her gentle smile.

"There is no need for fear," Aliana said, taking Semina's hand in her own as the peasant woman started kneel, her musical voice gentle as though speaking to a child. "You are among friends."

Semina allowed herself to be raised to her feet, but lowered her eyes, at once self-conscious of her filthy garments and stained hands.

"Come," Aliana continued. "You have journeyed far and are weary. You and your son shall share my quarters tonight, for I do not require sleep and the bedchamber is wasted on me. Willerth shall bring food to the room. After you eat, you should rest."

Semina turned uncertain eyes on her husband-to-be.

Earon brushed back her hair and kissed her cheek. "We will talk tomorrow. I am sure everything will be clearer in the morning."

Semina conceded at last, with weary, though still confused relief, to be led away with her son.

As they left the Great Hall, Earon returned to the table where Brendys sat and picked his mazer up from the floor, refilling it as he sat down.

"I doubt *your* head will be any clearer in the morning, Your Highness," Lord Dell remarked wryly.

The Harvathine Prince gave him a wan smile. "Perhaps not, but this one last drink I *need*."

Dell shook his head and returned to join the other guests.

Earon's gaze followed the Hagane Lord and he noted that all eyes were still upon him. He barked a sharp, drunken laugh and raised his cup to his fellow guests, shouting, "To family!"

The guests raised their cups and drank to the toast, then slowly returned their attention to the matter at hand, which was Brendyn's birthday.

Earon drained his cup, then placed it on the table shoving it and the wine ewer away from himself. He turned his bleary eyes to Brendys. "You have again helped remove a burden from my heart and allowed me to prove myself a true man. Thank you, my friend."

An evil grin crept across his lips. "But I *will* have my revenge on you before the night is over."

Before Brendys could respond, Berephon suddenly leapt atop a table calling for attention, keeping his wine from spilling with practiced grace.

"And *I* am accused of drunkenness," Earon muttered.

"My dear friends," the Bard's apprentice began. "Most of us know each other well . . . or so we have thought until tonight."

Brendys glanced at Earon, but the Harvathine Prince either was not paying attention or was too intoxicated to comprehend Berephon's quip.

"In my travels with Master Fennis," Berephon continued. "I have had the opportunity to study many ancient texts in libraries and vaults throughout Milhavior, and over the past year I have learned a story which has been lost for many generations of Men. Tonight seems the appropriate time and place for this tale as it is a family history of sorts . . . a tale perhaps of greatest interest to my King."

Brendys glanced at Quellin, who now sat at full attention, his eyes fixed firmly on the aspiring Bard.

Berephon took a sip of wine before beginning his story. "Many centuries ago, near the end of the Second Age of En Orilal, in Mingenland of old ere the population of Milhavior, a Lord of the Firstborn Elves named Dothager fell in love with a woman of the young and mortal race of Men. She was called Ronna and was acclaimed to be the most beautiful of mortal women in that day. Against the wishes and warnings of his own people, Dothager took Ronna to wife.

"The union brought dire consequences in the years to come, for it diminished the grace of the Elves, and there was a great division among them. From this division was born the three kindreds of the Elves as they are today: the *Caletri*, the High Elves, who remained true to their purpose as the counselors of Man and retained the greatest portion of the grace allotted them; the *Saraletri*, or Wood Elves, who chose to isolate themselves from Mankind and fell into a more rustic existence; and the *Analetri*, or Sea Elves, who with the Saraletri departed from Mingenland and voyaged northward by the Western Sea to make their home in the land that would later be known as Milhavior.

It is said that Men chosen by the Dawn King Elekar journeyed with them and built a great city on the Holy Isle of Athor, and that these Men were the forefathers of the Great Wizards.

"It is also said that this division turned many against Dothager and Ronna, and that they were banished from the lands of the Elves for their defiance. But banishment mattered little to Dothager and his mortal wife for their love for each other was greater than their love for either of their peoples. They lived as outcasts, but in happiness for many years before Ronna finally bore a child, a son—an event which drew the attention of both their peoples, for such progeny was not deemed possible. The child's eyes were the color of emeralds, sparkling as if they were gems themselves. Because of this, they named him Trost, after the greatest and purest of Stajouhar gems—green Elvinstone, which to this day remains the symbol of the House of Trost . . . the direct bloodline of my Lord and King, Quellin of Gildea.

"Though his coloring was more like unto his mother, he was Elvin fair and in body aged slowly. As he grew, he was treated as a child by Men, though his mind aged no more slowly than any Man's. At first, he resented this gift of youth, but then learned to use it to his advantage. As a youth, he became ambitious and used the guile of innocence to garner power and possessions for himself."

It was clear to Brendys that Quellin was becoming quickly uncomfortable with the story, though his brother-by-marriage did nothing to hinder Berephon's tale.

Berephon fell silent for a moment, his visage becoming grim. He took another quick drink, then continued. "When Trost was fourteen years of age, Lord Dothager and Lady Ronna were taken captive by the hosts of Thanatos. They were imprisoned in the dungeons of the Deathlord's fortress, Chi Thanatos, and tortured until their bodies could no longer bear it, and they perished. Trost swore an oath of vengeance against his father's murderers, and that oath became the sole motivation of his life from that day forward.

"Trost became mighty among both Men and Elves alike, for the blood of both ran strong in his veins. It was during those days, as the Third Age began, when Thanatos himself returned to the Mortal Realm and spread his lies and evils throughout the whole of Mingenland. The younger races of Men and Dwarves and a few among the Caletri—from whom are descended the Dark Elves—turned against the Dawn King and followed Thanatos."

Brendys noticed Karel, Novosad's step-daughter, abruptly stand up and march from the Great Hall. He caught a glimpse of her pale face beneath her hood as she passed him, and her cold expression chilled him. Unnoticed by any but Brendys, Shannon followed after her, his own face a mask of concern. Brendys silently wished his nephew good fortune . . . but he did not think the girl would respond well to his concern.

Brendys turned his attention back to Berephon, who continued without a glance at the departing youths. "But there were a few Men and even fewer Dwarves who remained faithful to Elekar. These people joined together under the leadership of their greatest rulers: Ascon for the Men, Râsheth Joahin for the Elves, and Graemmon Laksvard for the Dwarves. Trost and his people followed Ascon, but even the combined forces of Men, Elves, and Dwarves could not withstand Death's Legion. It took the direct intervention of the Dawn King to once again banish Thanatos from the Mortal Realm and bring peace to the lands.

"After the Dawn King had defeated the power of Thanatos, he returned among mortal Men and divided the nations of Milhavior among the leaders of the race of Man. To Trost, he gave Kingship over one of the southernmost nations and made Gildea and his brother Horack, Trost's only friends, Lords of that land.

"Trost ruled for many years in wisdom, but eventually he fell back to his old ways. Conflict arose between the King and his Lords, and in the end, Trost imprisoned Gildea and Horack and enslaved their peoples. But the Gildeans would not succumb to oppression and revolted against the Trostains. They overthrew Trost and released Gildea, making him their King.

"Trost was condemned to live out his remaining years in his own dungeons, but in deference to their former friendship, Gildea allowed Trost's children to remain free as Lords of Gildea. But Gildea's kindness would prove disastrous in its own way. As they grew, the sons of Trost became more decadent and wicked than their father had ever been.

"In the dungeons, Trost repented of his evil, and Gildea was moved to accept back his friend of old, but Trost refused him, determined to live out the judgment which he had brought upon himself. Shortly thereafter, the sons of Trost, seeking to undermine Gildea's rule and incite a new rebellion, plotted to murder their own father and lay the blame upon Gildea and Horack, but they were thwarted in a way none expected. Before their plan could be executed, the Alar Uhyvainyn appeared before Trost to test his heart, and when she found his repentance was true, she took him into Alaren Orilal, the High Realm, where harm could not befall him."

Quellin's head hung low, and Arella wrapped her arms around him in comfort. Brendys shook his head. It was a dismal history, but the truth at last was known.

Berephon then smiled. "Throughout the centuries, the history of the Trostains was much the same—of greed and treachery—but a seer of the Caletri of Dun Sol prophesied that one day a Prince born in the lineage of Trost would come to right a great wrong and turn to good a great evil. Many believe that day came when Quiron, called the last Lord of the House of Trost, and his wife Arlena brought forth into the world a son whose likeness was said to be the very image of Trost of old . . . my Lord and King, Quellin of Gildea."

Berephon dropped from the tabletop, putting down his mazer, and knelt before his King.

Quellin raised his head and placed a hand on the young man's shoulder. "It was a hard tale to hear, Bipin, but a truth that needed to be heard. My thanks to you."

The Gildean King turned to say something to his son and noticed for the first time that Shannon was not present. "Where is Shannon?"

"He went with that *girl*," Brendyn piped up, a note of disdain in his voice.

Brendys sighed. Evidently, he was *not* the only one who noticed Karel and Shannon leave.

After a quick survey of the room, Novosad sheepishly added, "I believe that would be my daughter."

* * * *

Shannon paused outside Karel's chambers. Through the closed door, he could hear her pacing within. He hesitated, uncertain whether to trouble her or not. She had not responded well the last time he had come to her aid.

Bolstering his courage, he straightened his tunic, then reached up to straighten his crown, but thought better of it and knocked on the door. Without waiting for an answer, he opened the door and stepped into the room.

Karel spun to face him, startled by the intrusion, her heavy cloak whipping around her at the motion. "How *dare* you? Because you are a Prince, do you think that gives you the right to barge into my room, boy?"

No matter how prepared he had been, her words flustered him. "I-I saw you leave during Berephon's story and thought you might like someone to talk to. You looked upset."

"Did I ask you to follow me?" Karel responded harshly. "I do not need your pity, boy."

Shannon rankled at that. "I did not offer it. And stop calling me *boy* . . . I am not *that* much younger than you."

"Oh yes, the blessed Half-Elf," the girl sneered.

"You are half Elf, too," Shannon returned hotly.

"Half *Dark Elf*!" Karel shot back, tearing the cloak from her shoulders and casting it at Shannon's feet. "Do you think that gives us some kinship? Hardly!"

Shannon stared at her, open-mouthed. Her skin was whiter than the linens on her bed, and she had the cold, black eyes of her blood father's race, but her hair gleamed like copper in the lamplight. There was no question of her Elvin heritage . . . she was the most beautiful girl he had ever laid eyes upon.

"You cannot begin to imagine what it is like going through life knowing that you sprang from the seed of evil!" Karel ranted, her voice raising in volume and pitch. "I cannot even walk beneath the sun without feeling as though my very skin is being scorched from my flesh, while everyone stares at me in hatred and distrust . . . what it is like to be forced wherever I go to endure the assaults of bullies and ruffians like those boys at the fair! To be called *demon* . . . and worse. . . ."

She slumped down on the edge of her bed, her brow furrowing more deeply in anger, though her voice lowered. "Even my parents cannot abide me. Every time my mother looks upon my face, she is reminded of what my father did to her. And my step-father . . . he thinks I am evil incarnate!"

"Is that what you really think?" Shannon said in disbelief. "If so, you are a fool! I saw no hatred in that room when your mother put her arms around you, and Novosad loves you as his own . . . if it were not for him, you would have been slain at birth by superstitious idiots. Instead, you have Lord Dell's protection because your father believes there is no evil in you!"

"He is not my father," the girl snapped, though with less conviction.

"Yes, he *is*," Shannon returned. "It matters not whose blood flows in your veins, Novosad is the man who has raised you, cared for you, protected you, and loved you! And here you sit, scorning that love . . . you are *pathetic*."

Without reply, Karel set her jaw and turned her face away, trembling.

After a moment, Shannon realized she was crying. At once, his own anger melted away. Feeling like a cad, he sat down beside her, casting a guilty glance in her direction. "I-I am sorry. I was wrong to have spoken to you like that. Forgive me . . . please."

The girl did not respond.

Shannon looked at his hands, folded in his lap. "If it matters to you at all, *I* do not hate or distrust you, and I don't really think you are pathetic."

Karel turned her tear-streaked face to him, confusion setting in. When she spoke, her voice was barely audible. "What, then, *do* you think of me?"

Shannon licked his dry lips nervously and swallowed before replying. "I-I think you are beautiful."

Fresh tears began to well in the girl's black eyes.

"Hasn't anyone ever told you that?" Shannon asked, cocking his head in curiosity. "Other than your parents, I mean."

Karel shook her head.

"Well, it is true," the young Prince assured her. "I think you are the most beautiful girl I have ever seen."

The new tears finally escaped Karel's eyes and trailed down her cheeks.

"Oh, please don't cry anymore," Shannon pleaded. "It makes your face all grey, and that doesn't look well on you at all."

Fumbling, he pulled a kerchief from his sleeve and raised it to wipe the tears away, but Karel grabbed his hand. Her touch sent a thrill through him like an electrical charge. Her hand was warm . . . he almost expected it to be as cold as her gaze.

"Then what color would you say does look well on me?" she asked quietly.

Shannon stared at her for a moment, surprised by the change in her demeanor. At last, he replied, "Red. . . ."

Karel frowned. "Like blood?"

Shannon shook his head slowly, leaning closer, his eyes locked with hers. "Nay . . . like a rose."

* * * *

Brendys stood between Quellin and the doors of the Great Hall. "Quellin, leave them be. Or are you afraid of Karel like everyone else in this place? Are you afraid the girl might put a curse on Shannon or murder him?"

Quellin wrinkled his brow. "Of course not, don't be ludicrous . . . *that* is *not* what worries me."

At that moment, one of the doors creaked open and Shannon strode lightly in, fairly beaming. His silver crown was still tilted, but backwards rather than at its usual sideways angle. His normally perfect mane of hair was slightly ruffled as well.

"I am sorry for disappearing like that," he said brightly. "Has Brendyn started opening his gifts?"

"Where have you been?" Quellin asked him, an incredulous look on his youthful face.

"With Karel," his son readily replied. "She was weary and decided to retire, so I thought I should come back."

Quellin's eyes grew wider. "Indeed? And what were you doing?"

"Talking mostly," came the reply.

The Gildean king stared at his son, his face reddening. "*Mostly?*"

"*Father!*" Shannon exclaimed in a disapproving tone, shock registering on his young face.

Arella took her husband's arm and steered him back towards the rest of the guests. "This is neither the time, nor the place, husband."

As they moved out of ear shot, Shannon let out a sigh of relief. Then he noticed his uncle's gaze upon him. Blushing, he ducked his head, and hurried to join the others.

Brendys turned and looked at his Harvathine friend.

Earon raised his hands before him and shook his head. "Do not look at me, Prince of Horses . . . I am not the one spreading the seeds of romance tonight."

He chuckled lightly to himself. "Not yet, at any rate."

The Harvathine Prince started towards the door.

"Where are you going?" Brendys asked.

Grinning, Earon glanced back over his shoulder as he walked away. "You do not think I came empty-handed, do you? I must retrieve Brendyn's gift."

Brendyn shook his head and went to join his guests. The usually dignified Earon was hopelessly drunk, that was all there was to it.

111

As Brendys came to stand behind his son, Lord Guthwine knelt before the boy and held forth a cupped palm. "This is not a gift to awe a mortal child, young Prince, for the Caletri are a practical people. This ring is meant to be a lesson . . . to remind you that strength must be tempered with gentleness."

Brendyn picked the ring up. It was hard to tell the color of the ring, whether gold or silver, and it bore the same coat-of-arms as Brendys's own signet. The blazon on his son's new ring, however, was crafted from a single clear stone. Brendyn looked startled when he took the ring. He looked at the Elvinlord. "It's warm, like Papa's ring!"

Guthwine dipped his head once. "Aye. It too is crafted of Gloriod, and the stone is Elvindiamond, found only on the Holy Isle of Athor. Only a few such stones have made their way to the mainland. Elvindiamond is as hard as Gloriod, if not stronger, but has an additional power: the touch of the stone may heal even the most deadly injuries and illnesses. It is said that a large enough Elvindiamond may cure the all-consuming death of Crorkin, black Elvinmetal. This ring is priceless . . . you should never lay it aside."

The ring itself looked sized for a grown man, but when the child tried it on, it fit snugly upon his finger. "It fits!"

"And ever it will," Lord Guthwine replied. "For such is the virtue placed upon it by our smiths. Neither may it be removed unless you will it so. But I give you warning . . . do not use the gifts of this ring without great need, for its virtue may be lost."

Brendyn considered the ring thoughtfully for a moment, then asked, "Can it make scars go away?"

The Elvinlord smiled sadly. "Alas, scars that already are shall ever be. The ring cannot take them."

The boy nodded, crestfallen. Brendys knew his son had hoped the ring could take away the terrible scars that riddled his young body, but he would have to be patient and allow them to fade with time. Though Brendys understood the ring was perhaps the least of the gifts in his son's mind, it was truly the greatest. It was valuable, yes, but it also had meaning. He knew that the Elves presented it not as a trinket to a seven-year-old boy on his birthday, but as a symbol of majesty to a child who would one day be the King of Men, Elves, and all the Free Kindreds.

Brendyn received many small toys and trinkets, and clothing was in abundance. Most of these things held little interest for the boy, but he accepted them graciously, bringing a measure of pride to his father.

As the night drew on, it became evident that Brendyn was growing tired. Brendys prepared to bid his guests good night and bring a close to the feasts, but his nephew stepped forward to present his gift, so he waited.

Shannon smiled at his younger cousin. "Brendyn, I have two gifts to offer, though one will be late in coming. You shall have my stallion's first foal out of our best mare."

Brendyn was awestruck, and even Brendys was greatly impressed. He had seen Millas. The stallion was a black of finer quality perhaps than any that had come from the stable of Brendyk of Shalkan, with a temperament every bit as volatile as Fracas, Brendys's grey. Brendys was already imagining what he could do by introducing that stallion's bloodline into his stable.

Shannon unbuckled his belt and removed from it a silver-handled longknife in an ornate leather scabbard, also trimmed in silver. Cradling the weapon in both hands, he presented it to his cousin. "I also want you to have this. Volker has been an heirloom of the House of Trost since the days of Trost himself, or so it is said. My father passed it to me on my birthday this very year, but you should have it. I shall one day inherit Kalter, my father's sword, but your father is destined to pass his sword to the Heir of Ascon . . . it is not right that a Prince of Gildea should not have such an heirloom to pass to his son."

Shannon glanced shyly at Brendys. "I mean no offense, Uncle . . . you bear the mightiest heirloom in Milhavior, but it is not yours to pass on."

Brendys's eyes flicked quickly towards Dell, then to Quellin. The face of the Lord of Hagan was almost purple, and he looked as though he wanted to shout the secret he shared from the highest turret of the Keep. Quellin, on the other hand, beamed at his son with pride. Shannon's gesture was unnecessary, but noble.

Brendys wanted to laugh, but he restrained himself. He gently gripped his nephew's shoulder and smiled broadly. "No offense is taken, lad. You are right . . . Denasdervien is not mine to give. Indeed, it shall even pass to others before it comes into the hands of Ascon's Heir."

Brendyn looked up at his father, and Brendys gave him a nod. The boy took the Elvinknife from his cousin with wonder in his eyes and began to draw it from its sheath, but Quellin reached out and stopped his hand before the blade was more than an inch out of the scabbard. The deep green crystal of the Stajouhar blade glittered in the dim firelight.

Quellin's gaze was serious. "Shannon's gift is an admirable one, but also very dangerous. You must understand, Brendyn . . . should you even scratch yourself with Volker's blade, it could mean your death. Wounds caused by a Stajouhar blade burn with an unseen flame, and the pain is such that it can drive a man mad. With a child your age, I fear death would be instant."

Brendyn, his blue eyes wide, slowly resheathed the knife. "I will be careful, Uncle Quellin."

Quellin smiled and nodded. "I am sure you will be."

"It is long past Brendyn's bedtime, so I think it is time we bid you all a good night," Brendys announced. He took

Volker from his son and carefully placed it among the other gifts, then steered Brendyn towards the great doors.

As they walked away, Brendys heard Novosad instruct the twins, Copanas and Lehan, to gather the gifts and deliver them to the Horsemaster's quarters.

"I thought this is what castle servants were for," Lehan muttered to his brother.

"Be of good cheer, soldier," Novosad said good-naturedly. "Or you will *be* a castle servant."

"I think leadership has gone to his head," Copanas answered Lehan.

Brendys grinned to himself. Sometimes wearing the mantle of a Prince was not a bad thing. As he and Brendyn neared the doors, they swung open and Prince Earon entered.

"Oh! It looks like I made it back just in time," he said, striding up to the pair. "Brendyn has one more present . . . the best one of them all, if I might say so myself!"

That piqued the boy's interest. Brendyn looked up expectantly at the Harvathine Prince. "Where is it?"

Earon smiled down at him. "You will find it in your room . . . it is a very *special* gift."

"A very, *very* special gift," a voice, aged but full of authority and wisdom, concurred.

Brendys's gaze darted to the old man standing in the entryway. His white robes gleamed beneath his grey cloak, complimenting the snowy locks which fell around his shoulders and the long, white beard dangling below his belt. In his right hand, he held a staff carved with runes of an ancient tongue. The old man's piercing, steel-grey eyes glittered as he smiled.

Brendys hardly noticed the strong smell of wine as Earon leaned towards him and clapped a hand on his shoulder, saying in a low voice, "Turnabout and all that."

115

After Brendys recovered from the initial shock of seeing Odyniec there in the Great Hall of Racolis, he started moving again towards the open entrance, gaining speed until he was at a full run. When he reached his quarters, he threw open the door and halted just inside. Willerth and Aliana were there, as well as a golden-haired woman and a little girl, but Brendys paid no notice to any of them. His senses were aware of only one.

She had not changed. Her chestnut hair cascaded down her shoulders, framing smooth, fair-toned cheeks, which radiated Elvin youth and beauty. But it was her eyes, more than anything else, that drew him in . . . deep, green gems, glittering like the purest emeralds. If she was in pain, it did not show, or he could not see.

She rose from the couch, slowly and carefully, and threw herself into his arms. Brendys drew his wife to him and kissed her, abandoning himself to the moment.

Willerth grinned broadly and quietly ushered everyone out of the room, leaving Brendys and Mattina alone.

At last, the couple parted. Brendys ran his hand through her hair, watching the silky strands slip through his fingers, then caressed her cheek. "It has been months since Odyniec sent word of your condition . . . I did not know what to think. . . ."

Mattina smiled at him. "By the time Master Odyniec was certain I was out of danger, it was too late to send a message. It would not have arrived before you left Shalkan."

She lowered herself to the couch, drawing her husband down beside her. "We decided instead to come here directly. Since dear Englar was unable to come, he sent us to Harvath with an escort where we found Prince Earon preparing to depart."

Brendys looked at her in disbelief. "You have been here since last night, and Earon knew all along?"

"And Dell also," Mattina added, resting her head on his strong shoulder.

"I am betrayed," Brendys muttered.

Mattina laughed lightly at his side. "Perhaps it was cruel, but do not judge them too harshly, my love. I slept most of the day away . . . I am weak still, and a fever comes and goes. Master Odyniec thinks that with a month or so of rest, I should regain my strength."

Brendys rubbed his cheek against her head. "Then you shall have it."

"You know, when first I met Prince Earon, I didn't much like him," Mattina quipped. Brendys chuckled, remembering his first experience with the Crown Prince of Harvath. "But when he came to me a little while ago, he seemed changed."

Mattina looked up into her husband's eyes. "Willerth and Aliana told me what you did for him."

Any guilt he felt over putting his Harvathine friend through that emotional trial had vanished. Brendys kissed his wife on the forehead. "He deserved it."

At that moment, a small form came flying through the door, catapulting itself at Mattina. "*Mama!*"

Brendyn buried his head in his mother's shoulder, sobbing uncontrollably. Mattina clutched her child to herself, stroking his hair. "Oh, my darling, I have missed you so much."

"I want you to come home," the boy cried, his voice muffled. "I don't want you to go away again!"

Mattina pulled him away. With one hand on each of his cheeks, using her thumbs to wipe away his tears, she looked him squarely in the face. If she noticed his scars, she did not betray the fact. "Master Odyniec says that I am well enough to go home. I will not leave you again, my son."

*   *   *   *

From the doorway, Willerth smiled. His family was now complete. But his smile did not last. A strange feeling came over him, a feeling that something was . . . *missing*.

He turned to look behind him. He was alone.

Chapter 7

Brendys lay in bed, staring at the canopy above him, his right arm around Mattina's shoulders, her head resting on his chest. It was a strange sensation to feel the warmth of her body beside him once more, but it was not uncomfortable. Quite the opposite . . . it made him feel whole again.

The first rays of dawn began to filter in through the window. Brendys glanced towards the light. He had not slept at all the night before. So much had happened that his mind would not let him rest. He had questions and concerns, confusion that needed to be sorted out. Some of his questions he had answered himself, but others lingered.

Carefully, he slid out of bed, gently laying Mattina's head upon the bed. He walked to the narrow window and stared out at the slowly brightening landscape. If anyone stirred yet in the city, they did not pass within his limited view.

After a minute, he heard the bed linens ruffle and the slow padding of bare feet approaching. Mattina wrapped her arms around his strong body and pressed close to him. He draped his arms across her shoulders and held her.

They stood together in the growing sunlight, silent, content in the knowledge of each other's presence.

At last, Brendys broke the silence. "How much do you know about me?"

Mattina drew back, puzzled by the question. "All that I need to know."

Brendys shook his head. "I mean, how much do you know about my destiny? How much did Elekar reveal to you? How much did Odyniec say?"

Mattina paused a moment before replying, a slightly fretful look on her face. "Of *your* destiny, Elekar revealed to me only what I needed to know to prepare for your arrival at Lener Keep. Odyniec has told me nothing."

"And what of our son's destiny?" Brendys asked. "At Lener Keep, you told me that everything depended on my protecting Brendyn."

Mattina looked even more uncomfortable with that question, but she did not answer. Nevertheless, he saw the truth in her eyes.

Brendys nodded. "Then that makes six of us who know our son's destiny."

Mattina started at his words, but he placed his fingers over her lips before she could speak. "We will not speak of this again . . . already Machaelon sets its agents against us. The longer we can keep this secret, the safer Brendyn will be."

His wife nodded her understanding.

After a moment of tense silence, Brendys spoke again. "How much do you know of what happened after you succumbed to the Plague?"

"I heard stories," Mattina answered, with a slight shake of her head. "But many were so incredible I might not have believed them if Englar himself hadn't sworn to them."

"Aye," Brendys replied, nodding slowly, memories of that time flooding back to him. "It *was* incredible . . . it seems so distant now, like it was only a dream."

Mattina traced the scars on his face and chest. "These are not a dream, nor are the scars that mark my son's face. How did you come by them?"

Brendys closed his eyes, shuddering against the grim memory. "Brugnara . . . he . . . he had us tortured. He put the scourge to Brendyn himself, and I know not what else. Brendyn will not speak of it . . . and knowing Brugnara, I cannot say I blame him."

He opened his eyes to look into his wife's horror-stricken face. "When I at last confronted Brugnara and saw Brendyn stretched out upon the Black Altar, his small body was so torn that I wonder yet that he lived. Denasdervien's flame healed the worst of his wounds, but the scars are terrible still. You have seen but the least of them."

Mattina went back to the bed and sat down, wrapping her arms around herself, shivering as though a chill had come over her, despite the warmth of the summer morning. "My poor little boy. . . ."

My poor little boy. The words echoed in Brendys's mind. His heart wrenched within him. He did not want to bring more grief to Mattina so soon, but he had one last question to which he needed an answer. He needed to know the truth.

He sat down beside his wife, wrapping an around her shoulders. "Mattina, why did you not tell me about . . . about the other?"

Mattina's face snapped towards him. She blinked back her tears, a haunted look in her green eyes, her fair cheeks paling further. "What other. . . ?"

Brendys bowed his head. "Our . . . our other son. Brendyn's twin."

Mattina gave a startled gasp. "How did you know? I told no one. . . ."

"The night Brendyn and I arrived, I had a dream," Brendys replied slowly. With his free hand, he reached up and stroked her cheek. "But I have to know, I have to be sure . . . tell me . . . tell me about it."

"Brendyl was stillborn," Mattina rasped, grief overwhelming her. She collapsed against her husband's chest and wept. "They wouldn't let me hold him, Brendys . . . they wouldn't even let me bury him. They just took him away like refuse to be discarded. . . !"

Brendys squeezed his eyes shut, holding his wife to himself. The dream had been true then . . . Elekar had spoken to him again. But what had it meant? He would have to remember to consult Odyniec, but not now . . . the pain was still too great.

After a few minutes, there was a soft knock at the bedroom door, and Willerth's voice drifted through. "Master Brendys, Mistress Mattina . . . you will be expected at breakfast."

Brendys sighed in frustration, wishing they had never come to Racolis Keep.

Mattina pulled away, wiping her eyes. "I am all right now."

"Are you sure?" Brendys asked with concern. "I can have Willerth convey our regrets, if you don't feel up to it."

"Nay," Mattina replied with a shaky smile. "I will be fine."

After dressing, they stepped out into the anteroom where they were greeted by their son's excited voice. Hauling a young girl with him by the hand, he rushed to his parents. "Papa, can we go to the fair again today? I want to show Lonel the games."

Brendys raised a brow. He did not recognize the girl. She looked to be about the same age as his son, with golden hair and large brown eyes. Her dress was plain, but clean and well-sewn. Brendys wondered if perhaps she was one of the castle children. Then he noticed a woman, dressed similarly to the girl, also brown-eyed and golden-haired, standing to the side with Willerth. He vaguely remembered her presence in the room the night before, but he had been so focused on Mattina that he had paid no heed to her.

Mattina noticed his look and hurried to introduce the woman and child. "Brendys, this is Lara and her daughter Lonel. They helped Odyniec care for me at Lener Keep."

The woman did Brendys a curtsy. "Your Highness."

Brendys inclined his head in return. "My thanks to you, Lara."

"Brendys," Mattina said, taking his hand. "Lara's husband was a Shadine man-at-arms slain at the Harvathine border. She has no means to care for Lonel, and I thought that, perhaps, she could return with us to Shalkan . . . I am sure there would be more than enough work she could help with at the farmstead."

Brendys looked at the woman with a newfound admiration. It must have been difficult for her to journey to Racolis under the escort of the men who had slain her husband. "Of course! It has been far too long since my home has had the benefit of a lady's touch."

Lara curtsied again, the light of gratitude in her eyes. "Your humble servant, Your Highness!"

"Does this mean we don't have to eat Willerth's cooking anymore?" Brendyn quipped, eliciting a wry face from the young man.

*   *   *   *

Prince Earon was notably absent from the morning meal, and it was not until afterwards that Brendys learned why. The Harvathine Prince met his friends outside the Great Hall when the meal was ending. Brendys was taken aback at once by the severe expression on the younger man's face.

Earon sketched a bow as his friends gathered to the side. "My friends, my company prepares to depart at once. I have to come to bid you farewell and beg you to accompany us just beyond the gates of the city."

"So soon?" Arella responded in surprise. "But you have only been here a day!"

"Circumstances demand we leave immediately," Earon replied curtly. He cast a disparaging glance at the steady stream of nobles exiting the Great Hall. "Last night, I decided I must wed Semina before returning to Harvath. I am sure my father would not permit our union. If we wait until we return to Harvath, my father would be able to hinder our marriage."

His jaw tightened. "Unfortunately, King Kosarek is of the same mind as my father, and with the High Steward's support has forbidden our wedding within the walls of this city. The local Oranite priests will not defy their King, but Master Odyniec has agreed to perform our ceremony beyond the city gates. Afterwards, we shall leave."

Brendys's features darkened in anger. "And you shall not be the only ones leaving."

"Brendys!" Dell barked sharply, though in a low voice. "Do not antagonize Kosarek . . . he is not a forgiving man."

"I care not whether I incur the displeasure of an old man who will likely not live to see another year," the Horsemaster snapped back, ignoring the shocked glances of Kosarek's departing guests.

"Brendys, you would risk angering King Mathai as well," Quellin reminded him quietly.

Brendys faced his brother-by-marriage, making no effort to quiet his voice. "Mathai has already cast his lot against me."

In one movement, he drew forth Denasdervien and easily plunged the tip of its mirrored, Silver-gold blade into the flagstones before him. "But as long as I wield *this*, he dares not openly defame me."

Mattina clasped both of her hands over her husband's. "Brendys, please . . . you let anger control you."

Brendys met his wife's gaze. "What Earon does is a thing of honor, yet that old vulture is turning it into a scandal. Of course I'm angry!"

"Uncle Brendys," Shannon broke in, his soft voice a marked contrast to the heated energy in his uncle's.

Brendys looked at his nephew. The youth glanced briefly at his cousin before continuing. "This *is* Brendyn's birthday celebration."

Brendys allowed his attention to be drawn to his son, who followed the conversation with growing distress. He sighed, anger draining away. "Very well. For Brendyn's sake and in deference to Dell's friendship, we will remain . . . but I will have *nothing* more to do with Kosarek and the rest of these pompous fools."

Pulling Denasdervien out of the floor and returning it its scabbard, he turned back to Earon. "My family shall be honored to stand with you at your wedding."

Quellin quietly voiced his agreement.

Dell gave the Harvathine Prince a stiff bow. "I regret I cannot attend, Your Highness. While I, too, strongly disagree with Kosarek's decision, I cannot go against my King's will."

Earon gave him an acknowledging nod. "I understand, My Lord, and I harbor no ill will against you for it. It is the duty of every man to obey the will of his King."

Dell glanced at Brendys, a flicker of conflicting emotions fluttering across his face, but at last sketched another bow to his companions. "Farewell, Your Highness. I will speak with the rest of you later. In the meantime, I feel I should attempt to belay any ill-will on the part of my King."

He frowned darkly. "I seem to be doing a lot of that recently. . . ."

As Dell excused himself, Brendys inclined his head to his Harvathine friend. "Well, if we are to be a-party to this scandal, let's to it."

Coaches transported Brendys, Quellin, and their families and servants to a field beyond the city gates, where Earon's company waited. Odyniec was already there, as were Folkor, Asghar, and Guthwine's family.

Before the wedding began, Earon properly introduced Semina and Earek to his friends. The woman and her son had changed their appearance overnight: washed and refreshed, hair brushed and combed, and garbed in simple, yet elegant traveling garments. Looking with clearer mind and eyes, Brendys was not at all surprised that Earon had fallen for the young woman. Semina's copper-toned face was shapely with full lips and small nose. He noticed that her black hair had a silky sheen to it that his own did not.

When Earon named his friends to her, she started to kneel, but her husband-to-be caught her and raised her to her feet. "But for King Quellin and Queen Arella, these are now your peers . . . kneel not to them."

Quellin inclined his head to Semina. "Indeed, and we are friends . . . we would not have our friends kneel before us."

The woman blushed, a timid smile crossing her lips. "This be a change, to be sure . . . frightens me fierce."

Mattina laughed gently, taking her by the hands. "I can imagine. It will take time to accustom yourself. But think of *my* change . . . Brendys and I have chosen to live a common life in Shalkan, where royalty and nobility are unknown."

"Truly?" Semina exclaimed, dark eyes wide in amazement.

Mattina nodded. "Truly."

"Despite my wishes," Quellin muttered half to himself.

Mattina shot her brother a sharp glare.

Brendys bit back a sharp reply of his own. He knew that, despite Quellin's best efforts to maintain civility among his nobility, the same arrogance, underhanded intrigue, and complete asininity that he had witnessed thus far at Racolis Keep was no less rampant in Gildea. He had no desire for his son to be raised in such an environ.

He knew that Quellin only wanted what he thought was best for his sister—and perhaps it *was* best—but it would not happen, not unless the full power of Machaelon were thrown against Shalkan. Then, perhaps, Brendys might retreat to Trost Keep as Quellin wished, but not before then. Shunting aside his uncalled-for resentment of Quellin's persistence, he turned to Earon. "I *am* a little confused, Earon. I thought that your people would have to accept Semina as a Princess of Harvath before you could be wed?"

"It is thus in Gildea, Brendys," Quellin answered him, a momentary look of shame crossing his youthful features. "But only because of the troubles my ancestors caused in the past. It is not so in other lands. Earon's father may allow—or *disallow*—their marriage."

"Then what is to keep Welmon from simply declaring the marriage annulled?" Brendys returned, wondering if this whole wedding was simply to spite Kosarek—a thought which was not entirely unappealing to him at the moment—or whether Earon actually clung to some increasingly futile hope that his father would simply accept what had happened and permit the marriage to stand.

"The High Laws set down by Ascon himself," Odyniec said as he joined the fellowship, leaning on his staff. His grey hood was drawn for shade against the rapidly warming sun, but Brendys did not fail to notice his smile.

Earon grinned. "The very . . . *indiscretion* . . . which has brought us to this pass is what will protect us from my father's wrath."

Brendys was beginning to feel the onset of a headache forming behind his eyes. He found the answer to his question wanting for a simpler clarification. Rubbing his temple, he said, "Please . . . my knowledge of the High Laws is not what I suppose it should be. What the blazes are you saying?"

Lady Reatha gave him the patient smile of a parent preparing to explain a simple lesson to a slow-witted child. "Do you recall, Brendys, what I said of Elvin marriages at your wedding?"

Elvin marriages? He vaguely recalled that Guthwine's wife *had* mentioned something, but many of his memories from that time had been subdued and buried by Brugnara's sorcerous manipulations of his mind over the years. What was it she had said? She had said something about vows exchanged in seclusion, because . . . because Elves practiced marriage by *consummation*. Brendys gave her a startled look. "But what does that have to do with Earon and Semina? They are not Elves. . . ."

"Aye, Brendys," Guthwine answered him, calm amusement playing on his lips. "But our people taught the Men of the Second Age. The rituals and ceremonies you mortals of this Age practice did not come into being until your alleged *old gods* sprang into being."

"Indeed," Odyniec agreed. "It is true that the vows you took were indeed prescribed by the High Laws, but the ceremony was little more than pomp to satisfy the increasingly arrogant mortal mind."

The Wizard turned to Earon and Semina and smiled. "The vows that shall be given here will be the final cord that binds your spirits, and not even Welmon may break it. Young Earek is the only evidence you shall need of your marriage."

His expression turned more severe, his gaze focusing more strongly upon Earon. "But understand, words and mortal passion alone are not enough. They may be easily given without love and discarded again without feeling. What you seek must begin in the heart. Do you understand?"

Semina looked as confused by the proceedings as Brendys felt, but she nodded silently.

Earon solemnly inclined his head to the Wizard. "I understand, Master Odyniec. I *do* love Semina, and I will not fail her again."

Brendys looked from Odyniec to Earon and back again. "Are you saying that Mattina and I could have avoided that whole affair just by. . . ."

Mattina gave him a sharp jab in the ribs, hissing angrily, "*Brendys!*"

The Horsemaster glanced down into his wife's red and disbelieving face and grinned.

Quellin's eyes narrowed threateningly, but his voice remained calm as he said, "I am sure you valued your life enough in those days to think better of it, however."

Brendys smirked, but did not reply, eliciting another jab from his wife.

"Brendys of Shalkan, you are a rat!" Mattina bit out, glowering at him.

Brendys smiled and put his arm around her. "Aye, I know. I shouldn't be so cruel."

He noticed Earon glance towards the sky, then offer Semina his arm. The Harvathine Prince drew in a nervous breath, then said to his companions, "The day is wearing on. We should begin."

"Indeed, we should," Odyniec agreed, beckoning for the group to follow him. "This way, please."

Brendys noticed that the Wizard was leading them to a small hillock nearby, prominently within view of the open city gates and the streams of people beginning to make their way into the city from the outlying lands. Odyniec was clearly enjoying his own part in this rebellious moment.

As Brendyn, Lonel, Sîan, and Earek ran past him, laughing, Brendys smiled. Earon's son had at least found a measure of comfort in the company of the other children. He only hoped that he would find welcome in Harvath, as well.

Brendyn stopped a moment and turned to call back, "Come on, Shannon!" before following the others again.

Brendys glanced back over his shoulder and saw his nephew facing the city, a distracted look on his face, completely oblivious to the fact that he now stood alone. He had no doubt what—or rather, *who*—Shannon was thinking about, but what those thoughts might entail disturbed him, particularly in the wake of the recent conversation. He told Mattina to go on without him, then strode back towards their nephew.

As he approached, he reached out and gave the youth a sharp whack to the back of the head, just below his tilted crown, his face and voice severe. "Don't even think it."

"*Ow!*" Shannon said, rubbing his head where the blow struck. He turned to his uncle, his expression both annoyed and confused. "What are you. . . ?"

His eyes suddenly widened, and his cheeks began to darken, turning nearly purple. "*Uncle Brendys!* You are as bad my father!"

Glowering and rubbing his head, he stalked after the retreating wedding party, muttering, "Of all the stupid, inconsiderate, completely thoughtless. . . ."

Brendys let his gaze follow his nephew for a moment, hoping that the lesson would sink in, then trailed after him. He rejoined the wedding party just as Odyniec drew back his hood and tossed his cloak back behind his shoulders, revealing his white robes to the sun. Brendys felt Mattina lean against him, and looked down into her smiling face. He draped his arm around her shoulders and smiled back, then returned his gaze to the wedding.

Odyniec raised both of his hands, his staff uplifted in his right, and cried out in a voice that could be heard for some distance. *"Gwikas boFäno, där mäs nwäsoi!"*

The runes around the head of his staff flared with white fire, then dimmed again. The Wizard indicated for Earon and Semina to stand before him, while saying in a loud voice, "We are here to recognize the union of Earon, son of Welmon, Crown Prince of the House of Harvath, and Semina, daughter of. . . ."

Odyniec raised an eyebrow in Semina's direction, and the young woman stammered out something that Brendys could not make out. Odyniec smiled and continued. "Semina, daughter of Geneta, of Corimuth. In token of the vows you are about to take, will you, Prince Earon, claim and acknowledge Semina's son, Earek, as your own, blood of your blood and heir to your legacy?"

Earon, his face paling a little, drew in a deep breath and replied in a strong voice. "I will."

Odyniec looked again at Semina. "Semina, daughter of Geneta, do you understand and accept in whole the role this marriage shall bestow upon you as a Princess of Harvath, wife of he who will one day be King of Harvath?"

Trembling, dark eyes wide in fright, Semina nevertheless replied in a barely audible voice, "I-I will."

Brendys heard movement behind him and an increasing number of quiet voices exchanging wondering words. He grinned at Odyniec. The wedding was beginning to draw a small crowd from among the peasantry making their way into the city from the outlying farms.

The Wizard lowered his staff between the man and woman before him. "Kneel and place your hands upon the staff."

Brendys felt a buzz of nostalgia. As Earon and Semina knelt, he could almost imagine himself and Mattina years before kneeling across from each other upon the steps leading up into Gildea Keep, their hands atop each other's, preparing to take their own vows.

Odyniec muttered a few words in Athorian, then spoke to Earon. "Earon, son of Welmon, will you swear to love Semina as yourself and to remain faithful to her alone, never putting her aside for another, according to the will of the Lord Elekar?"

Brendys looked down at his wife, recalling grimly that he had ignored that final phrase when he had responded, having sworn himself against the Dawn King from a young age, blaming him for the death of his mother. Earon did not hesitate, however, and readily responded to the Wizard with fervor. Almost without realizing it, he found himself reaffirming his own vows to Mattina in a whispering voice.

Mattina heard his voice and returned his steady gaze, tears welling in her eyes.

It was Semina, this time, who stumbled over her vow, wondering if by swearing an oath in the name of a being at war with the gods she had been raised to serve would bring condemnation down upon her, but Earon's encouraging smile helped ease her conscience. As she finished her response, Odyniec spoke a benediction in Athorian, then drew his staff away, saying, "May these holy vows which you have made never be broken as long as death abstains. By the High Law of Milhavior and by the grace of the Dawn King Elekar, I proclaim you husband and wife.

Arise, Earon of Harvath, and receive your wife unto yourself."

As Earon drew Semina to her feet and kissed her, a loud cheer went up from the gathering crowd. The Prince and his new wife turned with looks of astonishment, for so intent on each other had they been that they had not been aware of the crowd, now numbering over a hundred in attendance. Brendys could not help but grin again. Word that the Crown Prince of Harvath had taken a common woman as wife would now spread throughout Racolis Keep, much to the consternation of Kosarek and his noble cronies.

As Earon and Semina descended from the hillock, the Harvathine Prince swept his young son up into his arms. The boy's excited grin abruptly vanished in favor of the trepidation he had shown his father the night before, but he did not offer resistance. The wedded couple received congratulations from those who had chosen to stand with them, though Semina, like her son, was quickly becoming almost as overwhelmed as she had been the previous night. They stopped at last before Brendys and Mattina.

Earon gripped the Horsemaster's hand. "Words alone are not enough to thank you for what you have done for me, Brendys of Shalkan. Is there aught else I can do?"

Brendys smiled in return. "There is nothing, my friend. I have all I need. Elekar go with you . . . it will be a difficult road. Quellin's nobles do not truly accept me as a Prince of Gildea, and I have the feeling Semina and Earek will meet with the same resistance."

Earon gave him a solemn nod. "I know, and were it not for the responsibilities of my rank, I think I would follow your lead, disinherit myself, and retire to the country. But my father does not have many more good years in him—more than the Crow King of Racolis, to be sure, but not many more—and I must be prepared to take the throne."

He smiled sadly as he looked from Brendys to Mattina. "I wish that we could remain even a little longer so that Semina might come to know you as I have. I fear she will have need of such friends."

"You and your family shall ever be welcome in the home of Brendys of Shalkan," Mattina replied with a gracious smile.

Earon and his wife exchanged a look before Earon answered, "We will remember that, Your Highness. Now, farewell, my friends. May the Dawn King watch over you."

"And you," Brendys and his wife both responded.

Earon, Semina, and their son joined their waiting escort and began their long journey home to Harvath.

As Brendys and his companions watched the Harvathine company wind away to the south, Guthwine stepped forward and clasped the Horsemaster's hand. "We, too, are called to depart. We have fulfilled our duty here, and others await us in Dun Ghalil."

"I wish you could stay, my friend," Brendys replied, an unnerving sensation coming over him. "I would feel more secure."

Guthwine smiled, but shook his head. "But for the distant shadow over the High Steward's heart, Darkness has not returned, and I do not think it will. Be at peace, but go with caution when you leave this place."

Brendys nodded his understanding.

"Father," Aliana said from her place at Willerth's side. "I would remain for awhile longer."

Guthwine glanced sharply at Willerth, bringing a tinge of color to the young man's cheeks, before turning his sky-blue gaze upon his daughter once again. Though the Elf looked barely older than himself, Brendys could see the depth of his age in his eyes, an ancient light which seemed suddenly burdened with fatherly anxiety. "My daughter, I do not. . . ."

Reatha placed a hand upon Guthwine's forearm, interrupting him with a firm voice. "Husband, leave them be. Aliana and Willerth are, by the standards of both our peoples, old enough to decide their own fates. Memories have been shared . . . our daughter's path is no longer ours to guide. Is her choice truly any different than the one that *you* have made?"

Guthwine looked at his ageless wife as though he had been stung with a dagger. Brendys was startled by the passion of his emotion, for he thought he saw tears begin to rise in the Elvinlord's eyes before he turned away and strode to his waiting steed. No further words of farewell did he give before turning his mount southwards and departing.

"Forgive my husband," Reatha said to those remaining. "He has lived a very long time, by the standards of your Kindred, and has seen much change . . . he will come to accept this as well."

Brendys could see the same pain in her eyes that had shone so strongly in Guthwine's, but she kept a stronger hold upon her emotions. Reatha bid them all a final farewell, lightly swung up upon her horse's back, and rode to join her husband.

Willerth turned his gaze upon Aliana. "They do not know then?"

She blinked at him, her face as emotionless as an owl's, as though her parents discomfiture had not affected her in the least. "Do not know what?"

Willerth's lip curled. "That our *fates* have been chosen."

The servant's answer drew a flicker of sorrow from her, but Aliana quickly covered it behind a musical laugh. "I

135

have chosen *my* fate, aye . . . but I will not believe that you have yet chosen yours."

Willerth shifted uncomfortably, avoiding eye contact with everyone, his cheeks reddening again, but he did not debate with the Elfess.

Brendys felt a hand on his shoulder and turned to find Quellin beside him. The Gildean King's expression was serious. "Brendys, we have had our amusement at Kosarek's expense, but it is time we return to the fair. No matter your feelings, you cannot simply ignore Kosarek and Mathai."

"His Majesty speaks truly, Brendys," Odyniec agreed, with a grave nod of his head. "You must remember that it was *your* decision to accept Kosarek's invitation. You are here as *his* guest, are partaking of *his* hospitality, in *his* home. Your welcome may now be dubious, but for your part, you must behave as an honored guest."

Brendys glared at both of them, but at last sighed, letting go his anger. His cheeks burned, but he refused to let his wrath control him. "Very well. I suppose I *do* owe Kosarek at least a *show* of respect."

Odyniec turned his steely eyes towards Racolis Keep, his white brow wrinkling in grim thought. Quietly, he said, "I am more concerned with Mathai at the moment."

"You have heard the same rumors that have made their way to the Crystal Mountains?" Asghar put in, frowning through his red beard.

"What rumors?" Brendys and Quellin said simultaneously.

"Why, that the High Steward has been entertaining priests from the temples of the gods," Asghar replied, looking startled that neither of them had heard the same. "They say that he professes to serve Kolis Bazân, yet consorts with the gods."

"Mathai?" Quellin said with a quizzical frown. "He is a brash man, but I do not think he would resort to such treachery."

Brendys looked at Odyniec, who was staring fixedly in the direction of the city. "Master Odyniec? What say you?"

"Hrm, eh?" the Wizard replied as if waking from a dream. "Eh? Aye! Aye, my concern is just that. I have heard the rumors of which Delvecaptain Asghar speaks, and more . . . I have heard rumor that Mathai intends to ask the Kings of the Free Lands to declare him High King. These are rumors which fret me. I fear time is running out. We should be watchful."

"I agree," Quellin answered, then fixed Brendys with his emerald gaze. "And it will be easier to watch him if we adhere to protocol."

The Gildean King turned his head and called to his escort commander. "Gowan! Send the carriages away . . . we will walk back. You and Kovar shall accompany us."

Quellin took his wife's arm in his own, then beckoned to his companions. "Come . . . we can talk on the way back"

Quellin and Arella led the way with Odyniec at their side. Brendys and Mattina came next, flanked by Asghar and Folkor. Behind them, Lara kept an eye on the children, Brendyn and Lonel at either hand, while Shannon walked with his sister. Willerth and Aliana followed them, while Kovar and Gowan brought up the train.

Odyniec and Quellin continued their conversation regarding the High Steward's potential treachery, but Brendys paid them little heed. He felt his wife's gaze upon him, but he did not turn his attention to her either. He was unhappy. He knew he could not avoid peaceable contact with Kosarek and Mathai for the remainder of his stay at Racolis Keep, and the thought of having to put on a display of civility to them for a week was almost too much to bear.

As they passed through the southern gate of the city, Brendys saw movement off to his right and looked over just in time to see Karel's cloaked and hooded form fall into step beside and a little behind Shannon. He wondered that she could bear to be out in the blazing sun in her woolen garments and muffler. He would have thought she would have found it much more comfortable in a sheltered part of the Keep.

"Shannon," she whispered to the youth, drawing the young Prince's attention.

"Karel, what are you doing here?" Shannon hissed to her, casting a wary eye towards his father before falling back to walk beside the girl.

Brendys could see that Karel was actually a few inches taller than Shannon, which stood to reason as she was also almost two years his elder. Karel gave him a quick glance, her eyes glittering in the shadows of her hood with a mixed look of fear and mistrust. Brendys turned his gaze forward, but kept his attention on the youths' conversation.

"I-I wanted to talk to you again," he heard the girl respond, a tremor in her voice betraying a measure of startled disappointment. She had apparently been anticipating a warmer reception from Shannon.

"I know," Shannon replied hastily. "But *here?*"

A touch of bitter sarcasm entered Karel's voice. "Well, I am sorry if my presence causes you embarrassment."

"Nay, that-that's not what I meant," Shannon stammered in return, his pride stung. "I mean, isn't it too hot out here for you? You should not be out in this sun dressed like that . . . you might get sick."

"I cannot exactly be *out in this sun* dressed any other way," Karel responded wryly.

"You know what I mean," Shannon said in a reproving tone. "Surely there is someplace we could go where you could take off that blasted cloak."

There was a pause before Karel said, a hint of humor in her voice, "There are many shaded places in the Keep library . . . the scribes would leave us be. They are afraid of the dark corners when I am there."

There was another pause, and Brendys ventured a second glance back in their direction. Shannon was staring nervously at his father's back, but he seemed prepared to speak when Brendys felt his wife's elbow dig into his side. He grunted and turned his puzzled gaze on her.

Mattina gave him a disapproving glare. "Mind your own affairs, Brendys."

Quellin turned at the sound of his sister's voice. Seeing Karel beside his son, he came to a halt, his face beginning to darken.

Shannon gave him a startled look, then cleared his voice and said, "Father, might I be excused to return to the castle with Karel? To the library . . . to talk . . . it is cooler there."

"And what of your cousin?" Quellin replied sternly.

Shannon glanced a little guiltily at the younger boy, but he stood his ground. "Father, I am really not up to more children's games. . . ."

Arella gripped her husband's arm, silencing the lecture rising to his lips, and said, smiling, "Go on, you two. We are all here to enjoy ourselves."

Shannon took Karel's hand and started to move away without waiting for his father's input. "Thank you, Mother. . . ."

Quellin scowled at his wife, but did not gainsay her. Instead, he turned his emerald gaze on his escort commander. "Go with them, Gowan."

Shannon grimaced as the warrior fell in behind him, but he did not argue.

"Quellin," Arella started in a soothing voice.

"Enough," Quellin snapped back. "I will not be manipulated by my own family. When Shannon is a man, he may choose his own way . . . until then, he follows my rules."

After a moment of uncomfortable silence, Mattina turned to her handmaid. "Lara, perhaps you should take the children on. . . ."

Quellin nodded in agreement. His face was still red, but his voice was now calm. "That is a good idea. Kovar, you are responsible for their safety . . . do not allow them out of your sight for one moment."

Brendys looked sideways at Willerth, a stern tone entering his voice. "The same goes for you. Do not disappoint me."

Willerth bowed his head, shamefaced, his memory still stinging from his last failure. "I won't let you down, Master Brendys . . . you have my oath on that."

Brendys was sure his servant would keep his word. His past neglect aside, it appeared Aliana was quite willing to include herding three young mortal children through the festival grounds as part of her fellowship with Willerth.

The Elfess surprised Sîan and Lonel—not to mention Willerth—by taking them each by the hand. She leaned down to them, smiling, and said, "Come, let us away. Games and treats await us at the fair."

Brendyn grabbed Willerth's hand and began tugging. "Come on, Willerth, come on!"

A smile tugged at Brendys's lips as he watched the children lead Willerth and Aliana away, followed by Lara and Kovar. At last, he sighed and turned to his wife. "If we are to maintain an illusion of peace with these stuffed hypocrites, I suppose we shall have to make an appearance at the tournament."

"It would be a good thing," Quellin acknowledged. "Besides, Dell crosses lances with Mathai today, if they have not done so already. He will need support. Most of Mathai's opponents yesterday either withdrew or allowed themselves to be unhorsed, though they need not have . . . Mathai is a masterful lancer. It is likely he would have defeated them anyway."

The claws of worry fretted at Brendys. He may not have been an expert in the art of the joust, but he knew enough to understand *why* the knights who faced Mathai had given way before him. To strike any royal, much less the High Steward of Milhavior, even be it in tournament, could result in a charge of high treason and execution, if the mood fell upon the royal. In Mathai's current state of mind, Brendys was not sure what he might be capable of.

He looked at Mattina again. "I will meet you in the grandstand . . . I wish to speak with Dell."

"Brendys," Quellin said offhandedly. "Dell takes tournaments very seriously. I doubt very much that he would intentionally lose a match."

Brendys gave him a grave look. "That is exactly what I fear."

Quellin's youthful features hardened in understanding. "Do you want me to accompany you?"

Brendys shook his head. "Nay. Dell will likely ride anyway, but he should at least hear a voice of reason before he does so."

Quellin's lips quirked in an odd smile. "I have never exactly thought of *you* as a *voice of reason*."

If the Horsemaster had not been distracted by his concern for his old friend, he might have laughed at the irony of his own statement. Instead, he just answered in a quiet voice. "I have grown, Quellin. I do not have great wisdom, but neither do I think I am as foolish as I once was."

Quellin eyed Brendys for a moment before giving him a quick nod. "Aye . . . you *have* grown. Very well. We will await you."

He took his wife's elbow and reached a hand out to his sister. "Come. Let us join the throng. Brendys can deal with Dell well enough alone."

Mattina allowed her brother to take her arm, but before they left she turned towards Asghar and Folkor. "Are you joining us?"

The Dwarf shook his bald head, his red beard wagging. "Nay, Your Highness. I have a melee to champion."

"And I doubt an old sea dog like myself would find a warm welcome amongst the high company," Folkor rumbled in reply. "Truthfully, I am more of a like mind with Asghar. I find the melee much more to my liking."

Brendys was fairly certain the big man would have declined a seat among the *high company* regardless . . . he had as little use for the nobility as they had for him.

"As you will," Quellin answered with a nod. "We will speak later."

As the wedding party went their separate paths, Brendys made his way to the challengers' pavilions beyond the tourney field, seeking out the red and blue banner of the House of Hagan. He found the Lord of Hagan at his tent, his squire assisting him with his mail.

"Dell," Brendys said as he approached. "I would have a word with you . . . do you have a moment?"

Dell dismissed his squire with a wave of his hand. As the young warrior walked into the pavilion, Dell turned a dry smile on Brendys. "I was not sure I would see you again today. After this morning, I still half-expected you to be leaving."

"I will not say that the thought had not crossed my mind," Brendys replied with a shrug. "But it would be better to try and keep the peace. To anger the royalty and nobility could put those I care for at greater risk than they are already. The common folk may yet be enamored with the legend of the Bearer of the Flame, but I believe the reality of Brendys of Shalkan is already wearing thin on Kosarek and Mathai."

Dell's lip curled into a grimace. "Aye. Kosarek and Mathai. I almost regret that I did not have the courage to defy Kosarek. I am still not convinced that the reality of Brendys of Ascon should not be revealed."

"Dell, you gave me your oath," Brendys said in reproach.

"And I will keep it," Dell replied, raising his hand to forestall the Horsemaster's protests. The vestiges of sorrow entered his brown eyes as he added quietly, "Better than I kept my oath to your father."

A rueful smile tugged at one corner of his mouth. "Besides, I shall have my justice when Mathai is staring at the sky from the midst of a dust cloud."

Brendys turned a serious eye on his old friend. "Dell, perhaps you should not ride against Mathai. In his frame of mind, who knows what he might do. . . ."

Dell laughed in response. "Brendys, lad, do not take me for a fool. I appreciate your concern, but I am quite safe. I do not believe Mathai has completely lost his wits, and I am far too trusted among many of the Free Lands. If he were to declare me outlaw for striking him in tourney, he would risk his own throne. I do not think he is yet that desperate."

Despite the Hagane Lord's assurances, Brendys could not shake the uneasy feeling that Mathai was capable of

143

more than Dell was giving him credit for. He shook his head slowly. "Still, will you not at least consider. . . ."

Brendys had his response cut short by a familiar and unwelcome voice. "Ah, Prince Brendys. I did not expect to find you here . . . have you then decided to grace Kosarek's tournament with your meager talents?"

Brendys turned to face Mathai. The King of Ascon was already mail-clad in preparation for his match against Dell. His surcoat bore the arms and colors of the House of Evola-Ascon: muted silver-gold blazoned with a brown hawk perched upon a sword, a brown crown above its head, and a brown star in the base. He wore neither crown nor circlet, allowing his grey-tinged black hair to fall about his shoulders. While the presence of grey in his mane was sparse, it still made him look older than a man in his mid-thirties.

Brendys could see in the man's narrowed blue eyes and tight smile his usual poorly-hidden disdain. The Horsemaster refrained from the antagonistic remark which first started to rise to his lips and instead, with a shake of his head, began to reply, "As I said before, I will not. . . ."

"Fight?" The High Steward's lips curled into a contemptuous sneer. "*Hah!* I believe you will not fight because you are not what you claim. You are nothing but a common man from a common land, married into a title which you have no right to bear."

Mathai's sneer deepened into an angry scowl. "Do you think I have not seen through the deception that is being played out before me? Know this, Brendys of Shalkan, be you a-party to this travesty or merely a gull used by the conniving charmer, you will never sit upon the High Throne of Milhavior."

Deception? Charmer? Confusion settled in on Brendys. "I have never laid claim to the High Throne, Your

144

Majesty, nor will I. I am but a herald, a messenger of the one for whom you reserve the Throne. The Dawn King chose me to bear the Living Flame only until the Heir of Ascon returns."

"I am not deceived by the Wizard's tricks and illusions," Mathai snarled in return. His gaze flicked briefly to Denasdervien. "Nor by clever properties in the hands of commoners."

Brendys's growing sense of uneasiness rapidly passed into full alarm. Did the High Steward actually believe that the manifestation of the Dawn King's avatar at Lener Keep had just been an elaborate illusion summoned by Odyniec in a ruse to unseat him from power and that Denasdervien was nothing more than a clever forgery? If so, then Mathai had truly become a threat.

The King of Ascon drew himself up and inhaled deeply, bringing his emotions under control. "However, I am not an unjust man and am willing to give you the benefit of a doubt. *Prove* to me that you are the prophesied Bearer of the Flame. Prove your mettle . . . ride against me in Dell's place. As Dell is my witness, I grant you full amnesty from any retribution for attacking my person, whether you should win or lose, for the Dawn King will have judged the truth before all men."

Brendys touched Denasdervien's hilt and felt the black metal throb a little more strongly than usual beneath his hand. The sensation was not quite the same as it was in the presence of true Evil, but still it seemed to speak of danger. He met Mathai's gaze with cautious trepidation and saw there growing impatience, but also cunning.

"Well, what will it be?" Mathai said at last. "Will you accept my challenge?"

Without quite knowing why, Brendys slowly nodded his head once and replied, "If that is what it will take to convince you, then aye, I accept."

A fleeting look of astonishment passed across the High Steward's face, melting into a tight, but pleased smile. "Very well then . . . by the Nodrun rules?"

Keeping his gaze even with Mathai's, Brendys replied, "By whatever rules you choose."

The High Steward's smile broadened. "Very good . . . you have more courage than I anticipated. I will leave you to prepare then."

Mathai inclined his head to both Brendys and Dell, then strode purposefully back in the direction of his own pavilion.

Brendys turned towards Dell and found the Hagane Lord staring at him in utter disbelief, his rugged features ashen.

"Elekar save us from your idiocy!" Dell cried out. "Do you know what you have done? The Nodrun has not been invoked since the days of High Steward Ailon . . . it was *banned* by Ailon for the risk it posed to the stability of the Free Lands."

Banned? Brendys had the uncomfortable feeling that Mathai had just cozened him into a trap. "He has granted me immunity from retribution. You are witness. . . ."

Dell gave a frustrated sigh and shook his head. "You do not understand. In the early days, the Nodrun was used to settle disputes between nobles. To the victor was granted the lands, titles, and possessions of the vanquished . . . how do you think the House of Racolis-Hagan came to rule this nation? The royal title was won away from the House of Hagan by one of Kosarek's ancestors."

Understanding dawned at once upon Brendys. "So, Mathai seeks to take Denasdervien from me through this joust. But he should know that Denasdervien is not mine to give."

"It does not matter," Dell replied. "The people will not recognize that fact. They will view *whoever* wields

146

Denasdervien as the Bearer of the Flame. Indeed, they may even see a victory by Mathai as a sign that *he* is the Heir of Ascon. If Mathai defeats you and you refuse to yield up Denasdervien, you will not only be discredited and disgraced, but you might even be declared outlaw."

Brendys drew in a deep breath and let it out. "Then I will simply have to unhorse Mathai, while remaining in the saddle. I do not doubt I am the better horseman."

Dell barked a rueful laugh. "I grant that you *are* the better horseman, but it is not as simple as you seem to believe. Jousting is not simply knocking your opponent off his horse with a stick. It requires a certain skill which Mathai has in quantity and you lack completely.

"Also, the Nodrun does not end when one lancer is unhorsed. If one or both of you are unhorsed, the Nodrun continues in melee until first blood is drawn or one challenger yields to the other. After what I have heard here, I do not doubt that Mathai will try to kill you and make it appear an accident."

"Kill me?" Brendys echoed, half in disbelief. "Would he dare, do you think? And is he not then also risking the High Throne? What if *I* should defeat him?"

"Nay, the Throne of Ascon is exempt from the Nodrun, for it was remanded to the regency of the House of Evola-Ascon by the Dawn King himself," Dell replied. "And to answer your first question, aye, I *do* believe he would dare to kill you. He sees you as a threat to his power . . . he will not let go that easily."

The Lord of Hagan grimaced. "King Mathai has trapped you in corner, Brendys. If you had not agreed to the Nodrun, you could have withdrawn from the challenge. Now, if you withdraw, it would be the same as declaring Mathai the victor."

Brendys cursed himself. He had done it again. He had allowed himself to be led into a trap from which it appeared he could not escape. "Then tell me what I must do."

Dell rubbed his chin for a moment, then called for his squire. "Parnin!"

Parnin emerged from the tent, his brown eyes wide. The lank youth reminded Brendys of Kradon, Dell's son and his best friend, slain during the Siege of Gildea. He had the same wheaten hair, fair skin, and intelligent face, which was agape in shame-faced fear. He had clearly been eavesdropping on the conversation.

Dell turned his eyes on the youth. "Parnin, fetch a suit of mail to fit Prince Brendys."

"Aye, My Lord," Parnin answered, striking his fist to his heart, then dashing away.

Dell faced Brendys again. "You *do* have the advantage of horsemanship, weight, and strength. Try to center your lance at his chest, and keep it low. I have studied Mathai's technique. If your lance is too high, he will be able to deflect the brunt of your blow.

"If you manage to unhorse him, I suggest you also dismount and take him on foot. Denasdervien will be your advantage. If *he* unhorses *you*, then we must pray that Elekar protects you, for Mathai will not hesitate to ride you down. He will have the advantage, and unless you manage to drag him from his saddle, he will simply wear you down until your strength is gone.

"Under *no* circumstance strike his horse. If you wound his mount, Kosarek's archers will be ordered to execute you immediately. It is considered treason in the Nodrun."

Brendys rubbed his scarred temple with his right hand, trying to relieve the building pressure. He knew the odds of his victory were slim. His only hope was to bring

Denasdervien to bear against Mathai in melee, and to do that, he would need a miracle.

* * * *

Brendys had little time to prepare for his run against Mathai. It had taken Parnin nearly twenty minutes to find mail large enough for Brendys, reminding the Horsemaster just how much smaller the Racoline people tended to be in comparison to him. The suit provided to him included leather vambraces and greaves and a visored jousting helm. Over the chain, he wore the livery of the House of Hagan: an azure fess, wavy, between three azure roundels on a field of red. Denasdervien's battered black scabbard hung at his waist. Shortly after donning his armor, a page arrived, summoning him to the tourney field.

As they neared the lists, Dell assisted Brendys into his saddle. Brendys had considered having Parnin fetch Fracas from the Keep's stables, but though the grey had been in battle before, he was not disciplined and would be more likely to jump the lists and attack Mathai's horse. Vesper, Dell's bay charger, obeyed his every command with but a little pressure from his knees.

Dell lifted his lance up to Brendys. "Remember what I have told you. I can only hope it will be enough."

Brendys took the spear and looked across the field to see Mathai emerge from the circle of challengers' pavilions. "Aye, so do I."

He urged Vesper towards King Kosarek's grandstand. As he and Mathai approached each other and the Racoline King's seat, Kosarek's herald announced their Nodrun challenge, eliciting a wave of awed gasps and whispers from the spectators. He saw Mattina blanch in fear and start to rise, but Arella gripped her hand, keeping her in place, though her own expression was no less anxious.

Even Quellin looked stunned. Odyniec was grim-faced, but Brendys could not tell if it was due to the gravity of the challenge or because of the presence of the blue-robed Oranite priest seated next to him.

As Brendys and Mathai stopped before the grandstand, Kosarek slowly rose to his feet. For the first time since Brendys had met the old King, he thought Kosarek looked truly pleased.

"Sire, Your Highness," the old man said, a somewhat malicious grin splitting his frail and hawkish features. "This is a most unusual challenge. I assume that you are both in agreement and that the High Steward has approved the Nodrun?"

Old viper, Brendys thought. *You know well that Mathai has approved this debacle. I doubt not that you knew of it before I did.*

Nevertheless, both men solemnly nodded their affirmation.

"Then may the favor of the gods shine upon the victor," Kosarek said, saluting the two riders.

Brendys and Mathai lowered their lances in salute to the Racoline King, then faced each other and did the same. The High Steward's arrogant smile screamed of treachery, but Brendys knew it was too late to turn back. He was committed, whether he liked it or not.

Both men retreated to their own ends of the lists, facing each other. Brendys slapped down his visor and abruptly realized that he could barely see straight ahead of him, much less anything to either side. Trumpets sounded and the herald cried out, signaling the charge.

Brendys spurred Vesper into a gallop, carefully bringing his lance down into a couched position, but even as the blunted point dropped before him, he knew he had begun lowering it too late. His blow slid off Mathai's tilted shield with little effect, while the High Steward's lance impacted against his own shield like a battering ram. He felt himself helplessly lifted from his saddle and thrown backwards through the air.

He struck the ground heavily and nearly blacked out as every ounce of breath was driven from his lungs. Nevertheless, dazed and gasping for air, every bone and muscle in his body screaming in agony, he struggled to his feet, for he knew his life depended on it. He lifted his visor and saw Mathai bearing down upon him, spear lowered. The jousting lance had broken about a foot from the point, leaving a jagged shard in its place.

Brendys managed to dive out of the path of the charger, dropping his shield as he rolled to the side. Struggling against his pain and the weight of his mail, he pulled himself back to his feet, tearing off his helmet. Again, he found himself staring at the broken shaft of Mathai's lance as it was brought to bear against him.

His hand flew to Denasdervien's hilt and at once he felt the sword's life surge into his arm, and he knew he was no longer in control. In one fluid motion, he drew his sword, sidestepped the oncoming charger, severing the High Steward's lance, then spun around and slashed at the cinch-strap of Mathai's saddle. He heard angry cries from the spectators as Mathai, still in his saddle, was flung from his horse's back.

Above the din, he heard Kosarek's herald start shouting, *"The horse is unharmed! The horse is unharmed!"* As he turned to look, he saw the Racoline archers relaxing their bows and realized how close he had come to being shot. His gaze flicked up to his wife, who was shouting something at him, though he could not hear her words.

A jolt of power from Denasdervien warned him of danger, and he swept the sword around in a wide arc. Its Silver-gold blade burst into white flame as it struck

151

Mathai's swiftly descending sword, shattering the High Steward's blade as though it were made of glass. He leveled Denasdervien's point at Mathai's throat, but the Asconi King did not seem to notice. Mathai was staring, dumbfounded, at the useless weapon in his hand. Only the barest fragment of the blade remained attached to the hilt, and that but barely, smoke rising from the shard.

"I warned you that any weapon brought to bear against Denasdervien would surely perish," Brendys gritted out, his chest still heaving for breath.

Mathai's azure gaze slowly met the Horsemaster's, and his face began to twist in rage, then just as suddenly, his anger vanished. He barked out a jovial laugh and cried in a loud voice, "*I yield to the Bearer of the Flame! Let no man doubt his worth!*"

Brendys's brow beetled in confusion and suspicion. Denasdervien's flame flickered out, leaving its mirrored blade gleaming in the sunlight, but Brendys could still feel the weapon throbbing in his hand, warning of danger. Nevertheless, he slowly lowered his sword, returning it to its sheath, though his eyes remained on the High Steward.

Mathai clapped him on the shoulder with a gauntleted hand , grinning broadly. "Well fought and well played. Let no man doubt your destiny, Brendys of Shalkan. You have wielded the Sword of the Dawn with skill and honor."

"Thank you, Sire," Brendys politely responded, inclining his head to the High Steward, despite his reservations towards the man. However, something in Mathai's eye still bothered Brendys, an insincerity or duplicity that the Asconi King was masking well.

He excused himself and started back towards the challengers' pavilions. Parnin fell in beside him, leading Vesper back to his Lord's tent. The youth stared up at Brendys in awe and reverence. "That . . . that was *amazing*, Your Highness, if I may say so."

Brendys grimaced in frustration. Did anyone under-stand? *He* was nothing. He was a simple man with no skill or knowledge of arms. *He* did not wield the sword . . . the sword acted *through* him. When Denasdervien was in his hand, he became an extension of *it*, not the other way around.

Dell soon joined them, saying to Brendys as he fell in step, "From the look on your face, I would guess that you are not convinced by King Mathai's sudden change of heart."

Brendys cast a grim glance at the Hagane Lord. "You would guess right. Whether he is now convinced that I *am* the Bearer of the Flame or not, I cannot say, but Denasdervien warns of danger when I am in his presence."

A puzzled frown twisted his lips. "The Flame senses little evil though . . . it is confusing."

"Perhaps not," Dell replied with a grimace. "I do not believe that Mathai has yet fallen to the Shadow, but it may be that he is deceived by an evil intent."

Brendys wrinkled his brow. "You mean that another influences his actions?"

Dell nodded sharply. "Ever since the High Steward arrived at Racolis Keep there has been an Oranite priest in his entourage wherever he goes. There are whispers that he has been taking counsel from the priest."

"Aye, Odyniec said as much this morning," Brendys affirmed. "And judging from what I saw of Odyniec in the grandstand, he is none too pleased about it."

Brendys fell silent, his thoughts turning inward. If the High Steward was indeed being influenced by the counsels of the Oranite priest, it would explain the danger Denasdervien warned of. The very existence of the Bearer of the Flame was blasphemy in the sight of the priests, for the Bearer represented the power of the Dawn King, whom the priests declared to be a myth. To the priests of the old gods, Brendys was anathema, and they would do whatever was in their power to destroy him.

"*Brendys!*"

The Horsemaster raised his head suddenly at the sound of his wife's voice. Mattina was hurrying towards him, her young face pale, her expression a mixture of fear and anger. Quellin and Arella came behind her, the Gildean King no less outraged. Odyniec followed last, leaning heavily upon his rune-marked staff. The old Wizard's face showed grim concern, but neither the fear nor anger his companions expressed.

"Brendys, you rat! You terrified me!" Mattina cried out, slamming her fists against her husband's mail-clad chest. She winced at the pain, then glanced down at her hands as if they had offended her.

Quellin, crimson in anger, was quick to concur with his sister. "That was madness! What were you thinking? Do you not know what might have happened?"

"More than you realize," Brendys replied quietly. "If he had been able, Mathai would have killed me."

Odyniec nodded his agreement. "It is clear that King Mathai's will is being bent to serve the priests, and they will not hesitate to do whatever is in their power to arrange your death. They will not yet act openly, but they are not to be trusted. I was able to wean from the Oranite in attendance that the High Priests of the High Temples have forged an alliance, a *Council of the Gods* so to speak, putting aside their differences, in an attempt to undermine Fanos Pavo's power in the Free Lands. This can only serve to strengthen the cause of Thanatos."

Brendys gently grasped Mattina's shoulders, looking down into her face. "We should find Brendyn and take him back to our rooms. Between wild-men, Dark Alar, and treacherous priests, I think the danger has become too great. We should leave tomorrow."

"Dark Alar?" Odyniec echoed, alarm showing on his wizened face. "What is this? You have actually *seen* a Dark Alar here?"

Brendys inclined his head. "Aye, the children did. That and a wild-man who had frightened Willerth and Brendyn back home."

Odyniec's visage darkened. "Wild-man? A man dressed in wolf skins, with a cowl of three wolf heads?"

Brendys nodded again, surprised that Odyniec knew the description.

"Kerebros the Wolf," Odyniec said in disdain. "He is called the least finger on the Hand of Thanatos. He is the least of the Sorcerers of Thanatos, a brute, relying more on his physical strength than upon the power the Deathlord has granted him. If he is here, then you should indeed bring Brendyn where you can best protect him."

"Guthwine and Reatha assured me that both the wild-man and the Dark Alar are no longer within the walls of Racolis Keep," Brendys replied. "But I still do not trust the Oranites or Mathai."

Arella turned to her husband, her brown eyes reflecting the general sense of alarm. "We should go with them, Quellin. It would be safer for them if they journeyed with our escort."

"Aye," Quellin agreed. "I will have Folkor bring the *Sea Dog* to the Shipyard of Ilkatar."

He turned his emerald gaze on Brendys. "For this, I will risk Kosarek's wrath . . . I, too, would feel more at ease if I knew you had an armed escort."

"You should leave at the first light of dawn," Dell inserted. "That you participated in Earon's wedding was enough to garner Kosarek's wrath . . . one more affront

155

will mean little, though I will be sure to salve his wounded ego ere I take my own leave."

"And so the Bearer of the Flame sneaks away like a thief," Brendys ended wryly. He removed a gauntlet and stroked his wife's cheek. His brow furrowed in concern. "You are fevered. . . ."

Mattina leaned wearily against her husband's chest. "I will be fine. I just want to go home."

Brendys held her close. "And so we will."

Chapter 8

The cave chamber was dark, but for a handful of torches spaced out along its walls. Five bodies arranged in a semi-circle adorned the barren floor. The men wore sleeveless, black, leather jerkins and trousers, and four of them had the image of a wolf's head burned into their foreheads. All of them had bleeding claw marks running down their bare chests where a large animal has slashed them. Their hair was drenched and their flesh glistened with perspiration.

Kerebros the Wolf leaned over the one who did not bear the brand of the wolf and pressed his open palm against the man's forehead. A flare of red light surged forth from his palm, and the man screamed, his back arching. At last, the man's eyes rolled white and he fell still.

Kerebros stood at the feet of the five men, smiling in satisfaction at their still forms, now all bearing the mark of the wolf. "Soon, my Children, your suffering will end and your new lives will begin."

"Do you truly believe these savages will gain you your prize?" a pleasant voice said behind him. "What if they should prove unappreciative of the change you have made in them?"

Kerebros turned to look at the hooded and cloaked form of Krifka, Sorcerer, Dark Alar, and Emperor of the Dagramon. Beside the dark spirit stood Archa, Captain of the Dark Elves who inhabited this outpost, his chalk-white face and dead, black eyes showing open disdain. Kerebros smirked. "These men willingly chose to follow me, and I have marked them. They are mine completely. Even those who do not follow willingly cannot resist the power of my curse. The Wolves of Kerebros have no equal, and they serve *only me*."

The Dark Elf raised a brow. "Why, then, do you feel it necessary to sacrifice my people to the Flame? If your Wolves have no equal, let *them* deal with your quarry."

"Oh, but they will," Kerebros replied with a wolfish grin. "Your kindred serve only to flush my quarry and provide a diversion. Do not fear, Archa, your people's sacrifice will not be in vain. When eternal night is brought to this Sphere, they will return on the wings of the Shadow . . . or do you perhaps believe that the Master will not honor his oath to your kindred?"

Archa glared coldly at the Sorcerer, then turned on his heels and strode from the chamber.

"Your attempts at cleverness amuse me, Wolf," Krifka said as the Dark Elf departed. "However, I do not believe you have the wits to bring this venture to a successful conclusion. Have patience, Wolf . . . Black Cragg awakens and gathers his kind in the Far North. Not even the Flame can stand against *them*. The Dark Ones are not a resource to be lightly thrown away and will be needed for the final battle."

Kerebros scowled in return. "This is *my* hour, Demon. We will see who is the least finger on the Hand of Thanatos."

He spun around to face his unconscious victims, crying out, his muscular arms raising before him, amber eyes bursting into red flame, "*Arise, my Children, and join your brethren!*"

*   *   *   *

Brendys felt terrible about sequestering his son on their last day at Racolis Keep, but he comforted himself with the understanding that it was the only way to protect Brendyn from the dangers springing up around them. Quellin's children and Lara's daughter, Lonel—who was quickly becoming Brendyn's soulmate, due in part to their age and also because of their mutual opinion of Sîan's less-than-hospitable attitude towards anyone of common blood—provided some distraction during the long hours remaining in the day.

As evening drew on, Berephon came to their quarters to fulfill his promise to Brendyn. The Bard's apprentice taught Brendyn a song entitled *The Lay of Zhayil-Khan*, a ballad which told the story of Michuda's two-hundred year siege of the fortress nation which would become known as Shalkan and of High Steward Ailon's eventual victory against the Dark Elf Sorcerer. Berephon played the song upon his flute, while Aliana sang, though the words were in the Caletri Tongue and incomprehensible to everyone present. The song was slow, the melody haunting and mysterious. Berephon then aided Brendyn through the song and when the boy finally had the basic melody well enough in hand, the Bard's apprentice admonished him to practice every day, then took his leave. Not long thereafter, the company took their beds, for they would be rising early to depart from Racolis Keep before Kosarek had arisen from his own bed.

*   *   *   *

The morning sun was just beginning to peek above the horizon as a caravan of five wains and twenty horsemen prepared to depart from Racolis Keep for the long journey to Shalkan. Already warm, almost stiflingly so, the day

159

promised to be a miserably hot one, not at all ideal for traveling. As supplies and Brendyn's gifts were being loaded into one of the wagons, Willerth and Lara, with Shannon's help, corralled the younger children, while the rest of the adults stood aside to say their farewells to Odyniec and Lord Dell.

The Lord of Hagan shook hands with the men and kissed the hands of the ladies. "Safe journeys, my friends."

He turned his brown eyes on Brendys. "Kosarek was not at all pleased with the outcome of your ride against King Mathai. I think he would have been much happier if you had not survived the bout."

Odyniec nodded in agreement. "Aye, the same is true of Mathai. While he publicly pronounced your victory against him as proof of your claim as the Bearer of the Flame, he still harbors dark feelings against you . . . intentions which the Oranite priest has been all too ready to seize upon. That is why I shall return to Ascon with King Mathai. I believe he will need a voice of wisdom to counter the madness which has fallen upon his throne."

"I do not believe Mathai will openly or actively threaten myself or my family," Brendys replied. "But neither do I trust him. Still, I have greater worries than two disgruntled Kings."

"That is true," Quellin admitted, casting a grim glance in Brendys's direction. "I, too, feel there are greater threats at hand."

Brendys knew of what his brother-by-marriage spoke. Since that first day of the fair, Kerebros the Wolf had not been seen, nor had the Dark Alar returned—at least as far as any of them knew, for not even Aliana had sensed the demon's presence again. He felt an inevitability of danger on the return journey to Shalkan, and Guthwine had warned him of as much. It was not like the agents of Thanatos to sow the seed of fear in the hearts of their victims, then vanish without a trace, without bringing harm to anyone.

"On this, I agree with you," Dell replied. "That is why I have instructed Novosad and the twins to accompany you. There is no better swordsman than Novosad, and Copanas and Lehan are the sharpest-eyed of my scouts."

"We appreciate the offer, Dell," Quellin replied. "But it is quite unnecessary. Gowan's men are more than capable, and Kovar and Amrein shall be our eyes."

Dell nodded, but refused to be denied. "I understand, Your Majesty, but my heart would be more at ease knowing I had done my part to safeguard my friends."

Brendys interrupted before his brother-by-marriage could respond. "We shall be honored to have their company, Dell."

"That is well," Dell replied, one side of his mouth curling into a smile. "For I delegated one-half of my personal escort to Novosad's command."

Before Quellin could object, they were joined by Gowan and Novosad. The commander of the Gildean escort saluted his King. "Your Majesty, all is ready for our departure. One of the covered wains has been prepared for Queen Arella and Princess Mattina as you requested. There are plenty of cushions should the Princess become weary."

Brendys glanced at his wife. It was clear that she was already weary. The stress of the eventful days had taken a toll on her still weakened condition. He had no doubt his wife would sleep for most of the journey.

Quellin nodded to him. "Very well, we shall depart soon."

With a slight bow, Lieutenant Gowan again struck his fist to his heart, then turned on his heels and rejoined his company. Novosad remained before Quellin, looking as though he would rather have been anywhere else.

Quellin took note of his discomfort almost at once. "What troubles you, Novosad?"

"Your Majesty, I . . . Karel, my daughter . . . sh-she requests permission to journey with us," the soldier stammered. He quickly added before Quellin could speak. "I thought it so strange, Your Majesty, as she seldom cares for the company of others and the clothing she must wear to protect herself from the sun forces her to endure such heat, that I did not wish to deny her."

Not that strange, Brendys thought. Since that first night, Karel had endured *such heat* to spend as much time with his nephew as she could—a fact of which Quellin was quite aware and with which he was clearly uncomfortable.

But Quellin did not have the opportunity to refuse the Hagane scout's request. Arella gave Novosad a gracious smile. "Of course . . . it would please us to have her company. In fact, she should ride with Mattina and I. We could keep the flap closed so Karel would not have to wear that awful cloak."

"Absolutely!" Mattina agreed. "It would give us a wonderful opportunity to become acquainted."

Brendys stifled a laugh as Quellin glared darkly at his wife and sister, but the Gildean King held his tongue.

Novosad bowed to Arella and Mattina. "Thank you, Your Majesty, Your Highness . . . I will let Karel know at once!"

The warrior struck his heart in salute, then marched away.

The companions bade Dell farewell, then went to join their escort. A ramp led up into the back of the wagon prepared for Mattina and Arella to allow easy access. A Gildean warrior stood at the head of the ramp, holding back the heavy cloth flap which covered the back of the wain. He helped his Queen up the ramp and into the wagon, then turned to assist his Princess.

Brendys felt his wife hesitate beneath his touch and noticed the apprehension in her face as she stared at the wagon. He knew her mind was not seeing a wain prepared for the comfort of royalty, but a slaver's wagon . . . a mobile prison full of the stench of terrified captives and human refuse. He touched her cheek and she started, as if waking from a dream. "Are you all right, Mattina?"

Taking a deep breath, she nodded. "Aye. I survived the journey from Harvath in such as this. . . I can survive one more fortnight."

She kissed her husband on the lips, then allowed herself to be assisted into the wagon.

The warrior at the head of the ramp held out his hand one more time to assist Novosad's step-daughter up the ramp. The girl again wore heavy winter clothing, cut for a boy, and a woolen cloak and muffler which covered most of her face. Brendys could only see the glitter of her dark eyes beneath the hood, staring after Arella and Mattina with a mixture of admiration and trepidation. At last, squaring her shoulders, she strode up the ramp, ignoring the Gildean warrior's proffered hand, her pack clutched in her arms.

As the Gildean warrior dropped the flap and removed the ramp board, Aliana approached, leading both her own horse and Fracas. Willerth walked beside the Elfess, leading Hashan. To Brendys's surprise and admiration, Fracas seemed quite at ease under Aliana's handling, a testament to her Elvin grace, for usually Fracas suffered no one to handle him but his master and Kanstanon.

"We had a terrible time keeping those two devils apart," Willerth said, nodding towards Shannon's black stallion, as he mounted his own horse. "If not for Aliana, I think they would have been at each other's throats."

Brendys could easily believe his servant as he looked at Millas. The great horse was clearly bred and trained as a warhorse, but despite his instinct to fight, he obeyed Shannon's command, even as Fracas obeyed Brendys. Brendys nearly laughed . . . his slight nephew might have been lost on the black stallion's back were it not for his glaring yellow tunic and blue hosen which shimmered slightly in the sunlight.

"Thank you for your assistance, Lady Aliana," Brendys said, turning a curious eye on the Elfess. She wore a tunic and hose made of the same strangely-hued material as the cloaks of the Elves he had met thus far, which seemed to shift between all the hues of nature. Brendys noticed for the first time that the cloth was very light, almost satiny in appearance, its color changing subtly with Aliana's every move. Her bow and quiver was slung across her back, and she wore two long knives at her belt, one of which, like her father's, was crafted entirely of Elvinsilver. The second was forged of ordinary steel, though elegantly so after the manner of the Elves. "So, you are leaving as well?"

Aliana cracked a slight smile and inclined her head to him. "I have decided I wish to see this land that tugs so strongly at my beloved's heart and keeps him from me."

A tinge of red colored Willerth's cheeks, and he looked away.

Brendys's own smile faltered a little. Aliana seriously misread Willerth if she believed Shalkan is what kept him from following his heart. That Willerth had loved Aliana from their first meeting, he had never doubted, evidenced by the constant presence of the pendant she had given him at their first parting. However, Willerth had married himself to duty and would not allow himself to diverge from his chosen path, not even for the shining star for whom his heart burned. "You are, of course, most welcome on our journey. I only hope you will not be disappointed with what you find."

Aliana's smile turned sad. "I am sure I will be, but not with Zhayil Khan, the great Land of the Mountain."

Brendys noticed his servant's blush deepen, but Willerth still said nothing. Casting a frown in his servant's direction, he swung up onto his grey's back and spurred Fracas forward.

"Where is Brendyn?" Brendys asked his servant as they rode towards the head of the column to join Quellin.

"Unhappily in Lara's keeping," Willerth replied. "He wanted to ride with Shannon, but I thought it would be best if he rode in the wagon with the other children . . . Princess Sîan was none too happy at the prospect of riding out the journey with naught but servants for company."

Brendys shook his head. He was certain that one day his young niece would make the perfect companion for some stuffy Lordling with plenty of honor, but little love. But Sîan's petty attitudes were of little concern to him. He was more concerned with his son's safety, and the wagon would be much more defensible.

As he, Willerth, and Aliana joined Quellin, the Gildean King signaled for the column to move out.

* * * *

Mattina made herself comfortable in the bed of cushions prepared for her, relieved to be able to rest at last. Arella, meanwhile, lit the lamp affixed to the roof of the wain to provide them with better light, then sat down on the side bench opposite Karel. There was a small hole above the lamp to allow heat and smoke to escape, but the beam of sunlight it allowed into the large wagon would be easily avoidable by the women's young companion.

Arella looked across at Karel. The girl sat with her head bowed and turned slightly towards the rear flap, completely motionless, but for the jostling of the wagon as it began to move. "Karel, with the flap closed, it will get quite stuffy in here very quickly . . . you should at least take off that cloak."

The girl did not respond in any way.

Mattina and Arella exchanged a glance, then the younger woman turned her emerald gaze back on Karel, a gentle smile on her rosy lips. "Karel, no one here would make a mockery of you, if that is what you fear."

Still, the girl did not react.

Arella sighed. "Very well then . . . in your own time. If you feel the need for refreshment, there is water at the end of your bench."

Arella and Mattina spent the first part of the day trading stories from the past seven years . . . something they had not had much time to do during the past couple of days. Mattina pointedly avoided discussing the Great Father, and despite Mattina's prompting, Arella refused to tell her about Brendys's descent into darkness after Mattina's presumed death. Throughout it all, Karel did not speak or move at all that either of the women could tell.

At midday, the caravan halted briefly for a noontide meal. Karel took her meal in the wagon, despite the stifling heat. She would not come out of the wain for anyone, including Shannon. For some reason known only to herself, she had chosen to completely isolate herself from everyone else.

After eating, Mattina went back to the wagon to take a nap. Since her sister-by-marriage was still asleep when the caravan resumed its journey, Arella once again attempted to draw Karel into conversation . . . still without success. To stave off boredom, she resorted to knitting, though with the bumping of the wagon and the flickering lamplight, it was at best a challenging task.

As the afternoon wore on, she noticed that Karel's breathing was becoming labored. She put aside her knitting and turned a stern frown on the girl. "This has gone on long enough, Karel. You are going to suffocate in that muffler. . . ."

Even as she spoke, Karel's shoulders slumped, and she began to tilt forward. Arella stumbled across the wagon bed and caught her, drawing her back to the bench. The girl's head lolled back, her hood falling away. Her clothing was completely drenched with perspiration, and her coppery hair clung to her scalp in dark tendrils. Her white flesh had taken on a slightly greyish hue, flushed from the heat and streaked with perspiration, and her eyes were rolled back.

Arella soaked a kerchief in water and started mopping Karel's face. "Oh, child! Foolish, stubborn child!"

The Gildean Queen's outburst awoke Mattina. When she came fully to her senses and noticed Karel, she abruptly sat up. "What happened?"

"Precisely what I feared," Arella replied, stripping the sodden cloak and garments from the girl. "The foolish girl was overcome by the heat. There should be a bundle of Shannon's clothes beneath those cushions . . . see if you might find something lighter in there that may fit Karel."

Seeing her this closely, Arella realized that Karel actually looked a little older than Shannon, as she rightly should. Her face had lost more of its childish roundness than Shannon's and was beginning to gain the sharpness and maturity of adulthood. She was also just beginning to develop a womanly figure.

When Arella had gotten Karel free of the heavy garments, she draped a linen around the girl, then reached into the water bucket and withdrew the cup which lay within. Karel's eyes began to roll into focus as Arella brought the cup to her lips. The girl choked on the first sip, but when the Gildean Queen started to pull the cup away, Karel drew it back, gulping the water down.

"Not too quickly," Arella cautioned her.

The girl obeyed and took smaller sips. When she had drained the cup, Arella refilled it and handed it to Karel. The girl accepted it and took another sip before sitting upright. She leaned forward on her knees, the cup grasped in both hands before her, her head bowed, gasping to regain her breath.

"Child, why would you not heed us?" Arella asked, placing gentle hand on the girl's shoulders. "We knew the heat would become too great. That is why we suggested you ride with us . . . so you would not *have* to suffer it."

"I just . . . I just couldn't," Karel rasped in reply, closing her eyes. Her lip trembled as though she was struggling to keep back tears. "You . . . you are both so beautiful. . . ."

"I am flattered, child," Arella said with raised eyebrows, giving the girl's shoulders a light squeeze. "But you are no hag yourself. You are half Elf, which is more than I can say for myself."

"Dark Elf," Karel bit out.

"Elf or Dark Elf, it matters not," the Gildean Queen pressed. "You are lovely in such a way as only an Elf can be."

"I look like a walking corpse," the girl gritted through clenched teeth. A sob wracked her body.

"Never say that again!" Mattina said in a firm tone, choking back dreadful memories of the Great Father. "I have had the occasion to *meet* a walking corpse, and I assure you there is *no* resemblance."

She knelt forward, cupping her hand beneath Karel's chin and raising the girl's face to meet her own. Her eyes widened in surprise. "You *are* beautiful! It is no wonder Shannon is so enamored of you."

Karel lowered her eyes. "Shannon said I was beautiful, too. No one had ever said that to me before . . . not even my parents, that I can remember. But I have become so used to

168

scorn that it is hard for me to see kindness when it is laid before me."

She reached a pale hand up to wipe her eyes. "First, Shannon, and now the two of you. . . ."

"You will find there are caring people all around you," Mattina said, smiling. "You may be looking in the wrong places."

Arella wiped a few stray wet hairs back out of Karel's eyes. She felt a question rise to her lips, and she could not help but ask it. "I am sorry if this is too personal a question, Karel, but I must ask it. What *did* happen when you were alone with Shannon?"

The girl was slow to answer, but finally she did. "At first, we argued. He came to me out of kindness," Arella stifled a laugh behind Karel's back, "but I berated him. He grew angry and said some things that he did not mean, then he did something no one else has ever done before to me . . . he apologized."

Arella cast an amazed look at Mattina. She would have thought her son too proud.

Karel sighed. "I suppose it was really at that moment that I understood that he really did care. We talked a little . . . he said things that made me feel like a lady for the first time."

Arella smiled.

Karel hesitated again. "Then we stopped talking. . . ."

Arella's smile vanished and gave Mattina another startled look.

"He . . . he kissed me," Karel continued nervously. "I had never been kissed like that before. I . . . I liked it. A lot. So I kissed him back."

She swallowed nervously before continuing. "I . . . I wanted more. . . ."

"But . . . ?" Arella said slowly.

Karel looked over her shoulder at Arella and smiled shyly. "But your son is a Prince and a gentleman."

Arella leaned down to whisper in the girl's ear. "Good."

She leaned back with a light laugh. "You have answered my question, now let us see what we can do for *you*. What do we have to work with, Mattina?"

Mattina found the drawstring sack full of Shannon's clothes. "Ah! Here it is."

She opened it and looked inside. At once, a look of horror swept over her youthful features. "Oh, no!"

"What is it?" Arella asked in concern.

Mattina began to draw articles of clothing out of the sack one-by-one. Every one was garishly bright, often with gaudy trim. "It appears your son has inherited Quellin's lack of taste in clothing!"

The first tunic she withdrew that was *not* hideously bright brought Karel to immediate attention. "That one! Please. . . ."

Mattina held it up. The shirt was a deep red color, almost a light burgundy. It was a long-sleeved, plainly-cut tunic of a sturdy cloth that Shannon used for more rigorous activities.

Arella took it from her and looked at it for a moment in thought. "What *can* we do with this?"

She held it up before her, smiling as an idea came to her.

And so Arella and Mattina busied themselves with the transformation of Karel.

* * * *

When evening fell, the caravan halted to make camp. Cookfires were set at one end of the camp for the preparation of the evening meal, while several watchfires dotted the encampment. At one fire near the children's wagon, Lara and Willerth kept watch over their young charges. Brendys sat with Quellin at a fire outside the Gildean King's pavilion, waiting on their wives. Lanterns hung outside the pavilion, as well, brightly illuminating the grounds around them.

Brendys stared into the flickering glow of the campfire, conscious only of the crackling and popping of the fresh wood. A shadow covered his spirit which he could not explain. His family was together once more—for that, his heart should have been filled with joy. But he could not dispel the strange anxiety that had come over him. Perhaps he was still incensed over Kosarek's and Mathai's treatment of Earon or Mathai's blatant attempt on his own life, or maybe was just worried about the fact that Kerebros had dared to reveal himself at Racolis Keep, but had not shown himself since.

But no, he had long since put aside any concern for the attitudes or opinions of the Kings, and while he could not put fear or vigilance aside, it was not Kerebros the Wolf that troubled him either. It was his dream, his vision from that first night at Racolis Keep. Its meaning, if any, still eluded him.

He was still sorrowed by the loss of his second son, but the sharpest pain of grief had passed. Brendyl walked the Road to Elekar—the full pain of grief could not last with that reminder—but he could not understand the connection between the vision and the Dawn King's message. Brendyl was certainly silent, for he was stillborn . . . was the kingdom of Milhavior dead as well? If so, there was little Brendys could do, for he did not have the power to breathe life back into it.

"Brendys? What troubles you?"

Brendys started from his thoughts as if from a dark dream, turning his blue eyes to his brother-by-marriage.

Quellin's brow furrowed. "Brendys, I have not seen you look so careworn since before you found Mattina. What is wrong?"

The Horsemaster lowered his gaze before answering. "While at Racolis Keep, I had a . . . a *dream*."

Quellin barked a short, nervous laugh. "As did we all, I am sure!"

Brendys glanced at him. Though Quellin spoke lightly, his expression was tinged with concern. Brendys shook his head slowly. "Nay . . . *he* spoke to me again, Quellin."

Quellin's emerald gaze intensified. "Elekar appeared to you again?"

Brendys shook his head. "Nay. He spoke to me, but did not show himself."

His brother-by-marriage looked at him thoughtfully for a moment, before speaking again. "Tell me your dream, Brendys . . . if you feel you should."

Brendys knew what Quellin meant. The Dawn King had given *him* the dream. Should he tell Quellin? Brendys did not have the wisdom to decipher the vision's meaning on his own. The Gildean King's wisdom had proven far greater than his own in the past . . . if ever he needed it, that time was now.

Quellin sat with his head bowed and eyes closed, hands folded together before him, as he listened to Brendys. If he was surprised or disturbed by the imagery of the dream, he did not show it. When Brendys finished his story, Quellin drew in a deep breath and raised his head. He shook his head, clearly as confounded as Brendys. "I have no answers for you, Brendys. The Silent could refer to Brendyn's twin, but I cannot begin to guess in what way he is connected to Elekar's message. Perhaps the key is not Brendyn's twin, but Brendyn himself. But again, I do not know in what way."

He turned his emerald gaze on Brendys. "You should have brought this to Master Odyniec. If anyone would have an answer for you, it would be the Wizard and Prophet of the Dawn King."

Brendys answered with a nod. He knew Quellin was right. Who better to interpret the messages of the Dawn King than the Dawn King's representative to Milhavior.

"Father?"

The young voice drew both men's attention to Shannon, who stood before them. His silver crown rested upon his head, as usual, at a slight sideways tilt, but he wore no air of vanity, but rather apprehension.

Brendys noticed Quellin's jaw muscles twitch. Few words had passed between father and son since the night of Brendyn's birthday feast . . . it was clear that Quellin was still angered by his son's apparent tryst with Karel, though perhaps more with Shannon's refusal to discuss the matter.

"Aye?" Quellin said a in slightly terse tone.

Shannon sat down, giving his father a sidelong glance. "I know you are still upset with me, Father. I have been trying to decide what to say, but it is hard. Karel confided things to me, Father, things that she has not been able to tell anyone . . . should I break confidence?"

"I care not what *words* passed between you," his father replied. "I only want to know what *happened*."

The youth met his father's gaze—a feat which impressed Brendys, for he had looked directly into those eyes himself and would never forget the experience, a feeling as though Quellin could see into his very soul. "We talked almost the entire time I was in her room, Father. Nothing happened."

Shannon's cheeks turned pink as a small grin passed his lips. "Well, *almost* nothing. I . . . I *did* kiss her. . . ."

Quellin did not relax his gaze. "And that is all?"

"Aye, Father," Shannon replied with a firm and sincere nod of his head.

Brendys could not help but feel that Shannon was leaving something out, but Quellin appeared satisfied. The

Gildean King's expression softened as he placed a hand on his son's shoulder. "Shannon, you are yet young and easily led by your feelings, but you should be wary. I must confess that I believe Lord Dell is right . . . Karel has a choice set before her whether to follow her mother's path or the ways of her blood father."

Shannon's face darkened, and he grew serious. "She is not evil."

"I did not say she was," Quellin replied, firmly but with gentle restraint. "I said only that I believe the choice still lies before her. She has not been truly tested."

Brendys could sense a stubborn will growing within his nephew. The conversation was not his to intrude upon, but he could not let Shannon throw caution aside. "Shannon, your father is right. I can personally attest to how quickly an evil will can prevail against the unsuspecting—as you well know, I myself fell victim to Brugnara's will and it nearly cost me everything I love. I do not think your father is saying to forget your feelings, but rather to not be blinded by them. That is sound advice for anyone."

His nephew stared sullenly into the fire. "She will not turn to evil . . . I shan't let her."

Brendys looked at his brother-by-marriage. He saw worry in Quellin's face, but he also saw a touch of pride. One corner of the Gildean King's mouth curled upwards in the beginnings of a smile as he looked upon his son.

"You look a miserable lot. Who died?"

Mattina's voice brought the men to their feet. Mattina and Arella stood together, with Karel just before them. It was hard for the men not to stare at Novosad's step-daughter, for she no longer wore the heavy winter garments they had become accustomed to seeing on her, but was instead transformed into an elegant vision of a young woman, despite the boy's clothes she wore.

Her tunic fell just below her hips and was bound at the waist with a silver belt. The sleeves had been removed, revealing her smooth, milky-white arms, and the shoulder hems were embroidered with a simple pattern in silver. Both the tunic and hosen were deep red in color. The garments, tailored for the slightly smaller Shannon, accentuated the femininity of her form.

Her coppery hair, cropped at her shoulders was brushed and combed straight, and her bangs were braided back out of her face with garnet-studded strings of silver. A necklace of silver and garnet adorned her white throat. The color of her garments brought a glimmer of warmth to her black eyes, as did the shy smile she wore and the slightly ashen hue in her cheeks which passed for a blush.

"Well, do not just stand there gawking," Mattina chided the men. "Say something."

Shannon was the first to stir. He took a step closer to Karel, his eyes surveying her in wonder, awed by the change despite the fact the clothes had once been his own. Lacking the words to describe his feelings, he simply said in a near whisper, "Red!"

"Like a rose?" Karel questioned in return.

Shannon nodded slowly, a grin creeping over his boyish face. "Aye . . . very."

The young Prince offered his arm to Karel, and the girl took it. Arm-in-arm, they walked towards the cookfires.

"Quellin," Arella addressed her husband. "You may look at *me* now."

Quellin turned his gaze back to his wife, and he offered his own arm to her. "My dear, my eyes are always for you alone. I am just amazed that you managed to find a young woman beneath those wrappings. Besides, she looks far too young for my taste."

"She looks only a few years younger than you do," his wife reminded him as she took his arm.

Quellin shrugged nonchalantly. "Youthful beauty is not everything."

Arella knit her brow as she looked at him, trying to decide whether to be flattered or insulted.

Glaring, Mattina thrust a finger up at her husband's face, startling him. "Not a word from you."

Brendys gently closed his hand around hers and drew it away. Leaning forward, he kissed her on the lips, then said quietly, "Not a word."

Mattina's icy glare melted into a pleased smile.

* * * *

The wolf padded through the night shadows of Ilkatar Forest. It was a powerful beast and completely unnatural. The muscular animal was nearly the size of a pack pony, but that was not the strangest aspect of the silver-grey creature. This wolf sported three heads, all lowered to the ground as though tracking a quarry.

As the wolf entered a clearing, it raised its center head to gaze upon the lone, rocky cliff which rose up before him. At the base of the cliff was the entrance to a small cave. All six of the wolf's baleful, red eyes glared at the dark hole. A growl rumbled deep within the wolf's chest, then a rough, growling voice issued from the center jaws of the beast. "Betrayer, come forth!"

There was no answer.

"Come forth, Demon!" The wolf barked again. "It is nearly time for you to redeem yourself."

Almost instantly, a pair of glowing red eyes appeared at the cave mouth. A shrill voice, halfway between a hiss and a whine, spoke out of the darkness. "What do you desire of me, Mortal?"

The other creature's insolence raised the wolf's hackles. "Speak with respect, Demon, or the Black Pits of Hál will seem like the High Realm compared to the fate that I will reserve for you."

176

The eyes quailed back, and the voice became more whine than hiss. "Speak, and I will obey."

"Of course you will, Betrayer," the wolf growled in satisfaction. "Soon, a company of Men will come to this wood. The Dark Ones prepare a trap to provide me with a precious hostage. But the Living Flame journeys with the caravan, and they cannot stand against it. They will see to it that my prize enters this forest . . . a mortal child of great value to our master. You will capture this child for me, Demon. The Bearer of the Flame will trade his own life for that of his son. Do this, Betrayer, fulfill this test of loyalty, and all shall be forgiven you."

"It shall be as you demand," the shrill voice trembled in reply as the eyes vanished back into the cave.

*　*　*　*

The journey to Shalkan drew on with wearying slowness. Brendyn's daily, lengthy attempts to practice with his flute, despite the jarring bumps and rocking of the wagon, were driving nearly all of his wagonmates to madness . . . all but young Lonel, who listened intently, enraptured by the off-key and discordant notes as if they were played by a master Bard. Lonel's attention to Brendyn and the boy's returned friendship to a common servant resulted in sour looks and frequently sour words from Sîan, but no one paid her increasingly foul temperament any heed.

By nightfall of the eighth day from Racolis Keep, the company reached the head of the forest which lay between Ilkatar Keep and the great Barrier Mountain of Shalkan. Brendys suggested taking the caravan further south, away from the forest, but Quellin gainsaid him, citing the chances of one or more of the horses stumbling in the dark. Brendys knew he was right, but it made him no less wary of the forest.

177

The Horsemaster stood at the edge of the camp, beside Novosad, who was standing watch, and Aliana. He stared into the dark woods, trembling slightly. "You know, Novosad, I once told Willerth that I feared this place. I still do. It gives me an evil feeling."

He gripped Denasdervien's hilt with his left hand. "Even the Flame speaks of the presence of Evil here, though distant . . . it is still too close for me."

"You worry too much, Your Highness," the Hagane warrior replied. "I doubt there is much in this part of the land that we cannot deal with.

Novosad's words were not at all comforting to Brendys. "Worry has become a necessary part of my life, my friend, and I cannot help but feel I do not worry needlessly here."

"Prince Brendys is right," Aliana said suddenly. "I too sense a great Shadow here. Nay, *Shadow* is too light a word. There is, as Prince Brendys has said, a great *Evil* here. And it is nearer than I, too, would like."

Novosad placed a hand on Brendys's shoulder, a grave look in his eyes. "Brendys, if it will ease your mind, I will take Copanas, Lehan, and a few others and scout the forest as far as we might before morning."

Brendys stared off into the dark forest, his blue eyes searching the shadows. After a moment of nervous silence, he gave a slight nod of his head. "Aye, my friend, it *would* put me at ease."

"Then it shall be." Novosad saluted Brendys, then turned to gather his men.

Aliana glanced at Brendys, then back at the forest. "I will go with him. I sense something in this wood that does not belong."

As the Elfess and the Hagane scout departed, Willerth took their place. His voice sounded distracted. "Master Brendys, Mistress Mattina was wondering where you wandered off to."

Brendys turned to look at his servant.

The slight young man's gaze had followed Aliana and Novosad with concern. Willerth glanced at his master. "Is there something wrong, Master Brendys?"

Brendys shook his head and smiled sadly. "Nay, probably not. I am beginning to see Kubruki in every shadow, Willerth. Novosad and Aliana are going to take some men and scout the forest. I am troubled, but for naught, I am sure."

Willerth smiled in return. "No doubt. Ordinarily, I might share your concerns, Master Brendys, but I doubt that, even were there danger near, anyone in this land would assault thirty-five trained men-at-arms, the King of Gildea, and the Bearer of the Flame."

Brendys laughed and turned to rejoin his wife, placing an arm over his servant's shoulders. "I am sure you are right, Willerth. Though I am beginning to wonder if I shall ever again live a normal life."

Brendys paused for a moment to watch the children gathered at a nearby watchfire. Shannon and Brendyn were sparring playfully with sticks, while the girls looked on. Brendyn wore a light tunic and hosen with a waistcoat sewn for him by Arella. A summer traveling cloak, also made by Arella, was fastened around his shoulders. Volker hung, sheathed, at his belt, and the flute given him by Fennis the Bard hung on a string around his neck. From another cord suspended the ring given him by Guthwine. Brendyn grinned and laughed, the campfire shining in his eyes, and he wildly swung his makeshift weapon at his older cousin.

Shannon's attire was a tunic and hosen of the more subdued green and brown of his mother's House, but he still wore his silver crown, cocked at a rakish angle on his immaculately-groomed chestnut hair. He easily parried Brendyn's blows, but pretended to have difficulty.

Brendys knew that his nephew was, as Crown Prince of Gildea, undoubtedly already being trained to wield the weapons of war. In but a few months, he would turn thirteen and enter manhood, as per the customs of most of the Free Lands.

Lonel, the young servant girl, laughed and cheered for Brendyn, but Sîan and Karel watched in open disdain at the juvenile display. Mattina and Arella had converted more of Shannon's gaudy wardrobe for Karel. Despite the boyish cut of the clothing, the girl did not appear anything but feminine in them. Yet Brendys could see in her bearing something that reminded him of nothing other than a lioness waiting to pounce.

Brendys smiled to himself. Perhaps life was getting back to normal. His family was together again, and they would be home soon. Even the threat of Kerebros the Wolf seemed distant now.

He glanced at his servant. "Let's join the others, shall we?"

* * * *

As the evening drew on, the travelers took to their blankets, while Gowan and Kovar ordered the watch rotation for the night. Sîan and Lonel shared the children's wagon with Lara, while Willerth slept in a tent just outside. Brendyn and Shannon lay near their fire. Quellin and Arella retired to their pavilion, leaving the women's wain to Karel. Brendys and Mattina chose, as the boys, to sleep beneath the stars.

Nothing could be heard but the sounds of crickets and night birds.

Chapter 9

The wagon trundled down the bare wagon ruts which passed for a trade road, leading from the northern Keeps of Fekamar through several small Fekamari and Ilkatari towns and villages to the northern marches of Ilkatar Forest, through the forest and on to Shalkan. The driver, a tall, muscular man with golden hair and a large, drooping mustache, stared at the approaching line of shadow which marked the forest in the night-darkened distance. A farmstead belonging to a friend sat on the edge of that wood, where he had intended to stay the night, but as he neared the forest, he felt something which troubled him.

There had always been a presence in the forest which did not belong, but this time, the Shadow seemed to be stronger, more active. It was something which would require his attention. What he had seen on his journey into the Far North had necessitated his return to his home between Shalkan and the Shipyard of Ilkatar—there were precautions to be taken and plans to be laid—and he could not help but believe that the disturbance he felt in Ilkatar Forest was somehow related to his discoveries in the north.

The wagon creaked to a stop before the small cottage belonging to the driver's friend. As the tall man dropped to the ground, the cottage door opened and the old farmer stepped outside, peering cautiously into the night. "Eh, what ye be wantin'?"

The driver turned, flashing the farmer a broad smile and a booming laugh that was ever ready to his lips. "Come, good Faygrin, is that any way to greet an old friend?"

The old man squinted at the driver, then broke into a smile himself. "Elgern! What in Heil's stormy wrack be ye doin' up in these parts? Ne'er mind that. Get ye inside, an' we'll 'ave a nip'r two."

"Nothing would please me more," Elgern replied, his gaze drifting towards the dark line of the forest. "However, I have business elsewhere. Have you heard of any disturbances in the forest of late?"

"Disturbances in the forest?" the farmer repeated with incredulity. "I daresay I 'ave! With me own eyes an' after dark, I've seen a winged demon flittin' 'bout the treetops and terrible white ghosts a-wanderin' through th' wood. An' monsters!"

"Monsters?" Elgern said, raising a thick, golden brow.

Faygrin nodded sharply. "Aye, monsters. A few nights agone, I 'eard me cows bellerin' out in the field and went t'look . . . afirst me thoughts it 'uz wolves, but if'n they 'uz wolves, they 'uz th' first 'uns I'd ever seen what walked a-right!"

"Wolves that walk upright, eh?" Elgern replied. "This is a sight I must see for myself. I would that you care for my horses and wagon until I return, Faygrin . . . I will pay you for your trouble."

"Eh? Ye're goin' inna tha' 'aunted wood?" the old farmer said, his eyes wide in disbelief. He shook his grey head and made a dismissive gesture. "Ach, ye've al'ays been a strange 'un, Elgern. If'n ye come outta tha' place alive, ye're beasts'll be a-waitin'."

Elgern laughed. "And then we shall have that nip or two."

Faygrin snorted, then turned his back on Elgern and disappeared back into his home. Elgern grinned at the old farmer, then trotted off into the deepening night.

*　*　*　*

Brendys found himself in the midst of a battle between two armies. One army wore white, the other black. He himself wore the livery of the white army and wielded a longsword of common steel and a white shield. Warriors from both armies fell maimed or slain all around him. He pushed through the forces, defending himself with both sword and shield. Despite his lack of skill with the sword, his foes fell about him.

As the battle raged around him, he saw an unusual sight. At the center of the bloody struggle, there sat on the ground a dark-haired young beggar boy, dressed only in breeches. The child wept in terror, tears streaming from his green eyes, cutting through the dirt on his cheeks, but his voice could not be heard above the din of the battle. Brendys tried to reach the boy to take him to safety, but he kept getting driven back by the press of the battle.

Suddenly, Brendys heard the shrill cry of a charger and saw one of the black knights, mounted and wielding a long lance, charging across the field, his path taking him directly towards the child. Brendys shouted at the boy, telling him to move out of the way, but if the child heard him, he was too frightened to heed the cry. Brendys wanted to turn his eyes away as the charging horse neared the boy, but he could not.

A white knight leapt between the boy and the charging warrior at the last moment, causing the black knight's mount to rear up, dumping its rider. A golden crown was

183

set upon the white knight's greathelm, and he held a shining sword in his right hand. Without turning around or speaking, the knight motioned for the boy to get behind him.

The child grasped the back of the knight's surcoat and pulled himself up. All of his weight was placed upon one leg, for the other hung limp and useless. The boy clung to the knight for protection and did not let go, and the knight did not leave him. All foes fell before his blade.

A familiar voice spoke to Brendys, drowning out the sounds of the battle. "A King must know his people's needs, though he cannot hear their cries. A King must make known his will, though his people cannot hear his voice. A King must feel his people's pain to also share their joy. Without him, his kingdom shall fall."

Brendys awoke to find the stars twinkling in the black veil of the night sky above him. Another dream, another message. This one was less disturbing to him than the first, but no less cryptic. He wondered if Quellin was perhaps right, and Brendyn was indeed the key to the first dream. It would certainly explain the image of the warrior King with the blazing sword in this second dream.

He rolled his head to look at his wife. Mattina lay beside him, but not close. The hair near her forehead was slightly damp, and she had kicked off her blanket. Her sleeping face bore signs of discomfort and dark dreams. Brendys gently touched her face—she felt slightly feverish.

He sighed. She had warned him she might still occasionally fall into a fever for awhile yet. The long journey from Harvath to Racolis, the stressful events at Racolis Keep, and now the final leg home to Shalkan . . . it must have taken its toll on her at last.

Somewhere within the forest, not too near, but closer than comfort would allow, a pack of wolves howled, and from within the camp, a child's voice cried out in surprise.

Brendys at once leapt to his feet, grasping Denasdervien's hilt as he rose, whipping its scabbard away with a hard flick of his wrist. An argent flame ran down the sword's blade, driving back night shadows.

* * * *

Young Prince Shannon tossed on the ground, his sleep troubled by dreams of terrible woodland spirits, glowing a sickly white in the shadows of the night, descending upon the camp while everyone slept. Wolves howled in the depths of the forest, and Shannon found the ghostly face of one of the spirits hovering over him, its eyes black holes opening into a void. As the spirit prepared to plunge its sword into his heart, he suddenly realized he was no longer asleep, but staring up into the face of a Dark Elf.

Crying out as loudly as he could, he swung both of his feet up with all his strength between the Dark Elf's legs. The pale one grunted and nearly doubled over. Shannon immediately drove his feet in the Dark Elf's kneecaps, toppling the warrior backwards into his comrades.

The young Prince rolled to his feet, dragging his cousin up beside him. Brendyn stared at the Dark Elves in dazed fear, still half-asleep, but Shannon shoved him away. "Run, Brendyn!"

Brendyn hesitated, his uncertain gaze redirected towards his cousin.

"*Run!*" Shannon shouted. "I will be right behind you!"

With his cousin's second shout, Brendyn dashed off towards his parents' campfire.

Shannon turned back towards the group of Dark Elves, only to find the black blade of a Dark Elf's sword descending upon him. He tried to leap back, but was not fast enough. The ebon blade threw sparks as it struck his crowned brow with a loud ring. The youth collapsed to the ground, a web of blood quickly trailing down his boyish features.

The Gildean Prince's cries and the clamor awakened the camp and brought the warriors to alertness in time to defend themselves against the Dark Elves' assault. Willerth came out of his tent, longknife in hand, just in time to see Shannon cut down. Crying out, he launched himself at the nearest Elf, plunging his weapon into the pale being's back with such force that they both fell to the ground.

Before Willerth could rise completely to his feet, one of the Dark Elves swung at him. The young man ducked forward, avoiding the Elf's blade, but the weapon's steel hilt caught him in the side of the head, sending a burst of light and a crushing pain through his mind. He collapsed upon the corpse of his victim, darkness overwhelming him.

Before the Dark Elves could finish Willerth, a large shadow rose up behind them with an inhuman scream. Millas, Shannon's black stallion, had broken free of his tether and had raced to defend his master. The warhorse's hooves struck out at the Dark Elves, crushing one's skull and scattering the others before his fury. Fracas, Brendys's grey, likewise broke free and struck out at every Dark Elf that dared to near him, as did most of the chargers. The drayhorses bolted in terror without their masters to guide them.

Quellin erupted from his pavilion, half-dressed, Kalter bared in his hand, the Elvingold sword blazing with the fury of its master. As Arella came out behind him, he directed her towards the wagons. "Help Mattina into the cover of the wagon. *Go!*"

Without question, his wife hurried to Mattina's side and helped her sister-by-marriage to her feet. Fevered, Mattina looked around in confusion, her eyes unable to focus on anything, but she allowed herself to be led to the wagon.

Karel drew back the curtain and helped Arella get Mattina into the wain, but as the women squeezed past her, her gaze fell on the caravan's assailants. She froze, her eyes drifting across faces that mirrored her own, but twisted in merciless rage. Arella yelled at her to come away from the opening, but she would not . . . she could not tear her eyes away as the ghostly figures flooded into the camp from out of the forest, only to fall beneath the blades of the caravan's defenders.

The Dark Elves kept coming, though they had little chance. Despite their greater numbers, the camp was now alerted, and the Gildean and Hagane escort were prepared. As well, Kovar's white falcon, Amrein swooped among the assailants, slashing at them with her Elvinsilver-tipped talons, while Kovar and Gowan engaged them at swordpoint. Not too far from them, the Dark Elves fell in droves to Quellin's Elvingold blade, and spear, sword, and flesh parted at Denasdervien's touch as though they were but a passing mist.

*   *   *   *

At Shannon's shouted command, Brendyn took off at a run. He set his gaze on Denasdervien's white flame across the camp, but his passage was blocked at every turn by battling warriors, mortal and immortal, and he could not get through. Panic overcame him, and he froze in his tracks, sobs born of dread wracking his body.

A terrible form rose up before his tear-blurred eyes, a figure clothed and cloaked all in black, wielding a black-bladed sword in its pale hand. The ghost-white face shone clear even through the boy's tears, though the black eyes appeared like the empty sockets of a skull. The nightmare face leaned forward, causing Brendyn to take a step back.

"Run, Man-child," the being's fair voice said in a steady tone, barely audible to Brendyn over the din of the battle. "We shall slay all we may, but you at least shall have a chance to live. Run, boy! The forest is your only hope for escape. . . a second chance you shall not have. The blood of my brethren shall not be in vain."

The Dark Elf slowly lifted his ebon sword, and Brendyn broke into a run back the way he had come, dashing past the place where he had slept but a few minutes before, unaware of Willerth and Shannon lying amidst the bodies with bloodstained faces. He ran in blind terror, not looking back. Even when he passed into the protective shadows of Ilkatar Forest, he did not stop.

*   *   *   *

Novosad and his scouts carefully scoured the forest near the campsite for nearly two hours without finding sign of any threat, though what signs they may have missed in the dark, no one could tell. At last, Dell's chief scout signaled for his men to regroup. As the warriors gathered together, Novosad noticed that Aliana was missing.

"Has anyone seen Lady Aliana?" he asked his companions.

"I am here," the Elfess said, directing the attention of the others to herself. In her Elvin garments and cloak, she was nearly invisible against the backdrop of the dark forest. Kneeling, she stared intently at something on the ground before her.

Novosad and his men hurried to Aliana's side. As they approached, Aliana pointed at a set of large paw prints in the earth. Novosad's eyes widened. "Wolf tracks."

"If that is so, the wolf they belong to is larger than any I have ever seen," Copanas remarked.

Novosad's jaw set in a grim line. "I wager this is no worldly creature."

"And you would wager well," Aliana answered, looking up at him. "It is said that Kerebros the Wolf is able to take the form of a great, three-headed wolf. If it was indeed

Kerebros that approached Prince Brendyn at Racolis Keep, then I deem these tracks belong to him. It may be that he plans to spring some sort of trap here."

"If that is so, we should head back to camp and warn the others," Lehan said, receiving nods from most of his companions.

"Do what you must," Aliana replied, standing and staring off into the forest. "I sense more than just the Sorcerer's presence. There are many Shadows here, and there is *something* else . . . something I have never felt before. I must discover what it is."

"I agree," Novosad said with a solemn nod. "The twins and I shall accompany Lady Aliana. You four return to camp and assure King Quellin and Prince Brendys that we shall be back by dawn. Let them know we believe Kerebros to be in the vicinity and that Lady Aliana feels there is something more as well."

With an affirmative reply, the four junior scouts immediately retraced their steps towards the campsite at the edge of the forest.

Novosad and the twins followed Aliana through the forest, trusting that the Elfess could either see or sense something that they could not. All three of the Hagane warriors were expert trackers, but none of them could see much of anything in the darkness of the night and forest shadows. Aliana's Elvin eyes, on the other hand, seemed to miss nothing. Her gaze most often tracked the ground along barely seen paths, but occasionally she would stop and scan the trees around her, her sky-blue eyes almost completely closed.

Finally, they stepped out into a clearing. Almost straight ahead, at the eastern edge of the clearing, a rocky cliff rose up from the ground, perhaps thrice the height of a man and a little more than half that wide, tapering to ground level at the back. At the base of the cliff was a small cave mouth, like the lair of a forest animal.

"The Wolf stopped here for a moment, facing the cave," Aliana said pointing at a spot near the center of the clearing. "It looks as if he then moved on around the northeast edge of the cliff."

Novosad stared apprehensively at the cave, which was little more to his eyes than a dark hole in the night shadows. A slight chill ran down his spine, though he could not say why. Slowly, he drew forth his sword, a vicious trophy taken from a Dark Elf years before when Lord Dell's host had marched to Gildea's aid against Iysh Mawvath, Warlord of Thanatos. The blade's double edge was serrated and keen as a razor. "We shall see where the tracks lead . . . there is little sense in exploring this rock at night."

"The deeper we go, the darker it will get," Copanas reminded him. "There is little sense in going on as is."

Novosad glanced at Copanas's twin. "Lehan?"

Lehan exhaled, uncertainty on his face. "Copanas is right . . . unless you want to risk a torch, there is little use wandering around in these woods. Even *I* would miss the tracks in the deeper wood."

Novosad looked distracted. "These tracks make me uneasy. They are unnatural, that much is clear from their size. And if they *do* belong to this Kerebros. . . ."

He fell silent for a moment, his head bowed in thought. He had to admit to himself that he was more than a little anxious about continuing on. The thought of running into a Sorcerer of Thanatos in this wood was unsettling at the very least, and there was little he or the twins could do in the dark, except act as bodyguards for Aliana. He did not wish to risk torches, for the dark was their ally if it came to spying on the enemy—if there *was* an enemy—without

190

being discovered. Aliana herself did not appear to need a torch to see by, which was an advantage.

Novosad looked at the Elfess. Aliana was staring in distracted curiosity at the cave opening. "What is it, My Lady?"

Aliana turned her gaze on him. "I . . . I am not certain. There is . . . *something* in there."

"Do you think it is dangerous?" Lehan asked her.

The Elfess shrugged helplessly. "I do not know. I have never felt its like before . . . it is strange. . . ."

Novosad cast one last fearful glance in the cave's direction, then said, "Leave it. Let the dawn deal with whatever dwells there. The Wolf is our quarry. Let us return to the hunt. No torches unless absolutely necessary . . . unless you have need of more light, My Lady?"

Aliana shook her head. "What light the moon and stars grant is enough for my eyes. I will not lead you astray."

"Very well, My Lady," Novosad replied. He looked at the twins. "Lehan, Copanas, arm yourselves. We shall be Lady Aliana's guardsmen. Our eyes may be hindered, but we do have other senses which may avail us."

The wheaten-haired twins glanced at each other uncertainly, but nevertheless obeyed their Captain.

Aliana led her mortal companions into the dark wood, following the tracks past the northeastern edge of the cliff. The task was difficult and slow, for much of the ground had been dried from the summer heat, hardened so that tracks were scarce. When tracks failed, Aliana followed her Elvin senses, the presence of Evil unmistakable in her mind.

For three hours, the scouting party haltingly followed the trail before their hunt yielded results. Quite suddenly, they heard voices not too far in the distance. Slowly, silently, and ever watchful, they advanced. The voices became clearer as they neared the source. Beyond a crafted barrier, expertly disguised to look like natural foliage, they could see the flickering, orange glow of a watchfire. The speakers, two or three at their best estimation, were not yet visible, but their speech was quite clear. The voices themselves were quite fair, almost musical in quality, but the language they spoke was the harsh, guttural speech of Machaelon.

Novosad and his companions exchanged nervous glances. They had heard voices like these speaking in the same tongue many years ago and had not forgotten them. The chief scout motioned for Lehan to wait until he, Copanas, and Aliana were closer to the barrier, then loose an arrow over the barrier. It was not important that the shot be accurate . . . only that it provided a brief distraction.

As Novosad and his companions crept up to the chest-high barrier and peered over the top, they could see the speakers—a pair of Dark Elf sentries—silhouetted by the fire. One stood beside the dark entrance to a camouflaged outpost. The other was seen only by its shadow cast upon the vine-covered wall of the outpost. The second sentry sat beside the watchfire. When Novosad deemed they were close enough, he nodded to Copanas and Aliana, then waved his left hand at Lehan.

Lehan let fly his arrow into the trees above and behind the outpost. The Dark Elves' startled attention was drawn to the sound of the missile ripping through the leaves above their heads. During the brief moment of distraction, Novosad and Copanas charged the barrier and dove over the top. Copanas hit the ground on the far side of the barrier and rolled to his feet facing the Elf standing near the outpost entrance, though his foe deflected his first attack.

Novosad misjudged the distance, striking the inside edge of the barrier, and was thrown off-balance. He tumbled across the ground, bowling into the Elf by the fire, knocking him back towards the outpost wall. The odd fall knocked the wind from Novosad's lungs, and he gasped for air, trying to regain his breath.

The hiss of steel being unsheathed drew his gaze towards his intended opponent, and he was able to react in time to avoid a blow from the Dark Elf's slender, serrated blade, despite his lack of breath. He came to his feet, hunched and coughing, but sword held ready. As the Dark Elf lunged again, Novosad dodged aside. The scout fought defensively until he had regained his breath. At last, he circled around the watchfire, keeping it between himself and his enemy.

The Dark Elf spat out a curse in the language of Machaelon, then said in the Common Tongue, "You fight like a coward, Mortal."

Novosad stared intently into the cold, black gaze of the Dark Elf before him. Fury transformed the face of his enemy in his mind's eye. Memory carved a deep, grey scar from the Dark Elf's temple, down his jaw, ending at his chin. He saw before him Lord Chol, the one who had used the woman who would be his wife and spawned the child who would become his stepdaughter. Novosad's blood raged within him, and in unbridled fury, he leapt across the fire with a cry.

The Dark Elf sentry, taken off guard, threw up his sword to parry aside Novosad's stroke, but too late. The serrated blade of the Hagane scout's weapon plunged through the Dark Elf's chest, pinning him to the wall of the outpost. Novosad braced his foot against the body of his foe and wrenched his blade from the corpse. Holding his sword in a two-handed grip, he hacked savagely at the body in blind rage, until his hand was at last stayed by his companions.

Copanas and Lehan each grabbed one of their captain's forearms as he raised his sword above his head for another stroke. Novosad jerked to a halt and looked at his

193

companions' fearful faces as though suddenly awakened from a dream. The twins released his arms as he slowly lowered his weapon. He stared down at the mutilated corpse of his foe and at his crimson surcoat, darkened with the blood of his enemy.

He felt suddenly weakened as the adrenalin rushed from his body, and his knees buckled beneath him. He drove the point of his sword into the ground before him, using the weapon to hold himself upright, his forehead tilting forward to rest upon its pommel. Perspiration trickled down from his sweat-soaked hair, cutting through the blood staining his face, and his breath came in gasps.

When he had at last recovered his strength, he rose to his feet. He cleaned the blood from his sword and returned it to his sheath. Noticing his companions' concerned looks, he raised his hand before him, shaking his head. "I am all right."

His voice sounded uncomfortable and unconvinced in his own ears. He had lost control, and he could not bear that. Worse yet, he had given in to utter hatred . . . not just hatred for Lord Chol and what he had done to Titha, nor for the Dark Elf he had just slain, but for their entire people. He wanted nothing less than the destruction of the entire Dark Elf race. And why not? Was that not the fate *they* sought for the race of Man?

Novosad shook off the thought. There were greater matters at hand. That the Dark Elves had an outpost that deep in the Free Lands, previously undetected, was unthinkable. The danger had grown from a single shapeshifting Sorcerer to a Sorcerer aided by deadly immortals.

He glanced once more at Lehan and Copanas, his brow wrinkling in confusion. "Where is Aliana?"

The twins glanced around the small clearing in bewilderment, but all they saw were the corpses of the two Dark Elf sentries. Aliana seemed to have vanished.

Novosad made his way carefully around the barrier, followed by his men, and found the Elfess still standing there, her gaze, alert and sharp-eyed, flicking back and forth through the gaps in the trees. The chief scout touched her arm. "My Lady? What is it?"

She turned her eyes on him, her gaze focusing on his face. She wore a grave expression. "We should not stay too long in this place. There is Evil afoot. I fear we may be discovered soon."

Novosad nodded, then inclined his head towards the entrance of the outpost. "Let's have a look inside, then report back to the caravan. Stay wary."

Without another word, they each took a brand from the watchfire, then slipped into the dark entrance of the outpost. The entrance opened into a tunnel formed of intertwined branches and vines, but that rapidly dropped into an earthen cave, reinforced with carved stone. The cave consisted of a common room, a supply room, an armory, and a small room which seemed to have little purpose at first glance.

The common room to the left was very large and spacious, littered with numerous tables. Another doorway led out of the common room into the smallest chamber. As they stepped inside, they found it barren but for five blood-stained pallets lying on the floor, arranged in a semi-circle.

"An infirmary?" Lehan offered.

Aliana shook her head and shuddered. "Nay, this room was used for a ritual of some form . . . I can still feel the vestiges of the sorcery used here. We should not stay in this place."

"I agree," Novosad said, motioning for the others to leave. "Let us check the other rooms, then get out of here."

The other rooms told more than either the common room or the ritual chamber. The storeroom to the right was stocked for no less than a hundred men. The armory, also on the right side of the tunnel, was no smaller than the store room, but it was nearly empty. Novosad exchanged alarmed glances with his companions.

"We must get back to the camp!" Novosad said, his voice laden with urgency.

As they turned to leave the armory, they found three mortal Men standing just inside the entrance. They all wore sleeveless, black, leather jerkins, open down the front, and black leather trousers. Their feet were bare. The torchlight glistened off the perspiration drenching their exposed skin and thick manes. Thick, bristling sideburns ran down their cheeks, and black brands in the shape of a wolf's head were burned into their foreheads. They wore short swords in scabbards on their backs, but none of them reached for their weapons.

The man in the center bared his teeth in a grin, a hungry light in his amber eyes. "You ain't goin' anywhere . . . leastways, not 'til the Great Wolf has had a chance to question you."

Novosad slowly raised his serrated blade before him. "I somehow doubt your ability to hold us here."

"Let them try to escape, Vrash," one of the other men said to his leader. "I've a hankerin' for some fresh meat."

Fresh meat? At first Novosad thought the man was simply yearning for a fight, but a second look into his amber eyes convinced him that the man was speaking quite literally. *Leave it to Dark Elves to ally themselves with cannibals.*

Novosad shot a glance at his companions, who had apparently come to the same conclusion as he had, and noticed that Aliana was not to be seen. The Elfess had simply vanished. He was careful not to let his bewilderment show and possibly betray Aliana's escape.

"Whether these live or die be the Wolf's decision," Vrash snapped back at the other. "No killin' 'less Kerebros says."

He turned his wolfish gaze back on Novosad. "But there's nothin' sayin' we can't have sport of you. You'll be cooperative enough when we're done with you."

Vrash's comrades, still unarmed, slowly circled around each side of Novosad and the twins, splitting their focus. Novosad kept his gaze on Vrash, leaving the other two to Copanas and Lehan. Something felt terribly wrong to him, for these men were far too confident for common brigands.

Novosad did not have to wonder long at his foe's demeanor, for even as the man poised himself to spring, a red light sprang to life within his amber eyes, and he began to change. Vrash began to grow, his face distorting into something more animalistic. Coarse hair began to sprout from his exposed flesh, while his hand and feet enlarged, his nails becoming taloned claws. His leather clothing was stretched so near to bursting that Novosad had to wonder if Kerebros had ensorceled them against such an event.

A curse from one of the twins alerted him that Vrash was not the only one of the brigands to transform. Novosad drew back his sword, moving the torch in his left hand in front of him. Vrash took a step backwards, snarling, apparently more intimidated by the flaming brand than he had been of the jagged steel of the sword.

Before any of them could make another move, a shrill cry drew their startled attention. A shadow detached itself from the back wall, hurtling between the two man-wolves

197

threatening Lehan and Copanas. A pair of longknives, one of ordinary steel, the other Elvinsilver, leapt from the folds of Aliana's Elvincloak, an argent light bursting forth from the Elvinsilver blade. Aliana's hood fell back, revealing her shining face, hardened with focus and determination.

The twins fell back beyond the range of the Elfess's cyclonic assault. As he dodged away, Copanas glanced back towards Novosad and cried out a warning.

Novosad spun around in time to see one of Vrash's large claws flying towards him. He ducked forward, avoiding the sharp talons, but Vrash's broad palm struck him in the side of the head, throwing him sidelong against the near wall with immense strength. Novosad's sword and torch flew from his limp grasp in opposite directions as he struck the wall. He wavered on the edge of consciousness, unable to focus his vision on anything, barely cognizant of Copanas and Lehan turning their attacks on Vrash. He could do little more than lie there, braced against the wall, struggling against the massive ache in his skull to maintain consciousness and regain his wits.

As his senses began to return and his vision to come back into focus, Novosad saw a double image of Aliana whirling and spinning between her two opponents, her knives flashing out at the creatures. The steel knife sliced into the beasts' flesh, leaving raw, pink slashes which healed almost instantaneously, while cuts inflicted by the Elvinsilver knife bled profusely and healed far more slowly.

On his other side, the twins were fighting a defensive battle against Vrash, one dodging Vrash's claws while the other lashed out at the man-wolf. Their blades, like Aliana's steel knife, did little more than inflict temporary wounds which rapidly vanished. As well, Vrash adeptly avoided thrusts of the twins torches, keeping the deadly flames away from his vulnerable fur.

As his vision began to come more into focus, Novosad looked about for his sword, spotting it farther along the wall, several feet from where he lay. His head still pounding in agony, he crawled towards the weapon, though somewhere in his foggy mind he knew his weapon would be of no more use against Vrash than a willow switch. As his hand grasped his sword's hilt, a strangled roar caught his attention, and he looked back.

Aliana had driven her Elvinsilver knife into the heart of one of her foes, striking a mortal blow. The beast collapsed to its knees, then fell backwards, transforming again into the form of a Man. The second man-wolf took the opportunity and seized the Elfess with both claws, its talons piercing into her flesh, then clamped its fanged jaws onto her shoulder. Aliana cried out in pain, but kept her wits about her, plunging her Elvinsilver longknife into the creature's throat. The beast fell atop her, knocking her to the earthen floor of the chamber, then reverted to human form.

Novosad grabbed his sword, then painfully rose to his feet and lurched to Aliana's side. He collapsed to his knees and dragged the corpse from atop the Elfess. The sleeves and shoulder of Aliana's tunic were in tatters, and the pale flesh below was torn and bleeding.

Aliana's eyes fluttered open, and she looked up at Novosad, her gaze clear, though not without signs of pain. "Do not fear for me. If I live, I shall not die. You must kill the beast . . . these men are cursed, and they bear the venom of their curse in tooth and claw. Even now, I can feel it in my veins. I cannot be overcome, but you would become as they are if you are thus wounded."

As the words left Aliana's lips, Novosad heard a cry behind him, and he turned to look, fear gripping him, though the cry had sounded more startled than hurt. Vrash's claws had sheared through Lehan's surcoat and mail and through the outer layer of the quilted gambeson below. He did not think the man-wolf had pierced through to Lehan's flesh, but it was hard to tell in the torchlight.

Copanas pressed the attack, allowing his brother to step back for a moment and gather his wits. Novosad ripped Aliana's Elvinsilver longknife from the throat of the corpse in which it was lodged and leapt to his men's defense. Novosad thrust his sword into Vrash's back, near the spine, jamming it in as far as he could. Vrash howled in pain and rage and spun around to slash at the Hagane warrior, but Novosad held to his sword's hilt and braced his feet against the man-wolf's back, staying out of Vrash's reach. With Aliana's knife, Novosad speared at Vrash's throat, but the man-wolf's movement threw off his aim, and the Elvinknife plunged into Vrash's shoulder. Vrash backhanded Novosad in the face, dazing him again, but the scout managed to maintain his hold on his sword and the Elvinknife.

Suddenly, a wave of heat washed over Novosad, and orange flames filled his vision. He pushed off Vrash with his feet, wrenching both sword and knife from the man-wolf's flesh and fell backwards to the floor. He rolled away from the creature, then looked up to see Vrash enveloped in flame, flailing blindly, roaring in hatred and agony. At last, the man-wolf collapsed into a burning heap, reverting to human shape, the stench of his burning hair and flesh stinging eyes and nostrils of Novosad and his companions.

The twins skirted around Vrash's charred and burning corpse to join their Captain. Copanas helped Novosad to his feet, then looked at the man's brother. "Are you hurt?"

Lehan fingered the rent in his mail and shook his head. "His claws missed me . . . though barely. If I had not dodged away, I think he would have ripped my heart out."

"Nay," Novosad replied grimly. "They were not trying to kill us . . . Aliana says that a bite or scratch from them would change us into creatures like them."

He turned away from his men and knelt down beside Aliana, who was trying to raise herself up. "Lie still and let me tend your wounds."

Aliana smiled weakly and shook her head. "You worry needlessly. I will mend . . . though perhaps you should return to the camp without me, for until my strength returns I shall only hinder you."

"And if the Dark Elves return while you are in this state, they would kill you," Novosad returned. "We will not leave you behind."

A cloud of doubt passed over the Hagane's face as he quietly added, "We are likely too late to warn the others now. Our swords will make little difference against so many, especially if there are more of these creatures among them."

Fear shone briefly on Aliana's face as well, but quickly vanished. "Your daughter and my beloved are in far less danger than ourselves, for they at least are under the protection of the Living Flame. If Kerebros sends my cousins against the camp, they will fail, no matter their numbers or their allies."

"I pray you are right," Novosad replied, unconvinced.

"I am," Aliana replied with certainty. "Now, please help me to the storeroom. The Dark Ones will have medicines which will help quicken the healing and restore some strength to my limbs."

Novosad returned her longknife to her, then assisted the Elfess to her feet.

* * * *

Flames burst in Shannon's mind, and he slowly came to. His eyelids fluttered open briefly before he squeezed them shut against the wracking pain in his head. He had been fortunate—when he had tried to duck away from the Dark Elf's blow, his crown had taken the brunt of the strike.

He raised his hand to his forehead, but quickly drew it away again, sticky with blood. The cut was small, but it bled profusely. Gritting his teeth against the pain, he adjusted his dented crown so that it put pressure against the wound. It was not a proper dressing, but it was all he could manage in the midst of battle.

The youth slowly rolled over and started to raise himself up on his arms. As he did, he saw his cousin's small form run past him, followed at a distance by the Dark Elf with the black sword. Shannon tried to rise, but he was still too dazed. As he watched his cousin disappear beneath the eaves of the forest, it occurred to him that the Dark Elf was not making a real effort to catch Brendyn, but rather seemed to following the boy's progress.

Painfully, Shannon began to drag himself along the ground towards the forest. As he neared the place where he thought Brendyn and the Elf had entered the wood, he used a tree trunk to pull himself to his feet, then stumbled into the forest after them. Not far into the wood, he heard human voices shouting through the trees to his right, the sound fading as the men left the forest, joining the battle in the encampment.

In his path, he stumbled across the body of the Dark Elf that had been chasing Brendyn, though there was no sign of his sword. The body was badly slashed as if he had been overwhelmed by mortal blades. That was some relief at least—his cousin was no longer being hounded by the enemy—but there was no telling what other dangers lay within the forest.

Shannon continued on, trying to follow his cousin's tracks, but the night shadows and his own blurred vision made it almost impossible. He stumbled through the wood, occasionally trying to call out his cousin's name, but his voice was little more than a painful creak. All sense of time was lost to him as he wandered through the wood, seeking his young cousin.

A crippling pain shot through the youth's body, and he collapsed into a bed of fern, shutting his eyes. He tried to stand again, but to no avail. His body would not respond to his will. Unable to control his own body, he stopped struggling against the darkness grasping at his mind and slipped into unconsciousness.

*   *   *   *

Brendys and Quellin stood back-to-back, the light of their Elvinswords blazing in terrible wrath, streaks of white and gold fire darting to and fro. Every weapon which chanced to meet Denasdervien shattered on contact with the unbreakable Silver-gold blade of the Living Flame, but the Dark Elves came in such numbers that Brendys was hard put to avoid a stray blade. He took many minor wounds, but ignored the pain and stood his ground.

Behind him, Quellin fared much the same, though he had to rely more on his own skill as a swordsman to defend himself, for it was not Kalter's power to shatter steel. The Gildean King's Half-Elvin reflexes were nearly a match for the Dark Elves, however, and he sustained fewer cuts and slashes in the fray.

Both men were cut off from the women's hiding place and could not force their way through the fray, but their wives were not without defense. Gowan and Kovar held back the flood of Dark Elves with the help of the great hawk, Amrein.

The brunt of the attack was being directed against Brendys and Quellin, and it was not long before the rest of the combined Gildean and Hagane escort were able to bring their swords to bear on the rear ranks of the Dark Elves. The pale enemy did not turn to face them, but continued to press their attack on the Bearer of the Flame and the King of Gildea, who were quickly weakening beneath the assault.

As the pre-dawn light began to grow in the sky, nearly a hundred Dark Elves lay scattered upon the ground in bloody heaps, as well as fifteen Gildean and Hagane warriors. Brendys collapsed to his knees, overcome at last by the pain of his wounds. Denasdervien's flame died away, leaving its mirrored Silver-gold blade clean. Brendys slid the weapon back into its battered, black scabbard and bowed his head, breathing hard.

Beside him, Quellin resheathed Kalter and received Arella into his arms. His wife embraced him, and he held her for a long moment, both arms entwined around her, before she turned away from him.

"Brendys," she said, touching the Horsemaster's shoulder, her voice heavy with concern. "Mattina has fallen into a terrible fever. . . ."

Brendys placed his hand over hers, and smiled weakly. "I do not think there is need to fear. The stress has been too much, and she already warned me of her fevers. She will be well once she can rest."

"*Murderer!*" a voice screamed out.

Startled by the cry, Brendys looked up in time to see Karel throw herself at Gowan, striking his chest with both fists. His old companion stood still beneath the girl's futile blows, a look of surprise and confusion on his face.

Brendys dragged himself to his feet and followed Arella and Quellin back towards the wagon.

Arella pulled Karel away from Gowan, holding the struggling girl back with both arms wrapped around her. "Calm yourself, child!"

Karel stopped struggling and gave in to Arella's firm, but comforting embrace, breathing heavily.

Quellin looked at his escort commander. "Gowan, what is this about?"

The brown-haired warrior shook his head in stark confusion. "I know not, Your Majesty, I swear!"

"*Liar!*" Karel shrieked, spinning to face him, her white face contorted in fury. She pointed to the nearby corpse of a slain Dark Elf. "That man was defenseless, and *he* murdered him . . . I *saw* him!"

Gowan looked down at the body, understanding flooding his features. He turned his brown gaze to his King. "Your Majesty, he was dying. He begged me for a swift death . . . I think he feared the coming dawn."

"He was wounded!" Karel shouted accusingly. "You could have tried to help him!"

Quellin turned his attention to the girl, but though his face was a mask of compassion, Brendys saw beneath a strange and dark fear. His voice was gentle when he spoke. "To what end, Karel? Even if we could have saved him, what then? Let him go?"

Karel's hatred melted away to uncertainty and confusion. "I don't know . . . aye, perhaps . . . why not? Maybe such an act of mercy would have been enough to turn his allegiance. . . ."

Quellin shook his head. "Do you not understand, Karel? These are not creatures of mercy . . . we are little more than animals to these monsters, cattle to be enslaved at best. Look around you, girl. They sent no less than a hundred men against us and fought until the last fell. They did not come here to take captives . . . they came here to kill. Do you truly believe they would have stopped with the deaths of the men? Nay, they would have slain us all, warrior or child. . . ."

Brendys suddenly forgot his pain. His gaze darted to the children's wagon and saw Lara climbing out to hurry to the side of one of the fallen. Fear gripped him.

"Brendyn," he said, his voice barely above a whisper. Without another word, he broke into a run across the camp.

Quellin, too, realized the implications of his own words and dashed after his brother-by-marriage. Behind him, he heard his wife tell Karel, "Come, child, this field of carnage is no place for us. The sun will be up soon, and you must be covered. Come . . . help me with Mattina."

As Brendys reached Lara's side, he found her kneeling beside Willerth. The young man was bleeding from a wound above his left ear. His grey eyes were having trouble focusing, until his gaze rested on his master's face. "Master Brendys. . . ."

Brendys knelt beside his servant, across from Mattina's handmaid. "Willerth, lie still. Let Lara tend that wound."

Propping himself up on his elbows, the young man shook his head. "I will be fine, Master Brendys. I have taken worse than this in my life, and you know it. Is Master Brendyn all right?"

Brendys gripped his servant's arm, a deep foreboding seizing his heart. "Then you have not seen him?"

Willerth's grey eyes widened in fear. "Did he not come to you? When the Dark Elves attacked, Prince Shannon told him to run, and so he did . . . straight for *you*."

Brendys's blood ran cold. He let go his servant's arm and slowly rose to his feet. A shudder ran through his body as his gaze swept across the field of carnage, his mind

conjuring images of his little boy's body amongst the
slain.

Chapter 10

Brendyn crashed through the dense underbrush, ducking under low branches, sometimes crawling, blindly pressing onward. No thought of reason entered his young mind. Only the relentless scourge of terror drove him onward, abject fear and weary confusion. His young limbs ached and faltered beneath him, but he could not stop. White death followed him. There could be no rest.

Time was lost to Brendyn. How long and how far he had run, he did not know. At last, the little boy stumbled into a small clearing, collapsing as he came out of the woods, breath and strength completely escaping him. He could go no farther, though he knew his life depended on it. Panting, he came to his knees and rested there for a few minutes with his eyes closed, expecting at any moment for his Dark Elf pursuer to spring into the clearing and end the chase. But all he could hear were the noises of insects, nocturnal animals, and his own heavy breathing.

It finally occurred to him that he may have actually lost his assailant. Perhaps he could sneak back to the campsite and find his parents. Still sobbing and gasping for air, he opened his eyes and looked around. In every direction, trees closed in about him, except at one side of the clearing where a small, rocky cliff rose up to the tops of the trees around it. If there were any signs as to which direction he had come from, they were hidden by the night shadows from his unskilled eyes. He was *lost*.

A fresh wave of fear and anxiety swept over him. His blue eyes again scanned the dark forest around him while he wept in bitter terror, his imagination transforming every shadow into an unknown evil. The forest itself closed in around him like a predatory beast stalking its helpless victim.

The sudden beating of heavy wings behind Brendyn elicited a terrified shriek from the boy. Brendyn fell away from the noise, sprawling on his back. Through his tear-blurred vision all he could see was a great shadow and a pair of red eyes, burning like hot coals, looming over him. His crying intensified, great sobs wracking his small frame and resounding in the still of the night.

"No, no, foolish child!" a shrill, but raspy voice hissed angrily from the shadow above him. "You mustn't cry so, Little One. It shall bring the Dark Ones, or worse, the *Wolves*. They will find you."

As the eyes drew closer, Brendyn fumbled with the Elvinknife at his belt, still crying loudly. At last, Volker slid free of its scabbard. In the boy's trembling hand, the Stajouhar blade slowly blazed forth with an emerald radiance. The hovering shadow quailed back in the light of the Elvinknife's gemblade.

"No, child, no!" the creature hissed. "Do not be foolish! Skrak is harmless . . . *he* will not hurt you. You must listen to him! They come even now. You must trust Skrak!"

Brendyn slowly climbed to his feet, Volker thrust out before him. His weeping subsided, though not completely. Sobbing, his lip trembling, he wiped the tears away from his eyes. In the emerald fire of his Elvinknife, he could see the creature clearly. It was about the size of a small man and was covered in a fine black fur. It cowered back, its arm raised defensively before it. The creature was generally man-shaped, but for its nightmarish face and the bat-like wings stretched from its sides to its wrists. The creature's head was a bizarre mixture of a man's and a bat's. Its red eyes gleamed over the edge of its upraised arm.

Brendyn's eyes widened. "Y-you're a *Jaf!*"

A Jaf, a demon akin to the Drolar, a creature of the supernatural, impervious to all mortal harm, seen by few, feared by all. But there was something strange about this creature. Brendyn fancied the creature was truly frightened, but there was more. His young mind was slowly beginning to wrap itself around the situation, and something seemed different about this creature than what he had learned from stories.

"Yes, yes," the Jaf replied. "The Dark Ones call him Skrak . . . the Betrayer. Now, you must hurry to hide!"

Suddenly, Brendyn realized what bothered him about the creature . . . it spoke with its own voice. Like the Drolar, a Jaf could only mimic what it had heard recently. Only once had such a creature been known to speak with its own voice, and that was because it had not been a true Drolar . . . it had been the disguise of the Sorcerer called the Great Father, Brugnara, Willerth's father—the man responsible for Brendyn's own scars.

"Jaf can't talk!" Brendyn cried out. "You're a Sorcerer!"

The creature hissed in response. "Nay, Little One! Skrak speaks because he is the Betrayer, he is accursed. Sorcery made him, but is no longer *in* him. Please, you must trust him!"

The sound of a large animal passing through the wood, accompanied by a low growling, drew slowly closer, too near for comfort, though not yet upon them.

Skrak's gaze began to dart to and fro in fear and agitation. "They come. The Wolves . . . they will kill you if they find you! You must hide . . . you must trust Skrak!"

Brendyn hesitated. He detected a strange sincerity in the creature, but fear would not allow trust just yet.

Skrak turned his hideous gaze fully upon the child, his grating voice growing calm. "Little One, if Skrak wished you harm, you would not have had a chance to draw your knife. Please, you must trust him . . . he has a hiding place where neither the Dark Ones nor the Wolves will look. It is near."

Brendyn hesitated, then slowly sheathed Volker. Though he knew he should be terrified, fear was beginning to subside. Something within told him this strange creature was a friend. "All right . . . but if you eat me, I hope you get sick."

As the Elvinknife's light was quenched, Skrak cautiously approached the boy. His raspy voice held a tinge of sorrow. "Child, no sickness is worse than being cursed with this form."

In the night shadows, Brendyn could see the creature point its winged arm towards the cliff. "There, Little One, lies my den . . . the Dark Ones do not trouble me, for I am still more powerful than they."

The Jaf moved past Brendyn and disappeared through the small cave entrance.

Brendyn took a nervous step towards the cave. Cautiously, he dropped to his knees. A rank animal smell exuded from the entrance. He was still not sure whether he wanted to go in or not.

Suddenly, he heard movement behind him and looked back. He could see some large animal, like a wolf, pacing in the shadows of the forest, not far away. Brendyn quickly crawled through the opening and into a long, dark tunnel.

When the boy disappeared into the tunnel, the animal came into the clearing. It was a dog, a strange looking animal. It had a beautiful, golden coat and was powerfully built, but it also had a very flat face with a heavy upper lip and eyes that almost appeared human. The dog stared at the cave entrance for a moment, then bobbing its head almost in a nod, it trotted away.

It took Brendyn a few minutes to traverse the shaft he had entered, for it was as black as pitch, completely blinding him. When he came to the end of the tunnel, he found himself in a small chamber. Skrak was huddled down beside a small fire at the center of the chamber. The Jaf looked up when Brendyn entered his cave, his small, red eyes examining the boy.

"Come, Little One. You have had a trying day—or is it night? Time slips from Skrak sometimes," the Jaf croaked, beckoning the boy to the small blaze. "Day is night and night is day. He has made a fire to comfort you. Come! Come and sleep. Skrak will make sure that the Dark Ones do not find you."

Too worn out to argue, Brendyn obeyed the Jaf's instructions. No sooner had he stretched out beside the fire than he had fallen into a deep slumber. If he dreamed any dreams, he did not remember them. His sleep was peaceful, despite the terror he had experienced that night, but all too short. He was awakened by the gentle touch of a rough-skinned hand on his cheek.

Brendyn's eyes flew open. In the dim firelight, he saw Skrak leaning over him. The Jaf drew his clawed hand away from the boy's face and sat back. Startled to alertness, Brendyn reached for Volker, but the longknife was gone.

Skrak waved a claw across to the other side of the chamber. Volker sat as far from Brendyn's reach as possible, its dark gemblade glittering faintly in the firelight. Skrak squatted on the floor, his shoulders hunched. A strangely sad look, or the closest thing his visage could manage, passed across his features. His voice was barely more than a whisper. "Take your weapon, Little One. Slay Skrak. He is deserving of death."

Brendyn looked at him in confusion. Slowly, he rose to his feet and crossed the chamber. He bent down and picked up Volker, then turned his puzzled gaze back on the Jaf. Sheathing the Elvinknife he returned to the fire and sat down cross-legged. "Why should I kill you? You haven't hurt me."

Skrak let out a rasping sigh, bowing his head. "Skrak has hurt you more than you know, Little One. He did not save you from the Dark Ones. He is truly a betrayer . . . he first betrayed his King and his family, then his master, and now you."

The Jaf made a harsh croaking sound, and Brendyn realized the creature was weeping. He felt oddly stirred to pity, rather than fear. He leaned forward and gently laid a small hand on the bristly fur of the creature's arm. "What have you done?"

Skrak slowly raised his head and looked at the boy, wondering at the compassion he saw in the child's face. He lowered his gaze again. "What has Skrak *not* done, Little One? Not many yet live that remember the beginning, but perhaps that must change."

The Jaf fell silent for a moment. "The first betrayal came many of your mortal centuries ago . . . indeed, *Ages* ago. Near the end of the First Age, before Man walked the face of En Orilal, and dominion was held by the Firstborn Elves, there was strife between Elekar and the chief of the Alar—Skrak will not speak his true name, for it has long been denied him. The Elves call him Machaelon, the Men of Athor name him Thanatos, but all living creatures know him as the Deathlord.

"Machaelon sought to be the Lightlord's equal in all things, and so powerful did he seem that many of the Alar and the Firstborn followed him . . . including this one."

Brendyn stared at the creature in wide-eyed astonishment. "Do you mean you were an Elf once?"

The Jaf bobbed his head in response. "We Jaf and our cousins, the Drolar, were not always the beasts which you see now, Little One. Nay, we were once of the first race of the Elvinfolk—the mighty race, the noble race—until the betrayal.

"Machaelon was aware that Elekar planned to bring a new race to En Orilal, the race of Men, and so he plotted to bring his own form of life to the world. From the roots of the mountains he formed the shells, deformed mockeries of what he perceived the form of Man to be, but he did not have the power to create life. Instead, he convinced those of the Firstborn who served him to forsake the bodies given them by Elekar and take the form of the creatures made by his hand.

"But Elekar was aware and his vengeance was swift. He came upon the rays of the sun in fiery wrath. He cast Machaelon into Mâelen Orilal, the Under Realm, along with the Alar who followed him—those which have become the Dark Alar—and drew forth the spirits that inhabited Machaelon's creatures and cursed them to the form of the Drolar and Jaf. Skrak—though he was not called that then—knew at once that he would forever be parted from his wife and son and fled in bitter anguish. Indeed, his wife took their son and walked the Road to Elekar, where Skrak could no longer follow.

"When Machaelon brought his Kubruki and other creatures from Mâelen Orilal into En Orilal to wage war against the servants of Elekar, he summoned the Drolar and Jaf to him, but Skrak betrayed him . . . he understood the evil he had committed against Elekar and refused to be

214

led astray once more by the Deathlord. Machaelon then made Skrak doubly cursed, for he took away his immortality—there is little power left in Skrak, very little. Just enough to make the Dark Ones fear him still."

The Jaf fell silent for a moment, his eyes almost completely closed, showing only the slightest sliver of red.

Brendyn cocked his head in puzzlement. "But how did you betray *me?*"

Skrak's eyes opened wide and he turned his fiery gaze on the boy. "Little One, Skrak *lied* to you. The Dark Ones do not hunt you, for they are dead . . . every one of them. They could not stand against the Living Flame and knew it when they set upon your caravan. The one who sent them also would fall before Denasdervien. Kerebros the Wolf commanded Skrak to take you unharmed, for he would trade your life for that of your father's. In return, Machaelon would return my power and immortality."

An image flashed through Brendyn's mind, the image of a wild-man dressed in wolf skins. His blue eyes widened in fear and his trembling hand reached again for Volker's hilt, but the small voice within stayed his hand yet again. He could no longer find it within him to either fear or hate the miserable creature. With head bowed, tears began to run down his cheeks as hopelessness overcame him.

Brendyn felt his chin gently lifted by Skrak's rough hand. The Jaf stared into his young face, head cocked curiously, the light of his eyes dimming slightly. He looked into the boy's eyes for a long moment before squatting back. His fanged maw parted in an expression of anger, his eyes narrowing. "No, it cannot be this way. I cannot listen again to Machaelon's deceptions. There will be no redemption. Skrak is cursed to be alone, to live out his long life, then die and dwell forever in Darkness.

"No, Skrak must betray once more, and this betrayal will likely mean his death. He will not sacrifice you, Little One

. . . you must escape. It is no use going back to the caravan. Skrak does not doubt that the Wolf or his pack watches that path. You must find your own way back to the lands of Men and leave Kerebros and his Wolves to your father. Come with Skrak . . . at once."

Scuttling on fours, the Jaf vanished into the tunnel leading out to the clearing. Staring after the creature in wonder, Brendyn followed Skrak out of the cave. Skrak led the boy around to the southwestern edge of the cliff and pointed into the dark forest. "Do your eyes see that path?"

Brendyn squinted into the shadows, but all he could see was the tangle of the wood and darkness beyond. Slowly, he shook his head. "I can't see anything."

"It is there, but it is hidden," the Jaf hissed in reply. "The Dark Ones made it, but they hid it so eyes untrained might not see it. It is marked by large stones of similar size and shape, first on one side of the path and then the other . . . do you see it now?"

The Jaf patted a large round rock at the edge of the wood. "See?"

Brendyn looked at the stone, then again stared into the wood, this time seeking a similar stone. At once, his eyes found what he sought about ten feet into the forest. Ten feet farther, gleaming in the moonlight streaming through the trees, he saw another stone. "Aye! I see them now!"

"If you follow stone to stone, you will not lose your way," Skrak rasped. The Jaf placed both his clawed hands on Brendyn's shoulders and turned the boy to face him, leaning his fanged maw closer to Brendyn's face. "Skrak has no food or water to give to you. It will be a hard journey for one so young, but you must go this way. It is your best hope. If you travel quickly, the stones will lead you to a pond within two days' time . . . the water there is good, and you may well find berries there that are good to eat. There

216

is also a wagon trail there that will lead you out of the forest."

Skrak spun the boy back towards the forest and gave him a light shove. "Now go, Little One! Do not tarry here! I will delay Kerebros as long as I can . . . perhaps he will decide you are not worth hunting. *Go!*"

Brendyn looked back, but Skrak had already vanished from sight. Staring into the terrifying darkness of Ilkatar Forest, he drew in a deep breath and plunged into the wood.

*   *   *   *

An excruciating pain coursed through Shannon's body, waking him from his dark slumber. It was morning, or least the first rays of the dawn were breaking, for though light filtered through the trees, it was dim and unfocused. Moaning, he forced himself into an upright position, wincing at the burning pain in his head.

"Blast," he rasped, looking around himself, his eyes squinting painfully. "I've gone and slept the night through. *Now* how am I to find Brendyn?"

Slowly and painfully, Shannon climbed to his feet. He wobbled for a moment, his knees unsteady beneath him, but he finally gained his balance. He suddenly realized he could not even remember the direction from which he had come. He glanced through the treetops and tried to gauge the direction in which the sun was rising. When he thought he had his bearings, he stumbled off in what he believed to be a westward direction, deeper into the forest, with no thought but to find his younger cousin, his own health and safety completely forgotten.

He wandered through the woods, calling out his cousin's name, though his voice was still hardly more than a croaking rasp, with no thought of being heard by unfriendly ears. How long he stumbled along, he could not tell, though when he at last stepped into a clearing in the wood, the sky was showing the blue of morning and the sun was shining brightly through the leaves of the forest. He noticed a cliff at the far side of the clearing, and at its base, a small cave.

Shannon looked at the cave for a long moment, wondering if his cousin had perhaps taken shelter there in the night, or whether it was the lair for some forest animal. He slowly stepped towards the dark opening. "Brendyn? Are you in there?"

He frowned. His voice was barely audible to his own ears. No one could possibly have heard him unless they were standing near him.

As he neared the cliff, his vision began to fade. Suddenly, a sharp pain streaked through his head, bringing a brief, strangled shriek to his lips before darkness took him, and he collapsed into a limp heap upon the ground.

But the Prince's cry had not gone unheard. Almost instantly the burning red eyes of the cave's occupant appeared in the shadows. In the safety of the dark hole, the creature stared at Shannon for a long moment, pondering the appearance of the youth. "What is this? This child should not be here. . . ."

The Jaf shuffled as close to the mouth of his cave as he dared to get a better view of the boy. Seeing Shannon's bloodstained face, Skrak started in alarm. "The child is hurt!"

"Aye, he is," a deep, gruff voice responded.

Skrak looked up to see the brawny form of the Sorcerer, Kerebros, emerging from the forest. The man's amber eyes were as baleful as the wolves' heads that adorned his head and shoulders. At either side and slightly behind him strode two men in black leather, wolves' heads branded upon their sweaty foreheads.

The big man crossed the clearing to stand beside Shannon, his minions in his wake. With one foot, he roughly shoved the youth onto his back.

"Have a care, Wolf!" Skrak pleaded. "The child is no good to you dead!"

Kerebros grunted. "He is no good to me as is, Betrayer. I can sense the presence of the death that has no cure . . . he will not live to see another sunrise."

Ice clutched at Skrak's heart. The boy was dying, and there was nothing he could do to save him. But no . . . there *was* a chance, slight though it may be. "Leave him here then . . . there is one in the Land of the Mountain who might save him. Leave the child here, and I will carry him there myself when the sun fails."

The Sorcerer barked laugh in return. "Do you think I care about this boy, Betrayer? It would please me to see the Crown Prince of Gildea dead. If it were not for the venom in his veins, I would consume him now. Nay, I think I will offer him with the son of the Bearer of the Flame . . . I will gain the satisfaction that Quellin of Gildea will feel the bite of the Master's vengeance. Now, bring me my prize."

Skrak hissed in anger. "The Little One is not here, Wolf . . . I let him go! You will not find him now before the Bearer of the Flame. You know he searches even now."

The Sorcerer's face reddened in fury. "Well they name you Betrayer! I should blast you now and be done with you! But I have not the time to deal with you, Jaf. This damaged prize will have to do for now. But never fear, Betrayer . . . I *will* return to deal with you!"

Skrak's heart pounded within him as Kerebros bent over and grasped Shannon by the front of the tunic. A mixture of fear, helplessness, and fury burned in his veins. *Skrak cannot let this be! He must do something . . . Skrak must save the child!*

219

Without another thought, the Jaf launched himself from his lair, screeching in terrible agony as the sun-death instantly began in his flesh. Kerebros fell away from the Jaf's beating wings, allowing just enough room for Skrak to grasp Shannon with his taloned feet. With a mighty heave of his wings, summoning the last shreds of his power to lend him strength and life, he rose into the air, bearing Shannon with him. Below him, he could hear Kerebros bellow out in fury, cursing him as he winged his way westward towards the Land of the Mountain, Shalkan.

Despite his burden and the fire burning in his flesh, Skrak flew with the speed of his kind, the sprawling trees of Ilkatar Forest speeding past below him. Somewhere in the distance behind him, he heard a scream like that of a bird-of-prey, but he paid it no heed. Already, as his wings beat past his vision, he could see tendrils of smoke rising from his flesh. Soon, he knew white flame would begin to consume his flesh, and he would die.

No! No! his mind screamed to the dawn. *Do not let me fail this child! Do not let my last betrayal lead to his death!*

As if in answer, his waning power waxed again, and the burning agony subsided. The smell of his charred flesh was strong in his nostrils, but he ignored it as easily as he would the smell of an animal's rotting carcass, grateful for the brief respite from the Curse of Darkness, to which he knew he must eventually succumb. Funneling his power into the strength of his wings, Skrak pushed himself to greater speeds.

Ilkatar Forest passed behind him, opening into the sprawling fields between the wood and Barrier Mountain. In but four hours, he had crossed a distance that would have taken the Gildean caravan no less than four days. Already, he could feel the sun-death once again taking hold. Indeed, he caught glimpses of white flames licking at the edges of his wings and bone beginning to show in spots.

With determination, he used his last surge of power to soar over the edge of Barrier Mountain and into the canyon that was Shalkan. Spying the place he sought, he wheeled towards the ground, though more quickly than he intended for his strength was quickly leaving him. He tried to slow his descent, but still landed heavily. Shannon slipped from his grasp as they struck the ground, and Skrak tumbled head over heels until coming to rest in a wasted heap.

The Jaf's vision was rapidly darkening, but before it forsook him completely, he saw the shadow of a man standing near. He croaked out a few last words before he lost the strength to do even that. "*Save . . . the boy . . . save him.*"

"*Prince Shannon!*" he heard the man exclaim. "*Master Gwydnan! Master Gwydnan! Come quickly!*"

There was a momentary pause, then an elderly voice joined the first. "*By all that is holy! Kanstanon, take Prince Shannon to my room . . . do not argue! I will deal with this creature.*"

The last few words were almost inaudible to Skrak. There was no doubt in his mind as to his fate. He gave up his struggle to live and let the fire consume him. There was burning pain, but also silence. He expected at any moment to see the Black Pits of Hâl open before him and draw him into his final punishment.

But they did not. Instead, the elderly voice spoke again, this time in his mind, stronger, more clearly. "*You have proven your loyalty with this act, and your heart repentant for your past transgressions. Fanos Pavo shall grant what your heart most desires. But Skrak of the Jaf must still perish, for he is a Creature of Darkness and cursed forever. . . .*"

Now, it is time, the Jaf thought. *Now Skrak shall die.*

But instead, a bright flame of white blinded his mind's eye. He felt a searing heat, a sensation that his flesh was indeed being scorched from his bones, and an inhuman scream escaped his jaws. But even through his agony, strength began to return to him and life and . . . *power*. He felt a power rising within him that he had not felt in many centuries. Not the cold, dark fire of the Jaf. . . .

"*Arise now, Anselm of the Firstborn. You have been forgiven.*"

He who was once Skrak the Betrayer opened his eyes and found himself standing upright in the full light of the sun. He raised his hands before him and saw not the coarse, black, fur-covered flesh of a Jaf, but skin both fair and smooth, shining with the glory of the Elves. In utter amazement, he raised his sky-blue eyes to the old man standing on the porch of the house and spoke, his voice melodic in his own ears after the centuries of Skrak's rasp. "How . . . how can this be?"

"It is no doing of mine, Elf," the old man replied shortly in a weary voice, leaning heavily on his cane. "You are free . . . do what you will with your freedom. Right now, I have a child on the verge of death to care for."

"Yes, yes, of course," the Elf, Anselm, responded, a wave of concern shoving away his amazement and joy at his miraculous release. "Can you save him?"

Gwydnan turned and started to hobble back into the house. "I do not know, Elf."

Anselm followed the old man into the house and to his chamber near the dining room. Kanstanon had laid the youth on Gwydnan's bed. Shannon's face, beneath the dirt and dried blood, was pallid, his eyes sunken and dark.

Kanstanon gave a start when he saw the naked Elf, but Gwydnan cut him off before he could speak.

"There is no time," the old man barked. "Now, out! Both of you . . . and for goodness' sake, Kanstanon, get the Elf some clothes."

The stablehand did not question his master. He hurried out of the room, drawing the strange Elf with him.

Gwydnan closed the door, then went to Shannon's side. He gently tried to remove Shannon's crown, but it held fast. He gave the boy a look of sad compassion. "Ah, lad, I fear this is going to be painful. The blood has sealed the crown to the wound."

With a firm hand, he slowly forced the crown away, but the act brought only the vaguest moan to the boy's lips, which brought graver concern to Gwydnan's heart. Blood trickled anew from the cut on Shannon's forehead, but not as heavily as before . . . he had lost much, perhaps too much. Gwydnan reached over to his wash basin and withdrew a rag. He washed the remaining blood from the boy's forehead and face, then bent nearer to examine the surprisingly tiny cut just above Shannon's right brow— his battered crown had clearly taken the brunt of the blow. He gently rubbed a bit of black, metallic residue from the wound with his forefinger.

"Blast!" he muttered.

The old man seemed to struggle in indecision for a few minutes. Finally, taking a small knife from a pouch at his belt, he cut away Shannon's tunic. Leaning heavily on the edge of the bed, Gwydnan began whispering in the Athorian Tongue. "*Fänos Pävo, apä de maphe eäthen gwokhen panwoth. Hyobjas eäth ekweos bo ekek eäthen peth meekaen.*"

After he had spoken, Gwydnan placed his right hand over Shannon's heart and his left hand upon the boy's wound. He could feel the last remaining spark of a once great Fire slowly begin rising to its former glory, filling his

223

whole being. Then the heat began to flow from him into Shannon.

He stood there for a long time with his hands upon the boy, the Fire within him growing steadily stronger. Finally, it flared to its peak, then slowly began to weaken until it died away entirely. Gwydnan slumped down into a soft, high-backed chair, too weak to even move.

* * * *

Kerebros the Wolf stared up at the sky, his amber gaze following the vanishing silhouette of the Betrayer, amazed at the vain boldness shown by the creature, yet cursing at his final betrayal. At last, he turned to his Wolves, glowering. "I will *not* have my victory stolen from me. Prove your worth. Find the boy. I shall deal with the Bearer of the Flame."

His minions said nothing, but dashed into the forest, following Brendyn's scent.

* * * *

Brendyn followed Skrak's instructions and traveled as far as his young legs and weary mind could take him, which was surprisingly far, for fear of the evil that he was sure pursued him, and the hope of finding his way out of the forest lent strength to his limbs. He journeyed for hours, heedless of anything but the round stones that marked his path. The ground soon became rocky, but that did not slow his pace. Only when the first rays of the dawn began to filter through the trees did he stop.

The realization that he had walked all through the night seemed to drain what energy had been granted him, and he collapsed to the ground, his vision quickly blurring as weariness settled fully upon him. Heedless of any danger, he allowed himself to drift off to sleep, a deep and dreamless sleep. He awoke a short time later.

From what he could see through the green canopy above him, the sun was still not very high. He could not have slept for more than an hour or two, but while he was still tired, strength enough to continue a little while longer returned to him. Worse than weariness was the realization that he was very hungry and thirsty, but had no food with which to satisfy that hunger, nor water to quench his thirst.

Nevertheless, he pressed on, reminding himself that he would find something to eat when he reached the pond Skrak had spoken of. He labored along for another couple of hours before again becoming too weary to continue on. He curled up beside one of the marker stones and went to sleep again, but this time when he awoke night had fallen.

Rubbing his eyes and yawning, Brendyn climbed to his feet, then slumped down onto the marker stone, staring dully into the darkness. After crashing through the forest, pursued by Dark Elves, then coming face-to-face with the nightmarish visage of Skrak the Jaf the night before, there was very little left in the night shadows and rustling of nocturnal animals to inspire fear in the child. Hunger, thirst, loneliness . . . these things he felt intensely, but fear he had put aside. In his short life, he had faced an undead Sorcerer, survived the Great Father's scourge, and now had eluded Dark Elves and yet another Sorcerer with the aid of a Creature of Darkness, cursed by both the Dawn and the Night. Even *his* vivid imagination could not at that moment conjure up a greater or stranger threat than those from which he had escaped.

He knew he should try to walk farther, but his legs ached, he was tired, hungry, thirsty, and was quickly losing hope.

At that moment, a rustle in the nearby foliage startled him to alertness. He came to his feet, his eyes scanning the forest shadows, his hand grasping the hilt of his sheathed Elvinknife. As he peered into the woods around him, a large, four-legged shape came out of the trees. Fear began to creep into Brendyn as he recalled Skrak's talk of wolves, until the creature came into the moonlight. What he at first took to be a wolf was, in fact, a dog, and a very strange-looking dog at that.

The animal stood almost as tall as the boy and was muscular with short, golden fur. It's large head had a flat face with a heavy, drooping upper lip and large, sad eyes with an almost human quality to them. The dog sat down several feet away from Brendyn and whined at the boy, its head cocked in curiosity.

Brendyn let go of his weapon's hilt and sat back down on the rock. The dog did not seem at all aggressive, and it occurred to the child that it might be just as lost in the forest as he was. He offered the back of his hand for the animal to sniff and called out to the dog in a soft voice. "Come on . . . I won't hurt you."

The massive animal started to rise, still whining, then sat back down again. After another moment, it rose and slowly, sporadically wagging its stubby tail, stretched forward to sniff the boy's hand. Finally, it stepped closer and began to lick Brendyn's face with a long, large, wet tongue. Brendyn fell to the ground laughing, trying unsuccessfully to push the dog's head away.

Finally, the dog sat down, grinning at the boy, its tongue lolling as it panted. Brendyn dried his face on the ragged remains of his sleeve, then rose to his knees and hugged the dog around the neck. "I'm glad you found me . . . now I won't be alone."

Slowly, he pulled himself back onto the stone he was using as a seat. The dog turned its head to him and looked at him a moment more before standing up and trotting a little along the path Brendyn had been following. Brendyn started in alarm. "Where are you going?"

The dog stopped and looked back at him, then turned around and went back to the boy. It took Brendyn's cloak in its teeth and gently tugged on it, then let go and turned back to the path, looking back at Brendyn again.

"You want me to follow you?" Brendyn asked.

The dog cocked its head again, then looked down the path and back at Brendyn once more.

"But my legs hurt," Brendyn said in response to the look. "And I want to rest some more."

The dog whined at him again, then circled in place for a moment before lowering itself to the ground, crouching on all four forelegs, offering its back to the boy. It looked up expectantly at Brendyn and waited.

Brendyn stared at the animal in amazement. He had never seen a dog that seemed to understand what he was saying as well as this one, and its behavior was every bit as strange as its looks. Nevertheless, he threw one leg over the dog's broad back and gently sat down.

The animal stood up with no apparent effort under its burden, causing Brendyn to grasp the loose skin at the nape of the dog's neck to balance himself. The dog trotted into the woods once more, following the stones that marked the boy's path.

Brendyn watched in wonder as the marker stones passed by quickly on either side of them, until understanding came to him. "I wager you're getting as thirsty as me way out here, and you know where that pond is, don't you?"

The dog's short ears twitched at the sound of the boy's voice, but it kept its eyes straight ahead as it jogged through the forest.

The dog trotted easily along for hours without stopping and without the showing the faintest sign of weariness. Brendyn, on the other hand, at last began to grow tired again and started to slump forward even as the first rays of dawn were beginning to peek through the foliage. The dog stopped and gently lay down, allowing the boy to fall forward on its back, his head resting between the animal's strong shoulders.

Brendyn awoke as the sun rose to its zenith, stiff and sick with hunger. Grimacing, he sat up slowly on the dog's back, his arms wrapped tightly around his stomach. The dog lifted its large head and tilted it back slightly, whining sympathetically.

Brendyn let go of himself and grasped the dog's ruff. He licked his parched lips with an almost dry tongue. "I don't feel very good . . . I think we better find that pond soon."

As if on queue, the dog carefully rose to its feet, then loped away again, slowly gaining speed until is was running at a fair pace. Brendyn was amazed, for he barely noticed the movement of the animal beneath him, though the air whipped at his hair and stung his dry eyes.

The dog sprinted on for nearly three hours, but showed no signs of flagging. But Brendyn did not notice. His thoughts were wholly occupied with his overwhelming hunger and thirst and with how he was going to find his way home. He was not entirely without hope. His new friend was exceedingly fast and seemed to be aware of the boy's needs, but Brendyn was not sure what direction to go from the pond.

At last, they arrived at their destination. The dog slowed almost to a stop as it approached the clearing. Brendyn, as soon as he saw the pond, tumbled from the dog's back and staggered as quickly as he could to the water's edge, practically dunking his head in the water. He gulped down the precious liquid until his thirst was quenched, then turned his attention to finding food.

He knew a little of what berries and such were good to eat and what were poisonous, but there was nothing to find. What berry bushes were near the pond had been laid bare by birds and other foraging animals. Distraught by the discovery, Brendyn sat down at the edge of the pond and began to cry, fatigue and hunger finally overcoming him.

The dog whined and licked at the boy's face, but Brendyn did not respond. His blue eyes stared at the gently rippling surface of the pond, completely oblivious to anything around him, as hope was sapped from him. The dog lay down beside him, resting its large head in his lap.

Brendyn did not stir for some time, but at last the sound of a pair of heavy wagons rattling along the trail Skrak had spoken of drew him abruptly from his forlorn thoughts. Hope again kindled within him, and he leapt to his feet, turning to run towards the high hedge that separated the trail and clearing. But before he had gone a few feet, the dog bounded forward and grabbed his tattered cloak in its powerful jaws, sending the boy sprawling to the muddy ground.

The dog jumped over Brendyn and placed itself firmly between the boy and the hedge, hackles raised, its teeth bared in a snarl. The sudden change in the animal's demeanor alarmed Brendyn greatly. This dog that had been his friend and companion for the last day or so now appeared ready to savage him.

The wagons halted almost directly across the hedge from the boy. Brendyn opened his mouth to call out for help, but the dog immediately took two steps towards him, snapping its jaws menacingly. The boy froze, not daring to move or speak, though he trembled from fear of the seemingly crazed animal before him.

Soon, he heard strangely-accented voices on the other side of the hedge.

"Ye cain't do it, Brun," a high-pitched, elderly, male voice said. "'ee's jest a younger. Ye cain't jest leave 'im 'ere t'die!"

"Oh, I cain't, cain I?" the one named Brun shot back, his voice much deeper than the first. "An' jest what am I 'sposed t'do wi' th' li'l wretch? We cain't sell 'im—'ee ain't nae use t'any'un."

"But—"

"Nae buts," Brun interjected. "Bloody 'ál, Kregor, 'ee's crippled, deaf, and mute! Nae 'un wants 'im. Why I e'en let ye talk me into keepin' the runt in th' first place is beyond me. I should'er killed 'im when 'ee 'uz born, then there wouldn'er be nae trouble right now!"

"But, Brun—!" Kregor whined.

"But nothin'!" Brun growled. "I let ye talk me into keepin' th' brat as a pers'nal slave, an' I've kep' 'im now fer se'en years, but 'ee cain't do nothin'—naught 'cept eat up me vittles! Th' boy goes, an' 'ee goes now. An' if ye gots any objectens, Kregor, ye kin join 'im!"

There was a pause before Kregor spoke again. This time his voice was heavy with sorrow. "Sorry, lad. I did what I could."

Brendyn's attention was focused entirely on the conversation now. He did not notice as the dog relaxed and came to lie down beside him again.

Suddenly, he heard a thud, then the shape of a child crashed through the base of the hedge, rolling down the slight incline. The boy slid into a thicket of vines at the base of the incline, the thorny cords wrapping themselves around his body. The boy lay still, not daring to move lest he cut himself.

Brendyn flinched. The very sight caused his skin to prickle, as if the thorns wrapped around the other boy's body were poking into his own flesh.

"C'mon, Kregor," he heard Brun say again. "We'd best be movin' . . . these 'uns 'ere 'bouts nae take kindly to our sort."

A moment later, the wagons started off again, trundling northward through the forest.

As the sound of the wagons faded, Brendyn turned his gaze to the dog now lying next him, whining apologetically. "You knew they were bad men, didn't you?"

The dog's stubby tail wagged slowly as the boy rubbed its head.

Brendyn slowly rose to his feet and approached the place where the other boy lay. The other child looked to be about the same age, though perhaps a bit smaller and clearly underfed. His hair was a thick, tangled, black mop that hung down in his face. From between the unruly strands that dangled past his brow, piercing green eyes stared back.

The boy was clad only in breeches, and Brendyn could see clear signs that he had not been treated well, though none of this child's scars were anywhere near as terrible as his own. Masses of thin, thorny vines securely held the boy where he lay. The boy stared back at Brendyn in apprehension, but still he did not move.

Unable to shake the uncomfortable sensation of thorns pricking his flesh and no little trepidation of his own, Brendyn chewed on his lower lip, trying to reason his course. "Well, I can't leave you there like that. I guess I'm going to have to cut you out of those vines."

He took a step towards the boy, drawing Volker from its sheath.

Tears began streaming from the child's eyes at the sight of the weapon in Brendyn's hand, and he started to wriggle backwards, entangling himself even more. Small rivulets of blood began to appear where the thorns cut into his flesh, but the boy made no sound, though pain showed clearly on his face, mixed with terror.

Brendyn stopped his advance, wincing in empathy, the thought of the thorns biting into his flesh making him slightly ill. He placed his hands on his hips, careful to avoid the razor edge of Volker's Stajouhar blade. "Now look here, I'm not going to hurt you. I'm trying to get you out of there."

He knew the boy could not hear him, for Brun had said he was deaf, but the sound of his own voice in the relative silence of the clearing was somewhat comforting to himself. He looked down at the dog who had come to sit beside him, its long wet tongue lolling from between it's strong jaws, and displayed his Elvinknife to the animal. "He thinks I mean to use this on him. What am I supposed to do? I can't just leave him there, but I can't get him out of those vines if he won't let me."

The dog lowered its head and whined helplessly.

Brendyn turned his gaze back to the other boy, who had been curiously watching Brendyn's dialogue with the dog, and heaved a sigh. "Well, he's just going to cut himself up in those vines, but there's nothing for it . . . I can't help him just standing here."

As Brendyn continued forward, knife in hand, the other boy to pull back again, but the vines now held him fast. Brendyn knelt down just beyond the edge of the briars and stretched out to start cutting the vines from around the boy's ankles. A look of surprised understanding crossed the deaf mute's face, and he carefully slid back towards Brendyn.

Brendyn again winced sympathetically. It was painful just to watch the other boy writhing in the grasp of those thorns, but the boy understood that Brendyn could not reach the bulk of the vines if he did not move closer. Carefully, Brendyn cut away the vines from around the boy's torso and arms and finally a single cord that had wrapped itself around the other boy's throat. He breathed a sigh of relief as he lifted the last vine away from the boy, then sheathed his Elvinknife and helped him out of the thicket.

Brendyn assisted the other boy to the shade beneath a tree near the pond. The child shivered a little. Despite the heat of the summer day, a cool breeze did pick up a little. Brendyn removed his tattered cloak and fastened it around the other boy's bare shoulders. "That should keep you a little warm anyway."

The boy wrapped the cloak around himself and smiled at Brendyn.

Brendyn returned the smile. "My name is Brendyn—what's yours?"

The boy cocked his head as if trying to understand the words spoken to him.

Brendyn sighed. "You can't even hear what I'm saying, or answer me if you could. But still, I can't just call you *you*, so I guess I've got to give you a name. Let's see. . . ."

He took a moment to ponder several names he knew, trying to match them with the boy's face, but nothing seemed to fit. The boy was rather nondescript . . . or at least Brendyn could not seem to focus well enough on the child's face to describe it. It was the gleam in the boy's green eyes that finally brought something to his mind.

"That's it!" Brendyn exclaimed. "*Arban!* I will call you Arban! That's Elvin for *Bright-Eyes*, you know—I learned that from Lord Guthwine. Mama calls me that sometimes—Bright-Eyes, that is, not Arban."

The boy sat there, watching in silent amusement while Brendyn babbled on, oblivious to what was being said, but understanding that Brendyn was trying to convey something to him.

Brendyn jabbered on, his only audience an old dog and a deaf-mute, but it did not matter. His stomach ached and growled from hunger, but he was no longer alone. Talking kept his mind off his hunger, and so he kept on, until he noticed the Arban glance at the pond and lick his dry lips. The mute boy turned imploring eyes back on Brendyn, who sighed and motioned towards the water. "You don't need my permission to get a drink. Go on."

Arban smiled and scurried surprisingly quickly on his hands and one good knee to the edge of the nearby pond, his left leg dragging limply behind him.

As the boy drank, Brendyn leaned back against the tree and tried, without great success, to keep his thoughts from his stomach. Thinking of nothing better to do, he took up the flute that Berephon had given him, which hung around his neck by a leather thong, and tried practicing the song the young Bard had taught him. The song was a slow and haunting melody as Berephon played it, but Brendyn had difficulty remembering all the notes. What he played was at least recognizable, but halting and severely discordant.

Noticing movement in front of him, Brendyn glanced up. Arban had seated himself directly across from Brendyn, watching him play in curiosity. After a moment, Arban held his hand out, glancing from Brendyn to the flute, then back again.

Brendyn slowly drew the flute's cord over his head and started to hand the instrument over to the other boy, but paused, a suspicious look in his gaze. "Are you *really* deaf?"

Arban cocked his head as if trying to comprehend the question, but did not reply. His gaze returned to the flute, and slowly he took it from Brendyn. He began to run it beneath his pursed lips as he had seen Brendyn do, but no sound came forth.

Brendyn fell on his back laughing, then raised himself to a sitting position again, shaking his head. "No, no . . . you have to *blow* in it."

He reached and grabbed both the flute and Arban's hand and drew them to himself. Brendyn lightly blew on the other boy's hand, then across the flute's pipes. Surprised understanding came over Arban's face, and the boy raised the flute to his lips once more.

Brendyn giggled again, expecting to hear a racket worse than his own, but his grin was rapidly replaced by stunned amazement, for what he heard was the very song he himself had been trying to play, note-for-note as Berephon had played it, with all the young Bard's intensity and emotion. Even the dog raised its head and stared at the mute boy. After a few strains, Arban noticed Brendyn's look and abruptly stopped, holding the flute out to Brendyn, a slightly fearful look on his face.

Brendyn slowly shook his head and gently pushed the other boy's hand back. His wonder was no less than it had been a moment before, but he managed a shaky smile. "Nay, you keep it . . . you are better at it than I am."

Arban looked at the flute, then looked back up at Brendyn and pointed to himself.

Brendyn gave him a nod. "Aye, it's yours."

The other boy beamed as he slipped the flute's thong over his head.

Brendyn sat back and looked around, his gaze finally landing on the high bushes that hid the clearing where the boys sat from the road. He stared thoughtfully at the vegetation for a long moment before rising to his feet. "The wagon trail Skrak told me about must be on the other side of those bushes. That's the way we have to go to get out of this forest."

He glanced down at Arban. "But you can't walk. I guess you'll have to ride the dog, and I'll walk."

Brendyn helped his new friend onto the back of the dog, though Arban resisted, reluctant to climb astride the large animal. When Arban was finally situated straddling the dog, Brendyn turned and walked a few steps towards the hedge line. The dog, however, did not follow him.

Brendyn turned and looked at the animal, hands on his hips. "Well, come on."

The dog raised its head again and looked at him expectantly, but did not otherwise move.

Brendyn sighed. "We can't stay here. There isn't any food, and I'm hungry. I want to go home."

The dog raised itself up, eliciting a look of surprise, then a delighted grin, from Arban. It trotted to Brendyn, then lay down again in front of the boy, looking up at him.

"You want me to ride, too?" Brendyn said, raising his eyebrows in surprise. "But I don't know if you can carry both of us."

The dog did not budge.

"Well, all right," Brendyn said with a shrug. He sat down behind Arban on the dog's broad back, then waited for the dog to struggle to its feet.

The big animal stood up effortlessly, much to Brendyn's surprise, and trotted through a break in the hedge line and started jogging southward along the wagon trail—the opposite direction from that taken by Brun and Kregor. The dog's pace was much slowed, but Brendyn suspected that the dog was simply taking care not to lose either of its passengers, rather than struggling beneath the weight of the two children. With smooth strides, the animal trotted quickly down the worn and rutted trail, bearing its wards as swiftly as it dared towards the southwestern edge of Ilkatar Forest and to the grasslands beyond.

As the day wore on, it became more and more difficult for Brendyn to ignore his rumbling stomach. He felt ill with hunger, a condition doubled by the loping movement of the dog beneath him. He felt bile rising to his throat and swallowed, but his queasiness grew persistently worse.

The boy seated before him, as if sensing his distress, craned his head around to look at Brendyn, a worried look on his face. He lowered his gaze again, staring hard at the back of the dog's head, then looked back in forlorn helplessness. The dog, however, also seemed to detect that something was amiss and gradually slowed to a halt.

As the dog lowered itself to the ground, Brendyn again felt his gorge rising and knew he could not hold it back this time. He desperately slid off the dog's back and tried to scramble to the side on his hands and knees, but had only gone a couple of feet before vomiting the liquid contents of his otherwise empty stomach, gagging on the bitter juices. When he was finished, he rolled over onto his back, grimacing in disgust, wishing he had some water to wash the sour taste from his mouth and relieve his burning throat.

His stomach ached terribly, but he decided he no longer had an appetite for food even if it were available. He rolled over on his side, curling into a ball in an effort to relieve the cramps in his stomach, but to no avail. Tired, hungry, and in pain, he began to cry. Even as a slave at Lener Keep, he had never been without the necessities of life, not even for a short while, and despair had firmly planted its claws into his young heart. Through his suffering, he was sure he would die.

Brendyn felt a gentle touch and opened his eyes. Through tear-blurred eyes, he could see Arban sitting beside him, his lame leg folded beneath him at an awkward angle, though he did not seem to notice. Brendyn wiped his eyes and nose on his tattered sleeve. With his vision somewhat cleared, he could see that Arban also had tears in his eyes.

The deaf-mute reached his hand out and awkwardly patted Brendyn's head, trying to console him. When that did not seem to work, Arban pulled his hand away. He looked down at the flute dangling at his chest, then slowly raised it to his lips and began to play the *Lay of Zhayil-Khan*, the haunting notes filtering through the trunks and branches of the wood like a ray of sunshine.

Brendyn, still sobbing, listened to the song, allowing its soothing melody to flow over him. Through his pain and distress, he felt a strange peace come over him, as though the music had some hidden, gentle power which drove away fear and doubt. Brendyn closed his eyes, putting aside thoughts of his pain, of hopelessness, secure in the knowledge that he was not alone.

Chapter 11

Brendyn was awakened by a wet assault from his canine companion as its large tongue slathered his face. Barely conscious, his sticky eyes still tightly closed, he shoved the dog's muzzle away, mumbling, "Go away. I want to sleep."

The dog whined and tugged hard at the boy's sleeve, raising his head a little. The dog let go, and Brendyn's head thudded back to the ground. Brendyn sat up, his hand flying to the back of his head. "*Ow!* All right, I'm awake already. Stupid dog."

He noticed movement next to him and turned his head to watch Arban rising into a sitting position, rubbing the back of his head, glaring accusingly at Brendyn.

"It wasn't me," Brendyn replied to the look. He pointed to the dog. "It was him."

The dog looked back in the direction from which they had come and sniffed the air, then let out a low growl. It pulled on Brendyn's sleeve again, let go and looked southward along the road, then tugged again, whining.

Brendyn pulled away and slowly, weakly, rose to his feet. "All right. I suppose the sooner we leave, the sooner we'll get home."

He glanced back into the forest, a brief stab of fear piercing his heart. Skrak had told him that Kerebros would hunt him. He wondered if that was perhaps what the dog smelled . . . the Sorcerer or his Wolves. He felt a wave of worry pass over him, and he turned and looked at Arban, putting on a brave smile, though he knew he could not hide his feelings from his new friend. Arban knew he was afraid—he could feel it, just like Brendyn could feel his friend's care and anxiety.

The dog lowered itself onto its belly, allowing Brendyn and Arban to remount, then rose up and started down the road. The animal trotted along at a slightly faster pace, forcing the boys crowded on its back to cling to its fur to remain seated. Hours later, as night fell, they left the forest and started across the grasslands which lay between Ilkatar Forest and Barrier Mountain, their destination.

The night deepened around them, and still the dog ran on. Not until the boys were teetering dangerously on their perch did the dog finally stop. Brendyn and Arban both slid down from the animal's back and sprawled on the dry ground, quickly embracing the oblivion of sleep.

Neither of them noticed the dog leave.

*   *   *   *

Novosad and his companions retraced their steps through the forest, leaving behind the Dark Elf outpost, wondering whether they would return to find the caravan destroyed, or whether the Dark Elves had failed, as Aliana suggested they would. Though the path looked different in the morning light, their tracks were fresh enough and undisturbed that Copanas and Lehan were able to discern their path. Though fear and uncertainty drove them on, Aliana's wounds slowed their pace.

At last they arrived at the clearing from which they had followed the trail of the wolf to the Dark Elf outpost. As they stepped to edge of the clearing, Lehan came to an immediate halt, splaying his arms to hold back his companions. He pointed to the dirt floor of the clearing, gaping. "Look!"

Novosad followed Lehan's gesture and started in surprise, his mind almost immediately registering what was before him. Where several hours before there had only been their prints and those of the wolf they followed, now he saw many more. Slowly, careful not to disturb the prints any more than necessary, Novosad and his companions advanced, examining the new marks.

Novosad knelt down and touched two sets of prints which disturbed him greatly, both smaller and lighter than any of the others, human in shape. "The smaller of these could be Prince Brendyn, Princess Sîan, or the servant girl, but the larger could only be Shannon or . . . or Karel."

"I would venture Prince Shannon," Aliana offered, kneeling down beside Novosad. "The boots that made these were heavier than your daughter's."

Novosad nodded, feeling some small relief at the observation. "Aye, I agree. Karel wears archer's boots. They leave a much lighter track."

"It looks like he may have collapsed here," Copanas said, closely examining the ground about ten feet away from the cliff. "There are gouges in the ground where his head would have lain . . . I would guess imprints from his crown."

Novosad rose to his feet and went to examine the marks his companion had found. "Aye, so it would appear. My guess is that Prince Brendyn ran into the forest and Prince Shannon followed him . . . but Shannon was either hurt or was struck down at this spot. There *is* a set of prints belonging to a man here as well . . . but nay, there is no sign of violence."

"And what of these prints?" Lehan asked gesturing to two more sets belonging to nothing resembling a human.

One set was large and canine, but different from the wolf prints they had found earlier, and the second set belonged to some large creature with taloned feet.

Novosad shook his head. "I do not know what to make of these, particularly these clawed prints. I have never seen the like."

"The Wolves of Kerebros?" Copanas ventured.

"Possibly," Aliana affirmed. "There are two more sets of prints here belonging to Men . . . their feet are bare."

Novosad followed the taloned tracks a short way, then turned back to his companions, pointing out the trail the prints took. "Look here. Whatever the creature was followed the younger child's steps into this cave, but then both come out again . . . only the clawed tracks stop at the forest's edge, while the child's continue on. And they seemed to be no hurry . . . the child was not running. The clawed tracks then return to the cave, only to come out again and vanish at the place where Prince Shannon fell."

Aliana frowned, a puzzled look entering her sky-blue eyes. "The creature is not one of the Wolves then, for I do not believe they would allow the child to walk away. The Wolves that were here, however, were hurried, for they pursue the child's tracks into the forest . . . and they *were* running."

She stared hard at the mouth of the cave. "Whatever I sensed here before is no longer present. I think that this was perhaps the lair of the creature with the taloned feet. Its presence was . . . strange. It did not feel evil, but it also did not seem quite . . . *right*."

"Perhaps one of us should search the cave," Lehan offered.

Novosad inclined his head to his companion. "Aye, do so. You may want to make a torch."

Lehan looked more than a little uncomfortable. "I was not volunteering. . . ."

His Captain pointed to the cave. "I was not asking for volunteers."

"Do not fear," Aliana assured the scout. "The presence I felt no longer dwells here."

Lehan cast her a rueful grimace, but did not answer her. Instead, he set himself to making a brand with which to search the cave.

While his brother was investigating the cave, Copanas followed the last set of tracks, the booted prints of the third Man. Finally, he stopped and shook his head. "These are no Dark Elf's footprints . . . much too large. They lead east, back towards the camp, but vanish shortly after they enter the forest."

"That is because he is no ordinary man," Aliana answered him. "He is Kerebros the Wolf, Sorcerer of Machaelon. He seeks the blood of the Bearer of the Flame."

Before either Novosad or Copanas could respond, Lehan emerged from the mouth of the cave, extinguishing his torch in the dirt as he did so. He held up his right hand, displaying a ring. "There was nothing in there but the ashes of a fire and this. . . !"

The ring glittered in the sun, Silver-gold and Elvindiamond.

"Prince Brendyn," Novosad breathed. "I thought it likely, but I could not be sure until now."

"What do we do now?" Copanas asked.

Novosad glanced at him. "What do you mean?"

"Do we return to camp and gather a search party, or do we follow Prince Brendyn ourselves?" Lehan answered for his twin.

Novosad looked eastward into the woods, in the direction of the camp. He yearned to find out whether all was well with his daughter, what had happened in the night, and with more men, they might have better luck locating the children.

"I do not believe we have a choice," Aliana's voice broke into his thoughts. "The camp has Denasdervien to protect it. Young Prince Brendyn is alone in a hostile forest, hunted by a Sorcerer and his cursed minions."

Novosad turned his gaze briefly on the Elfess, then sighed and looked westward. "We find the Princes . . . Brendyn, at the least. Shannon, if the gods will."

Silently, the four companions plunged into the forest. Relentlessly, they tracked Brendyn, for they hoped to find him before he could go too far. The child's trail was easy to follow for awhile, but soon the ground became rocky, and Brendyn's tracks were lost. Even the trees thinned to a few scattered and sickly saplings.

"Even this ground should yield some clue as to Prince Brendyn's direction," Lehan grumbled. "It is as if he simply up and flew away."

"We are missing something," Novosad replied. "It is here, but we are not seeing it."

"Begging your pardon, Captain," Copanas returned, placing his hands on his hips. "We have searched this area a hundred feet in every direction. There is scarcely a tree to be seen, much less a little boy's footprints."

"Captain Novosad speaks true," Aliana said, wearily lowering herself onto a large, round, white stone, bracing her head with one hand, her eyes closed. "Mortal children do not grow wings. The signs are here . . . we are simply missing them. There are few signs that I should miss, but my sight is clouded. I have failed you . . . for that I must apologize."

Novosad stepped towards the Elfess, dropping to one knee before her, eyeing her closely in worry. Aliana's skin had taken a slightly ashen hue, and her inner light seemed somehow dimmed. "Lady Aliana? You look ill . . . perhaps Copanas or Lehan should take you back to the camp."

"Nay," Aliana replied, shaking her head. "I will live. If this what you mortals call weariness, I do not envy you your state. I need only to rest awhile."

Aliana's weakness troubled Novosad, but he knew it was useless to try and further dissuade her from going on with them. "Very well. We will rest here for an hour, then continue westward. Hopefully we shall find some sign of Prince Brendyn's passing ere sundown."

*　*　*　*

Elgern leaned with his back against a tree at the edge of the forest, staring into the night-darkened wood, twisting his drooping, golden mustache in thought. Things were worse than he had first imagined. He should have returned from the Far North sooner. He had known for some time that Dark Elves had dwelt in the forest, but they had thus far posed no threat, and so he had placed them farther down his list of priorities to be dealt with . . . but now they seemed to be moving, and they had allies.

He had also known of Anselm's presence, the cursed one who was called Skrak in the tongue of Machaelon—the Betrayer, betrayer of two masters and his own kith, had now betrayed a third master, Kerebros the Wolf. Elgern had long felt that Anselm's repentance had been true, but the creature he had become was afraid, afraid of both the Flame and the Shadow. Still, he had proven himself by letting the Bearer's son go free and by sacrificing himself to save the young Prince of Gildea.

In a twist that Elgern had not expected, Brendyn of Shalkan had found a very special friend in the strangeness that had been his escape. Brendyn was safe, for now, as was the fate of Milhavior, but he would have to be brought to civilized lands quickly, for he was succumbing quickly to dehydration, and the Wolves were gaining on him.

Elgern had not the healing gifts of his cousin in Gildea, but the Wolves were a threat he could deal with.

A rustling in the underbrush nearby drew his attention. He looked up through his thick brows and broke into a jovial grin as two men stepped out of the shadows of the forest, as of yet unaware of his presence. There was no doubt . . . these were the spawn of Kerebros. The dark fire of the Sorcerer's curse burned in their veins, perspiration from the terrible heat drenching their flesh and matted hair. Their amber eyes gleamed faintly in the darkness.

"Well now," Elgern said, still grinning. "What have we here? Cubs of Kerebros? Don't you know this is the territory of Elgern Warhound? What business have you here, pups?"

Startled, the bandits looked in his direction, quickly shielding their eyes as though Elgern shone with a blinding light. The nearer of the pair growled out, "Don't get 'tween us and the Great Wolf's prey, dog of the Dawn."

"Or what?" Elgern laughed. "You are but a nuisance, pup. Abandon your hunt and return to your master. You shall not have the children. They are well beyond your reach."

The Wolves glanced at each other with a slightly bewildered look, then the first one replied, "We want only the son of the Bearer of the Flame. We will allow any others to go free . . . for now."

So, they do not know of the other. It is also likely then that they do not know his significance. Elgern's grin broadened. "Why should I give you the son of the Bearer? So that you may destroy Brendys of Shalkan and the hope of Milhavior? So that the Deathlord may return and bring eternal night to this world? I think not, Whelp of Kerebros. I will not let you pass."

The Wolf's eyes narrowed. "Then we'll have to move you out of the way."

Elgern chuckled. "You are welcome to try."

The eyes of the Wolves burst into red flame and they began to change, to grow and distort, transforming into the bloodlusting monsters Kerebros had made of them. Elgern poised to leap, still grinning, a golden light growing in his eyes, spreading out around his body, enveloping him in its powerful embrace.

*   *   *   *

Brendyn was awakened once more by the dog licking his face. He felt the animal's tongue, wet against his painfully dry skin, but it was several minutes before he was able to open his eyes. He felt drained of all strength, barely able to move. His lips were dry and beginning to crack, his tongue felt thick and swollen, and the inside of his mouth was like cotton. The morning sun had not yet begun to heat the air, and there was a faint, slightly cool breeze, renewing a little of his strength.

The boy slowly pulled himself up into a sitting a position, rubbing his dry and gritty eyes. When he finally looked up, he saw the form of Barrier Mountain rising up in the west and found hope renewed. Silently, he shook Arban until his friend also awoke. With little ceremony, both boys dragged themselves onto the dog's back, and their canine companion arose and jogged westward, careful to keep its weakened and precarious passengers from losing their seat.

In only a couple of hours, the sun had begun its ascent into the heavens. Without the shading foliage of the woods, the sun beat down oppressively upon the boys, swiftly lending strength to their ever-growing thirst. Eventually, it became difficult for Brendyn to remain upright on the dog's back. In the firm grasp of dehydration and hunger, Brendyn slid from the dog's back and collapsed to the ground, sprawled on his back. He was vaguely aware of Arban stretching out beside him on one side, his head resting against Brendyn's shoulder, and the dog laying down on the other before slipping into unconsciousness.

Dark dreams plagued the shadowy corners of his mind for what seemed an eternity, made more frightening by his inability to wake himself. He stirred a little as he felt himself raised from the ground. From someplace beyond his nightmares, he heard a faint, gruff voice say, "I have you. . . ."

Chapter 12

Brendys swept his gaze across the multitude of
bodies littering the field, fear wracking his heart,
but something told him that his fear was
unfounded . . . perhaps something in the warmth of
Denasdervien's hilt or maybe just a vain hope.
Nevertheless, neither hope nor fear abandoned him
completely. He turned again at the sound of Quellin's
voice behind him. The Gildean King was kneeling beside
Willerth, his youthful, blood-smeared face bearing the
same fear and anguish that burdened his own heart.

"Willerth, what of Shannon?" Quellin asked. "Where is
my son?"

Sorrow mixed with confusion settled over Willerth's
features. "Your Majesty, his body lies beside me. . . ."

Shock registered on his face as he rolled to look upon the
place where the Crown Prince of Gildea had fallen. "I saw
him struck down as I came from my tent . . . I swear it!"

"Struck down, he may have been," a girl's voice
answered him. "But slain, he most definitely was not."

Brendys saw then that Karel had joined them. She had
donned her cloak and gloves once more and a long-sleeved
tunic, though she left her muffler behind, trusting only to
the shadow of her hood to protect her from the rays of the

early morning sun. Her gloved finger was pointing to the ground where Shannon had lain. There in the blood-soaked mire were prints that even an untrained eye could see, too small for a man, clearly a child's.

Karel followed the tracks for a few steps, then looked up towards the forest. She glanced back at the men, and Brendys saw worry in her black eyes, though her voice did not betray it. "The footprints lead that way."

"Then that is where we shall go, as well," Quellin said, rising to his feet. He glanced at his escort commander. "Gowan, take the rest of the men and escort the women and children on to Shalkan. Head to the river, away from this forest . . . there is no telling how many more of these creatures dwell within. Kovar, I want you and Amrein to remain with us. . . ."

As he spoke, four Hagane warriors approached them and saluted.

"It appears we arrived only in time, Your Majesty" their leader said, sketching a quick bow at the shoulders.

Brendys recognized the men as the scouts who had accompanied Novosad. It did not take him long to miss the presence of Aliana, Novosad, or the twins. "Where are the others?"

The soldier turned to face Brendys. "Captain Novosad sent us back to report what we found. When we arrived, the battle was already joined."

Brendys and Quellin exchanged hopeful glances, then the Horsemaster spoke again to the scout. "Did you see aught of my son or nephew in the forest?"

The man started to shake his head, but stopped an odd look coming over his face. "Perhaps, Your Highness . . . I did not give thought to it before, but not too far beneath the eaves of the forest we stumbled across a Dark Elf. He was leaving the battle, but did not seem to be in much of a hurry. More like he was tracking something. It may well be that he was following the Princes. We could have easily missed them ourselves in the commotion."

Quellin nodded thoughtfully. "Very well, our course is clear."

He pointed at Gowan. "You get the caravan moving. Break camp at once. I want my family taken as far from this place as possible by nightfall."

"Your Majesty, perhaps you should allow me to lead the search," Gowan said in a grim tone. "I am not sure it would be in the best interest of Gildea for her King to go wandering about in a wood full of Dark Elves."

"Do you dare gainsay me?" Quellin snapped back. A look of immediate regret fell over his features, and he said in a gentler voice, "I am sorry, Gowan. I know you are only doing your duty, but my decision is made. Brendys and I will fare better than any with Denasdervien and Kalter. Do as I command."

Reluctantly, Gowan struck his heart in salute and strode away, shouting orders to his men.

The Gildean King's gaze next fell on Kovar. "Kovar, you will come with Brendys and me. I want Amrein searching from above. Gather some provisions . . . there is no telling how long this will take."

To the Hagane scouts, he said, "You four will first locate Lady Aliana and the others . . . if they are well, let them know what has happened, then split into two parties. We need to cover as much ground as possible. If ill has befallen either of the boys, seek us out at once."

"I am going with you," Karel added, her voice quiet, but resolute.

"We haven't time for this, child," Quellin replied in exasperation. "You are going on to Shalkan with the other women and children."

Karel put her hands on her hips, and even within the shadows of her hood, Brendys could see the defiant set of

251

her jaw. "First off, Your Majesty, I am *not* a child, as you well know. Secondly, you will need the best eyes available to you, and there are none better here than mine, as these men can attest."

The leader of the Hagane scouts looked uncomfortable, but did at last reluctantly agree. "Aye, Your Majesty, those eyes of hers aren't human—begging your pardon, young lady—and Captain Novosad has taught her tracking as well as any of us."

Karel flashed her icy gaze at the man only briefly before fixing it once again upon Quellin.

As Quellin stared into the girl's black eyes, Brendys knew he was not seeing the eyes of a tracker, but the progeny of a Dark Elf, wondering her intentions. Despite his assurances at Racolis Keep that he did not fear her as others did, it was clear to Brendys that there was indeed more than just a shadow of doubt. The Gildean King's gaze became suddenly and piercingly intense, and Brendys felt a momentary pang of sympathy, for he himself had felt the power of that gaze. Perhaps it was a shadow of his Half-Elvin heritage, but Quellin seemed to have a gift to discern the very souls of Men.

But Karel was not a Man. She, too, was a Half-Elf, and of far more recent lineage than Quellin. She met his gaze without flinching. After a moment, Quellin turned from her and pointed to the white hawk perched upon Kovar's arm. "There are my eyes, girl . . . we cannot be saddled with a *child*."

Brendys was taken aback by Quellin's expression and understood why he had turned away from the girl. The Gildean King's face was pale and fearful, and Brendys began to wonder what he had seen.

Kovar clearly saw the look on his King's face as well, for the falconer could not meet his King's gaze. With a nervous glance at Brendys, Kovar hesitated, then spoke.

"Your Majesty, I . . . I am afraid I must agree with the young lady. The canopy of the forest is dense . . . there is simply too much that will be hidden from Amrein that would not be hidden from trained eyes upon the ground."

Quellin's green eyes darted to the hawk, who uttered a few strange sounds. Brendys assumed that the highly-intelligent creature was affirming her master's concerns, for Quellin squared his shoulders and drew in a deep breath, composing himself. After a brief moment, the Gildean King turned back to Karel, some color returning to his features. "Very well. As it seems there is no alternative, we shall follow you. We have wasted enough time with this debate . . . as soon as Kovar has gathered our provisions, we will begin the search."

The hardness drained from Karel's face, replaced instead by a look of half-fearful relief. The girl started to survey the ground, but slowly turned to face Quellin again.

"You *do* understand, Your Majesty?" she said quietly, her black eyes almost pleading. "I *have* to go. . . ."

Quellin gave her a stiff nod, but Brendys could not read his expression.

Karel turned back to her task, slowly wandering more closely to the edge of the forest, head bowed, eyes fixed upon the ground, ignoring everything but Shannon's tracks. Amrein took to wing to begin her search from the sky, while her master hurried to the supply wains to pack some rations and water for the search parties.

Baris, the senior of the Hagane scouts, cast a nervous glance at Quellin and Brendys. "Your Majesty, Your Highness, 'tis best you hear the tidings Captain Novosad sends. . . ."

"Go on," Quellin replied, his expression unchanging, still unreadable.

"We found the tracks of a large wolf," Baris continued. "They were monstrously large. Lady Aliana and Captain

Novosad believe they may belong to the Sorcerer, Kerebros. They think he may still be wandering about the wood . . . Lady Aliana was determined to hunt this Kerebros down, so Captain Novosad and the twins went along with her."

It is no surprise, Brendys thought. *We knew he would not simply vanish.*

It was obvious to the Horsemaster that his brother-by-marriage was no more surprised than he, for if there was any change in his expression, it was only a subtle twitch in his jaw. "Does anyone have any *good* news to share?"

He sighed, then waved off the Hagane scouts.

Baris and his men saluted, then hurried away to meet Kovar at the supply wagons.

Brendys cast his eyes on his brother-by-marriage. "Clearly, you already suspected the hand of Kerebros in the attack . . . I am guessing that you are more troubled by Karel. What did you see?"

Quellin did not look at him, but Brendys could see a haunted look hiding in his green eyes. "Too much. I saw hatred, an almost savage hatred. Fear, a terrible, gnawing fear. The shadow of Evil is restless within her."

He bowed his head, closing his eyes. "I also saw love, a bright burning fire. All of these are in great conflict within her. Having seen what I have, I would be lying to say I do not fear her."

At last, he looked at Brendys, unbridled fear in his eyes. "The sooner we find Shannon, the sooner we can return to Gildea. I will never again bring my son within a stone's throw of Racolis."

"The choice may not be yours to make, Quellin," Brendys reminded him. "He will soon turn thirteen. If he were my son, growing up in Shalkan, he would be a child still and under my domain, but in your land, he will be a man . . . that is something you cannot change."

254

Quellin turned towards Karel, who was now nearly to the eaves of the forest. "You need not remind me."

Footsteps approaching from behind drew their attention. Arella was carefully picking her way to them through the carnage. Her face was pale, but it was not from the sight of the mutilated remains scattered across the battlefield. She had seen enough blood and death during the Siege of Gildea to have grown accustomed to such a sight.

Quellin took a step towards her, and she threw herself into his arms, sobbing. "Our little boy. . . ."

Quellin held his wife, soothing her. "Do not worry yourself, Arella. We will find Shannon. I promise you, we will not stop looking until we have found him . . . even if it means my own life."

Arella jerked her head back, a shocked look on her face. "Do not speak so!"

"We do not know what we may be facing in those woods," Quellin replied as calmly as he could. "It may well be that none of us returns. I make my will known now . . . if neither I, nor Shannon return, Brendys shall become King of Gildea in my place. If he, too, is lost, Shanor shall take the throne. Make known my will to Gowan so that there can be no question."

Blinking back her tears, Arella nodded silently.

Brendys did not fail to notice that Quellin did not mention Kerebros, though he also knew Arella was no fool and had likely reasoned the Sorcerer's involvement on her own already. Nevertheless, he decided it was unnecessary to mention it himself either. Instead, he reached out and touched Arella's arm, drawing her attention to him. "Is Mattina awake?"

Arella shook her head. "Nay. She was sleeping when I left the wagon. Her fever has taken a toll."

"Then there is no choice but to place this burden on you, Arella," the Horsemaster replied. After a moment's hesitation, he said, "When she awakens, she must be told that Brendyn, too, is missing. We think Shannon and Brendyn went into the forest, perhaps together. Will you do this?"

Arella took Brendys's hands in her own, giving them a squeeze. "Of course, Brendys."

Kovar rejoined the group, handing over heavy packs to both Brendys and Quellin. "Baris and his men are retracing their steps. It shouldn't take them too long to find Novosad and the others."

Quellin slung his pack over his shoulders, then embraced his wife. "We must go now before the trail becomes too cold."

Arella nodded, then kissed her husband.

Without another word, Quellin, Brendys, and Kovar turned away from the camp and hurried to catch up to Karel, who had already disappeared into the forest. Not far into the wood, Brendys and his companions came upon the place where the Hagane scouts had slain the Dark Elf. Karel was there, leaning against a tree, her gaze averted from the sight.

The sun filtering through the trees had already blackened the flesh of the corpse, and the smell of burnt flesh filled their nostrils. The flesh and bones of the creature, before their eyes, turned to ash, then crumbled, leaving no remains but a pile of smoking ash.

Swallowing back her disgust and fear, Karel leaned over the place where the Dark Elf had lain, coughing from the reek and waving the tendrils of smoke away from her. "Shannon certainly passed this way . . . and *after* the Dark Elf was slain."

"Why do you say that?" Quellin asked, knitting his brow. Then understanding dawned upon him. "The ground is hard here, except where the creature's blood was spilt. That is why Shannon's prints are so clear there."

Karel nodded and pointed further along the path. "And look there . . . the prints leading onward into the forest are not pressed into the ground, but are rather marked by the blood soaked up by his boots."

"But if the tracks fade on the hard ground, how will we trail him?" the Gildean King asked as Karel continued forward.

The girl stopped and touched a leaf on a bush to her right. Her voice wavered a little when she spoke. "There are other signs. This blood was not from his boots. I feel Willerth was right . . . Shannon is hurt, and by the looks of this trail, badly. Come. We must take care not to miss the signs, but neither can we waste any more time."

"What of Brendyn?" Brendys asked anxiously. "Do you see any sign that may lead to him?"

Karel shook her head. "Nay, but that is not to say much. His footsteps may be too light on this hard ground to leave a noticeable imprint at all. We may yet find his trail deeper in the woods. Please . . . we must continue."

Brendys thought he saw a nervous look in her eyes, but only briefly, but neither he, nor Quellin questioned her. Kovar glanced through the canopy for a sign of Amrein, but he could not see the great hawk through the treetops. Carefully following the trail of blood and quickly fading footprints left by Shannon, Karel led the men deeper into the woods.

Despite her promptings to quicken their pace, Karel led the men slowly and carefully, and Brendys noticed her occasionally hesitate and glance back the way they had come. After some time, they came to the place where Shannon had first lost consciousness. It did not take a trained eye to see the crushed vegetation and the bloodstains in the fern.

Quellin knelt beside the bed of fern, brushing the bloodstained plants with his fingers, fear openly displayed in his youthful features. His voice cracked at a near whisper. "Shannon. . . ."

Brendys put his hand on the Gildean King's shoulder. "Quellin, do not despair on me yet . . . Shannon is not here, and that is a good sign. He was able to walk again."

Quellin swallowed, then nodded.

Brendys turned his eyes to Karel, and the girl quickly looked away. "Have you seen any sign of Brendyn's passing here?"

The girl remained silent, her face averted, hands grasping her own shoulders.

Despite his own anxiety, Quellin took notice of her reticence and turned his rapidly hardening gaze on her. "Karel . . . answer him."

The girl still did not look at any of the men, but she did finally reply, her voice quavering. "I am sorry, Your Highness . . . I didn't mean to lie . . . but I . . . I *have* to find Shannon. . . ."

A chill started to spread through Brendys at her words.

"Look at me and speak plainly, girl!" Quellin barked. "What have you seen?"

Karel looked up, and Brendys could see the glistening moisture of tears in her dark eyes. "I-I saw faint signs of Brendyn's footprints back on the path where we found the Dark Elf . . . and broken and trampled underbrush heading due westward from there."

Brendys just stared at her in astonishment, torn between anger and indecision. He was furious that the girl would be so selfish as to pursue her own ends, withholding a chance of discovering Brendyn, yet at the same time he recognized his own selfishness, for to turn aside now would be to abandon his nephew, wounded, possibly dying.

Quellin stood up and closed his eyes in grief, shaking his head. "Foolish girl . . . you do not know what you have done."

The Gildean King fell silent, his eyes still closed.

Brendys turned his gaze on his brother-by-marriage. He stared for a long moment, before coming to a decision. He could not leave his son—his only living son and future King of Milhavior—to the wild, but neither could he abandon Shannon. "Quellin, you and Karel continue after Shannon . . . I will take Kovar, and we will hunt for Brendyn."

Quellin shook his head and opened his eyes, a tear escaping down his cheek. He met Brendys's gaze unwaveringly. "Nay, my brother. There is danger in this forest—too great a danger—and we are too few as is. We both know Brendyn *must* be found . . . no matter the sacrifice."

Karel started to object, but fell silent. The anguish in Quellin's face made it clear his decision did not come as easily as it fell from his lips.

Brendys, too, would have objected, but was cut short by an inhuman scream, a sound of sheer agony, followed by the screech of a bird-of-prey. All four companions abruptly turned in the direction of the sound. Brendys's first thought was that Brendyn or Shannon had been brought to harm, but he could not imagine that cry coming from human lips, no matter the pain.

The bird cried out again, and Kovar took a step forward listening intently. "Amrein has found something, though I dare not guess what."

Brendys touched Denasdervien's hilt and felt its warmth quickly rising. "Come! Evil is near, and I fear it will lead to one or the other of the boys."

259

"Agreed," Quellin replied, drawing Kalter and plunging westward into the forest, followed quickly by Brendys, Kovar, and Karel.

The journey was not short, but at last they came to Skrak's clearing, where they found Amrein waiting for them, perched in the branches of one of the trees ringing the clearing. As they entered the open space, she swooped down and alighted upon Kovar's outstretched arm, chittering wildly. Quellin, Kovar, and Karel all stared at the bird in amazement.

"What?" Brendys asked. "What is she saying?"

Kovar turned his wide eyes on the Horsemaster. "A *Jaf!* She saw a Jaf flying from here in a southwesterly direction, bearing a great burden. . . ."

"A Jaf?" Brendys echoed. "In broad daylight? But how?"

Kovar shrugged. "I know not. She says the sun-death was clearly taking hold, for smoke trailed behind it as it flew, but it departed with such speed that she could not see clearly what it bore. She followed as far as she dared, but she could not keep up."

Brendys shuddered to think that his son or nephew may have been taken by such a creature, but at the same time, he could not imagine what could cause the creature to wing its way to certain destruction in the full light of the sun. His thoughts were interrupted by Quellin's voice. The severity of the Gildean King's tone brought Brendys at once to attention.

"That is not all, Brendys," Quellin said. "She also saw Kerebros here in this clearing . . . and he was not alone."

Karel was already searching the clearing for any sign of either Brendyn or Shannon.

Fear gripped Brendys once more. "Then he may have the boys already."

"Or," Kovar started, a thoughtful look on his face. "He seeks to delay us, so that he may have a better chance of finding them before us."

"Here!" Karel called out. She stood near the northeastern edge of the cliff harboring Skrak's lair. "There are too many tracks in the clearing. I am not sure where they all lead, but *someone* passed through here, though these tracks *are* also disturbed badly enough that I cannot tell who. It may be the Sorcerer himself from what I can tell."

Quellin motioned her onward. "If that is all we have to go on, then so be it . . . we will accomplish nothing by remaining here. Lead on."

Karel gave him an uncertain look, but obeyed and started following the old and vanishing trail.

For a little under three hours, the party traveled at a quick, yet cautious pace. It became apparent to Karel that they were not tracking a single individual, but were more likely following the trail of a small group. She briefly knelt on the ground, examining one of the few fairly clear tracks she had seen along the trail. She glanced up at Quellin and Brendys. "I think we follow my father . . . these tracks are too large for a Dark Elf, and there is certainly more than one man. There are some lighter prints as well . . . Lady Aliana, I think."

"All the better," Quellin replied. "You have shown to us that you are your father's daughter, but I would still feel more confident with your father's skills added to our hunt."

"I will not argue against that, Your Majesty," Karel replied quietly. "I am indeed still a student."

Silently, they continued on until they came at last to the Dark Elf outpost, now completely empty and abandoned. Two piles of ash, somewhat scattered by the occasional breeze, were all that remained now of the Dark Elf sentries slain by Novosad and Copanas. Karel examined the ground and said with finality, "There was a fight here."

"And clearly your father was the victor," Quellin said motioning towards the ash piles.

Karel nodded. "Aye, but I see also signs that they returned the way they had come. How could we have missed them?"

"Mayhaps we did not," Kovar put in. "It may be that their prints were among those destroyed by Kerebros."

A spark of hope rose within Brendys's breast. "Perhaps, they found either Brendyn or Shannon."

Quellin sighed. "Would that I could have such hope. I would guess, at best, that they found the trail of one or the other, and Kerebros wished to keep us parted . . . the fewer in the party, the easier to deal with it."

He shook off his darkening mood. "Come, let us have a look at this outpost, then return to the clearing. Perhaps we missed a sign."

Brendys and Kovar guarded the entrance of the outpost, while Karel and Quellin went inside to check the stores. While he waited, Brendys drew forth Denasdervien. It's hilt still felt warmer than usual and vibrated slightly in his grasp. Stranger still, it's mirror Silver-gold blade had a very faint aura about it. It was as if there were a Creature of Darkness very near, yet somehow hidden. His blue eyes scanned the surrounding forest warily, but he could see nothing out of the ordinary.

Kovar noticed his look and dropped his own gaze to the sword in the Horsemaster's hand. "Your Highness, what is it?"

Brendys shook his head. "I do not know, Kovar . . . Denasdervien is not speaking clearly to me at all. It feels as though there is Evil near, yet at the same time distant."

"I am sure if there were anything to be seen, Amrein would have warned us by now," the falconer replied.

Brendys sheathed Denasdervien. "Perhaps, but you said yourself that this forest hides much from Amrein's eyes."

"That is true," Kovar acceded.

After several minutes, Quellin and Karel reappeared from the entryway. Both of them looked concerned.

"It is empty, but for three corpses," the Gildean King said. "Two were stabbed, the third was burned to death. They were all three Men."

"They had a brand like a wolf's head on their foreheads," Karel added.

"Then there is no doubt that Kerebros has been here," Brendys replied. "Nor that Novosad and the others fought here as well."

"They may have fought here, but it is clear they did not remain long," Quellin said. "I know we have not eaten yet today, but I do not think we should tarry here."

"For once, we agree, Your Majesty," Karel affirmed. "From all signs, my father and the others returned the way they had come . . . I suggest we do the same. If there are any further signs to be found, I think it will be at the clearing."

In mutual agreement, the four searchers began their journey back to Skrak's clearing. The journey back was uneventful, though unsettling, for as the afternoon sun traveled across the sky, giving way to dusk, the forest shadows began to deepen. They knew that any ambush Kerebros and his minions might have laid for them would most likely be sprung at night.

Brendys and his companions arrived at Skrak's clearing as the first stars of evening were appearing in the sky above. Amrein was there waiting for them, having taken up a perch for the night in a nearby tree. They set a campfire in the center of the clearing and ate of the dried rations they had brought with them, then decided among themselves how they would split the watches. Brendys took the first watch, while the others tried to get some sleep.

The Horsemaster sat on a piece of a rotted log, his back to the fire, Denasdervien thrust in the ground before him. The red light of the fire played at the keen edges of the sword's mirrored Silver-gold blade, causing it to glow as if it had just come from the smith's forge. Brendys stared at the Living Flame, his thoughts solely upon his missing son . . . his little boy lost in the forest, hunted by yet another Sorcerer, if not already dead.

At last, in anguish, he placed his hands upon the pommel of his sword and bowed forward, weeping. *Why? Is it forbidden that I have even one moment's peace? That I just once experience joy without sorrow? Am I given my family back only to have it taken away again?*

Even as the bitter thoughts ran through his mind, an overwhelming sense of peace came over him, a firm assurance that Brendyn was still alive and, as of yet, unharmed. Indeed, he reflected, had his son perished, there would be nothing to keep the Deathlord from returning to Milhavior even at that moment.

Brendys raised his eyes and found himself standing in a wide, green field dotted with patches of multi-hued wild flowers. The scent of the flowers swirled about him on a gentle breeze, while the midday sun warmed the weariness and grief from his spirit. The nearby bleating of sheep drew his gaze.

A flock of several hundred sheep, if not thousands, grazed in the pasture lands around him. In their midst stood a man that Brendys at first took to be the shepherd, but as the man slowly approached him it became quite clear that this was no ordinary shepherd. He was robed all in white, and his hair and beard were also snow-white, and in his hand was a shepherd's crook. His face was at once both young as the new spring and ancient as the mountains. His clear, blue eyes bore a timeless wisdom, and a light shone from him like the first rays of the dawn. Elekar, the Dawn King, had once again come to him.

But even as the Lightlord approached Brendys, a shadow fell across the field. A great cliff, where none had been before, rose up on Brendys's right. Upon a high ledge, a small lamb cowered in fear. All around the cliff and to either side of the lamb, ravenous wolves snapped and snarled, eager to make a feast of the helpless creature. On a ledge above the lamb, a great, black wolf with eyes and fangs of fire sat, glaring in hatred and fury at the lamb below it.

The sky turned black, and the breeze rose to a mighty gale. Upon the wind came the howling of many wolves, and many creatures likened to the black wolf raced upon the field, charging into the great flock, slaughtering the sheep with reckless abandon. The demon wolves at last withdrew to the right of the Dawn King, gathering in the shadow of the cliff, leaving the bloody field covered with the ruined carcasses of the slain.

To the left of the Dawn King, a great ram, its white fleece blotched red with its own wounds, gathered the remainder of the flock and planted itself boldly between the sheep and the wolves. The wolves again pressed their attack, but the ram rushed to and fro, denying them the flesh of its charges. But even as it defended its flock, it saw the lamb trapped on the cliff. Lowering its mighty, curled horns, it charged into the ranks of the wolves.

Brendys turned questioning eyes to the Dawn King.

Elekar smiled sadly. "This is your story as young Kradon saw it many years ago. You, my child, were the lamb."

"And the ram?" Brendys asked.

The Dawn King did not respond, but the sorrow in his eyes deepened.

265

*Brendys turned his gaze back to the ram for but a moment before understanding dawned on him. "**You** are the ram . . . you would not abandon me to the wolves of Machaelon."*

The Dawn King's face turned grim as if in memory of a great pain. "I have suffered much to ensure that you and others like you should live in freedom from the Shadow of Machaelon. But there is yet work to be done. Look now upon the future."

Elekar raised his crook and a great light flashed forth, then was gone. The sheep were transformed into Men and Elves and Dwarves, garbed in the colors of all the nations, and they made battle with the wolves, which had become Kubruki and Dark Elves and Men of the Dark Lands. Overhead, Jaf wheeled in the black sky, and among the battling forces, Drolar leapt upon the unwary.

The lamb upon the cliff became the crippled child of Brendys's previous dream, cowering in dread from the wolf upon the ledge above him, his mouth forming terrified shrieks, though no sound came forth. Below him, the ram became the white knight, his bright sword cutting a swathe through his foes as he fought to reach the cliff and save the child. The great, demon wolf above was changed into a large, grey, three-headed timberwolf. One head of the chief wolf howled orders to his forces as they gave battle to the Alliance, the second intently watched the progress of the white knight, while the third leered down at the helpless child.

"Heed the cries of the Silent, for they are the cries of the Kingdom lost," the Dawn King said, pointing his hand towards the child. Before Brendys could respond, Elekar spoke again, his aspect beginning to fade. "I will not say do not fear for your son, for grave danger does indeed await him, but for now he is safe. The greater danger is nearer at hand. . . ."

As Elekar faded completely from view, Brendys heard the beating of great wings, and the form of a tremendous, black dragon rose up from behind the cliff to rest upon its peak. The three-headed wolf at once turned all its attention upon Brendys. With a resounding snarl, it leapt down from the cliff. . . .

With a warning cry, Brendys snatched Denasdervien from the ground before him and swung the flaming blade upwards to meet the oncoming monster, but the jaws of one of the creature's heads snapped down upon his forearm, whipping him around like a rag doll. Denasdervien flew from his grasp and stuck in the cliff above the entrance to Skrak's cave. As the wolf's jaws closed on his arm, Brendys screamed in terrible agony, the beast's great teeth piercing his flesh and crushing bone.

But his first cry had accomplished its purpose. His companions awoke at once, practiced hands immediately taking up sword. Amrein swooped down from the branches, her Elvinsilver-tipped talons blazing with an argent light, reaching out to strike at the terrible creature, but the wolf swiftly lifted another head and snatched the great bird from the air with a vicious snap of its jaws, then tossed aside the broken and bloodied corpse of the white hawk.

With a cry of grief and hatred, Kovar charged the wolf with sword upraised, but the wolf snapped at him as he approached, clamping its jaws down upon his leg and throwing him aside as well. The falconer dropped his weapon and grasped his leg, crying out in pain. The wolf's violent motion dragged Brendys around by his torn and shattered arm, eliciting another agonized scream from the Horsemaster's lips.

While the wolf was occupied with Kovar, Quellin leapt forward and brought golden Kalter down upon the head holding Brendys, shearing completely through the muzzle. Terrible screams erupted from the two undamaged heads, and the great wolf fell away, a red glow enveloping the beast. As the blood-red haze vanished, the wolf was replaced by the human form of Kerebros.

The muzzle of the wolf head adorning the Sorcerer's left shoulder was shorn away, and his left arm hung limply at his side, drenched in blood. His amber eyes burned in fury as he looked upon the King of Gildea. "A lucky strike, *Trostain*, but it will avail you nothing!"

Quellin's heritage was a curse on the Sorcerer's lips, but one that the Gildean King had long ago become accustomed to. Quellin planted himself between his wounded comrades and Kerebros, raising Kalter defensively before him. "Would you care to test my luck again, Sorcerer?"

The Sorcerer's amber eyes glared at the slight King. "You are like a lamb before me, Trostain, and there is none left with the strength to stop me from ripping your throat out. But know this before you die . . . you wander this forest in hope, but hope has perished already. I myself have slain the four you sent to search for your son and your nephew, and the Betrayer, the Jaf of this forest, has carried your son to his doom. The son of the Bearer . . . he is lost to you already."

Quellin raised Kalter and charged the Sorcerer with a cry of anguish. Kerebros swept up his right hand and a bolt of black flame lashed out, striking the Gildean King in the chest, lifting him in the air and throwing him several feet backwards into a tree. Quellin collapsed to the ground, smoke rising from a scorched patch on his chest where his tunic had been blasted away.

Kerebros turned his malevolent gaze back on Brendys. "*You*, Bearer of the Flame, shall live . . . only long enough to feel the point of my dagger as it pierces your heart in sacrifice to the Master."

As Kerebros the Wolf came to stand over Brendys, a shrill scream erupted from the shadows behind the Sorcerer, and a blazing white light hurtled past his head, landing beside the Bearer of the Flame. Brendys snatched up the blazing form of his sword with his left hand, ignoring the white flames enveloping it, and lunged up at the Sorcerer. He saw a look of shock and pain on the man's face before a blast of white fire threw him back to the ground.

Red flames engulfed Brendys's vision, but he could not feel their heat. He knew at once he was dreaming again. He waited, staring through the glaring light of the fire into the blackness beyond, expecting at any time to hear the Dawn King's voice.

As he waited, the flames before him split down the center and retreated to the edges of his vision, like curtains drawn back by rough hands, opening into an unfathomable darkness. Two burning red eyes opened in the blackness before him, and a wave of malevolence swept over Brendys.

The eyes started to draw back, revealing the silhouette of the great draconic body to which they belonged, surrounded by roaring flames. A deep roar thundered out of the great creature's gaping maw. Beating its powerful wings, the Dragon launched into the air and swept down upon Brendys, taloned claws poised to strike.

Brendys sat up with a startled cry, which turned quickly into a cry of pain as the shattered bones in his right arm ground together with his abrupt movement. He fell back at once, his eyes squeezed shut, fighting the urge to retch. His arm was splinted and bound in a sling made from strips of one of his companions' cloaks, but it meant little. He knew from the terrible sensation of the bones shifting in his forearm, despite the tightly-wrapped splint, that he would never use it again.

He squeezed his eyes shut as stinging sweat ran into his eyes. He felt almost unbearably hot and knew that a fever had taken a strong hold on him. He wondered if his fever was brought on by his injury or whether Kerebros had infected him with the Plague as the Great Father had done to Mattina at Lener Keep the year before.

"So you have decided to join us at last?"

Brendys opened his eyes again to find Quellin kneeling over him. The front of Quellin's tunic had been blasted away, and the exposed flesh of his chest was badly scorched. His youthful features were taut with pain, but he was clearly bearing his injury better than Brendys was his own.

"From the looks of you, you had some nightmare," Quellin said, helping Brendys into a sitting position with his back against a tree trunk. Though the Gildean King spoke lightly, there was no hint of humor in his expression.

"What happened?" Brendys rasped, breathless from the agonizing task of sitting up. "What . . . happened to Kerebros?"

"I cannot say for sure," Quellin replied, his expression becoming grim. "As soon as Denasdervien pierced his body, he was enveloped in a red light. Then there was an explosion of white fire from Denasdervien. When it cleared, Kerebros was gone, and you were lying there unconscious."

Quellin paused for only a moment before speaking again, his voice lowering. "It is unlikely Kovar will ever walk again, and your arm. . . ."

He bowed his head. "We cannot continue the search, Brendys."

Brendys grasped the Gildean King's wrist with his left hand, a look of grim determination on his face. "Brendyn may still be alive . . . you and Karel *must* continue the search."

Quellin placed his free hand over the Horsemaster's, a grave and sorrowful look in his eyes. "Nay, Brendys, we cannot."

His eyes raised to look beyond the place where Brendys lay.

Brendys followed Quellin's gaze and saw Kovar and Karel lying together on a litter crafted of boughs bound with strips of cloth from one of their cloaks. Both of them were either asleep or unconscious, their hair and faces drenched with perspiration. Kovar's leg was bound in bloody rags, and both of Karel's arms were swathed from her elbows to her fingers.

"It was Karel who pulled Denasdervien from the cliff," Quellin continued. "Very nearly at the cost of her life. Brendys, we have all suffered wounds that are beyond my meager skills to tend. We must return to civilized lands."

His green eyes misted over, but he did not weep. "The search is over."

Brendys lowered his gaze, despair overcoming him. "Then all is lost. Without Brendyn, there is no hope. There is a Storm coming that we will be powerless to stop. My arm is destroyed, Quellin . . . I will never again wield Denasdervien."

There was a moment of silence before Quellin answered. "There is still hope for Brendyn, meager though it is. The Sorcerer said he killed the four we sent out . . . I think he spoke of Baris and his men. It may be that Novosad, Aliana, and the twins yet live. We saw ourselves the signs of their victory at the Dark Elf camp. Regardless, Brendyn's life has been taken out of our hands."

Brendys glanced up at his brother-by-marriage. "And what of Shannon?"

Life drained from Quellin's gaze. "Amrein witnessed the Jaf bearing him away. My son is dead. Do not use him against me, Brendys. Dead or alive, I do not wish to leave him in this wild place, but I have not the skill to continue the search alone, and I cannot leave the three of you here to die. The search is over."

Brendys stared at him, part of him crying out to continue the argument, but in his heart he knew Quellin was right. Brendyn's fate was no longer in their keeping. The Dawn King had told him Brendyn was safe, but if Kerebros had escaped, did that remain true? The thought sapped what energy he had regained since awakening, and he fought back a renewed flood of tears. At last, not daring to face his brother-by-marriage again lest he lose control of his emotions, he gave Quellin a brief nod.

"Very well," he said quietly, his voice hoarse with emotion. "Give me an hour to recover some of my strength. We shall leave this place."

"You shall have your hour," Quellin responded. "Regardless, we should eat something before we leave. I do not know how far I will be able to drag that litter, as it is. I, at least, will need strength."

Brendys did not reply.

*　*　*　*

Kovar awoke while Brendys and Quellin were eating, but refused any food himself. He just stared vacantly at the treetops above him and would not speak. Brendys had never fully understood the relationship between the falconer and his bird, but clearly Amrein had been more than a pet to the young warrior.

Quellin and Brendys finished their meal in silence, then the Gildean King loaded the remainder of the provisions on the litter with Kovar and Karel. He carefully assisted Brendys to his feet, then turned to heft the end of the litter at Kovar's and Karel's heads. He had used his own belt and Kovar's as makeshift shoulder straps, so that he would not have to rely on the strength of his arms alone to pull the litter.

As Quellin moved towards the litter, Brendys followed him. "Quellin, I have one good shoulder . . . we will last longer if you will let me help you drag this thing."

Quellin glanced at him. "Are you certain? If that injured arm is jostled too much. . . ."

"Nay, I am not sure," Brendys replied looking down at his immobilized arm. "But there is no more harm that can be done to it."

Quellin gave him a grimly uneasy look. "If the wound infects. . . ."

Brendys clenched his jaw at the thought, then replied, "Then it shall be your lot to remove it."

There was no mistaking the apprehension in the Gildean King's face. "Let us hope then that it does not come to that."

"It matters not," Brendys responded, his expression darkening. He bent down and shouldered one of the straps. "Let us go. These two need proper care, and Mattina . . . Mattina needs to know. . . ."

His words choked off, and his eyes began to mist.

Quellin nodded solemnly and slipped the other strap over his shoulder.

Together, they began to drag the litter westward into the forest.

Chapter 13

As the first rays of the dawn pierced the canopy of the forest, Novosad and his companions resumed their search. Novosad stared thoughtfully at trees around them for a moment before speaking. "It seems to me that the trees have been thinning out somewhat as we move westward."

Copanas gave him an acknowledging nod. "Aye, 'tis this ground . . . there is too much rock here for the trees to grow."

"But farther to the west the trees are beginning to deepen again," Lehan pointed out.

"Aye, I noticed that, too," Novosad replied, a hint of hope entering his eyes. "It may well be that we are coming once more upon softer ground. We should spread out and move westward in a line."

Then he quickly added, "But stay within hearing distance . . . there is a Sorcerer about, and we should not be taken unawares."

The twins nodded their acknowledgment, then Copanas said with a worried look, "We should have returned to the caravan. We have *some* water, but no food. It could be bad business for us."

Novosad looked eastward for a moment, then turned his gaze back to his companions. "It is too late to turn back now . . . keep your eyes out for any game, as well as any sign of the boys."

He gave Aliana a sideways glance and noticed something that alarmed him once more . . . she was perspiring and her breathing seemed slightly labored. He turned to face her fully. "My Lady, do not tell me that you will be fine. You are ill . . . and you should not be. I have never heard of an Elf sickening in all my mortal life."

He fished Brendyn's ring out of his pocket. "If the healing power of the Elvindiamond on this ring is as powerful as your father claimed, use it . . . it will do none of us any good if you die of an illness that should not be possible."

Aliana took a step backwards and raised her hand, palm out in refusal. "Your concern is appreciated, Captain, but while it may indeed heal my *illness*, the power of that ring is not yours to give, nor mine to receive . . . it was given to Prince Brendyn, and he may yet have need of it."

Novosad grimaced, but slipped the ring back into his belt pouch.

Aliana drew him aside, lowering her voice so that the twins could not hear what she said. "It is not a mortal illness which burns in my veins, but the curse of Kerebros the Wolf. I did not believe that such could affect me, but it seems it can and does, though it is only very slowly taking hold.

"I may weaken further before the end, for I must focus all of my strength inward to reject this poison, and even then, I do not know if I will succeed. If I begin to change into such as the Wolves, you must not hesitate to strike me down before the transformation is complete, for if I change, I do not know whether I will be in my own mind or not."

Novosad ran a hand through his matted, blonde hair, wishing that he had also been unable to hear her, but he knew she was right. He was responsible for the safety of the party, and if it meant killing Aliana to ensure the safety of the twins, he would do so. With a sigh, he nodded. "Very well. Stay near me."

"I shall walk before you," Aliana replied. Unexpectedly, she smiled. "Do not look so glum, Captain. Unless my will is not my own, I shall walk the Road to Elekar before I put your lives at risk."

She removed her Elvinknife from her belt and held it out to Novosad. "This will serve your purposes best. If you must strike, strike true."

Novosad took the Elvinsilver longknife and fastened the sheath to his belt, a hollow feeling forming in the pit of his stomach. Without a word, Novosad began to walk westward, his eyes scanning the ground and the foliage around him, trying to put Aliana's grim tidings out of his mind.

Copanas and Lehan followed Novosad's example, the first moving a little northward, the second southward. Aliana quickly moved ahead of Novosad, making sure to leave her back open to him. As Novosad had predicted, the ground soon softened considerably, making tracking an easier task.

They journeyed on for nearly twenty minutes longer, sighting a few animal tracks, but no animals and no sign of either of the children. At last, Novosad heard Lehan call out. Quickly turning northward, he yelled, "Copanas, your brother has found something!"

Novosad and Aliana waited for Copanas to join them, then together they headed southward until they found Lehan. Lehan was holding his bow in his left hand and an arrow in his right, with which he was pointing at the ground.

"I found some familiar tracks," he said as they approached.

Novosad knelt down and examined the animal tracks more closely. "The wolf?"

Lehan shook his head. "Nay, they are smaller and not shaped quite right for a wolf . . . a dog certainly, and a large one, but not the Wolf. Nay, these are the same as the second pair of animal tracks we found in that clearing."

He moved a little farther westward and pointed at some other marks with his arrow. "That is the least of it . . . the dog lay down here, and look here. . . ."

He pointed to some indentations on either side of the spot where the dog had lain.

Novosad again knelt down and took a closer look at the marks. His head abruptly snapped up and turned towards his companions, his brown eyes widening in surprise and confusion. "These were made by a child's boots!"

He looked back down at the marks and shook his head. "But I do not understand them . . . it would appear as though Prince Brendyn were sitting astride the dog."

Lehan broke into a slow grin. "Aye, that was my reading as well."

Novosad looked up at him in disbelief. "Are you saying that Prince Brendyn is *riding* this dog?"

Lehan inclined his head towards the dog's tracks. "Look at the depth of the prints, Captain . . . that animal is carrying a weight."

Aliana knelt down beside the prints, touching them with the tips of her fingers and closed her eyes in concentration. After a minute, she opened her eyes and looked at her companions. "The dog is not what it seems. A power for good indwells it . . . that much I can feel. I can also sense another power in this place. The Wolves of Kerebros have also passed nearby. We must follow."

Novosad drew a deep breath and stood up, again shaking his head. "We have seen stranger, I suppose. I guess there is nothing for it . . . we follow the dog."

Novosad and his companions followed the dog's tracks at a fairly rapid pace, slowed only by Aliana, emerging into a sudden clearing late in the afternoon. There was a pond in the clearing and the ground became muddier. The tracks there were numerous and clearer than any they had seen yet.

Lehan and Novosad hurried forward, their eyes sweeping the ground, while Copanas went towards the pond. Aliana knelt down where she had stopped, her hands on her knees, eyes closed and head bowed, breathing slowly and deliberately.

Lehan motioned around the clearing. "There is no doubt Prince Brendyn was here . . . his tracks are everywhere."

"Aye," Novosad said distractedly, his gaze focusing intently on the ground near a patch of briars. "And it appears he found a friend . . . these vines have been cut with a knife, and there is another print here beside Prince Brendyn's. This one is a little smaller than his and bare. It looks like the second child was dragging its left foot. The child may be hurt."

"Prince Brendyn may have found a friend," Copanas called from the pond's edge, a severe look on his face. "But he did not find food. There is nothing here."

Novosad understood his companion's concern. His own strength was flagging from lack of sustenance . . . he could not imagine what Brendyn had to be going through. But hunger was the least of the boy's troubles. There were other prints in the mud, as well—the tracks of grown men, bare-footed. The Wolves of Kerebros were close on Brendyn's trail.

He glanced back at Aliana. Her breathing was more labored than it had been earlier, and she was beginning to perspire more heavily. He considered resting at the pond for awhile to allow the Elfess a chance to fight the effects of the sorcery afflicting her, but with the Wolves ahead of them, they dared not stop yet.

Finally, he removed his water flask from his belt and tossed it to Copanas. "These tracks are no more than a day old, if that. They cannot be too far ahead of us . . . we need to gain as much ground as we can today. There are still a few hours of daylight left. Refill the flasks, then we'll move on."

He glanced at Lehan. "Let's see where these tracks lead."

Lehan nodded, then tossed his own flask to his brother and turned to follow his Captain.

As Novosad followed the tracks towards the hedgeline, he shook his head in wonder. "If I read these tracks right, the dog is now carrying *both* of the children. Aliana is right about one thing, at least. This creature cannot be an ordinary dog . . . it simply isn't possible."

Lehan shrugged. "Perhaps it was sent by the gods."

The chief scout snorted in return. "I find that unlikely. Why would the gods send aid to the son of their worst enemy? More likely, if this creature was sent to help him, it was Prince Brendys's Dawn King."

The trail passed through a break in the hedgeline, leading to the road on the other side. The two Haganes stopped and examined the ground.

"It looks like a pair of heavy wagons came through about the same time Prince Brendyn was here," Novosad commented. "But they continued northward . . . the dog went southward."

"Aye," Lehan replied. "But the dog came up here after the wagons passed. Its tracks are clear within the ruts."

Novosad rubbed his stubbly chin. "If I had to venture a guess, I would say the dog is taking the children to Shalkan."

"They are certainly headed in the right direction," Lehan agreed. "But without food and water—and *soon*—Prince Brendyn will not survive the journey."

Novosad nodded grimly in return.

Copanas joined them, passing his companions' flasks back to them.

As Novosad attached his flask to his belt, he motioned southwards. "From here on, we pick up our pace."

He stepped back through the break in the hedgerow and called to Aliana. "My Lady, we must go . . . are you strong enough to run?"

The Elfess raised her head, shifting her gaze to the man. "I have what strength I need for now."

She slowly rose to her feet, then lightly sprinted to Novosad's side. "Let us be on our way."

Novosad nodded in response, then took off at a jog down the road, following the dog's tracks, his companions following behind.

*   *   *   *

"We should stop here for the night," Quellin said, glancing around the stony clearing they had come upon. "Not the most comfortable campsite, but I want to get those rags changed while there is still light."

He and Brendys carefully lowered the end of the litter to the ground, then Brendys sat down, his back against a tree. Quellin knelt down beside him, reaching for the knot holding the Horsemaster's sling secure around his neck. He paused before untying the knot and looked Brendys straight in the eye. "This is going to hurt . . . badly."

Brendys nodded, closing his eyes and bracing himself for the agony he knew was coming. Quellin untied the knot, then used the loose sling to carefully lower the shattered arm into the Horsemaster's lap. Brendys winced at the shot of pain that ran through his arm, but it was nowhere near as terrible as he thought it would be . . . until Quellin began to unwrap the splint bracing the arm. He nearly passed out from the pain of it, but just managed to keep his senses about him.

He opened his eyes and looked down at the arm and felt worse. The rags Quellin was removing were stained with black and red clots of blood pulled away from the ugly wounds caused by the jaws of Kerebros. Fresh blood oozed from the gaping holes in his arm. Small shards of bone protruded from the flesh, the sight of which nearly caused Brendys to retch.

"Will you hurry?" Brendys muttered, swallowing back bile.

Quellin, looking more than a little green himself, eyed the wound closely. "I don't see any sign of infection. All right, this is likely to hurt even worse."

Brendys cried out as the Gildean King reset the splint and began to tightly wrap it with fresh scraps he had taken from a bundle between Kovar and Karel. The Horsemaster's vision faded to black, but still he struggled to remain conscious. At last his vision returned, going from black to red, then finally clearing up again.

"Wha. . . ?" Karel's dazed voice said from his left.

"I believe that was the sound of His Majesty torturing Prince Brendys," Kovar's wry voice responded.

Quellin rose to his feet and walked around to Kovar's side of the litter. "Aye, and you are next. Lay still."

The young falconer groaned only a little when his King removed the bindings from his leg. Quellin examined the wound, then began rebinding the leg. "No infection here either, and just as well . . . I was not looking forward to playing surgeon as well as physician."

"Your pardon, Your Majesty," Kovar grated between clenched teeth as Quellin knotted the new bindings. "But you are not much of a physician either."

Quellin did not reply, but stood up and walked around the litter to Karel's side, then knelt again. "All right, young lady . . . I think the sun has gone down far enough that we can risk removing those bandages. I doubt the pain will be any worse than if you were not of Dark Elf blood . . . but you should know that this *will* hurt. Are you ready?"

The girl set her jaw and gave a quick nod. Her face immediately twisted in pain as the Gildean King started to unwrap one arm and the next, but she did not cry out. Her arms, from elbows to fingertips, were masses of oozing blisters and cracked, bleeding flesh.

Brendys winced at the sight and groaned a little.

Quellin glanced over at him. "As bad as these burns are, I speak from experience when I say she will heal, and likely without a scar to show for it. One of the blessings of a Half-Elvin bloodline."

When Quellin had finished unwrapping the bandages, he helped Karel into a sitting position, then reached for his waterskin. "Hold out your arms."

She did so without question, but as Quellin began pouring water over the burns, she did let out a gasp of pain. Through clenched teeth, she muttered. "I think you are enjoying this too much."

"Do not make light of this, girl. Denasdervien's power could easily have destroyed you," the Gildean King snapped. His expression softened and his voice gentled. "That it did not is evidence, however, that the Shadow over you does indeed waver. What path you tread is yet yours to choose."

Brendys fixed his gaze on Karel as Quellin put fresh wrappings on her arms. As he looked at her, he was not certain whether the tears forming in her eyes were due to the pain of her wounds or Quellin's veiled words of acceptance. She noticed him staring at her and quickly ducked her head away from him.

When Quellin was done, he started rummaging through the packs, withdrawing a single decent strip of dried meat for each of them. "It isn't much, but we need to ration carefully. As it is, I don't know how long the food will last."

He looked once at Karel's bandaged arms and shook his head. She would not be able to feed herself. He handed two strips to Kovar. "You are on feeding detail."

"Aye, Your Majesty," the young warrior replied without hesitance.

Karel looked miserable, but acquiesced without comment.

Quellin slowly settled himself down beside Brendys, passing one of the remaining strips of meat to his brother-by-marriage. Brendys took it, but could not bring himself to eat . . . he had quite lost his appetite after watching Quellin tend to his arm.

Brendys looked at the Gildean King. Quellin also did not seem eager to eat, but clearly for other reasons. A terrible weight of weariness and grief had settled upon him, such that Brendys had not seen on his face since the Siege of Gildea. Rather than make him look older, the burden made him look even more boyish . . . a boy forlorn and neglected, full of despair.

Quellin bowed his head, staring at the ground between his drawn-up knees. After a moment, he spoke, his voice quiet. "How do you do it?"

"Do what?" Brendys asked in return, his brow furrowing in confusion.

Quellin swallowed, his green eyes misting. "Just in the time I have known you, your family has been shattered by death and tragedy more times than I care to count, yet you survive. Losing Shannon . . . I-I feel. . . I feel as though the Dawn King has turned his back, not just on me, but on the world."

Brendys leaned his head back against the tree. He knew exactly how Quellin felt. A remnant of the grief and terror tugged at him even now, but he still had Mattina to consider . . . he could not give in to despair, and neither could Quellin. He drew in a breath and turned his gaze back towards his brother-by-marriage. "Quellin, you know I blamed the Dawn King for every pain and loss that I suffered for many years . . . and you know as well as I that he was not to blame."

Brendys sighed and shook his head. "I feel foolish trying to counsel one who has been *my* counselor since my youth. I just do not feel that we have been abandoned."

Quellin was silent for a moment before speaking again. "Etzel told me that I would one day doubt Elekar. I never believed such a day could ever come, but it has . . . I do not have your faith, Brendys."

"If the Dawn King has abandoned us," Brendys responded, his gaze drifting into the deeper woods. "Then why has he given me the dreams?"

Quellin's head came up, his emerald eyes opening wide in surprise as he looked upon the dark-haired Shalkane beside him. "*Dreams?* You have had more than just the one?"

Brendys nodded slowly. "Aye. The second came shortly before the Dark Elves attacked the camp, the third right before Kerebros attacked, and the fourth just before I awoke after the attack."

The Gildean King's gaze intensified. "Tell me . . . what did you dream?"

If just to keep your mind off Shannon, Brendys thought. With a brief nod, he related each of the dreams as he remembered them in the order he had been given them.

Quellin listened patiently, his expression thoughtful. When Brendys finished, he nodded. "The dreams appear to be a chain. The first two are bound by the theme of the Silent, whatever that may mean. The second and third share the images of the knight and the child. The third and fourth both contain the image of a dragon. . . ."

"The *same* dragon," Brendys put in.

"Unless the dragon symbolizes the newest Warlord of Thanatos, I do not have an explanation for that image," Quellin said, rubbing his chin. "The dragons went into the wilds of the north during the Second Dawn War . . . none have been seen in two Ages. I must believe it is a symbol, rather than a literal dragon. And the boy . . . you are sure you did not recognize him?"

Brendys resolutely shook his head. "Nay, I have never seen him . . . of that I am sure."

"Then I cannot say his part in the dreams means anything to me either," Quellin replied. "The knight, however, tells me one thing . . . if he does, indeed, represent the Heir of Ascon—and I would tend to agree he does—then either Brendyn still lives or you will father another son before the Storm breaks."

Brendys lowered his head. "I pray the former is true . . . but even then, as you pointed out before, his life is out of our hands now."

To that, Quellin did not reply. He patted Brendys's good left arm, then stood up and walked back to the litter. He put his share of the evening's rations back in the pack, then looked at Karel. "Do you feel up to taking the first watch tonight?"

The girl looked startled, but replied, "Aye . . . I have slept most of the day. I'm by no means weary yet."

"Karel and I will split the watches, Your Majesty," Kovar put in. "You and Prince Brendys have greater need of your strength than either of us. Besides, I doubt we are in further danger, what with the Sorcerer dead."

A grim look passed over Quellin's features. "Of the Sorcerer's death, I am none too sure. Very well . . . take the watches, but stay wary."

Both Kovar and Karel acknowledged his instruction with a nod.

Quellin unbuckled his sword belt and lay down of the stony ground, his hand resting on Kalter's golden hilt.

Brendys looked at the strip of dried meat in his hand. With a sigh, he gnawed at the tough ration, finishing it in a few minutes. He did not bother to try and lay down, but simply leaned his back against the tree trunk he was propped against and waited for sleep to come

* * * *

Novosad and his companions steadfastly followed the tracks of the dog, watching for signs of both Brendyn and those with him and of the Wolves hounding them. The tracks of the two Wolves eventually moved off into the forest as if they had somehow lost the dog's trail, though the tracks appeared quite clear to the Hagane scouts. They came to the edge of the forest well before the end of the first day.

A horrible stench and the buzz of insects drew Novosad's attention. In the brush to the side of the road, he saw a body laying on its back, a cloud of flies swarming above it. He drew his sword and motioned for his companions to remain where they were, while he went to investigate the corpse. Despite his instructions, Aliana accompanied him.

As Novosad neared the body, he could see that it was one of the Wolves of Kerebros. The man had clearly fought something far stronger than he had been in bestial form, for his corpse was badly rent, his throat ripped out by a creature with powerful jaws. That the Wolf had fought in its altered form, he did not doubt, for the man's short sword was still sheathed.

The Hagane scout glanced at Aliana. "What do you think? The Wolves turned on each other?"

Aliana shook her head and pointed to the ground. "Nay, look here."

Novosad stepped closer to her, his gaze following her gesturing hand. His gaze widened. In the dirt near the place where the corpse lay were prints belonging to the dog they tracked. More astonishing were the prints beyond those, tracks belonging to a man wearing heavy boots. "Another shapeshifter?"

"I told you the dog was not what it seemed to be," Aliana replied matter-of-factly.

"That much was obvious," Novosad replied wryly. "But I must confess that I did not expect to find another shapeshifter. What kind of creature do you think it is?"

Aliana shrugged. "The only creature I know of with such a power that does not serve Machaelon is akin to my own people: a High Alar."

"An *Alar?*" Novosad responded with astonishment. "You mean to say we have been tracking an Alar?"

He shook his head in bewilderment. "Then it is no wonder this creature lost his battle."

He pointed to another set of tracks leading back into the forest. "It looks like the second Wolf may have escaped, though not uninjured, judging by the trail of blood."

Aliana nodded in agreement. "We should move on, Captain. There is still much daylight ahead of us, and it would be best if we were far from here before nightfall."

"I agree," Novosad replied. "I have no desire to face even one more Wolf if I can avoid it, and I deem we are gaining on Prince Brendyn."

Novosad and Aliana rejoined the twins, and they continued their journey into the open plains of Ilkatar. In the distance, they could see Barrier Mountain rising up from the horizon, a couple days distant at best. Unsheltered from the summer sun, the heat was almost too much to bear; nevertheless, Novosad did not allow his small party to slow their pace, nor to rest overlong in one place. They also drank sparingly from their waterskins, trying to make the precious liquid last as long as possible.

As afternoon began to fade on the second day, Novosad finally slowed to a walk, wiping perspiration from his brow, a wave of dizziness coming over him.

"Novosad, look!" Lehan said, his voice grating from weariness and lack of water.

The chief scout's gaze followed Lehan's outstretched arm. About forty feet away, he could see some shapes lying in the grass. At the sound of Lehan's voice, one of the shapes arose . . . a massive dog with a golden coat that shimmered in the dying sunlight. The animal glanced back at the three warriors for a moment, then trotted away. Novosad watched the dog until it disappeared beyond his view, amazed, for he knew the creature was indeed, as Aliana had said, far more than a simple dog.

Novosad and the twins hurried forward. The chief scout knelt beside Brendyn, placing his ear against the small chest. There was a heartbeat, though not strong.

"I have you," he rasped, gently raising the boy from the ground. He glanced over his shoulder. "One of you grab the other child."

He looked around for a moment, then noticed a tree only a few yards away to one side. Its shade was sparse, but better than nothing. He carried Brendyn into the shade, then set him on the ground. Raising the boy's head, he put his waterskin to Brendyn's parched lips and slowly allowed the remaining liquid to trickle into the boy's mouth. Brendyn swallowed reflexively.

Next to him, Copanas was doing the same with the other boy. When they had emptied their waterskins, they shared Lehan's between them. Finally, it too was empty.

Novosad slumped down beside Brendyn and shook his head. "Not nearly enough, and I gauge from the distance of Barrier Mountain that we still have about a two-day journey ahead of us, if not more."

He turned his gaze on Lehan. "In the morning, I want you to try and hunt up some game. I don't care if it is just a squirrel or rabbit . . . we need food."

His eyes turned to Lehan's brother. "Copanas you head out as well . . . I want you both to keep an eye out for a source of water or, preferably, a farmstead. Food we can do without, though the lack of it will only weaken us more, but we will none of us survive the journey without water."

The twins nodded in response.

After a moment's rest, the three men gathered enough wood to start a fire. Aliana remained with the children, kneeling upon the hard ground, meditating, her full concentration focused on purging her body of the Wolf's curse. Though they could have done without the heat of a fire, the light would perhaps draw the eyes of any travelers who were crossing through these lands. By the time the men had gathered enough wood for a decent fire, the sun had finally dropped below the horizon.

After he had gotten the campfire lit, Novosad sat back, wishing he could just lie down and go to sleep. He had not realized until now just how much the search had taken out of him. He looked at his men. "Sleep now. I will take the first watch. Lehan, you will take the second, and Copanas shall take the last."

"What about Lady Aliana?" Lehan asked. "I thought Elves did not sleep?"

Novosad glanced at Aliana, but it took no more than that to realize she would be of little use on watch. This was the first real opportunity she had to combat the Wolf's curse, and he would not begrudge her that time . . . all of their lives hung in the balance. He shook his head. "Lady Aliana, perhaps more than we, needs time to rest and regain her strength. Our breakneck chase has not afforded her that luxury, and she is hurt. Now, sleep . . . I do not know how long my own strength will hold out."

The twins silently acknowledged their captain's orders and lay down.

* * * *

Novosad sat on the ground before the small campfire, his legs drawn up, his head resting on his knees. His swordbelt lay next to him. It was hard to keep awake, but it was his watch and he had to remain awake for another hour. Lack of food and rest were taking their toll. He desperately wanted for water, as well, but that too was lacking.

He looked at Aliana. The rest seemed to be doing her some good. Her previously dimmed light was growing stronger, and her face appeared more serene, color returning to her fair cheeks. She still knelt with her eyes closed, hands on her bent knees, completely unmoving. He barely noticed her breathing. She, at least, was recovering.

The Hagane warrior's gaze strayed to the boys sleeping beside him—Brendyn and the mysterious friend the boy had found. Novosad was amazed that the children yet lived. The combination of the intense summer heat and near-complete lack of food and water would have stretched a grown man to his limits. Indeed, it had. He and the twins were nearly spent . . . the children should have died.

And they may yet, the Hagane scout thought. The children's exposed skin was red and blistered, unshielded from the summer sun as they left the forest. Their lips were cracked and scabbed, coated with dry matter. Novosad had seen men in this condition before, and even an abundance of water had been unable to save them. Their bodies rejected the very fluid that they craved for. Even if the boys survived through the night, and they were able to bring them to a farmstead, he was not sure anything short of a miracle could save them.

The ring! Novosad fumbled at his belt pouch. Aliana refused the power of Brendyn's Elvindiamond ring for the very reason that Brendyn himself might be in need of it. The clear Elvinstone was said to have the power to even purge the death of Crorkin, black Elvinmetal, from the veins of its victim.

As he withdrew the ring from the pouch and started to reach for Brendyn's small hand, he was startled by Aliana's voice. "It will not save him."

He looked at her, his brow wrinkling. "I thought it could heal any injury or illness."

Eyes still closed, Aliana gave a short nod. "Injury and illness, aye. But this is more. Their bodies have lost much of the water they need to remain alive. The ring will not restore that . . . not so small a 'Stone. At best, it may give Prince Brendyn the strength to live a short while longer."

Novosad looked down at the Elvindiamond signet, the light of the fire playing in its crystalline depths—so powerful a thing, and yet powerless to save its master. He took Brendyn's hand and slipped the ring onto his finger. A white light ignited in the heart of the 'Stone, faint, but visible. "I will take what is given me and pray that the gods have mercy on them."

Aliana opened her eyes, turning them on the Hagane warrior. Her gaze was clearer than Novosad had seen it in the past days. "Then you would place your hopes in false promises and dark spirits, Captain, for the gods seek the destruction of all this child's father stands for. The Heir of Ascon is the hope of Milhavior, yet if he comes, the gods shall be proven false, for the promise of his return is the promise of the Lord Elekar."

Novosad started to reply, but never gave voice to his response, the sound of an approaching wagon startling him from his line of thought. He rose to his feet, taking up his sheathed sword and Aliana's Elvinsilver knife as he did so, both relieved and cautious. He walked around the fire and nudged Copanas and Lehan. When the twins stirred to consciousness, he whispered, "A wagon approaches."

His men arose, making sure their weapons were handy in case the visitor was not friendly.

In a few minutes, the silhouette of the wagon came into view. The warriors waited as the wain approached, hands ready upon the pommels of their swords. Soon, they could make out the somewhat slight form of the hooded figure driving the wain. When the wagon had passed within several fcct of the camp, the driver brought his team to a halt.

The driver turned his head towards the men, and a fair voice spoke from within the shadow of his hood. "Greetings! This one . . . *I* see from your livery that you are men of Racolis. Did you happen to come from the caravan that I passed on my way from Shalkan?"

Novosad glanced at his companions, then turned his cautious gaze back on the driver. "Aye . . . we were scouting the forest and were delayed. I expect they think we are dead."

"I am genuinely surprised that you are not," the driver continued in a pleasant tone. "But it pleases me . . . it means you escaped the Wolf."

That brought Novosad and his companions fully awake and alert.

"The Wolf?" the chief scout echoed.

The hooded figure nodded his head once. "Aye, Kerebros the Wolf . . . the Sorcerer who orchestrated the Dark Elf attack on your caravan."

Suspicion took hold of Novosad. His hand slowly slid from the pommel of his sword to the hilt. "How do you know this?"

"Skr . . . *I* dwelt within the wood for many of your centuries," came the reply. "Little happens there that I am not aware of."

Centuries? Novosad drew his sword and raised it before him, taking a defensive stance. "Name yourself, stranger! What kind of creature are you, and whom do you serve?"

The driver withdrew his hood, revealing the fair countenance and golden hair of an Elf—one of the Caletri, the High Elves, Novosad judged from the light shining from within the Elf. The chief scout immediately lowered his sword, bowing to the immortal driver. "I beg your pardon, My Lord!"

The Elf smiled gently. "I do not blame you for fearing me. There was once a time when your fear would have been warranted. I am called Anselm. You need not treat me with the respect due an Elvinlord . . . I long ago lost any right to such a title."

Novosad gave him a puzzled look, but the Elf did not explain.

Aliana pushed past Novosad and the twins, her sky-blue eyes wide in wonder. She said a few astonished words in the Caletri Tongue, then fell to her knees, head bowed.

Anselm frowned. "Rise, daughter of the Caletri. I am outcast. I do not deserve your deference."

Aliana raised her face to look upon him, confusion on her fair face. "But you are Firstborn. . . ."

"And long cursed," Anselm replied. "The minions of Machaelon long ago named me in their tongue, Skrak—the Betrayer of All. This one has earned the pardon of Elekar for his crimes, but he . . . *I* cannot forgive *myself* that easily. I have too much to atone for."

Aliana arose and stepped back to join Novosad, her face as confused as the Hagane warrior.

"Now, need drives me to urgency. I have come from Shalkan, where I delivered the young Prince of Gildea," Anselm continued. "I now seek the Little One, the son of the Bearer of the Flame. Perhaps you have seen some sign of the child?"

"Indeed!" Novosad returned, both relieved and surprised. "That was why were delayed . . . we found Prince Brendyn's tracks in the forest on our way back to the caravan and chose instead to follow him. We found him only this afternoon."

The Hagane warrior half-turned and pointed back towards the watchfire. "The Prince was in the company of another boy as well. I am sure His Highness, like ourselves, has been without food and water for some time."

Anselm immediately dismounted and hurried past the warriors to kneel beside the sleeping children. "I feared this would be the case. It is fortuitous that the Bearer has someone as wise and powerful as Gwydnan of Athor in his employ, who keeps herbs of healing. There is water and a bundle of herbs in the wagon. There are also the tools of cooking. Bring everything here at once."

The Elf looked up at Novosad. "You and these children need nourishment, but solid food would be the worst possible until your stomachs have again become accustomed to food. With the herbs, I can make a broth which will be both nourishing and strengthening and will help your bodies retain the water. For the children, at least, water alone will no longer suffice."

Novosad yearned for the taste of meat, as he was sure his companions did, but he did not argue the point with the Elf. He motioned for Copanas and Lehan to bring the provisions as Anselm had instructed.

When the provisions had been brought to the camp, Copanas and Lehan tended to the wagon team, while Anselm set up the cooking gear and began preparing the broth. The Elf again looked up at Novosad. "I have no need of sleep . . . I will keep watch tonight. We need to bring the children to Shalkan as soon as possible, but we will stay here this night. When the broth is ready, I will wake you and your men."

Novosad stared hard at Anselm, not entirely without suspicion, wondering what *crimes* he had committed to bring the wrath of his Dawn King down upon him, but at last he acknowledged the Elf's instructions with a nod. When the twins came back from tending the horses, the three Men took to their blankets and finally gave in to their weariness. Sleep came, but hunger, thirst, and fatigue conjured bizarre dreams, keeping the Hagane scouts from resting well.

As Anselm finished mixing the fragrant herbs in the heating water, he said, half to himself, "This one feared he may have forgotten the remedies of his youth after three Ages as. . . ."

He hesitated, glancing sheepishly at Aliana, who watched him with curiosity and wonder. ". . . In such a state as *I* was."

He stirred the mixture in the kettle before him once more, then set aside the large spoon he was holding and turned to Aliana. "The broth must boil for awhile. Now for you."

Anselm reached out and placed his palm on her chest, just below her collarbone, closing his eyes, his brow wrinkling in concentration. He sat in that position for several minutes before sitting back, nodding in satisfaction. "The venom of the Wolves is purged. You did well, though you were nearly undone."

"I do not understand how their curse was able to affect me so," Aliana said, a troubled look on her face. "I did not think such as we were vulnerable to the curses of a mortal."

"The curses of a mortal, aye," Anselm said sharply in reply. "But the power that created these creatures is the magic of Machaelon, sorcery. Kerebros the Wolf serves the Shadow of Mâelen Orilal, and the power he wields is *of* the Under Realm."

He sighed, allowing his moment of emotion to pass, then said in a gentler tone, "You are an Elf and thus belong to Alaren Orilal, the High Realm, but you were born into En Orilal and all the ills the Mortal Realm has to offer. While the glory of the Caletri may protect you from mortal sickness, the grace of the Elves has grown thin with each generation born into this Sphere. Such as I or Râsheth Joahin may resist the power of the Shadow, but you are barely more than a child among your kin, daughter of the Caletri."

As Aliana silently contemplated his words, Anselm cocked his head, curiosity entering his sky-blue eyes. "Tell me, daughter of the Caletri, when you felt the venom of the Wolves burning in your veins, why did you not spare yourself the suffering and walk the Road to Elekar? The curse of Kerebros could not follow you into the High Realm."

"I cannot walk that Road," Aliana replied quietly, but without hesitation. "For the one I love cannot follow without the pain of death."

Anselm gave her a startled look. "You love a *mortal?*"

"A Man," Aliana replied with a short nod. "He was but a boy, and I little more than a girl myself, when we first met, but when we touched, the sign was given that our lives would be bound. We shared memories after the manner of the Elves."

Anselm stared at her in astonishment, then turned his gaze towards the kettle, sorrow entering his face, the light of the fire dancing in his tear-misted eyes. "Then I understand why you did not leave this Sphere. The pain of loss I know all too well. My wife took my son and retreated from the Mortal Realm after my first crime, for she could not bear what I had done and what I had become."

"If you have been pardoned, why do you not follow her?" Aliana asked, her voice puzzled.

Anselm bowed his head, his face twisted in sorrow and shame. "Because I am afraid, daughter of the Caletri. My shame is too great. I cannot face my love . . . the very thought is a terror to me. I have too much to atone for."

Anselm fell silent, and Aliana did not trouble him with more questions. Instead, she pondered the answers he had given her already. After a little while, Anselm broke the silence with a rueful laugh. "Is it not strange how the lives of our people become so entwined with those of Men?"

"How so?" Aliana returned. "Is it not our mandate to guide and protect the race of Men?"

"Oh, indeed," Anselm replied with a sad smile. "Men are the chosen of Elekar . . . even Râsheth Joahin must bend his knee to the High Throne of Men, for Elekar has placed the High King of Milhavior over all living things within its borders, including Elvinkind. To nurture and guide the race of Men is our sole purpose for existence, but since the *Pâred Talletri*, since the Sundering of the Elves, it seems many have forgotten their duty.

"However, that is not of what I speak. I speak of the inexplicable binding of fates we seem to attract. You have chosen to pursue the love of a mortal. A more difficult and troublesome path, I cannot imagine. As for this one, he has bound his fate to that of the Little One. It was because of the Little One that Skrak"—Anselm let out an aggravated sigh—"that *I* was redeemed. I was commanded by the Wolf to capture the child for him, but when I saw the Little One, I could not help but think of my own son, so small when his mother took him from En Orilal. I could not betray the Little One to his death. I allowed him to escape, then waited for Kerebros to come . . . I was prepared to die."

Anselm closed his eyes against the painful memory. "I did not anticipate the appearance of the wounded Prince, the young Prince of Gildea. He came to my lair and was nearly captured by Kerebros. The resolve the Little One had stirred in my heart would not allow me to sacrifice the Prince any more than I could have turned the Little One over to the Wolf, so I wrested him from Kerebros and brought him to the Land of the Mountain, risking the Curse of Darkness."

"*You?*" Aliana exclaimed, a startled look on her face. "*You* were the creature I felt in the cave?"

Anselm sank further into himself, overwhelmed by his shame.

Chapter 14

Anselm's cheeks burned in shame and guilt. *An Elf should not feel such things. But then, perhaps the greater the pride, the greater the shame after the fall.*

It amazed him how Men seemed able to so easily cast aside guilt after a short time and move on with their lives as though their crimes did not exist. Whether it was a resilience of spirit that Men were gifted with or a lack of conscience borne of their seemingly limitless capacity for vice and corruption, he was beginning to envy them that quality. He had been pardoned by the Lightlord Elekar and returned to his own proper form, and yet he could not forgive himself.

Anselm had garnered the courage to bear a little of his soul to young Aliana, but now he could not even meet her gaze. When he felt her eyes upon him, he sensed distrust and a measure of loathing, though he knew it was likely only his own loathing of himself that he projected upon her. Whether real or imagined, he was not yet prepared to face the contempt of the world around him.

After he had allowed the broth to cool some, he instructed Aliana to wake the Men. He ladled broth into a bowl for each in turn, then filled a last bowl for the children. He stood up, walked around the dimming fire, and knelt beside Brendyn. He slipped his left arm beneath the boy and carefully raised him up, cradling him.

Brendyn stirred, his eyes cracking open to look up at the Elf, and Anselm smiled down at him. "Do not be afraid. You are safe."

The Elf moved the bowl to his left hand, then picked up the spoon with his right and brought it to Brendyn's cracked lips. "Drink this . . . it will help you."

As the warm broth touched his dry lips, Brendyn opened his mouth a little wider, allowing the fragrant liquid passage. He swallowed painfully, but without hesitation. After a few more spoonfuls, his eyes opened a little more, and he worked his mouth as though trying to speak.

"Rest," Anselm said gently. "You need your strength. You need not fear. You are among friends."

"Wh-who are you?" Brendyn finally rasped out.

Anselm smiled again. "One who owes you his life, Little One, for you set his feet upon the path to redemption."

Anselm doubted that his answer meant anything to the boy, but Brendyn seemed to accept it without question. Brendyn closed his eyes for a moment, then reopened them and said, "Is Arban all right?"

"Your friend will be fine," the Elf replied gently. "You will *both* be fine. Can you take more of this broth?"

Brendyn almost imperceptibly nodded. Anselm fed him a couple more spoonfuls, but at last Brendyn laid his head against the Elf's breast and fell asleep. Anselm switched the bowl to his right hand, then gently lowered his young charge back to the ground.

Anselm placed his hand upon the boy's chest and closed his eyes. He could feel life once again pushing back the fingers of death, strength flowing through the child's body as the medicine did its work. "Sleep well, Little One, and grow strong."

He moved around to Brendyn's other side where the second boy lay. "You must be Arban, my young friend. Well, we shall have to see that you are taken care of, too."

Anselm started to reach down to lift Arban, but he quickly drew his hand back as his fingers brushed the boy's arm. He could hardly believe what he had felt in that one brief touch. He looked from Arban to Brendyn, then back again, in stunned amazement. Leaning forward, he looked more closely at Arban and could see a faint aura surrounding the child, an opalescent sheen which flickered at the edges of his vision.

The Elf slowly reached out and laid his hand on the boy's chest, his eyes closing. His spirit was faint but the sense was unmistakable. He opened his eyes, focusing them on Arban's face. *What are you, child? You are not what you appear. You wear a glamour like a skin . . . the like I have never seen. What are you? You are not of my kindred, neither are you a Creature of Darkness.*

Taking a deep breath, he exerted the full strength of the slowly growing spark of power within him to pierce the glamour and reveal the child's true form, but the glamour resisted with such power that Anselm at last had to desert his attempts.

"Adôn Anselm?" Aliana asked, concern in her voice. "What is it?"

Anselm looked up, startled. He quickly regained his composure and waved her away. "It is nothing. I have exerted my Fire too much . . . I am far from the Elf that I once was."

Carefully, he raised Arban's head into his lap and brought a spoonful of broth to the boy's lips. Like Brendyn, Arban cracked his eyes open at the Elf's handling, but Anselm felt no fear as the boy looked up at him. He felt peace and trust . . . a trust borne not of this child's spirit, but of Brendyn's.

Anselm's hand trembled, but he managed not to spill the contents of the spoon he held. What he felt was not possible, and yet here it was. Elekar's hand was upon this child—of that he was certain—but to what purpose, he could not ascertain. Gently, trying to calm his own senses, he continued to feed Arban. When the boy had finished the rest of the broth, Anselm laid the boy back on the ground, allowing him to sleep again.

The Elf turned again to the Men. "Sleep again when you have finished. I will wake you at dawn."

*   *   *   *

Brendys was awakened by Quellin shortly before dawn. He groaned a little as he came to his senses. His muscles and joints were stiff and aching, but more than that, he felt feverishly hot. After a moment, he opened his eyes, but quickly blinked them shut again as perspiration ran into them. He lifted his good hand and wiped away a virtual torrent of sweat.

He stared at his sodden hand for a moment, then looked around. Something was different. Despite his fever, his visual acuity seemed stronger. In fact, all of his physical senses seemed to be sharper than before. He turned his gaze on Quellin and saw anxiety in the Gildean King's green eyes. "Do I look as bad as I feel?"

"Worse," Quellin replied morosely. With his own eyes, he directed Brendys's attention towards Kovar.

From the perspiration drenching the falconer's curly, red hair and streaming down his face, Brendys felt it a safe assumption that he, too, was feverish, but it became quickly obvious that it was not the fever which worried his brother-by-marriage. When Kovar turned to look at him, he saw a faint amber light shining in the man's eyes.

Brendys felt his heartbeat quicken and looked at Quellin. "Both of us?"

Quellin nodded. "And only you two. There must have been some kind of poison in the Sorcerer's bite that is causing some kind of change in you. I dare not guess at its nature."

Quellin's expression became grimmer, his voice lowering. "Though the men Karel and I found at the Dark Elf camp had the same eyes. I do not believe it is coincidence."

Brendys shivered, despite the fire burning in his veins. He took a deep breath, fighting down the panic rising in his breast. "Nor do I, but there is no sense worrying ourselves about it . . . there is nothing we can do of our own power to stop it. Perhaps we shall find Aliana, and she will have a suggestion. Otherwise, if things go badly, you may not only have to play at physic and surgeon, but at executioner."

"Do not speak of such!" Quellin hissed angrily. "I *cannot* slay the Bearer of the Flame."

Brendys felt fear pass away, leaving behind only the dull ache of sorrow. "The Bearer of the Flame is dead already. I cannot wield the sword."

Quellin glared hotly at his brother-by-marriage. "What was it you told Mathai? The sword wields *you*. Do you think it cares whether the hand which holds it is left or right?"

Brendys blinked dumbly. He was often amazed at how slowly his mind grasped small facts, and this was no exception. Once again, he had focused on the negative and had not considered every possibility. It was true. So far, the Flame had guided his hand in almost every way . . . why *would* that suddenly be any different now that he was reduced to his off-hand?

Quellin sighed. "If it comes to trouble, we will deal with it then. Right now, we should break our fast, then get moving. The sooner we are out of this accursed forest, the sooner we may find a cure for whatever ails you and Kovar."

Brendys wiped the sweat from his face again, then turned his gaze back on Quellin. "Does this mean then that your faith is restored?"

The Gildean King glared at him for a moment, then said, "I will not surrender my wife and daughter to grief and a moment of weakness. If you perish, so does the world we know."

Without another word, Quellin retreated to the litter to begin rationing that morning's provisions.

Will it? Brendys wondered. If Brendyn yet lived, and if Aliana and Novosad had found him, then his loss would mean little. Brendyn was the important one. Still, it was a small relief that Quellin had chosen not to allow Shannon's loss to destroy him as Brendys had himself done when he thought he had lost Mattina in the destruction of Quellin's ship, the *Courser*, seven years before.

After a quick bite to eat, Brendys and his companions prepared to move on. As Brendys and Quellin approached the litter, Karel rolled slowly to her knees, then stood up.

"I will walk," she told them in a firm tone. "I am weary of being dragged, and perhaps your burden will be lessened."

Neither of the men argued with her, for Quellin's injuries had already weakened him, and with his fever, Brendys was not sure how long he would be able to bear his share of the burden. Brendys and Quellin shouldered the litter and began dragging it westward, Karel following them. Brendys was surprised as the day wore on, for rather than flagging, his strength seemed to be increasing with every hour, despite the fire in his veins. Still, pauses to rest were frequent, more to give Karel a moment to catch her breath, overheated from the heavy coverings she was forced to wear, than for the relief of either of the men pulling the litter. There was plenty of shade in the forest, but the air was still stuffy.

The woods began to thin quickly, and by late afternoon, they found themselves stepping into a large clearing. A large pond took up the majority of the open space, but there was also plenty of flat, soft ground along its banks. Up a slight incline from the clearing was a tall hedgerow.

Brendys came to an abrupt stop, his gaze riveted upon the muddy ground, as he and Quellin stepped into the clearing. Quellin stumbled, thrown off-balance for a moment by the Horsemaster's sudden halt.

Whether due to his seemingly enhanced senses or simple fact, the numerous tracks pressed into the ground were immediately clear even to Brendys's untrained eyes. "Quellin. . . ."

After recovering his balance, Quellin glanced at Brendys, then followed the Horsemaster's gaze. He looked down, then back, and saw without a doubt that whoever the tracks belonged to had come from the same direction. He cast an astonished look at Brendys.

Without waiting for instruction, Karel moved forward and began to examine the prints. "These larger prints were made by military boots, and there is another set that is much lighter and a little smaller."

She looked up at Brendys and Quellin, a hopeful expression on her face. "I think these belong to my father's party!"

"Kerebros mentioned killing four men," Quellin said. "That does leave Novosad and the others unaccounted for."

"The lighter set is very difficult to make out," Karel replied. "I am almost sure they belong to Lady Aliana.

Only an Elf could step so lightly. And as for the heavier prints, they clearly belong to Men, and if you recall, the Men we found at the Dark Elf camp were bare-footed."

She looked around some more, then abruptly stood up and turned to the men again. Brendys could see the glitter of her wide eyes from within the shadow of her hood. "I-I think Prince Brendyn was here too! There are booted prints belonging to a child here. . . ."

"You have quick eyes, lass," a deep, jovial voice interjected.

All eyes glanced up towards the hedgerow. A tall, fair man with thick, golden hair stood at a break in the hedges, his muscular arms crossed over his chest. His eyes sparkled in the sunlight, and he had a heavy drooping mustache. The man was grinning broadly.

Brendys stared in disbelief. It had been many years, but he could not forget the strange farmer who had given him and Kradon shelter on their fateful journey to the Shipyard of Ilkatar. The man did not appear to have aged a day, despite the passing of the years. "Master Elgern. . . ?"

The farmer laughed. "So, you remember me, Brendys of Shalkan?"

Brendys felt Quellin's eyes upon him and quickly explained. "Master Elgern owns a farm between Shalkan and the Shipyard of Ilkatar."

His gaze turned back to Elgern. "But what are you doing out here?"

The man gave him a mysterious smile. "I was returning home from a journey in the north. I came across a young boy wandering in these woods—your son, I believe, Master Brendys. I helped him along as far as I could, but it then occurred to me that you might have need of aid as well . . . and from the looks of you, it appears I was right."

"Where is Brendyn?" Brendys asked, his gaze looking beyond the big farmer, hope rekindled in his heart.

306

"I left him in the capable hands of your Hagane friends," Elgern replied, still smiling. "They will see to his safety."

Brendys felt a great wave of relief sweep over him. If Novosad and the twins were alive, Aliana was more than likely with them, and he could not hope for better guardians for his son. His relief was short-lived, for Elgern stepped closer, his smile fading as he examined Brendys.

"How many of you were bitten?" Elgern said, his eyes darting to each of the companions, his voice heavy with concern.

Quellin started in surprise. "How did you. . . ."

Elgern cut him off with a sharp glance. "Answer, for your lives may depend on it."

"Only Kovar and I," Brendys replied, motioning towards the litter.

Elgern hurried to Kovar's side and knelt down, staring intently at the falconer's shattered leg. Shaking his head grimly, he rose to his feet and turned back towards the others. "Was it Kerebros himself or one of his Wolves?"

Brendys understood Quellin's shock, for it seemed this *farmer* had encountered the Sorcerer before. Brendys had always thought there was something disturbing about the man, and Elgern's knowledge of Kerebros confirmed his feelings. "It was Kerebros. I think I slew him. . . ."

"I am not so sure," Quellin interjected. "He vanished in a red light, as we have seen another Sorcerer do."

"He may be wounded," Elgern replied. "But he is not dead. I think it more likely he has retreated to lick his wounds, but he *will* come hunting you . . . the venom of his curse burns in your veins, Master Brendys, and your friend's."

The farmer shouldered the litter. "I have not the gift of healing that my cousin Etzel in Gildea has. Your best hope is to return to Shalkan as quickly as possible. Gwydnan may be able to counteract the curse, but your time is short. Come, I have a wagon on the other side of the hedges."

"Etzel was your *cousin?*" Brendys said in stunned amazement. He noticed that Quellin's eyes had gone wide in awe.

"We are of the same Kindred," Elgern replied shortly, explaining nothing. "Now, come."

Still astounded by the sudden appearance of the farmer and the strangeness of the news he brought, Brendys as his companions followed the man through the break in the hedgerow. Quellin and Elgern managed to lift Kovar, litter and all, into the bed of the wagon, then Elgern picked up Karel by the waist as if she were a small child and put her in the back with the Gildean warrior.

Elgern turned to Brendys and Quellin and led them towards the front of the wagon. "Follow the road south out of the forest. Make your way as quickly as possible. There are enough provisions in the wagon to see you to Shalkan."

"You are not coming with us?" Quellin asked, a touch of worry in his voice. "If Kerebros is hunting us. . . ."

Elgern shook his head. "Nay, I have my own tasks to be about. A word of warning: if the curse is not purged from Brendys and your other friend—Kovar?—and Kerebros confronts you, they will become as his Wolves."

"What are these *Wolves?*" Brendys asked. The farmer's words disturbed him greatly.

Elgern turned his gaze on the Horsemaster. "If you have not met the Wolves of Kerebros, then pray you never do. Now, hurry."

"What of you?" Quellin asked.

Elgern's grin returned to his face. "I have Wolves to hunt. I slew one near the edge of the forest, but his companion escaped, and I must also deal with Kerebros."

The farmer turned and walked back towards the break in the hedgeline.

308

Quellin helped Brendys onto the seat of the wagon, then climbed up himself, taking up the reins.

Brendys looked back through the break in the hedgerow towards the clearing and saw a large, golden dog—an odd-looking animal he had seen once long ago outside the window of Elgern's home—standing just beneath the eaves of the woods on the far side of the clearing. The dog stared back at him for a moment, then turned and disappeared into the forest.

"Not a word," Quellin said, staring straight ahead, his face ashen. He flicked the reins and the horses started forward. "If Elgern is of the same Kindred as Etzel, I think things will go ill for Kerebros and his Wolves—whatever they may be—should Elgern find them."

Brendys could not disagree. The Gildean people had called Etzel a witch, and he had personally seen her hurl a fireball at a Kubruk during the Gildean rebellion against Iysh Mawvath . . . he doubted she was a witch, but that she was a being of great power, he could not deny. What confused him more was Elgern's faith that Gwydnan could remove the Sorcerer's curse from him and Kovar.

"Why Gwydnan?" Brendys mused aloud.

"There is more to that old badger than we can see on the outside, Brendys," Quellin replied.

Brendys nodded silently, wiping the sweat from his stinging eyes. After all he had witnessed, he would hardly be surprised to learn that Gwydnan was also one of Elgern's *cousins*.

* * * *

The sun had begun to peek over the eastern horizon. The dawn was muggy, but not unbearable, though Novosad knew the day would only get hotter as it wore on. It was strange weather for the region—the vast Western Sea was only a few days' ride from the camp—but the summer had been extreme even in Racolis, where drought had killed many a crop already. *Would that the west wind showed us some mercy this day*, he thought as he watched Anselm feed the children.

The Elf's medicinal broth had indeed worked a miracle in a short time. Both of the boys were fully alert, though still weak, but strength was quickly returning to them. Novosad himself had felt his own strength renewed after drinking his share of the fragrant liquid, though he would have liked something solid to go with it.

As Anselm turned away from Brendyn to feed the other child, Brendyn started to lay down again. The Elf reached out a hand and grasped the tatters of Brendyn's sleeve, holding him upright, and said, "Nay, Little One, do not sleep. You should try to stand, try to walk . . . it will help the medicine work more quickly."

"But I'm tired," Brendyn complained. "And I hurt. I walked a long way by myself before that dog found me. Where's the dog, anyway?"

A pained look entered Anselm's sky-blue eyes. "Skrak should not have let you walk at all. He should have carried you to the Land of the Mountain himself, but he was afraid."

"You know Skrak?" Brendyn said wonderingly. "Is he all right? Did that Kerebros hurt him?"

Novosad shifted his gaze to Anselm, confusion settling in, for Brendyn spoke as though he knew Skrak, but he clearly had never met Anselm, who had claimed *Skrak* as name given him by the minions of Thanatos.

"Kerebros the Wolf did not harm Skrak," Anselm replied, a hint of a blush rising to his fair cheeks. "Still, Skrak is dead. All that remains is Anselm. He is as he once was . . . before he became the Betrayer. He has you to thank for that. You guided his cowardly heart to courage and compassion, and that is a road which led to redemption."

Brendyn's eyes widened suddenly. "*You're* Skrak?"

310

"Once, but no more," Anselm replied, cringing under the child's gaze, a hint of a whine underlying his fair voice. "Skrak is dead."

From the edge of his vision, Novosad saw Aliana rise to her feet. The Elfess came to stand over Brendyn, offering her hand to the child. "Come, Your Highness, walk with me. I will try to explain what Adôn Anselm is trying to say."

Brendyn looked from Aliana to Anselm, then back, before he took Aliana's hand and allowed her to help him to his feet. As he and the Elfess slowly walked away, Anselm continued to assist young Arban with his bowl of broth. The mute boy stared at Anselm with the same confusion Novosad had seen on Brendyn's face before he had left with Aliana, and the Elf could not meet his gaze.

"Why, My Lord, do you speak as you do?" Novosad finally asked, breaking the nervous silence. "Why do you speak of yourself as another. You are unlike any Elf I have ever met before."

Anselm's shoulders hunched even further, and Novosad wondered that he did not drop the bowl in his hands. The Elf did not reply immediately, but continued to feed Arban. As the boy finished his breakfast, Anselm turned his shamed face towards Novosad, avoiding the Man's gaze. "Anselm . . . *I* am unlike any other Elf, for no other Elf suffers the mortal illness which I have suffered for four of your Ages. You see, I am mad."

The Elf suddenly became defensive. "And you would be no less mad had you worn the accursed shape I was condemned to wear since the early foundations of this Sphere. I could not accept that the creature I had become was truly *me*, and so could not speak of myself as myself. Four-Age-old habits do not leave so easily."

Novosad wrinkled his brow, trying to make sense of the Elf's confused words and failing. "I do not understand.

Are you saying that you used to be something other than an Elf?"

Anselm bowed his head, his cheeks turning red. "I was first as you see me now, but then Skrak . . . *I* betrayed Elekar, and he cursed me, and others like me, to the forms of Jaf and Drolar. For Four Ages, I have lived as a Jaf. My trust and my sacrifice have earned me redemption, but it seems madness and shame shall still be my punishment to bear."

A Jaf? It was no wonder that the Elf seemed strange.

Chapter 15

Arella stared out through the open flap at the dark line on the horizon that was all she could see of Ilkatar Forest and wondered for the thousandth time in four days if her son yet lived. Tears had flowed for the first two days, but then reason and despair had taken hold. Tears would not save her son, if he yet lived. All that she could do for him now was to pray.

She felt the small form of her young daughter nestling against her, and she turned to wrap her arms around her. She looked into Sîan's large brown eyes and saw her own fear and concern mirrored there. She gently stroked her daughter's cheek and kissed her on the forehead.

"Mother, will Shannon be all right?" Sîan asked in a tremulous voice.

Arella had heard that question many times in the last four days, almost as often from her own lips as from her daughter's. Every time, she had been quick to assure her little girl, but now she only responded with a sad smile. Her heart had grown numb with despair. She could no longer feel hope.

"Of course, Sîan."

Mother and daughter both turned their attention to the young woman lying on the cushions in the bed of the wagon. Mattina's smile was weak, but there was more life in her eyes than Arella had seen in the last few days. Her fever was beginning to recede.

"Your father and your Uncle Brendys will find the boys," Mattina continued in a reassuring tone. "The Dawn King will not abandon them in their hour of need."

Arella bowed her head, closing her eyes. She yearned to have the faith that her sister-by-marriage showed so readily, but blind trust and hope had abandoned her.

"Arella," Mattina said firmly, drawing the Gildean Queen's gaze back to her. The younger woman's green eyes were stern, as though she had read Arella's very thoughts. "They *will* be found."

Arella raised her eyes to Lara, who sat on the bench across from her with Lonel her daughter. The handmaid and the children had shared the wagon with Arella and Mattina since they had broken camp at the edge of Ilkatar Forest for the wagon they had occupied was being used to transport the wounded. From the expression Arella saw on the other woman's face, she was confident that Mattina was the only one in the wagon holding onto hope.

Very soon, the caravan began the long crawl up the East Road into Barrier Mountain, passing into the tiny country of Shalkan. They passed through many small towns and villages and watched the scattered farms along the east-west road drift by. By late afternoon, they finally arrived at their destination. Arella heard Lieutenant Gowan calling the company to a halt as the wagons trundled into the fenced confines of Brendys's farmstead.

The next voice Arella heard was that of Kanstanon, calling out, "There are not enough empty stalls in the stables . . . you will have to put most of these animals out in the paddock."

Without waiting for assistance, Arella climbed out the back of the wagon and dropped to the ground. She rounded the corner of the wagon and saw the brown-haired stablehand heading for the wagon bearing the wounded, a look of focused urgency on his face. She called out to him, motioning for him to come at once. "Kanstanon, come help with Mattina."

The stablehand's expression abruptly changed to one of wonder, and he hurried to join Arella. "Mistress Mattina? She is here?"

He quickly took down the ramp from its place on the side of the wagon and attached it to the rear of the wain. Before he was halfway up the ramp, Mattina appeared at the opening. Her eyes were dark from her recent feverish bout, but she had changed little since he had seen her last. He took her hand and slowly assisted her down the ramp.

As they reached the bottom, Mattina looked up into his face and gave him a wan smile, placing her hand on his cheek. "Oh, Kanstanon, it is good to be home at last."

She embraced the younger man, then stepped back again.

Kanstanon tried to return her smile, but he could not maintain it. "I only wish it were under better circumstances, Mistress Mattina."

"You appear to have been expecting us," Arella said, giving the stablehand a curious look.

Kanstanon replied with a nod of his head. "Aye, Your Majesty. Lord Anselm told us somewhat of your encounter at Ilkatar Forest. I have had a few days to convert the front room into a decent infirmary."

Arella's brow furrowed in confusion. "Lord Anselm? I am not familiar with the name. Did he say how he came by this knowledge?"

Kanstanon hesitated, an uncomfortable look on his face. "It is a rather complicated tale, Your Majesty. If you will give me leave, I will tell you the full story after I have seen to the wounded. You should know, however, that he brought Prince Shannon here four days ago."

"My Shannon is *here?*" Arella exclaimed. She turned and looked towards the house as though expecting to see her son emerge at any moment.

Kanstanon's discomfort grew. "Your Majesty, Prince Shannon has taken some small hurt. The wound itself is not bad, but he is overcome by an unnatural illness. His life even now hangs by the barest thread. It is taking all of Master Gwydnan's strength to keep him alive."

Arella looked as if she would go at once to the house, but Kanstanon grasped her arm, firmly, but gently. "I beg your pardon, Your Majesty, but you should not disturb them. Master Gwydnan must concentrate. His strength wanes, and I fear if his focus is disturbed, it will fail altogether."

"Listen to him, Arella," Mattina said in a tired voice from the stablehand's side. "And trust Gwydnan. He is a very special man."

Kanstanon avoided the women's gazes, muttering, "More special than you know."

Arella and Mattina both fixed their stares on him.

"How do you mean?" Arella asked cautiously.

The stablehand struggled in indecision for a moment, but finally answered. "Master Gwydnan will never forgive me, but you should know. He is—*was*—a Wizard. Master Odyniec was his apprentice."

There was a moment of stunned silence. Before anyone else could speak, Kanstanon gently took Mattina by the arm, and said, "Come, Mistress Mattina, I will help you to your room, then I must attend the wounded."

"Wait, Kanstanon," Mattina said, gripping his arm. "This Anselm . . . he . . . is Brendyn here as well?"

"Nay, Mistress Mattina," the stablehand responded. Seeing Mattina's eyes begin to mist over and her shoulders begin to slump worse, he added quickly, "But do not lose

316

hope . . . Lord Anselm swore he knew where to find Master Brendyn. He left here with a wagon and provisions almost immediately after delivering Prince Shannon. Given his most unusual entrance, I would not be surprised to see him return soon with Master Brendyn in tow."

Mattina nodded, but her gaze lowered, a tear escaping her eye.

"Your Highness?" a woman's voice said from behind them. "Are you all right?"

Kanstanon turned startled eyes to the golden-haired woman leading two little girls from the wagon.

Mattina wiped the tear from her cheek and straightened up as well as she could. "Aye . . . aye, of course. I am just weary from the journey."

She glanced up at Kanstanon, who was still staring open-mouthed at the handmaid. Despite her forlorn mood, she could not help but smile at the stablehand. "Kanstanon, this is Lara and her daughter, Lonel. They helped care for me at Lener Keep. You have already met my niece, Sîan, of course."

Kanstanon inclined his head to Lara, keeping his eyes upon her. "Welcome to Shalkan."

Lara gave him a shy smile and inclined her head in return. "Thank you."

Gowan soon joined them, approaching Mattina. "Your Highness, what should we do with the wounded."

"It seems that Kanstanon was prepared for our arrival," Mattina replied. "Take them into the front room."

"Very well, Your Highness," the soldier replied. He glanced at Kanstanon. "I could use a hand with Willerth."

"Willerth was injured?" Kanstanon said in alarm.

"Aye," Gowan replied. "He took a wound to the head while trying to protect the children . . . only he does not want to admit that it is as bad as it is. It has been a trial getting him to rest."

Kanstanon sighed. "I suppose I will have to deal with him. I know how obstinate he can be."

The stablehand turned back to Mattina. "Will you be all right now, Mistress Mattina?"

"Of course, she will be," Arella answered for her sister-by-marriage. "You go help with the wounded. Lara and I will take care of Mattina."

Kanstanon sketched a quick bow to Arella. "As you wish, Your Majesty."

As the young man hurried to see to his charges, Arella took Mattina by the elbow and began to lead her to the house.

"I can walk on my own," Mattina protested.

"Perhaps," the Gildean Queen returned. "And you could also just as easily fall flat on your face. Your fever may be receding, but it has taken the strength out of you, and you know it."

Mattina sighed in frustration, but allowed herself to be led like a feeble old woman to the house.

Once inside, they passed through the makeshift infirmary to the corridor leading to the master bedroom. Despite her protestations, Mattina sat on the edge of the bed, letting out a breath of relief. "Ah! It is *so* good to be home . . . my own bed, my own clothes, all the comforts that can only be found at home."

She looked up at her handmaid. "Lara, please fetch a basin of water . . . I really want to get this dust off."

"Aye, Your Highness," the woman said with a curtsy.

"Mistress Mattina, if you must use a title," Mattina corrected her. "In this house, in this land, I am not royalty."

"As you wish," Lara replied with a blush. She quickly left the room in search of the kitchens.

Arella stared out at the closed door of Gwydnan's room across the hall, longing in her heart.

"Arella," Mattina said from behind her, her tone a concerned warning. "Don't."

Arella turned to face her, her brown eyes misting. "I know. I . . . I am just afraid, Mattina, afraid that I may still lose my little boy."

Mattina motioned for her to sit beside her, and Arella obeyed. The younger woman put her arms around her sister-by-marriage, and said in a firm but comforting voice, "Shannon *will* be fine."

"I am ashamed of my selfishness," Arella berated herself. "My Shannon is here and in the care of a Wizard, while Brendyn remains lost in the wilderness, and I have given little thought to him."

A look of pain passed across Mattina's youthful features, but passed quickly. "Nay. Shannon is your son, and it is only reasonable that you think of him before all others. Besides, the Dawn King will deliver Brendyn safely . . . never you fear."

* * * *

The black mountain rose up above the rest of the range, a great, obsidian fortress, many-spired, snow filtering through cracks and gorges in its otherwise impenetrable surface. The violent north wind whipped around the mountain's sides, shrieking in the crevices like ancient, tormented spirits. One path alone was sheltered from the brunt of the northern storm, a narrow stairway of ice and stone leading up to the gaping entrance of the caverns within the bowels of the mountain.

Up this steep, frozen stair, a single man crawled on his belly, dragging himself inch-by-inch with one muscular arm. He was not clad for travel through the icy wastes of the Far North, though the cold did not trouble him. His body was covered only with a jerkin of wolf-skins and a cowl of wolf heads, one on each shoulder and the third adorning his head like a hood, leaving his arms and chest bare. The muzzle of the head seated over his left shoulder had been sheared away, the fur of the skull dark and matted with dried blood. Snow-wash had cleansed the blood from his arm, and the freezing winds had staunched the gaping slash in his bicep and the wounds where the Sword of the Dawn had pierced his body through.

Kerebros dragged himself on, but his strength was quickly leaving him. It had taken every last ounce of his magic to transport himself to mountainous barrens of the Far North, his life's blood draining from his body, barely escaping death at the hand of the Bearer of the Flame. At last, he collapsed against the rough stone steps and lay still.

One last choking laugh escaped the Sorcerer's lips. He might die in that cold place, but he would at least have the satisfaction of knowing that the great Bearer of the Flame was doomed, doomed to betray everyone he loved as the curse with which he had been infected gradually took hold and changed him. Brendys of Shalkan would never fulfill his prophesied destiny.

Kerebros felt the cold touch of gauntleted hands grasping his arms, tugging him upwards, dragging him up the cold stairs.

"I warned you, Wolf," came the calm, fair voice of Krifka, quiet, yet audible above the terrible winds. "Your brutish ways, uncontrolled and unguided, will always fail."

Kerebros wanted to laugh, but he lacked the strength. Nevertheless, his dying spirit would meet its Master with the knowledge that his *brutish ways* had brought about the downfall of the Lightlord Elekar.

*   *   *   *

Arella sat on the shaded porch of Brendys's house, her brown eyes fixed upon the east-west road that led past the farmstead. She wore a plain, light dress not at all appropriate for the Queen of Gildea, but certainly much cooler on a hot summer day than anything she had brought with her. Arella knew it could not have belonged to Mattina, for it fit her fairly well, and Mattina was a smaller woman than she. Perhaps it had belonged to Danel, Brendys's mother . . . if so, Arella had decided, common women had much more sense than those of the noble classes.

Since arriving at the farmstead the day before, there had been little for Arella to do, but to watch and worry for her son's life and her husband's return. No one but Kanstanon had been allowed into Gwydnan's room, and even he was only permitted to deliver somewhat for his master to eat. Mattina was in Lara's capable hands, and Willerth, despite instructions to rest, assisted Kanstanon in caring for those more seriously wounded than himself.

"Your Majesty . . . are you ill?"

Arella looked up at the handmaid standing just outside the open front door to her left. She shook her head. "Nay, Lara, just weary and worried."

"Worried about Prince Shannon?" Lara asked. "I am sure he will be well, Your Majesty. Master Odyniec was able to cure Prin . . . Mistress Mattina of the Plague. I am sure this Gwydnan will heal Prince Shannon. It just takes time."

Arella smiled wanly. "I am sure you are right, Lara, but still I cannot help but worry. Do not concern yourself. I will be fine."

"Aye, Your Majesty," the woman replied. She hesitated a moment, then spoke again. "Mistress Mattina is resting now, and I thought you might like some company, Your Majesty. . . ."

Arella's smile brightened a little, and she took Lara's hand in hers. "I would be grateful indeed. Come, sit beside me."

The handmaid's eyes widened a little, and she hesitated again.

"There are no niggling old noblewomen here to whisper about the impropriety of a servant sitting in the presence of a Queen," Arella assured her. Her gaze swept across the farmstead beyond the confines of the porch as she sighed. "Here, there is no royalty or nobility. All are the same, all common."

"Not the same, Your Majesty," Lara said earnestly. "These people treat you according to your rank."

Arella laughed softly at the handmaid's response. "They bow and call me *Your Majesty*, but they have not the loyalty to title that other peoples have. You have not yet met Gwydnan . . . I have no doubt the old badger would not hesitate to set me straight if he felt I were out of place."

Before Lara could contradict the Gildean Queen, the handmaid's daughter came dashing up the porch steps, followed in a more ladylike manner by Sîan. Lonel thrust a fistful of dandelions and other blooming weeds, mixed with a few wild flowers, up at her mother. "We picked some flowers for Princess Mattina, Mama. She's been so sad . . . do you think she'll like them?"

Arella leaned towards the girl with a kindly smile. "They are lovely, Lonel! I am sure Mattina will be delighted."

Sîan rolled her eyes and grimaced sourly, eliciting a warning glare from her mother. Arella noted that her daughter's bouquet was comprised almost exclusively of wild flowers, most of which she was sure Sîan had acquired from Lonel's hands. *So much for the equality of all in Shalkan*, she thought.

"Sîan, Lonel, why don't you have Willerth put those flowers in some water, then you can take them to Mattina," Arella suggested to the children. Even as the words left her lips, the faint clatter of distant wagon wheels drew her attention. At once, she rose to her feet and went to the porch railing, leaning out so she could get a better view. Behind her, she heard Lara shoo the children inside, then she also stepped towards the railing.

A wagon was coming down the road from the east. As the wagon turned through the gate at the end of the yard, Arella could see that the driver wore the mail and surcoat of a warrior, tattered and mud-darkened. She did not immediately recognize the driver, but the soft light which shone from the woman seated next to him, through the dirt and grime bespattering her face and her now-ragged garments, was unmistakable. As the wagon drew nearer, she could see the shoulders and heads of two more men above the sides of the wain . . . and with them, the heads of two children.

Her heart leaping within her breast, she called out in a voice accustomed to being heard from all quarters of a castle. "Kanstanon! Willerth! A wagon comes!"

Gathering her skirts, Arella hurried past Lara and out into the stableyard. Lara remained on the porch, staring out at the approaching wagon almost as anxiously as the Gildean Queen.

Kanstanon immediately emerged from the stable, trotting back towards the house. Willerth rushed out of the house and practically fell down the porch steps to meet Arella and Kanstanon in the stableyard. The amber-haired young man abruptly raised a hand to his bandaged head.

Kanstanon grasped Willerth's shoulder. "Are you all right?"

Willerth nodded in reply. "Aye . . . just a little too eager."

As the wagon came to a stop, Copanas and Lehan climbed out of the back, each one reaching up to assist the younger passengers down. Arella's hand flew to her mouth in shock and amazement when Brendyn stood up and turned towards Copanas. If it were possible, her young nephew looked worse than Novosad and his companions.

His eyes and cheeks were dark and sunken, his lips severely cracked and scabbed. His normally full hair was a tangled and lank mess, matted with mud. His clothes were in shreds, and the flesh showing beneath was covered with ugly scrapes and scratches and sores.

Willerth found his voice before Arella and gasped out. "Oh, Master Brendyn!"

Arella looked at the young man and saw a look of horror in his grey eyes such as she had not seen since Willerth had stumbled into the Great Hall of Gildea Keep covered in blood at the wedding of Mattina and Brendys.

Brendyn turned his weak gaze towards Willerth, and immediately upon seeing the manservant launched himself towards the young man, ignoring Copanas's outreached arms. The Hagane scout barely managed to catch the boy before he fell to the ground. Willerth rushed forward to receive the struggling child from Copanas.

Brendyn frantically threw his arms around Willerth's neck and clung tightly to him, great heart-wrenching sobs wracking his small frame. Willerth, too, wept as he hugged the little boy to himself.

"You are all right, Master Brendyn," the servant said, trying to soothe the boy. "You are home now."

Arella laid a gentle hand on her nephew's back. She wanted to say something to the boy, but could not find the words. She gave him a pat, then turned, a look of surprise on her face, as Lehan lifted the second boy out of the wagon. "Who is this?"

The scout shook his head. "I cannot say, Your Majesty. Prince Brendyn calls him Arban, but beyond that we know nothing. From what Prince Brendyn told us on the journey here, the boy was left for dead in the forest."

Arella looked the boy in the face. Arban did not return her stare, but fixed his green eyes on Brendyn's back. There was a sadness in the boy's eyes, and a yearning.

Arella shook her head sadly. If it were possible, his condition was even more pitiable, for it was clear he had not been kept well even before whatever ordeal had befallen her nephew and this child.

She reached a hand up and lightly placed it on the boy's filthy black mane. At her touch, Arban drew back, startled. Arella gave him a gentle smile. "Do not be afraid."

"He cannot hear you, nor answer you, Your Majesty. He is both deaf and mute."

Arella threw a startled look of her own in Novosad's direction.

"And he was not the strangest of Prince Brendyn's companions," the Hagane warrior continued. The man gave an exhausted sigh. "If you would forgive me, Your Majesty, it is a long tale, and I would rather have a decent meal and a good sleep before the telling of it."

"Of course," Arella replied, resting her hand on the warrior's arm. She turned towards the porch to call to Lara, but stopped before she spoke. Mattina was descending from the porch, using the stair railing for balance, Lara fretting beside her.

As Mattina reached the ground, she raised her eyes, her gaze landing first upon Arban. Her face paled, her expression a mixture of confusion and fear, and her legs became unsteady beneath her. She closed her eyes, averting her gaze.

"Mistress Mattina?" Lara asked with concern as she grasped Mattina's elbow to steady her.

Mattina reopened her eyes and looked up at her handmaid, a tremulous smile playing at her lips. "It is nothing. The fever . . . it plays tricks on my mind. I will be fine."

Brendyn's head jerked up at the sound of his mother's voice, and he let go his hold on Willerth. The servant set

325

his young charge on the ground, and Brendyn ran to his mother.

Mattina knelt to receive her little boy in her arms, hugging him close. "Oh, my dear . . . I was so afraid for you!"

While Mattina soothed her sobbing child, Arella turned to Willerth. "Fetch something for the men and boys to eat . . . they look famished."

"But do not allow the children to eat too quickly, nor too much," Aliana said, dropping down from the wagon. "They have had nothing to eat but a medicinal broth for a very long time. Solid food will do them good, but slowly."

Willerth stepped closer to Aliana, wiping the tears from his eyes. "Thank you . . . thank you for finding Master Brendyn and for bringing him home. Aliana, I . . . ."

The young man stammered to silence, a look of pain and longing flashing through his grey eyes before he turned away and walked back towards the house, Novosad and the twins following in his wake. Arella stared at the back of his tawny head for a moment, before looking away. That the son of a common vagrant and the daughter of a great Elvinlord could share such a love as they did was something she could not comprehend.

It was not the difference in their rank that troubled her— the Elves did not view rank in the same way as Men, and also she was quite accustomed to disregarding rank herself—but this was different. It was like trying to unite the new moon and the darkness surrounding it with the glory of the sun at its zenith. Willerth was a gentle soul, loyal and loving, but he could not seem to completely throw off the shadow of doubt and self-loathing his father had instilled in him, and it had clearly become a chain to imprison his heart.

Aliana, on the other hand, had refused to be defeated by Willerth's prison. Ever since that fateful night at Gildea

Keep so many years ago when love and terror had bound the hearts of a young mortal boy and an Elvin girl, Aliana had sought to break through the walls surrounding Willerth's heart, though it now was beginning to appear that the Elfess was starting to flag. Arella noted with some sorrow that Aliana's gaze had become despondent as she watched Willerth retreat to the house.

Arella briefly turned her gaze back to the road beyond the farmstead, wondering if her husband still wandered Ilkatar Forest, avoiding the dangers of the wood, seeking two children who had already been found. With a weary sigh, she reminded herself again that everything would be all right.

*   *   *   *

Brendys sat beside Quellin, his head bowed and eyes closed. The rattle of the wagon thundered in his ears, every bump jarring his insides. The constant stream of perspiration running down his face was maddening, the heat of his fever burning through his very being. He was changing . . . changing into *what*, he did not know. Elgern had said he was becoming as the Wolves of Kerebros, but what that meant, he did not know. Was he becoming such a creature as Kerebros himself could take the form of, or was it something altogether different?

His son had escaped the forest, his family was safe . . . for that, he should be rejoicing. But now he was bringing danger back to them. Whatever this venom was that was changing him physically, he could feel its sorcerous influence also tugging at his mind. His will was yet strong enough that he felt confident that he could resist it awhile longer, but how long? How long would it take for the change to become complete, for the will of Kerebros to conquer his own? Days, Months? Or just hours?

Even if he could hold out, could Kovar? Had the falconer's will been so weakened by his grief over

Amrein's death that he would fail sooner? In the last few days, Kovar had begged for his own death so many times he had lost count. Had he felt his will weakening further?

"Do not give up on me now," he heard Quellin say, his voice grim. "Gwydnan *will* be able to help. We are almost there."

Brendys opened his eyes, ignoring the sting of the sweat in his eyes. Though the sun was failing, his heightened sight let him see clearly the farmstead in the distance. *Home. . . .*

Chapter 16

The dimming red light of the sunset filtered through the room's single window, outlining the faces of the bed's occupants. Brendyn lay on his back, his face not looking nearly as sunken as it had before his meal and bath that morning. Arban, the strange boy he had found in the forest, was curled up beside him, the flute Brendyn had given him still hanging around his neck. Likewise, Brendyn still wore the signet ring Lord Guthwine had given to him on his birthday. The faint light emanating from the inset stone revealing that it was still healing some hurt.

I failed again. Tears welled up in Willerth's grey eyes as he looked down upon the sleeping children. *The children were my responsibility, and I failed to protect them. For what Master Brendyn and Prince Shannon have been forced to endure because of my failure, my life should forfeit.*

Willerth closed his eyes and wrapped his hand around the pendant hanging at his breast, seeking its soothing warmth. The Elvinsilver charm shimmered slightly at his touch. As usual, the image of Aliana's face sprang up before his mind's eye, her light and warmth filling him.

This time, however, it did not bring him peace, but rather a fresh wave of guilt.

Another failure. Aliana had ridden out that afternoon without even a word of farewell, but Willerth had no one to blame for that other than himself. Aliana had risked everything, suffered the venomed bite of a Creature of Darkness, bearing its curse in her own body, all to save Willerth's young master—all to sway his heart, he was sure, though it was a gesture she need not have made, for his heart belonged almost wholly to her—yet he had pointedly avoided her since she had arrived that morning, denying himself the things he yearned for most at that time: his beloved's soothing words, her soft caress, and gentle embrace. But these were things he could not have, and he knew it. He was not worthy of her love. He was so far below her that he could never hope to reach her.

Child of Darkness. That was what the Alar, Uhyvainyn, had called him as he despaired beside the grave of his master's father in Sharamitaro. He knew that the shadow of Evil he had for so long feared within himself was nothing more than an illusion, a trick of the mind planted there by the vicious man who had been his own father, but still he could not forget what had happened to him, his deepest shame, and that in itself was a kind of shadow, a kind of darkness. And that darkness separated him from the light that was Aliana.

Willerth felt a small hand slip into his own, and he opened his eyes, looking down.

Lonel stood beside him, holding his hand, her liquid gaze resting upon Brendyn, worry wrinkling her brow. Slowly, she looked up at the young man. "Willerth, is Prince Brendyn going to be all right?"

Willerth blinked back his tears and smiled at her, answering in a soft voice. "Of course, Lonel. He just needs to sleep."

The little girl frowned a little more deeply. "That's what Mama said about Princess Mattina, and she almost died."

Willerth sobered at the girl's expression. He looked down at her in silence for a brief moment, then sighed. "I will not lie to you, Lonel. If Master Brendyn had gone very much longer without water, he likely *would* have died. Even so, if Lord Anselm had not given him the medicine he made, he might still have died."

"The Elf Captain Novosad talked about?"

"Aye," Willerth said, nodding in response.

A thoughtful look crossed the girl's face. "Was Lord Anselm really a Jaf?"

That was a tale Willerth might not have believed had his own father not had the power to transform into a Drolar, a demon akin to the man-bat Jaf. He might still have doubted Novosad's story had not Kanstanon and Brendyn confirmed the Hagane's report. Brendyn had himself related a strange and rather confused story passed to him by Lord Anselm about how Jaf and Drolar alike had once been Elves. Willerth was sure that some details of his young master's story were muddled, but the gist of the tale corroborated Novosad's account.

Willerth shrugged. "I suppose he was. Master Brendyn told me that Anselm saved him from the Sorcerer when he was still a Jaf, and he brought Prince Shannon here also while a Jaf."

"Oh."

Willerth turned the girl towards the door. "Come. We should let the boys sleep . . . and you should be getting ready for bed yourself."

Lonel nodded, glancing worriedly at Brendyn once more before leaving the room.

Willerth slowly eased himself onto the edge of the bed, careful not to disturb its sleeping occupants. He reached out a hand and gently brushed a few strands of black hair away from Brendyn's face. The boy winced in his sleep and stirred a little, but he did not awaken. Simultaneously, the other boy also stirred, a painful grimace on his sunburned face, but unlike Brendyn, his eyes cracked open, the dim lamplight reflecting in the dark sliver of green showing between his eyelashes.

Willerth cursed himself inwardly. He should have known better than to touch his young master. The boy's skin had been scorched red by exposure to the sun, even blistering in some places, and it was extremely dry from dehydration. Though Anselm's medicine had restored much of the water to the children's bodies, their skin remained very sensitive.

That fact had become more evident when he gave the boys their bath. He had tried to explain to Brendyn that it was necessary. Their bodies were so riddled with sores and scratches that needed to be cleansed so as to avoid infection. Truthfully, Willerth was surprised none had already infected, perhaps another effect of Anselm's medicine.

Kanstanon had given Willerth some soothing powders from Gwydnan's strange medicinal supply which were supposed to help ease the children's pain, but they did not help as much as Willerth had hoped. Brendyn tried to put on a brave face and bear it, but the pain was simply too much. He wept terribly, sobs wracking his small frame.

Willerth had been so intent on caring for his young master that he had not immediately noticed that the other boy had also started crying. His young master's pain nearly set him to tears as well, and he had to pause to collect himself and to allow Brendyn some relief. That was when he first noticed Arban crying—in sympathy to Brendyn, he assumed.

I am so sorry Master Brendyn, he had told his young master, trying to comfort himself as much as Brendyn. *I know it hurts, but it must be done.*

I know, Brendyn had said through his sobs. Though his face was screwed in pain, the look he had given Willerth had been one of complete and utter trust. Willerth should have been comforted a little by that knowledge, but he was not. His heart stung the worse at the thought that he had to cause such pain to this child who trusted him.

He had steeled himself and set to work again. That was when he first realized that Arban was *not* weeping out of sympathy for Brendyn. As soon as the wash rag touched Brendyn's sensitive skin once again, both boys flinched in pain in precisely the same way at precisely the same time.

He had stopped again, staring dumbfounded at Arban. In response, Brendyn had choked out, *It's all right . . . he understands, too, Willerth.*

When Willerth had met Arban's green gaze, he saw the fear of pain, but he also saw the same trust Brendyn had shown. It was as if the boy truly had understood, despite his inability to communicate.

A movement on the bed drew Willerth from his memories. His gaze shifted to the boy lying next to Brendyn. Arban slowly sat up, rubbing his eyes with his palms, and yawned. When the boy noticed Willerth sitting on the bedside, he drew back a little, fear briefly crossing his features. Fear was soon replaced by recognition, and a shy smile crept across his cracked lips. Willerth tried to return the smile, but he managed little more than a grimace. There was something unnatural about this child, and it frightened him.

The clatter of a wagon entering the stableyard pulled his attention away from the boy. Willerth stood up—too quickly, he realized, for he heard Brendyn begin to stir— and went to the window, leaning over the table sitting in front of the sill to look out. The early evening shadows hid the faces of the wagon's occupants, but he did not need to see them to know who it was.

"Willerth?" he heard Brendyn sleepily ask.

Willerth looked towards the bed to see Brendyn also sitting up, rubbing the sleep from his eyes. "I am sorry, Master Brendyn, I did not mean to wake you. Master Brendys is home. . . ."

Brendyn became instantly alert, painfully trying to swing his legs over the side of the bed. "Papa!"

Willerth took a step towards his young master, holding out a restraining hand. "Master Brendyn, you should sleep. You can see your father in the morning. . . ."

"I want to see Papa," Brendyn pleaded, on the verge of tears. "*Please*, Willerth?"

Beyond Brendyn, Willerth could see that Arban was also beginning to fret. He looked at Brendyn for a moment, then sighed. "All right, Master Brendyn. Do you want me to carry you?"

Brendyn nodded and held up his arms to the young man.

Willerth bent down and carefully lifted his young master into his arms. Much of both boys' bodies were wrapped in bandages, smelling strongly of the pungent medicine Kanstanon had given him to help heal the most severely sunburned patches of their skin.

"Thank you, Willerth," Brendyn said, resting his head on the servant's shoulder.

"Of course, Master Brendyn," Willerth replied gently. The boy was heavy, but Willerth would have carried him to the ends of the world if it were demanded of him. Before leaving the room, he glanced at Arban, who smiled up at them, then laid back down.

As he carefully picked his way down the stairs, he saw Mattina and Arella making their way to the front door. Before the women stepped outside, Mattina cast a reproving look in his direction. "Willerth, Brendyn should be in bed."

Willerth felt his cheeks burning. "He would not be denied, Mistress Mattina."

Mattina's reproach melted into understanding, and she nodded her assent, then stepped through the front door with Arella. Willerth followed the women outside, down the porch steps, and across the stableyard. A small crowd was already beginning to gather around the wagon. The men gathered there parted as they approached, allowing them to pass.

Quellin had already dismounted and was waving everyone back. In the light of the lamps borne by Kanstanon and others, Willerth could see a large black burn marking the Gildean King's chest through the blasted front of the tunic.

At the back of the wagon, Novosad was assisting his step-daughter down. Both of Karel's arms were bandaged from her elbows down. As soon as the girl's feet landed upon the ground, she threw her arms around Novosad, ignoring the pain of her burns. "Father!"

The Hagane warrior hugged her to himself, a mixed look of surprise and tender affection crossing his ragged features.

Brendys came around the front of the wagon, his right arm bandaged and bound in a makeshift sling, his head bowed. His black hair and beard were drenched with perspiration and great streams of sweat ran down his face, and his breathing was slightly labored.

"Brendys!" Mattina gasped and hurried forward.

Willerth followed them, carrying Brendyn, who reached a yearning hand out towards his father.

Brendys looked up at the sound of their approach and raised a restraining hand, rasping out, "Come no closer!"

Willerth and the women halted abruptly, and Brendyn gave a frightened gasp and hid his face against Willerth's shoulders. Even in the dim light of the lamps, the change in his master was clear. The light gleamed in wolfish, amber eyes—eyes which reminded Willerth of nothing less than the Sorcerer, Kerebros—and glistened on his grim, perspiration-drenched face.

"Where is Gwydnan?" Quellin barked out, grim urgency in both his voice and expression.

"With Prince Shannon, Your Majesty," Kanstanon replied in a worried tone. "But. . . ."

"Shannon?" Quellin repeated, his eyes flying wide, his voice faltering. He seemed to grow a little faint for a moment, but recovered quickly, thrusting his personal feelings aside. He grabbed Brendys by the left arm and started to draw him towards the house. "Get Kovar out of the wagon . . . we must get them to Gwydnan right away."

Kanstanon stepped in his path, his look fearful. "I beg your pardon, Your Majesty, but you dare not. . . ."

"I *dare not?*" Quellin snapped back.

"Please, Your Majesty," Kanstanon replied worriedly. "Master Gwydnan must not be disturbed . . . Prince Shannon's life hangs in the balance."

Quellin hesitated, a stricken look passing over his features. Finally, he shook his head, agony and grief twisting his Elvin fair face. "Brendys cannot. . . ."

Brendys pulled away from his brother-by-marriage, taking a step back towards the wagon. "Quellin, I will not allow you to sacrifice Shannon for my life."

He glanced at his own son, then turned his sharp gaze back on Quellin. "There is hope without me. You know what you must do."

"*Manton's bloody hand!*" Copanas swore from the back of the wagon where he, his brother, and Gowan were lifting out Kovar's litter. "Novosad, they've been *bitten!*"

336

Novosad cast a stunned look in the twins' direction, then released his hold on his daughter, hurrying around to get a better look at Brendys. His face turned grim. "It may be too late already. The change has progressed much further than it had with Lady Aliana."

"Change? What do you mean?" Mattina demanded.

The Hagane warrior looked over his shoulder at Mattina. "The cursed ones we spoke of earlier, Your Majesty . . . as with Lady Aliana, they are changing into such as they. Lady Aliana's Elvin blood was able to defend her, but I know of no cure for mortals."

"Do what you must, Quellin!" Brendys gritted.

"Wait!" Lehan called out. "There may be a cure!"

Everyone turned their eyes on the younger scout, who was pointing in Willerth's direction. Willerth took a step back, half-fearful, wondering what he could possibly do to break a curse.

"Prince Brendyn!" Novosad said, moving towards the boy in Willerth's arms.

Hearing his name, Brendyn turned his frightened gaze on the Hagane warrior.

"Your Highness, your ring!" Novosad said as he closed the distance. "May I have your ring, Your Highness?"

Brendyn withdrew his arm from around Willerth's neck, staring down at the faintly glowing ring on his finger, his brow wrinkled in confusion. Then wonder grew in his young face as understanding dawned on him. He looked at Novosad. "It will help Papa?"

Novosad nodded. "I think it may, little Prince. I think it may indeed."

Brendyn hurriedly pulled the ring from his finger and held it out to the scout.

Novosad took the ring from the boy and hurried towards Brendys. Brendys quailed back, a wild and fearful look on his face, and raised his left hand to shield his eyes as if the faint light of the ring blinded him. Novosad thrust the ring into the palm of the Horsemaster's right hand and closed both of his hands about it so that Brendys could not drop the ring.

Brendys winced and gagged at the rough handling, but his gasp soon erupted into a drawn-out cry of agony as the power of the clear Elvinstone burst into a radiant fire, shining through the flesh of both his hand and Novosad's. The light slowly crept up through the Horsemaster's arm, shining red through flesh, bandages, and sling. His cry grew louder and he dropped to his knees, but still Novosad did not release him.

At last, Brendys fell forward, unconscious, and the light of the Elvinring winked out. Quellin knelt down beside Brendys and pulled back the Horsemaster's eyelids one at a time, revealing his deep-blue eyes. He pulled the wounded arm out of the sling and pulled away the bandages. The ragged gashes were gone and the bone was healed.

He looked up at the others, wonder and relief in his gaze. "It worked!"

Novosad pried the ring out of Brendys's clenched fist and called up to the twins, "Bring Kovar down here."

Gowan and the twins finished lowering Kovar's litter from the back of the wagon. After they placed him on the ground, Novosad removed the bandages from the falconer's wounded leg, then pressed the signet against the torn flesh, eliciting a cry of pain from Kovar's lips. The Elvindiamond flared up only briefly before winking out again. When the light faded, the injury had partially healed, but there was still an ugly scar. The Elvindiamond signet no longer shed any light . . . its power was spent.

Novosad felt the leg, drawing forth another gasp of pain from Kovar. "The leg has not fully healed."

"I doubt I will be walking around anytime soon," Kovar muttered through clenched teeth.

"But his eyes have returned to normal," Novosad finished, ignoring the falconer's cynical response. "We can only pray that the curse has been removed completely."

The scout motioned to the twins. "Take Kovar inside with the other wounded."

Copanas and Lehan lifted the litter and bore it to the house. Gowan's gaze followed them until they had vanished through the front door. He shook his head. "You would think he would be a little more grateful."

"His body will mend, but it will take his heart a little longer," Quellin quietly responded, a sad look on his face. "He mourns a friend."

Gowan turned a stunned gaze on his King, understanding dawning. "Amrein?"

Quellin nodded. "She was slain by the Sorcerer while trying to protect Brendys."

Brendyn again reached a worried hand down towards his father. "Papa?"

"He is just sleeping, Master Brendyn," Willerth said softly. "Your ring saved him."

Novosad stepped past the Horsemaster's prone form and took Brendyn's hand, slipping the ring back onto his finger. "Indeed, Your Highness. He will be fine."

Quellin reached out and gave his wife's hand a quick squeeze, then knelt down beside Brendys. He tried to wake the Horsemaster, but Brendys did not stir. He looked up at Gowan and Novosad. "Take him to his room."

*   *   *   *

Brendys awoke with a cry, grasping his right arm. He blinked in the sunlight streaming through the window of the room and looked around. It took him a moment to realize he was in his own bed in his own room in his own house. Memories of the previous night came flooding back.

Sighing, he rubbed his arm. It was whole and without pain. Clearly, his son's ring had proven its power.

Slowly, he climbed out of bed and found clothes laid out for him on the table. Beside the garments lay Denasdervien. He touched its hilt and felt the soothing warmth of its power. There was no sense of Evil near. If Kerebros had indeed survived, he had apparently decided to withdraw for the time being, perhaps to gather his strength.

It does not matter, Brendys thought as he drew on his clothes. *If not Kerebros, then another.*

He closed his eyes and rubbed his forehead. *I shall be seeing Sorcerers and demons in every shadow if I keep dwelling on this.*

He finished belting his tunic and stepped into the hallway leading to the front room, pausing only briefly to glance at the closed door of Gwydnan's bedroom. As he entered the front room, he noticed that the furniture had been rearranged to provide the most open floor space possible. Pallets had been laid on the floor for the wounded members of the Gildean escort. A few of the men had taken particularly grievous wounds, but they would live. Kovar was among the warriors laid out on the floor, and Karel was lying on the couch, her head propped up against a pillow, her white arms, properly bandaged from elbow to fingertips, resting atop her blanket. The light in the room was fairly dim, for the curtains had been kept closed to protect Karel from direct contact with the morning sunlight.

Brendys knelt beside his Gildean friend. The red-headed warrior stared vacantly at the ceiling, seemingly oblivious of the Horsemaster's presence. Brendys placed a hand on the younger man's shoulder. "Kovar, how are you doing."

340

Kovar's green eyes glanced at the Horsemaster, his vision coming into focus. After a moment, his gaze returned to the rafters above him. "There is pain, but I will live."

"I was not speaking of your leg," Brendys said, a grave look crossing his bearded face.

Kovar closed his eyes and swallowed. "Neither was I."

Brendys bowed his head. He, better than anyone he knew, knew the pain of loss, and he knew also that words could not ease that pain . . . only time. He gave his old friend's shoulder a sympathetic squeeze, then rose to his feet.

As he turned, his gaze landed upon Karel. He noticed the girl was staring towards the hallway leading back to the master bedroom and Gwydnan's room, her black eyes glistening ever so slightly in the dim light. He walked to the couch and sat down on the edge beside Karel, smiling down at her. "I am guessing Shannon is in there?"

Karel nodded, avoiding the Horsemaster's gaze. "Your stablehand tells us there is still a chance he may not live."

Brendys looked back towards the hallway, his smile vanishing. He raised his right arm before him and stared at it. *The ring should have been used on Shannon.*

He glanced back at the hallway one more time, then turned his gaze back on Karel, placing his hand on her shoulder. "If Shannon is in Gwydnan's care, then hope remains."

A tear escaped the girl's dark eye. "They won't even let me see him."

"That may be changing," Kanstanon's voice responded.

Brendys turned to see the stablehand coming out of the hallway behind him. Kanstanon's grim expression sent a wave of trepidation through the Horsemaster. "Shannon?"

"Prince Shannon has awakened . . . he will live," the younger man replied. "Master Gwydnan summons his parents."

Brendys heard Karel give an almost sobbing sigh of relief. A burden had been lifted from his own heart, but he could not help but be puzzled by the stablehand's demeanor. "Kanstanon, what is wrong?"

Kanstanon suddenly looked as though the full weight of world had fallen upon his shoulders. With bowed head and closed eyes, he answered, "Master Gwydnan . . . Master Gwydnan is dying. He used the last of his strength to save Prince Shannon."

Brendys slowly stood up and placed his hands on Kanstanon's shoulders. "I am sure he just needs rest."

Kanstanon shook his head. "Nay, he will not live through the day."

Brendys sighed. He had seen more grief and sorrow in his life than was right for any man, and he was weary of it. But Gwydnan was old, very old, and his health had been failing for a long time. Perhaps the stress of this latest incident had simply been too much for him . . . this day had been long in coming.

Kanstanon raised his head, drawing in a deep breath. "I should inform Queen Arella and King Quellin that their son is awake."

Brendys nodded and allowed the stablehand to continue on. He glanced at Karel and saw that her gaze was again fixed on the hallway, but despite the tears in her eyes, she was smiling. A slight smile crossed his own lips. No matter how often Death seemed to pass his way, Life always seemed to follow in its wake.

Brendys turned away from the girl and followed Kanstanon to the dining hall. As the two men entered the room, they found Mattina, Arella, and Quellin seated at the table, Novosad and Gowan standing nearby. Quellin's torso was bound in soft bandages, covering the large burn on his chest.

Mattina arose and threw herself into her husband's arms. Brendys kissed her, then held her close, burying his face in her hair. "It is over. For now, at least, it is over."

"Your Majesties," Kanstanon addressed the King and Queen of Gildea. "Gwydnan sent me to tell you Prince Shannon has awakened, and you may see him now."

Quellin and Arella looked at each other in surprise, then arose and immediately left the dining hall.

Brendys assisted Mattina back into her chair, then sat down himself, shaking his head. "The ring should have been used on Shannon first."

"It would not have been strong enough to save him, and Gwydnan would not have allowed it," Kanstanon said quietly. He blinked back tears and turned away. "I should have seen to the horses hours ago. Please excuse me."

"Of course," Brendys replied, his voice solemn. He wondered, however, what injury Shannon had taken that would have drained more power from the ring than the curse laid upon him and Kovar.

As the Horsemaster stared after his stablehand, he heard his wife's voice beside him. "Brendys? What is it?"

Brendys turned to look at Mattina, taking her hand in his. "Kanstanon tells me Gwydnan will not live through the day."

"He must have given too much of himself to save Shannon," Mattina replied, placing her other hand over her husband's.

Brendys gave her a curious look. "How so?"

"Gwydnan was once a Wizard . . . Odyniec's master, to be exact," Mattina replied softly. "From what I understand, he has been sustaining Shannon with the vestiges of his own power."

"And that power has now been exhausted," Brendys said, finally understanding. That Gwydnan was a Wizard did not surprise him in the least. It was obviously no coincidence that it was he who first delivered Denasdervien into Brendys's hands, nor that he had eventually found his way into the Horsemaster's household. Nevertheless, there was a hollow feeling within his heart . . . he would miss the old man. Gwydnan was a source of wisdom and guidance that he was not sure he could do without.

The sounds of children's voices and small, bare feet slowly pacing across the polished, wood floor of the front room brought the Horsemaster out of his sorrow. Soon, Brendyn appeared in the doorway. Much of his son's scarred body was wrapped in bandages, but a large portion was still revealed, blotched red and tan where his clothing had remained mostly intact. Enough of Brendyn's scarred flesh showed that Brendys was surprised his son's head was not hanging low in shame as he was paraded before so many people, but pain and trauma seemed to have driven shame from his young mind, at least for the moment. Behind Brendyn came Sîan and Lonel, herded by Lonel's mother. Willerth followed her, carrying another child, also bandaged like Brendyn, though perhaps a little more.

As soon as Brendyn saw his father, he ran forward and clambered into the Horsemaster's lap, wrapping his small arms around Brendys's neck, breaking into sobbing tears, ignoring the pain he caused himself. "Papa!"

Brendys gently held his son, soothing him. After a moment, Brendyn pulled back, allowing his father a better look at his bruised and scratched face, his scabbed lips and sun-reddened skin. Despite the pain and the still evident weariness, despite the tears moistening his cheeks, there was a glitter in Brendyn's blue eyes and a smile on his lips.

Brendys smiled back. "I was so afraid . . . why did you go into the forest?"

A look of recalled terror crossed Brendyn's features, and he shuddered slightly in his father's arm. "That white man said I would die if I didn't."

As Brendyn was speaking, Willerth situated the rest of the children at the table, while Lara went to the kitchen to fetch their breakfast.

The boy's face brightened a little with excitement. "But then Skrak rescued me. . . ."

"Skrak?" Brendys interrupted. That was a name he had not yet heard.

Mattina answered for his son. "An Elf named Lord Anselm found Brendyn and helped him escape Kerebros. He is also the one who brought Shannon here."

She hesitated a moment before adding, "Apparently, he was a Jaf at the time."

Brendys raised a hand to his scarred temple, his head beginning to throb a little. "Someone can explain *that* part of the tale to me later."

"*Papa!*" Brendyn said in a chiding voice. "I was telling my story!"

Brendys barked a short laugh and carefully ruffled his son's hair, eliciting a grin from the boy. "Then by all means, tell your story."

"Well, Skrak told me how to find that pond in the forest and how to get home," Brendyn continued as if he had never been interrupted. "But it was a long way, and I was getting hungrier and thirstier, and my legs started to hurt. Then this big dog found me."

Brendys nodded, the memory of Elgern entering his thoughts.

Brendyn kept talking, oblivious to his father's thoughtful expression. "The dog carried me to the pond.

There wasn't any berries or anything to eat, and I was hungry and lonely and tired. . . ."

The boy paused, suddenly shame-faced. "I cried."

The shame vanished as quickly as it appeared. "Then those bad men threw Arban through the bushes, and he landed in some thorns. . . ."

Brendys interrupted his son again, confusion again settling over him. "Arban? Now who is this Arban?"

"That's Arban," Brendyn replied, pointing across the table at the boy Willerth had carried in.

Brendys looked at the child in surprise, for he had not paid close attention to anyone but Brendyn as the children had entered the room. Arban responded by lowering his head, smiling shyly. There was something familiar about the boy, but the Horsemaster's muzzy wits could not sort it out.

"Can we keep him, Papa?" Brendyn spouted brightly.

The Horsemaster looked down at his son in disbelief. "He is not an animal to be made a pet of. His parents are probably worried sick about him . . . we should find out where he comes from so we can take him home."

"That is a little more difficult than you might think, Brendys," Mattina said in a quiet voice.

Brendys threw his wife a puzzled look. He was more surprised—even a little shocked—to see in her face a hint of the desire to keep the little boy that Brendyn had so openly displayed.

Mattina glanced at Brendyn's friend, then turned her green eyes back on her husband. "Arban can neither hear, nor speak . . . at all. He is completely deaf and mute."

From the recesses of his memory, Brendys heard the echo of a voice, faint yet clear. *Heed the cries of the Silent, for they are the cries of the Kingdom lost. The Silent. . . .*

Brendys gaped at the boy in utter shock. He had not recognized Arban at first, washed and groomed, bandaged

346

and burned, for that was not how he had first seen him. Now he remembered that face . . . beyond a doubt, he stared upon the child from his visions, living and in the flesh. As he gawked at the boy, he was only vaguely aware of Mattina speaking his name and shaking his arm and of Brendyn saying something to him. He heard Willerth, Novosad, and Gowan as well, but he did not respond until Quellin's voice came to his ear.

"Brendys? Are you all right?"

Brendys started as if waking suddenly from a strange dream. He looked numbly from Quellin to Arella to Mattina, noting their confused expressions. He slowly shook his head. "I . . . I've become a bit weary. I think I will rest for a little while longer."

He set his son in Mattina's lap, then stood up.

Brendyn looked up at him, his eyes pleading. "Papa, can we? Can we keep him?"

"Of course," Brendys replied, nodding dazedly, his haunted gaze darting briefly once more towards Arban. Slowly and carefully, trying to keep his balance, he turned and started for the door. "Of course."

He felt all eyes upon his back as he walked away, but he was not ready yet to answer the unspoken questions.

*   *   *   *

Quellin's gaze followed his brother-by-marriage until he passed from view around the corner of the doorway. He shifted his gaze to young Arban, his expression moving from confused to thoughtful. Frowning uncertainly, the boy seemed to shrink back in his chair, glancing fretfully at the staring eyes around him.

Quellin averted his gaze to stare at the floor, rubbing his smooth chin. *The Silent? Does this boy have something to do with your visions, Brendys? Is he the one? Elekar, what does this mean?*

"Quellin," Mattina said slowly, a suspicious look entering her eyes. "Do you have any idea what that was all about?"

The Gildean King raised his eyes to look at his sister. "Perhaps."

Arella huffed. "Do not bother asking, Mattina. Neither of those men are likely to tell you anything . . . they have been so secretive ever since Racolis Keep, it is becoming positively frustrating."

Quellin put an arm around his wife's waist and drew her close to his side. "There are things that it is not my right to tell, and others that are better left hidden."

Out of the corner of his eye, he noticed his sister look away. He was fairly certain he and Brendys were not the only ones keeping secrets.

Lara entered the room bearing plates of food that she placed before each of the children. As the handmaid moved around the table, Quellin started a little. "I nearly forgot . . . Gwydnan says the children may see Shannon."

Brendyn and Sîan both looked as though they would leap to the floor in their excitement, but Mattina stayed them with a firm hand. "They can wait until they have finished eating."

The children looked disappointed, but did not argue; however, Quellin looked at his sister and shook his head slowly, his youthful features turning grim. "Nay. They should go now."

Arella supported her husband with a solemn nod of her own.

Mattina looked at them each for a brief moment, her own expression turning serious. Finally, she looked at Willerth and gave him a slight nod. "Go with them, Willerth. Do not let them stay too long."

"Gwydnan also said to bring the other boy," Quellin told the servant as he was rising to his feet.

Willerth gave him a puzzled look, but scooped the boy up from his seat and started around the end of the table. He paused and looked at Quellin. "How did Gwydnan know about Arban?"

"There are also questions which should not be asked," Quellin replied.

Mattina kissed her son on the cheek, then allowed him to get down from her lap. "Wait for Willerth."

Sîan and Lonel were also climbing off their chairs, but Lara stayed her daughter. "You stay right here and finish your breakfast, young lady . . . you haven't any reason to be troubling Prince Shannon."

Lonel stuck her lip out in a pout, but obeyed.

As Willerth, carrying Arban, led Brendyn and Sîan from the dining hall, Quellin turned back to his sister and said in a quiet voice. "After today, I will never again consider Shalkan a place of safety for you. I wish more than ever that Brendys would bring you all to Gildea and take the Lordship of Trost Keep."

Mattina, refusing to meet her brother's gaze, only replied, "I know."

* * * *

As Willerth and his young charges passed through the front room on their way to Gwydnan's bedchamber, they were met by Karel. The girl was dressed in the sleeveless, deep red tunic and hose refitted for her by Arella and Mattina, though without any of the ornamentation. Her coppery hair was a mess, and her arms were still bandaged from elbow to fingertips and smelled strongly of Gwydnan's medicine, yet despite those things and her childlike appearance, Willerth was still amazed by her beauty.

"King Quellin told me to wait for you and the children," she said to Willerth as he approached.

Willerth nodded, then gave her a smile. "Then let us go in . . . Shannon will be very glad to see you, I am sure."

Karel's cheeks greyed in embarrassment, but she returned his smile nonetheless.

As they reached the old kitchenhand's room, Willerth knocked gently at the door. Gwydnan's voice answered, faint and sickly, through the heavy wood of the door. "Come."

Willerth opened the door and ushered Brendyn and Sîan into the room, then entered himself, Karel coming last. The first thing Willerth saw upon entering Gwydnan's room was Shannon lying on the bed, propped in a sitting position against a couple of pillows, the blankets pulled up over his waist, his head leaning back and to the side, eyes closed. His flesh was livid in hue, and his normally immaculate hair, pulled back a little by the bandage around his head, was extremely frazzled.

The children ran to Shannon's bedside, Sîan closest to her brother. Both of the youngsters looked uncertainly towards Gwydnan. Willerth was stunned by the old man's appearance. The normally tall kitchenhand sat stooped in his high-backed chair, thin and pale, his once strong shoulders hunched with weariness. He appeared to have aged another twenty years in the few weeks Brendys and his household had been gone.

Gwydnan stirred and nodded heavily in response to the children's questioning stares. His voice was weak and cracked when he spoke. "You may wake him, but do not stay long, nor weary him with needless prattle . . . he needs to rest."

The children acknowledged with silent nods.

"You need to rest as well," Willerth responded in a low tone.

The old kitchenhand's steel-grey eyes shifted to look at the young servant, a brittle smile crossing his lips. "Aye, indeed I do, lad. I shall rest soon . . .I shall walk the Road to Elekar, and then I shall rest."

His gaze moved to Karel and sharpened suddenly. He stared long at her, a hard look in his eyes from which the girl shrank. At last, the old man closed his eyes, resting his chin on his chest. He sat so still that Willerth would have thought he had died right then, if not for the harsh rasp of his breath.

Willerth shifted Arban into the crook of his left arm and placed his right hand on Karel's shoulder. "Do not mind him, Karel . . . Master Gwydnan is a strange creature."

The girl did not reply.

Sîan slowly reached out and laid her hand on her brother's arm, gently shaking it. "Shannon, wake up."

The youth did not immediately respond, but finally he stirred, raising his head. His eyelids parted just enough to reveal a glimpse of his green eyes. He turned his face towards his sister, his lips cracking into a faint smile. He reached his hand up and stroked the little girl's face. "Sîan . . . Mother tells me you were worried."

Sîan's lip trembled a little. "You were asleep so long, I thought you might not wake up again."

A shadow of recalled pain and darkness flitted across Shannon's boyish features, but was gone again almost as soon as it appeared. His smile returned. "Not wake up? Do not think of it! I was very ill, but I am getting better."

He patted the blanket next to him. "Come here."

His sister climbed up beside him, snuggling against him, her golden head resting against Shannon's chest. Shannon reached an arm around her small shoulders, gently hugging her. "I will be fine . . . you will see."

He turned his gaze on his cousin. "Brendyn, come here."

Brendyn obeyed, climbing onto the bed to sit with his legs curled beneath him at Sîan's feet. Shannon reached his right hand out to hold his cousin's. He took in the bruises and scratches on Brendyn's face and his cracked lips and his bandaged body. For that moment, Willerth saw in his expression a level of maturity beyond his physical appearance. "Brendyn . . . I am so sorry I could not protect you."

Willerth felt a strong pang of guilt stab at his heart. *You have naught to apologize for. It was my responsibility to protect you all, and I failed.*

"It's all right . . . you tried," Brendyn said, trying to smile, but failing. He laid across his older cousin's lap, hugging his legs through the blankets, while Shannon rubbed the boy's head.

Willerth let them be for a moment, turning his attention to the boy in his arms. Arban had discovered the polished pendant hanging around Willerth's neck and was now holding it, rubbing his fingers across the glittering surface of the Elvinsilver birch leaf. The little boy's green eyes seemed to reflect the sparkle of the pendant, and his small lips stretched into a contented smile.

Willerth watched him in curiosity. He wondered whether Arban was just pleased with the shiny, crafted metal, or whether he saw the beautiful and loving face of his dear Aliana. Perhaps that was the virtue of the pendant . . . that the memory of the Elfess who had stolen his heart would remain with him forever.

Arban noticed Willerth staring down at him and immediately let go of the pendant, his expression a powerful mixture of fear and guilt, as one who had been caught doing something he should not and anticipating punishment for his transgression. Willerth gave him a gentle smile and caressed his cheek. "It's all right, lad. I hold it all the time."

The boy's fear faded into surprise at the man's gentle touch. The surprise drifted into the shy smile that almost seemed a fixture on the child's face, and he wrapped his

352

arms around Willerth's neck, laying his head on the servant's shoulder.

"He seems to have taken to you quickly enough," Karel said quietly from Willerth's side.

Willerth turned his gaze on the girl. She abruptly looked away, her gaze dropping briefly to the floor, before raising again to light upon Shannon, who still sat with a comforting arm around his sister, conversing seriously with Sîan and Brendyn. There was a strange yearning in the black depths of her eyes, and Willerth knew what it was.

"Karel, just go talk to him," the young man told her. "That *is* why you are here."

Shannon's face at once turned towards them at the sound of Karel's name. His weak and weary face brightened.

Karel glanced once at Willerth, then slowly stepped towards the bed.

"Princess Sîan, Master Brendyn," Willerth addressed the children. "You have had your chance to visit with Shannon. Come along . . . give Karel some time, too."

Brendyn climbed down from the bed at once and hurried to join Willerth, but Sîan delayed. She scowled in Karel's direction for a moment, until Shannon chided her for her rude behavior. With a shame-faced apology to her older brother, she climbed down from the bed and walked across to the door.

As Karel was sitting down on the edge of the bed, Willerth started to turn away, but Gwydnan's ragged voice halted him. "Willerth, bring the boys here."

Willerth shot a glance towards the old man and saw Gwydnan's gaze fixed unblinkingly upon Brendyn. He nodded, then looked down at Sîan. "You go on, Your Highness. Master Brendyn will be along shortly."

Sîan frowned deeply, clearly displeased that her cousin would be allowed to remain behind and she would not;

however, she obeyed, strutting from the bedchamber in a huff.

Willerth guided his master's son before Gwydnan's chair, the old man following their progress across the room. Gwydnan reached his left hand out and placed it on Brendyn's shaggy, golden-chestnut mane. His right he placed on Arban's bandaged leg. He closed his eyes and muttered something in a language Willerth did not understand, then opened them again, his gaze moving slowly from Brendyn to Arban and back again.

At last, he nodded, a hint of a smile playing at his lips as he nodded weakly. "It is done."

Still smiling, he leaned his head against the back of his chair and closed his eyes again. Almost at once, his head lolled to the side and the deep sigh of his final breath escaped his lips.

Willerth gawked at the old kitchenhand, stricken by the suddenness of his passing. It was almost as if Gwydnan had been struggling towards this one brief moment, and now that it was over, he simply let go. The young man swallowed against the hollow feeling forming within him, absently pulling Brendyn to himself. The world had suddenly become a more threatening place.

* * * *

The shutters in the master bedroom were closed, keeping out most of the morning sun, but still Brendys could not sleep. His dreams and the appearance of the boy from those dreams in his own home troubled him still. No matter how much time he spent trying to decipher the meaning of his visions, he could not. He felt a deepening sense of foreboding, as though there were a vitally important task left unfinished, an urgent mystery unsolved, and time was rapidly slipping away.

His mind ran through the messages Elekar had given him in his dreams, but he could not determine their meaning or import. *Heed the cries of the Silent, for they are the cries of the Kingdom lost.* The message itself meant nothing to him at the time, for this Arban boy had not appeared in that vision.

A King must know his people's needs, though he cannot hear their cries. A King must make known his will, though his people cannot hear his voice. A King must feel his people's pain to also share their joy. Without him, his kingdom shall fall. This message was given in his second dream . . . the first in which the boy appeared. One piece of the puzzle at last fell into place. The boy clearly represented Milhavior—a Kingdom lost, for its King was lost—just as the knight in Brendys's second and third dreams had to represent Brendyn, the Heir of Ascon . . . the lost King.

The third dream did not explain the mystery any further that Brendys could tell. There was no message, other than that it began as a vision of the past and ended as a foretelling of the future. The Dawn King had repeated the message from the first dream, but how it related. . . .

Brendys sat up. *Of course!*

It was obvious. In the third dream, the boy was trapped on a ledge, Kerebros in his wolf form and a great, black dragon threatening him. If the dream-child represented Milhavior, then clearly the looming threat of the wolf and the dragon indicated that Milhavior would again be threatened by the forces of Machaelon. But that still did not explain the significance of the living, breathing, mortal boy in the other room.

And the dragon? What did it import? For it, and only it, appeared in his fourth dream. How did that relate to the other dreams? Unless. . . .

Brendys climbed to his feet. He had a suspicion, but he could not be sure, but there was one who could verify all that he had just deduced. He opened the door leading into the hallway and walked straight through the open door of Gwydnan's room.

He stopped just inside the door. On his right, Shannon was sitting up in bed, with Karel sitting on the edge beside him, her bandaged arms resting in her lap. They were talking quietly, but the room was not very large. Brendys could hear all they said.

"Father told me what you did," Shannon said in a very serious voice, glancing at the girl's arms. "You saved my father and Uncle Brendys at risk of your own life. It was very courageous of you."

Karel frowned and lowered her gaze. "Courage had nothing to do with it. I did not pull the sword from the rock to save your father or Prince Brendys . . . I did it for revenge."

Brendys was almost sorry he had overheard her, but neither could he blame her for her feelings. Still, no matter how much he wanted to believe she had finally refused her blood-father's heritage, there was something about her still that made him uncomfortable.

Shannon threw her a puzzled look. "Revenge?"

"The Sorcerer said you were dead," Karel replied. "How was I supposed to know that Jaf . . . Elf . . . whatever he is, carried you here?"

A movement at Brendys's left-hand drew his attention away. His gaze fell on Willerth's back. He was standing before Gwydnan's chair, holding Arban in one arm, Brendyn standing before him and slightly to the side. The movement had been Willerth pulling Brendyn to him.

"Willerth?" Brendys said, a heavy weight inexplicably dragging on his heart.

Shannon and Karel fell silent at the sound of the Horsemaster's voice and turned their gazes towards him.

Willerth did not reply at once. He stood facing Gwydnan for a moment longer before turning towards his master. Brendys could see the glistening of tears in his eyes. "He is gone. Gwydnan is dead."

Brendys looked past Willerth, his gaze resting on the peaceful, ancient face of the old man. He felt the bite of disappointment—his questions would have to remain unanswered for the time being—but he could not bring himself to grieve. Gwydnan had earned his rest. *Farewell, old friend . . . we shall meet again.*

Glossary

People and Creatures

Aden (Ay-den): A Man from Shalkan. Postmaster. Orphan once taken in by Brendyk.

Adina (ah-DE-nah): A Woman from Shalkan. Wife of Languedoc.

Adôn (AY-dohn): An Elvin title equivalent to lord.

Agidon (AG-id-on): A Man from Fekamar. A Fekamari nobleman.

Ailon (AY-lon): A Man from the early Fourth Age. A High Steward of Milhavior.

Alara (ah-LAR-ah): Immortal denizens of the High Realm from which the Elves originated.

Alaren Guardians (ah-LAR-en GARD-ee-ans): Alara entrusted with the protection of Sharamitaro.

Alerren (ah-LAYR-en): Captain of the *Courser*, Quellin's personal ship.

Aliana (al-ee-AN-ah): An Elfess from Greyleaf Forest. Daughter of Guthwine and Reatha.

Allard (ALL-ard): A Man from Matadol. A Fieldmarshal in the Matadane army.

Allic (ALL-ik): A Man from Shalkan. Innkeeper's assistant at the *Green Meadow Inn*.

Amrein (AM-rayn): A hawk once belonging to Malach. Companion of Kovar.

Analetri (ah-nah-LET-ree): The Sea Elves.

Anselm (ANN-selm): An Elf of the Firstborn. Cursed to the form of a Jaf.

Aragon (AIR-ah-gon): A Man from Gildea. Lord of the House of Gildea.

Arban (AR-ban): An abandoned child. Friend of Brendyn.

Archa (AR-kah): A Dark Elf. Captain of the Dark Elves at Ilkatar Forest.

Arella (ah-REL-ah): A Woman from Gildea. Queen of Gildea. Sister of Radnor. Wife of Quellin.

Ascon (ASK-on): A Man of the Third Age. First King of Ascon. First High King of Milhavior.

Asghar (AZ-gar): A Dwarf from the Crystal Mountains. Companion of Brendys. Son of Asghol.

Asghol (AZ-goal): A Dwarf from the Crystal Mountains. Father of Asghar.

Balgor (BAL-gor): A Man from Qatan. Lord of the House of Robel-Rigus.

Baris (BARE-iss): A Man from Racolis. A scout in the Hagane army.

Beelek (BEE-lek): A Man of the Third Age. First King of the land now called Ilkatar.

Belera (bel-AY-ra): A Woman from Gildea. Lady-in-waiting of Arella.

Berephon (BARE-eh-fon): A Man of from Gildea. Son of Runyan the Bard. Narrator.

Bernath (BER-nath): A Man from Gildea. Lord of the House of Gildea.

Bipin (BIP-in): The childhood nickname of Berephon.

Bjerkas (BYARE-kass): A Dwarf of the Podan Peaks. King.

Braden (BRAY-den): Name given to Brendys at Lener Keep.

Braya (BRAY-ah): The goddess of life.

Brendyk (BREN-dik): A Man from Shalkan. Horsemaster.

Brendyl (BREN-dil): A human child. Stillborn son of Brendys and Mattina. Brendyn's twin.

Brendyn (BREN-din): A human child. Son of Brendys and Mattina. Brendyl's twin.

Brendys (BREN-dis): A Man from Shalkan. Son of Brendyk and Danel. Prophesied Bearer of the Flame. Prince of Gildea.

Brugnara (broog-NARE-ah): A Man from Fekamar. Father of Willerth. The Great Father. Sorcerer.

Brumagin (broo-MAH-gin): A human child from Gildea.

Brun (BRUN): A Man from Bulkyree. A slaver. Partner of Kregor.

Caletri (ca-LET-ree): The High Elves.

Champa (CHAM-pah): Horse owned by Rister.

Chol (KOLE): A Dark Elf from Nightwood.

Copanas (co-PAN-as): A Man from Racolis. A scout in the Hagane army. Twin brother of Lehan.

Cragg (KRAG): Lord of all Dragons. Also called Black Cragg.

Dagramon (DAG-rah-mon): The Dragon-Riders of Krifka.

Dahmus (DAH-moos): A Man from Racolis. A Captain in the Hagane army.

Danel (DAN-el): A Woman from Shalkan. Brendyk's wife. Brendys's mother.

Dark Alara (DARK ah-LAR-ah): Alara who serve Thanatos.

Darmin (DAR-min): A Man from Gildea. Quellin's guardsman.

Deciechi (deh-SEE-eh-kee): A Man from Gildea. Guardsman of Henfling.

Dell (DEL): A Man from Racolis. Lord of Hagan Keep. Son of Hestin.

Deran (DAYR-an): A Man from Racolis. High Priest at the Temple of Oran.

Derslag (DER-slag): A Man from Gildea. Lord of the House of Gildea.

Dinugom (DIN-yoo-gom): A Man from Ilkatar.

Dothager (doh-THAH-jer): An Elf of the Second Age. Husband of Ronna. Father of Trost.

Dreiner (DRY-ner): A Man from Gildea. Lieutenant in the Gildean Royal Guard.

Drolar (DRO-lar): The Elvin name for a demonic being shaped like a man with the head of a panther.

Dykkie (DICK-ee): An old pet name for Brendyk.

Earek (AY-rek): A human child from Corimuth. Son of Earon and Semina.

Earon (AY-ron): A Man from Harvath. Crown Prince.

Ekenes (EK-en-eez): Horse owned by Brendyk and sold to Rister.

Elani (ay-LAH-nee): A name used by Mattina while in the household of Englar.

Elekar (EL-ek-ar): The Elvin name for the Dawn King, ruler of the High Realm.

Elgern (EL-gern): A mysterious farmer from Ilkatar. An Alaren shapeshifter. Also known as Elgern Warhound.

Englar (EN-glar): A Man from Shad. Lord of Lener Keep.

Erwin (ER-win): A Man from Gildea. Horackane guardsman of Quellin.

Etzel (ET-sel): A mysterious woman from Gildea.

Evin (EH-vin): A Man of Shalkan. Great-grandfather of Brendys. Horsemaster.

Evinrad (EH-vin-rad): A Man of Shalkan. Grandfather of Brendys. Horsemaster.

Evola (ay-VOLE-ah): A Man of the Third Age. Second King of Ascon. First High Steward of Milhavior. Brother of Ascon.

Falworth (FAHL-werth): A Man from Harvath. Nobleman.

Fanos Pavo (FAH-noss PA-vo): The Athorian name for the Dawn King.

Farida (far-EE-dah): A Woman from Shalkan. Brendyk's house servant.

Faroan (far-OH-an): Elf from Dun Rial.

Fayen (FAH-yen): A name used by Brendyn while in the household of Englar.

Faygrin (FAY-grin): A Man from Ilkatar. Friend of Elgern.

Fennis (FEH-niss): A Man from Gildea. A Bard. Mentor of Berephon.

Feranis (fay-RAH-nis): A Man from Harvath. Marshal of Yorg.

Fey (FAY): A human child from Gildea. Sister of Brumagin.

Folkor (FOLE-kor): A Man from Ovieto. Captain of the *Scarlet Mariner* and the *Sea Dog*.

Fracas (FRAK-ass): Brendys's horse.

Garrack (GAR-ack): A Man from Gildea. Royal Marshal in the Gildean army.

Geneta (jeh-NEE-tah): A Woman from Corimuth. Mother of Semina.

Gerren (GAYR-en): A Man of Gildea. Captain in the Gildean army.

Gildea (gil-DAY-ah): A Man of the Third Age. A King of Gildea. Brother of Horack. Friend of Trost.

Goffin (GOFF-in): A Man from Shalkan. Local drunk from Ahz-Kham.

Gowan (GOW-an): A Man from Gildea. Youth-hood companion of Brendys during the Siege of Gildea. Lieutenant in the Gildean Royal Guard.

Graemmon Laksvard (GRAM-mon LAK-svard): Warlord of the Dwarves during the Third Age.

Gramlich (GRAM-lik): A Man from Qatan. King of Qatan.

Grintam (GRIN-tam): A Man from Gildea. Royal Marshal of the Gildean army.

Grotan (GRO-tan): A Kubruk from the Blackstone Mountains. War-Chieftan under Iysh Mawvath.

Guthwine (GUTH-wine): An Elf from Dun Ghalil.

Gwydnan (GWID-nan): A Man from Athor. Mysterious kitchenhand in Brendyk's household.

Hagan (HAY-gan): A Man of the Third Age. First King of the land now called Racolis.

Haran (HAYR-an): A Woman of Gildea. Lady of the House of Trost. Mother of Quellin and Mattina.

Hedelbron (HED-ell-bron): Horse owned by Brendys.

Heil (HILE): The god of the sea.

Henfling (HEN-fling): A Man from Gildea. Governor of Gerdes.

Hestin (HEH-stin): A Man from Racolis. Lord of the House of Hagan. Father of Dell.

Horack (HOR-ack): A Man of the Third Age. Brother of Gildea. Friend of Trost.

Hugo (HYOO-go): A Troll of the Golden Hills.

Igin (IE-gin): A Man from Shalkan. Innkeeper at the *Green Meadow Inn*.

Iysh Mawvath (EESH MAW-vath): Man of Death. Warlord of Thanatos. Sorcerer.

Jaf (JAFF): The Elvin name for a demonic being shaped like a man with the head and wings of a bat.

Jaro (JAY-ro): A Man from Ilkatar. Warrior in the Royal Guard of Ilkatar.

Jholer (JOH-ler): A Man from Racolis. Lord of Daggs Keep.

Joahin (JO-ah-heen): Elf of the Caletri kindred. Chief of all Elves since the Third Age.

Jontn (YON-tin): The Dwarvin word for Men.

Kanstanon (kan-STAN-on): A Man from Ilkatar. Stablehand in Brendyk's household. Ward of Gwydnan.

Karel (kah-REL): Half-Dark Elf child from Racolis. Daughter of Titha and Chol. Step-daughter of Novosad.

Kerebros (KAY-reh-bross): A Man from Haff. A Sorcerer of Thanatos. Shapeshifter in the form of a three-headed wolf.

Kjerani (kyare-AH-nee): The Dwarvin name for females of their race.

Kjerek (KYARE-ek): The Dwarvin name for their race.

Kjerken (KYARE-ken): A Dwarvin title of honor given to Brendys by Asghar.

Kjerlinga (kyare-LIN-gah): The Dwarvin name for children of their race.

Klees (KLEESE): A Man from Qatan. Lord of Robel Keep.

Kosarek (KOH-sar-ek): A Man from Racolis. King of Racolis.

Kotsybar (KOT-sih-bar): A Man from Shalkan. Brewer in Ahz-Kham.

Kovar (KOH-var): A Man from Gildea. Apprentice to the Royal Falconer.

Kradon (KRAY-don): A human youth from Racolis. Lord of the House of Hagan. Son of Dell.

Kregor (KRAY-gore): A slaver. Partner of Brun.

Krifka (KRIFF-kah): A Sorcerer of Thanatos. Emperor of the Dagramon.

Kubruki (koo-BRUH-kee): A reptilian race originating in the Under Realm, but now inhabiting the Mortal Realm.

Lambeth (LAM-beth): A Man from Ilkatar. King of Ilkatar.

Languedoc (lan-gweh-DOK): A Man from Shalkan.

Lara (LAR-ah): A Woman from Lener. Mother of Lonel. Maidservant of Mattina.

Lathlean (LATH-lee-an): A Man from Shad. Crown Prince. Son of Micik.

Lehan (LEH-han): A Man from Racolis. A scout in the Hagan army. Twin brother of Copanas.

Lenharthen (len-HAR-then): A Man from Athor. Iysh Mawvath's former name.

Lonel (loh-NEL): A human child from Lener. Daughter of Lara.

Lorella (lo-REL-ah): A human youth from Shalkan. Languedoc's sister.

Malach (MAL-ak): An Elf from Dun Ghalil.

Manton (MAN-ton): The god of justice.

Marut (MAR-oot): A Man from Gildea. Master of the infirmiry at Gildea Keep.

Mathai (math-AYE): A Man from Ascon. King of Ascon. High Steward of Milhavior.

Mattina (mah-TEE-nah): A Woman from Gildea. Lady of the House of Trost. Sister of Quellin.

Merelda (mer-EL-dah): A Woman from Gildea. Nursemaid of the Royal Family.

Micik (MY-chik): A Man from Shad. King of Shad. Father of Lathlean.

Mikva (MIK-vah): A Man from Gildea. Doorwarden of King Treiber.

Millas (MILL-ass): Shannon's charger.

Molden (MOLE-den): A Man from Racolis. Guard-Priest at the Temple of Oran.

Montine (mon-TEEN): A human youth from Shad. Brother of Rovert.

Nathon (NAY-thon): A Man from Shalkan. Glazier in Ahz-Kham.

Nedros (NED-ross): A Man from Matadol. A Fieldmarshal in the Matadane army.

Nerad (NEER-ad): The Athorian word for a Wizard's apprentice.

Nibys (NIE-biss): A Man from Ilkatar.

Nisbud (NIZ-bud): A Man from Fekamar. A Captain in the Fekamari army.

Novosad (NO-voh-sad): A Man from Racolis. A scout in the Hagane army.

Odyniec (o-DIN-ee-ek): A Man from Athor. Wizard of the Dawn King.

Omusok (OM-yoo-sok): A Man from Ilkatar.

Oran (OR-an): The god of the sky.

Parnin (PAR-nin): A youth from Racolis. Dell's squire.

Pike (PIKE): A Man of Harvath. One of Earon's warriors.

Quellin (KWEL-in): A Man from Gildea. Lord of the House of Trost. King of Gildea.

Quiron (KWIE-ron): A Man from Gildea. Lord of the House of Trost. Father of Quellin and Mattina.

Radnor (RAD-nor): A Man from Gildea. Lord of the House of Horack-Gildea.

Rasheth (RAW-sheth): An Elvin title equivalent to chief or king, held by Joahin since the Third Age.

Reatha (ray-ATH-ah): An Elfess from Greyleaf Forest. Guthwine's wife.

Rister (RISS-ter): A Man from Ilkatar. Former horse-trader.

Roby (ROH-bee): A Man from Ilkatar. Dockhand at the Shipyard of Ilkatar.

Rodi (ROH-dee): A Dwarf from the Podan Peaks.

Romelda (roh-MEL-dah): A Woman from Shad. A noblewoman from Lener Keep.

Ronna (RAH-nah): A Woman of the Second Age. Wife of Dothager. Mother of Trost.

Rosa (ROH-sah): A Woman from Racolis. Queen of Racolis. Wife of Kosarek.

Rovert (ROV-ert): A human child from Shad. Brother of Montine.

Runyan (RUN-yan): A Man from Gildea. The most famous Bard of Milhavior.

Saereni (say-REH-nee): A small mortal folk not yet revealed to the other mortal folk.

Saraletri (sah-rah-LET-ree): The Wood Elves.

Sedik (SEH-dik): The god of the earth.

Selph (SELF): A Man from Gos. Horsemaster.

Semina (seh-ME-nah): A Woman from Corimuth. Daughter of Geneta. Mother of Earek.

Shannon (SHAN-on): A human youth from Gildea. Crown Prince of Gildea. Son of Quellin and Arella.

Shanor (SHAY-nor): A human youth from Gildea. Son of Radnor.

Shavane (SHAH-vane): A Man from Harvath. Captain of the Janish army.

Sherren (SHARE-en): A Woman from Gildea. Queen of Gildea. Wife of Treiber.

Sîan (SHE-ann): A human child from Gildea. Princess of Gildea. Daughter of Quellin and Arella.

Skrak (SKRAK): A Jaf. Cursed form of Anselm.

Skundrich (SKUN-dritch): A Man from Harvath. One of Earon's warriors.

Spiridon (SPEER-id-on): A Man from Matadol. Royal Marshal of the Matadane army.

Suria (soo-REE-ah): A Woman from Harvath. Queen.

Tally (TAH-lee): A Troll of the Golden Hills.

Tasic (TAZE-ik): Dockhand at the Shipyard of Ilkatar.

Taskalos (TAS-kah-loss): A Man from Matadol. King of Matadol.

Thanatos (THAH-nah-toss): The Athorian name for the Deathlord, ruler of the Death Realm.

Tinsor (TIN-sor): A Man from Ilkatar.

Titha (TIH-thah): A Woman from Gildea. Daughter of the Governor of Gerdes. Wife of Novosad.

Tonys (TOH-niss): A Man from Ilkatar.

Traven (TRAY-ven): A Man from Shad. Stablemaster of Lener Keep.

Treiber (TRAY-ber): A Man from Gildea. King of Gildea.

Triven (TRIV-en): A Man from Harvath. Captain in the Normant army.

Trost (TROST): A Man of the Third Age. First King of the land now known as Gildea.

Turan (TOO-ran): A Man of Gildea. Guardsman of Treiber.

Ubriaco (yoo-BRIE-ah-ko): A Man from Gildea. Lord of the House of Gildea.

Uhyvainyn (oo-hih-VAY-in-een): Elvin name of a High Alar.

Umbrick (UM-brik): A Man from Gildea. Captain in the Gildean army.

Valmen (VAHL-men): A Man from Harvath. Marshal of Yun.

Venloo (VEN-loo): A Man from Racolis. Temple Priest at the Temple of Oran.

Verak (VAY-rak): A Man from Shalkan. Carpenter in Ahz-Kham.

Vergan (VER-gan): A Man from Harvath. One of Earon's warriors.

Vesper (VESS-per): Dell's charger.

Vinad (VEE-nad): Gowan's horse.

Vrash (VRASH): A Man in the service of Kerebros. One of the Wolves of Kerebros.

Wargon (WAR-gon): A Man from Racolis. A Hagane nobleman.

Welmon (WELL-mon): A Man from Harvath. King.

Willerth (WILL-erth): A human youth from Fekamar. Son of Brugnara. Servant of Brendys.

Wolves of Kerebros : Men infected with the curse of Kerebros of Haff. Shapeshift into man-wolves.

Zanyben (ZAH-nib-en): The head of the Wizards of Athor.

Zoti (ZOH-tee): The god of death.

Places

Ahz-Kham (oz KOM): A town in Shalkan. Home of Brendyk and Brendys.

Alaren Orilal (AH-lar-en or-il-AL): The Elvin name for the High Realm.

Algire (AL-jire): A town in Gildea.

Anatar (an-AH-tar): The Great River. Spans the breadth of Milhavior.

Areth's Pool (AYR-eth's pool): A pond near Brendyk's farmstead.

Ascon (ASK-on): The High Throne of Milhavior, located in the Northeast Quarter.

Ascon Keep (ASK-on keep): A city in Ascon. Capitol of Milhavior.

Athor (AY-thor): The Holy Isle, home of the Wizards, hidden from the mainland. One of the Free Lands.

Bale Keep (BALE keep): A city in Matadol.

Bascio Keep (BASS-kee-oh keep): A city in Delcan.

Bhoredan (bor-eh-DON): An island nation in the Southwest Quarter of Milhavior. One of the Free Lands.

Bulkyree (bull-kih-ree): A nation in the Southeast Quarter of Milhavior. One of the Dark Lands.

Caladin (cah-LAD-in): A nation in the Southeast Quarter of Milhavior. One of the Free Lands.

Charneco (KAR-neh-ko): A nation in the Southeast Quarter of Milhavior. One of the Dark Lands.

Chi Thanatos (KIE THAH-nah-toss): The Tower of Death, fortress of Thanatos located in Machaelon.

Corimuth Keep (COR-ih-muth keep): A city in Corimuth. Capitol of Corimuth.

Daggs Keep (DAGS keep): A city in Racolis.

Dahl Keep (DAL keep): A city in Matadol.

Delcan (DEL-kan): A nation in the Southwest Quarter of Milhavior. One of the Free Lands.

Den Fantiro (DEN fan-TEER-oh): A river in the east of Milhavior.

Den Inkanar (DEN in-KAY-nar): A river in the south of Milhavior.

Den Jostalen (DEN jo-STAH-len): A river in the south of Milhavior.

Den Keplar (DEN KEH-plar): A river in the north of Milhavior.

Den Pelacor (DEN PEL-ah-kor): A river in the north of Milhavior.

Den Smih (DEN SMEE): A river in the Southeast Quarter of Milhavior.

Dun Ghalil (DUN GAH-leel): Greyleaf Forest. An Elvin forest in the Southwest Quarter of Milhavior.

Dun Rial (DUN ree-AL): An Elvin forest in the Northwest Quarter of Milhavior.

Dun Sol (DUN sol): An Elvin forest in the Southeast Quarter of Milhavior.

Ecavan (EK-ah-van): A town in Kahadral.

Elnisra (el-NIZ-rah): A town in Shalkan.

Elurdon (eh-LOOR-don): A country in the Southwest Quarter of Milhavior. One of the Free Lands.

En Orilal (EN or-il-AL): The Elvin name for the Mortal Realm.

Erutti Keep (eh-ROO-tee keep): A city in Delcan.

Far North: A frozen region far to the north of Milhavior.

Fedris (FED-ris): A town in Kahadral.

Fekamar (FEK-ah-mar): A nation in the Northwest Quarter of Milhavior. One of the Free Lands.

Gerdes (GER-deez): A town in Gildea.

Gildea (gil-DAY-ah): A nation in the Southeast Quarter of Milhavior. One of the Free Lands.

Gildea Keep (gil-DAY-ah keep): A city in Gildea.

Gos (GOSS): A country in the Northeast Quarter of Milhavior. One of the Free Lands.

Haff (HAF): A country in the Southeast Quarter of Milhavior. One of the Dark Lands.

Hagan Keep (HAY-gan keep): A city in Racolis.

Hàl (HAWL): The Athorian name for the Under Realm (or Death Realm.)

Harvath (HAR-vath): A country in the Southwest Quarter of Milhavior.

Harvath Keep (HAR-vath keep): A city in Harvath.

Horack Keep (HOR-ack): A city in Gildea.

Iler Hill (IE-ler HIL): The hill upon which Hagan Keep sits.

Ilkatar (IL-kah-tar): A nation in the Northwest Quarter of Milhavior. One of the Free Lands.

Kahadral (kah-HAD-ral): A nation in the Northwest Quarter of Milhavior. One of the Free Lands.

Ilkatar Forest (IL-kah-tar FOR-est): A forest in Ilkatar, northeast of Shalkan.

Ilkatar Keep (IL-kah-tar keep): A city in Ilkatar.

Janish Keep (JAY-nish keep): A city in Harvath.

Kahadral (kah-HAD-rahl): A country in the Northwest Quarter of Milhavior. One of the Free Lands.

Kahadral Keep (kah-HAD-rahl keep): A city in Kahadral.

Karuna (kah-ROON-ah): A town in Shad. location of the Black Temple of Zoti.

Kel Treibeirne (kell tray-BAYRN): A hill in Gildea where the new Gildea Keep was raised.

Lake Xolsha (LAYK ZOL-shah): A lake on the border of Gildea and Qatan.

Lener Keep (LEH-ner keep): A city in Shad.

Lewek Keep (LOO-ek keep): A city in Delcan.

Lind Keep (LIND keep): A city in Kahadral.

Machaelon (maw-KAY-el-on): The barren land between Milhavior and Mingenland of old; controlled by Thanatos.

Maelen Orilal (maw-EL-en or-il-AL): The Elvin name for the Under Realm (or Death Realm.)

Matadol (mat-ah-DOLE): A nation in the Southeast Quarter of Milhavior. One of the Free Lands.

Meyler Roam (MAY-ler roh-AM): A town in Ilkatar just outside the Western Pass of Shalkan.

Milhavior (mil-HAY-vee-or): The continent north of Machaelon and Mingenland given to Men by Elekar at the end of the last Dawn War.

Mingenland (MEEN-gen-land): The continent in the far south where Men and Dwarves originated.

Neza Bokân (NAY-zah BO-kawn): The Gate of the Arches. A minor portal into the Silver Mountains.

Neza Edvêjga (NAY-zah ed-VAY-ga): The Gate of the Golden Trove. A portal into the Silver Mountains.

Nordin (NOR-din): A town in Fekamar.

Normant Keep (NOR-mant keep): A city in Harvath.

Ona Orilal (OH-nah or-il-AL): The Realm Complete. The Elvin name for all of creation.

Oran's Refuge **(OH-ranz REH-fyooj):** An inn in Fedris.

Ovieto (oh-vee-EH-to): A nation in the Southeast Quarter of Milhavior. One of the Free Lands.

Phelan Keep (FEE-lan keep): A city in Caladin.

Podan Peaks (POH-dan PEAKS): A Dwarvinholt in the Northwest Quarter of Milhavior.

Qatan (kah-TAN): A nation in the Southeast Quarter of Milhavior. One of the Dark Lands.

Racolis (RAK-oh-liss): A nation in the Northwest Quarter of Milhavior. One of the Free Lands.

Racolis Keep (RAK-oh-liss keep): A city in Racolis.

Reanna Orilal (ray-AH-nah or-il-AL): The Elvin name for the Vision Realm.

Sapphire Lake (SAF-ire lake): A lake in Racolis.

Shad (SHAD): A country in the Southeast Quarter of Milhavior. One of the Dark Lands.

Shad Hills (SHAD hilz): A range of hills surrounding Lener Keep.

Shad Keep (SHAD keep): A city in Shad.

Shalkan (shal-KAN): A little country located in a box canyon at the heart of Barrier Mountain in the Northwest Quarter of Milhavior. Formerly the fortress retreat of a forgotten king.

Sharamitaro (shay-ram-it-AR-oh): The House of Sorrow. A cemetery honoring the fallen at Gildea Keep.

Tarlas (TAR-las): A fishing-village in Gildea.

Tesar (TESS-ar): A country in the Southwest Quarter. One of the Dark Lands.

Trost Keep (TROST keep): A city in Gildea.

Wegant Keep (WEH-gant keep): A city in Matadol.

Wills Keep (WILZ keep): A city in Kahadral.

Woodland (WOOD-land): An Elvin forest in the Northwest Quarter of Milhavior.

Yasgin (YAZ-gin): A town in Gildea.

Yun Keep (YOON keep): A city in Harvath.

Yorg Keep (YORG keep): A city in Harvath.

Zhâyil-Kan (ZHAW-yil kon): The original name of Shalkan.

Zirges Keep (ZER-geez keep): A city in Qatan.

Things

Crorkin (KROR-kin): Black Elvinmetal. Has the power to slay by only the merest scratch.

Denasdervien (day-nass-DER-vee-en): The Living Flame. Also called the Dawn Sword or the Flame of Elekar. Weapon of the Bearer of the Flame and the Heir of Ascon. Formed of Gloriod and Crorkin.

Denaseskra (day-nass-ES-kra): The Black Flame. The original name of Denasdervien, forged of Crorkin by the Dwarves to slay Elekar.

Elvingold (EL-vin-gold): Gold Elvinmetal.

Elvinsilver (EL-vin-SIL-ver): Silver Elvinmetal.

Golven (GOLE-ven): A summer month in the Milhaviorian calendar.

gona **(GO-nah):** The Gildean G.

Gloriod (GLO-ree-od): Silver-gold Elvinmetal. The most powerful of all Elvinmetals, unbreakable by any amount of force.

Holnar (HOLE-nar): Earon's Gloriod javelin.

Husrrom (HOOS-rom): A star.

Kalter (KAL-ter): Quellin's Elvingold sword.

Kjerekil (kyare-EH-kil): The Dwarvin language.

Koshyco (koh-SHEE-koh): A star.

Nodrun (NOH-drun): A set of tournament rules allowing the victor to take all lands and possessions of the defeated.

Pâred Talletri **(PAW-red tah-LET-ree):** The Sundering of the Elves.

Stajouhar (STA-yoo-har): Green Elvinstone. Has the power to burn wounds with an unseen flame.

Volker (VOLE-ker): Quellin's Elvinsilver and Stajouhar long-knife.

Phrases

"Anî âbahnir nâshiymër. . . ." (AH-nee aw-BAH-neer NAWSH-ee-mayr): "I will be your wife. . . ."

"Engen kellim Arzola, dellis el boradis!" (EN-gen KEH-lim ar-ZOH-la DEH-liss EL boh-RAD-iss): "Look to the Dawn, and all is possible!"

"Fänos Pävo, apä de maphe eäthen gwokhen panwoth. Hyobjas eäth ekweos bo ekek eäthen peth meekaen." (FAH-nohs PAH-voh AY-pah deh MAY-feh ay-AH-then GWOHK-hen PAYN-wahth HYOBE-jayse AY-ahth ek-WAY-ose bo EE-kek ay-AH-then peth mee-EK-AY-en): "King of the Dawn, I know now that my time has come. Give me to the strength to complete my final task."

"Goras Jundor! Jontn!" (GOR-ass YUN-dor, YON-tin): Untranslated Kjerekil expletive. (Jontn = Man).

"Gwīkās bō Fänō, där mäs nwäsoi." (GWI-case bo FAH-noh, dar MAS NWA-soy): "Look to the Dawn, and all is possible."

"Këlâbë hâlak teyanâsh" (kay-LAW-bay HAW-lak tay-ah-NAWSH): "I shall walk beside you"

"Kindone Getheirne un hason!" (KIN-done geh-THAYRN un HASS-on): "May the Dawn guide our hands!"

"Kuntok ê, Kolis Bazân!" (koon-TOK EH KOL-is BAY-zawn): "Hear me, King of the Dawn!"

"Mondone, Brendys du Prelarin!" (MON-done, BREN-dis du prel-AR-in): "Hail, Prince-to-be Brendys!"

"Mondone, Brendys Prelarin!" (MON-done, BREN-dis prel-AR-in): "Hail, Prince Brendys!"

"Mondone, Kiloni Velarin!" (MON-done, KIL-oh-nee veh-LAR-in): "Hail, Lord Quellin!"

"Mondone, Treibeirne Delorin!" (MON-done tray-BAYRN del-OR-in): "Hail, King Treiber!"

"Omdi kosumni udinor uktur!" (OM-dee koh-SOOM-nee OOD-in-or UK-tur): Nonsense phrase spoken by Odyniec.

"Shëd, yâkolëniren ârar enmâëlen!" (SHED, yaw-KOL-ayn-EER-en aw-RAR en-maw-AY-len): "Demon, may you be cursed to death!"

"Shilnuk!" (SHIL-nook): Untranslated Kubruk word.

"Shilnuk kubu mok!" (SHIL-nook KOO-boo MOK): Untranslated Kubruk phrase.

"Shilnuk nik Pragu!" (SHIL-nook NIK PRAH-goo): Untranslated Kubruk phrase.

"Skud!" (SKUD): Untranslated expletive.

"Tomeirne Hekdanatin!" (to-MAYRNE hek-DAN-ah-tin): "Hál-cursed devil!"

"Und Kjerlinga eschen ver Kjerkena, hjol Kolis Bazân." (OOND kyare-LIN-gah ESH-en VAYR kyare-KAY-na, HYOLE KOL-is BAY-zawn): "This child I name Kjerkena, before the Dawn King."

Songs

Elëkar yâkólëpâr nâkah âkëbel Ólayil
Est yâkólënir shâlëvë nólir Âzërem
Órë yâkólëshüb kâsal âfëlah Ókâshëkah
Nëfesh yâkólëmâr âlas Ëboelëkar

Layil kîdâshah yâtsah Mâëlen shë Talmâëlen
Yâshir ómikvë olâmë yâshabâr ëbir
Fë Anî nâtsabänë Dënäs shë Talmâëlen
Këlâbë yâkólësâraf lâhabë Îboelëkar

May the Dawn break free from the fetters of the Night
May it be a peaceful harbor from the Storm
May the Light turn back the gloom of the Darkness
May the Soul find solace in the morning Light

Though the Night brings forth Death and Shadow
A ray of hope forever abides beyond
As I stand between the Flame and the Shadow
May my heart burn brightly for the coming Dawn

Ëth yëshâwar üsârë
Est yëshâbar ëbir tordahâth
Ëkâshaklayil
Talmâëlen râkad ëmâkom ótâbah

Ahî kornëfesh âsaf
Nâshórë âbahnir në mâtsah
Înâshâkëb nâhal nâsh al
Alpâshat enelëkar

Nâsh yëshâbar ëbir

Time has left us
It has passed beyond our knowledge
In the darkening night
Shadows dance in the halls of waiting

Where the cold souls gather
Your light will not be found
For your footsteps guide you on
On the Road to Elekar

You have passed beyond

About the Author

Jonathan graduated with a B.A. in English from Southern Illinois University at Edwardsville and is publisher and Editor-in-Chief of Athor Productions. Inspired at a very early age by the works of J.R.R. Tolkien and C.S. Lewis, he became an avid reader—and later, writer—of fantasy and science fiction. As well as writing fiction, Jonathan also designs role-playing and trading card games.

9 781932 060058